ONCE UPON A CASTLE

And she was there, just there, conjured up out of storm-whipped air. Her hair was a firefall over a dove-gray cloak, alabaster skin with the faint bloom of rose, a generous mouth just curved in knowledge . . .

His heart leaped, and his blood churned with love, lust, longing.

She came to him, wading through the knee-high mists, her beauty staggering. With his eyes on hers, he swung off his horse, eager for the woman who was witch, and lover.

—from ''Spellbound'' by Nora Roberts,
New York Times Bestselling Author of *Sanctuary*,
From the Heart, and *Montana Sky*

ONCE UPON A CASTLE

NORA ROBERTS
JILL GREGORY
RUTH RYAN LANGAN
MARIANNE WILLMAN

JOVE BOOKS, NEW YORK

ONCE UPON A CASTLE

A Jove Book / published by arrangement with
the authors

PRINTING HISTORY
Jove edition / March 1998

The Penguin Putnam Inc. World Wide Web site address is
http://www.penguinputnam.com

ISBN: 0-515-12241-6

A JOVE BOOK®
Jove Books are published by
The Berkley Publishing Group, a member of Penguin Putnam Inc.,
200 Madison Avenue, New York, New York 10016.
Jove and the "J" design are trademarks belonging to
Jove Publications, Inc.

PRINTED IN THE UNITED STATES OF AMERICA

10 9 8 7 6 5 4 3 2 1

CONTENTS

SPELLBOUND
NORA ROBERTS

To all my wonderful friends
in this life and all the others

PROLOGUE

Love. My love. Let me into your dreams. Open your heart again and hear me. Calin, I need you so. Don't turn from me now, or all is lost. I am lost. Love. My love.

Calin shifted restlessly in sleep, turned his face into the pillow. Felt her there, somehow. Skin, soft and dewy. Hands, gentle and soothing. Then drifted into dreams of cool and quiet mists, hills of deep, damp green that rolled to forever. And the witchy scent of woman.

The castle rose atop a cliff, silver stone spearing into stormy skies, its base buried in filmy layers of fog that ran like a river. The sound of his mount's bridle jingled battle-bright on the air as he rode, leaving the green hills behind and climbing high on rock. Thunder sounded in the west, over the sea. And echoed in his warrior's heart.

Had she waited for him?

His eyes, gray as the stone of the castle, shifted, scanned, searching rock and mist for any hole where a foe could hide. Even as he urged his mount up the rugged path cleaved into the cliff he knew he carried the stench of war and death, that it had seeped into his pores just as the memories of it had seeped into his brain.

Neither body nor mind would ever be fully clean of it.

His sword hand lay light and ready on the hilt of his weapon. In such places a man did not lower his guard. Here magic stung the air and could embrace or threaten. Here faeries plotted or danced, and witches cast their spells for good or ill.

Atop the lonely cliff, towering above the raging sea, the castle stood, holding its secrets. And no man rode this path without hearing the whispers of old ghosts and new spirits.

Had she waited for him?

The horse's hooves rang musically over the rock until at last they traveled to level ground. He dismounted at the foot of the keep just as lightning cracked the black sky with a blaze of blinding white light.

And she was there, just there, conjured up out of storm-whipped air. Her hair was a firefall over a dove-gray cloak, alabaster skin with the faint bloom of rose, a generous mouth just curved in knowledge. And eyes as blue as a living star and just as filled with power.

His heart leaped, and his blood churned with love, lust, longing.

She came to him, wading through the knee-high mists, her beauty staggering. With his eyes on hers, he swung off his horse, eager for the woman who was witch, and lover.

"Caelan of Farrell, 'tis far you've traveled in the dark of the night. What do you wish of me?"

"Bryna the Wise." His hard, ridged lips bowed in a smile that answered hers. "I wish for everything."

"Only everything?" Her laugh was low and intimate. "Well, that's enough, then. I waited for you."

Then her arms were around him, her mouth lifting to his. He pulled her closer, desperate for the shape of her, wild to have whatever she would offer him, and more.

"I waited for you," she repeated with a catch in her voice as she pressed her face to his shoulder. " 'Twas almost too long this time. His power grows while mine weakens. I can't fight him alone. Alasdair is too strong, his dark forces too greedy. Oh, love. My love, why did you shut me out of your mind, out of your heart?"

He drew her away. The castle was gone—only ruins remained, empty, battle-scarred. They stood in the shadow of what had been, before a small house alive with flowers. The scent of them was everywhere, heady, intoxicating. The woman was still in his arms. And the storm waited to explode.

"The time is short now," she told him. "You must come. Calin, you must come to me. Destiny can't be denied, a spell won't be broken. Without you with me, he'll win."

He shook his head, started to speak, but she lifted a hand to his face. It passed through him as if he were a ghost. Or she was. "I have loved you throughout time." As she spoke, she moved back, the mists flowing around her legs. "I am bound to you, throughout time."

Then lifting her arms, raising palms to the heavens, she closed her eyes. The wind roared in like a lion loosed from a cage, lifted her flaming hair, whipped the cloak around her.

"I have little left," she called over the violence of the storm. "But I can still call up the wind. I can still call to your heart. Don't keep it from me, Calin. Come to me soon. Find me. Or I'm lost."

Then she was gone. Vanished. The earth trembled beneath his feet, the sky howled. And all went silent and still.

He awoke gasping for breath. And reaching out.

CHAPTER 1

"Calin Farrell, you need a vacation."

Cal lifted a shoulder, sipped his coffee, and continued to brood while staring out the kitchen window. He wasn't sure why he'd come here to listen to his mother nag and worry about him, to hear his father whistle as he meticulously tied his fishing flies at the table. But he'd had a deep, driving urge to be in the home of his childhood, to grab an hour or two in the tidy house in Brooklyn Heights. To see his parents.

"Maybe. I'm thinking about it."

"Work too hard," his father said, eyeing his own work critically. "Could come to Montana for a couple of weeks with us. Best fly-fishing in the world. Bring your camera." John Farrell glanced up and smiled. "Call it a sabbatical."

It was tempting. He'd never been the fishing enthusiast his father was, but Montana was beautiful. And big. Cal thought he could lose himself there. And shake off the restlessness. The dreams.

"A couple of weeks in the clean air will do you good." Sylvia Farrell narrowed her eyes as she turned to her son. "You're looking pale and tired, Calin. You need to get out of that city for a while."

Though she'd lived in Brooklyn all of her life, Sylvia still referred to Manhattan as "that city" with light disdain and annoyance.

"I've been thinking about a trip."

"Good." His mother scrubbed at her countertop. They were leaving the next morning, and Sylvia Farrell wouldn't

leave a crumb or a mote of dust behind. "You've been working too hard, Calin. Not that we aren't proud of you. After
your exhibit last month your father bragged so much that the
neighbors started to hide when they saw him coming."

"Not every day a man gets to see his son's photographs
in the museum. I liked the nudes especially," he added with
a wink.

"You old fool," Sylvia muttered, but her lips twitched.
"Well, who'd have thought when we bought you that little
camera for Christmas when you were eight that twenty-two
years later you'd be rich and famous? But wealth and fame
carry a price."

She took her son's face in her hands and studied it with a
mother's keen eye. His eyes were shadowed, she noted, his
face too thin. She worried for the man she'd raised, and the
boy he had been who had always seemed to have . . . something more than the ordinary.

"You're paying it."

"I'm fine." Reading the worry in her eyes, recognizing it,
he smiled. "Just not sleeping very well."

There had been other times, Sylvia remembered, that her
son had grown pale and hollow-eyed from lack of sleep. She
exchanged a quick glance with her husband over Cal's shoulder.

"Have you, ah, seen the doctor?"

"Mom, I'm fine." He knew his voice was too sharp, too
defensive. Struggled to lighten it. "I'm perfectly fine."

"Don't nag the boy, Syl." But John studied his son closely
also, remembering, as his wife did, the young boy who had
talked to shadows, had walked in his sleep, and had dreamed
of witches and blood and battle.

"I'm not nagging. I'm mothering." She made herself
smile.

"I don't want you to worry. I'm a little stressed-out, that's
all." That was all, he thought, determined to make it so. He
wasn't different, he wasn't odd. Hadn't the battalion of doctors his parents had taken him to throughout his childhood
diagnosed an overdeveloped imagination? And hadn't he finally channeled that into his photography?

He didn't see things that weren't there anymore.

Sylvia nodded, told herself to accept that. "Small wonder. You've been working yourself day and night for the last five years. You need some rest, you need some quiet. And some pampering."

"Montana," John said again. "Couple of weeks of fishing, clean air, and no worries."

"I'm going to Ireland." It came out of Cal's mouth before he'd realized the idea was in his head.

"Ireland?" Sylvia pursed her lips. "Not to work, Calin."

"No, to . . . to see," he said at length. "Just to see."

She nodded, satisfied. A vacation, after all, was a vacation. "That'll be nice. It's supposed to be a restful country. We always meant to go, didn't we, John?"

Her husband grunted his assent. "Going to look up your ancestors, Cal?"

"I might." Since the decision seemed to be made, Cal sipped his coffee again. He was going to look up something, he realized. Or someone.

It was raining when he landed at Shannon Airport. The chilly late-spring rain seemed to suit his mood. He'd slept nearly all the way across the Atlantic. And the dreams had chased him. He went through customs, arranged to rent a car, changed money. All of this was done with the mechanical efficiency of the seasoned traveler. And as he completed the tasks, he tried not to worry, tried not to dwell on the idea that he was having a breakdown of some kind.

He climbed into the rented car, then simply sat in the murky light wondering what to do, where to go. He was thirty, a successful photographer who could name his own price, call his own shots. He still considered it a wild twist of fate that he'd been able to make a living doing something he loved. Using what he saw in a landscape, in a face, in light and shadow and texture, and translating that into a photograph.

It was true that the last few years had been hectic and he'd worked almost nonstop. Even now the trunk of the Volvo he'd rented was loaded with equipment, and his favored Ni-

kon rested in its case on the seat beside him. He couldn't get
away from it—didn't want to run away from what he loved.

Suddenly an odd chill raced through him, and he thought,
for just a moment, that he heard a woman weeping.

Just the rain, he told himself and scrubbed his hands over
his handsome face. It was long, narrow, with the high, strong
cheekbones of his Celtic forefathers. His nose was straight,
his mouth firm and well formed. It smiled often—or it had
until recently.

His eyes were gray—a deep, pure gray without a hint of
green or blue. The brows over them were strongly arched
and tended to draw together in concentration. His hair was
black and thick and flowed over his collar. An artistic touch
that a number of women had enjoyed.

Again, until recently.

He brooded over the fact that it had been months since
he'd been with a woman—since he'd wanted to. Overwork
again? he wondered. A byproduct of stress? Why would he
be stressed when his career was advancing by leaps and
bounds? He was healthy. He'd had a complete physical only
weeks before.

But you didn't tell the doctor about the dreams, did you?
he reminded himself. The dreams you can't quite remember
when you wake up. The dreams, he admitted, that had pulled
him three thousand miles over the ocean.

No, damn it, he hadn't told the doctor. He wasn't going
that route again. There had been enough psychiatrists in his
youth, poking and prodding into his mind, making him feel
foolish, exposed, helpless. He was a grown man now and
could handle his own dreams.

If he was having a breakdown, it was a perfectly normal
one and could be cured by rest, relaxation, and a change of
scene.

That's what he'd come to Ireland for. Only that.

He started the car and began to drive aimlessly.

He'd had dreams before, when he was a boy. Very clear,
too realistic dreams. Castles and witches and a woman with
tumbling red hair. She'd spoken to him with that lilt of Ireland in her voice. And sometimes she'd spoken in a language

he didn't know—but had understood nonetheless.

There'd been a young girl—that same waterfall of hair, the same blue eyes. They'd laughed together in his dreams. Played together—innocent childhood games. He remembered that his parents had been amused when he'd spoken of his friend. They had passed it off, he thought, as the natural imagination of a sociable only child.

But they'd been concerned when he seemed to know things, to see things, to speak of places and people he couldn't have had knowledge of. They'd worried over him when his sleep was disturbed night after night—when he began to walk and talk while glazed in dreams.

So, after the doctors, the therapists, the endless sessions, and those quick, searching looks that adults thought children couldn't interpret, he'd stopped speaking of them.

And as he'd grown older, the young girl had grown as well. Tall and slim and lovely—young breasts, narrow waist, long legs. Feelings and needs for her that weren't so innocent had begun to stir.

It had frightened him, and it had angered him. Until he'd blocked out that soft voice that came in the night. Until he'd turned away from the image that haunted his dreams. Finally, it had stopped. The dreams stopped. The little flickers in his mind that told him where to find lost keys or had him reaching for the phone an instant before it rang ceased.

He was comfortable with reality, Cal told himself. Had chosen it. And would choose it again. He was here only to prove to himself that he was an ordinary man suffering from overwork. He would soak up the atmosphere of Ireland, take the pictures that pleased him. And, if necessary, take the pills his doctor had prescribed to help him sleep undisturbed.

He drove along the storm-battered coast, where wind roared in over the sea and held encroaching summer at bay with chilly breath.

Rain pattered the windshield, and fog slithered over the ground. It was hardly a warm welcome, yet he felt at home. As if something, or someone, was waiting to take him in from the storm. He made himself laugh at that. It was just the pleasure of being in a new place, he decided. It was the anticipation of finding new images to capture on film.

He felt a low-grade urge for coffee, for food, but easily blocked it as he absorbed the scenery. Later, he told himself. He would stop later at some pub or inn, but just now he had to see more of this haunting landscape. So savagely beautiful, so timeless.

And if it was somehow familiar, he could put that down to place memory. After all, his ancestors had roamed these spearing cliffs, these rolling green hills. They had been warriors, he thought. Had once painted themselves blue and screamed out of the forests to terrorize the enemy. Had strapped on armor and hefted sword and pike to defend their land and protect their freedom.

The scene that burst into his mind was viciously clear. The flash of sword crashing, the screams of battle in full power. Wheeling horses, wild-eyed, spurting blood from a severed arm and the agonizing cry of pain as a man crumpled. The burn as steel pierced flesh.

Looking down as the pain bloomed, he saw blood welling on his thigh.

Carrion crows circling in silent patience. The stench of roasting flesh as bodies burned on a pyre, and the hideous and thin cries of dying men waiting for release.

Cal found himself stopped on the side of the road, out of the car, dragging air into his lungs as the rain battered him. Had he blacked out? Was he losing his mind? Trembling he reached down and ran his hand over his jeans. There was no wound, and yet he felt the echoing ache of an old scar he knew wasn't there.

It was happening again. The river of fear that flowed through him froze over and turned his blood to ice. He forced himself to calm down, to think rationally. Jet lag, he decided. Jet lag and stress, that was all. How long since he'd driven out of Shannon? Two hours? Three? He needed to find a place to stay. He needed to eat. He would find some quiet, out-of-the-way bed-and-breakfast, he thought. Somewhere he could rest and ease his mind. And when the storm had passed, he would get his camera and go for a long walk. He could stay for weeks or leave in the morning. He was free, he reminded himself. And that was sane, that was normal.

He climbed back into the car, steadied himself, and drove along the winding coast road.

The ruined castle came into view as he rounded the curve. The keep, he supposed it was, was nearly intact, but walls had been sheared off, making him think of an ancient warrior with scars from many battles. Perched on a stony crag, it shouted with power and defiance despite its tumbled rocks.

Out of the boiling sky, one lance of lightning speared, exploded with light, and stung the air with the smell of ozone.

His blood beat thick, and an ache, purely sexual, began to spread through his belly. On the steering wheel his fingers tightened. He swung onto the narrow, rutted dirt road that led up. He needed a picture of the castle, he told himself. Several studies from different angles. A quick detour—fifteen or twenty minutes—then he would be on his way to that B and B.

It didn't matter that Ireland was dotted with ruins and old castles—he needed this one.

Mists spread at its base like a river. So intent was he on the light and shadows that played on stone, on the texture of the weeds and wildflowers that forced their way through crevices, that he didn't see the cottage until he was nearly upon it.

It made him smile, though he didn't realize it. It was so charming, so unexpected there beside the ancient stones. Inviting, welcoming, it seemed to bloom like the flowers that surrounded it, out of the cliffside as if planted by a loving hand.

It was painted white with bright blue shutters. Smoke trailed up out of the stone chimney, and a sleek black cat napped beside a wooden rocker on the little covered porch.

Someone made a home here, he thought, and tended it.

The light was wrong, he told himself. But he knew he needed to capture this place, this feeling. He would ask whoever lived here if he could come back, do his work.

As he stood in the rain, the cat uncurled lazily, then sat. It watched him out of startlingly blue eyes.

Then she was there—standing in the lashing rain, the mists swirling around her. Though he'd hadn't heard her approach, she was halfway between the tidy cottage and the tumbling stones of the old castle. One hand was lifted to her heart, and her breath was coming fast as if she'd been running.

Her hair was wet, hanging in deep-red ropes over her shoulders, framing a face that might have been carved out of ivory by a master. Her mouth was soft and full and seemed to tremble as it curved into a smile of welcome. Her eyes were star blue and swimming with emotions as powerful as the storm.

"I knew you would come." The cloak she wore flew back as she raced to him. "I waited for you," she said with the musical lilt of Ireland before her mouth crushed his.

CHAPTER 2

There was a moment of blinding, searing joy. Another of dark, primal lust.

Her taste, sharp, potent, soaked into his system as the rain soaked his skin. He was helpless to do anything but absorb it. Her arms were chained around his neck, her slim, curvy body pressed intimately to his, the heat from it seeping through his sodden shirt and into his bones.

And her mouth was as wild and edgy as the sky thundering above them.

It was all terrifyingly familiar.

He brought his hands to her shoulders, torn for a staggering instant as to whether to pull her closer or push her away. In the end he eased back, held her at arm's length.

She was beautiful. She was aroused. And she was, he assured himself, a stranger. He angled his head, determined to handle the situation.

"Well, it's certainly a friendly country."

He saw the flicker in her eyes, the dimming of disappointment, a flash of frustration. But he couldn't know just how deeply that disappointment, that frustration cut into her heart.

He's here, she told herself. He's come. That's what matters most now. "It is, yes." She gave him a smile, let her fingers linger in his hair just another second, then dropped them to her sides. "Welcome to Ireland and the Castle of Secrets."

His gaze shifted toward the ruins. "Is that what it's called?"

"That's the name it carries now." She had to struggle to

keep her eyes from devouring him, every inch, every expression. Instead she offered a hand, as she would have to any wayward traveler. "You've had a long journey. Come, sit by my fire." Her lips curved. "Have some whiskey in your tea."

"You don't know me." He made it a statement rather than a question. Had to.

In answer, she looked up at the sky. "You're wet," she said, "and the wind's cold today. It's enough to have me offer a seat by the hearth." She turned away from him, stepped up onto the porch where the cat stirred itself to wind through her legs. "You've come this far." Her eyes met his again, held. "Will you come into my home, Calin Farrell, and warm yourself?"

He scooped dripping hair out of his face, felt his bones tremble. "How do you know my name?"

"The same way you knew to come here." She picked up the cat, stroked its silky head. Both of them watched him with patient, unblinking blue eyes. "I baked scones fresh this morning. You'll be hungry." With this, she turned and walked inside, leaving him to come or go as he willed.

Part of him wanted to get back in the car, drive away, pretend he'd never seen her or this place. But he climbed onto the porch, pushed the front door open. He needed answers, and it seemed she had at least some of them.

The warmth struck him instantly. Welcoming warmth redolent with the fragrances of bread recently baked, of peat simmering in the hearth, of flowers just picked.

"Make yourself at home." She set the cat on the floor. "I'll see to the tea."

Cal stepped into the tiny parlor and near to the red eye of the fire. There were flowers, he noted, their petals still damp, filling vases on the stone mantel, pots on the table by the window.

A sugan chair sat by the hearth, but he didn't sit. Instead he studied the room with the sharp eye of an artist.

Quiet colors, he thought. Not pale, but soothing in the choice of deep rose and mossy greens. Woven rugs on the polished floors, mirror-bright woods lovingly cared for and smelling lightly of beeswax. Candles everywhere, in varying lengths, standing in holders of glass and silver and stone.

There, by the hearth, a spinning wheel. Surely an antique, he mused as he stepped closer to examine it. Its dark wood gleamed, and beside it sat a straw basket heaped with beautifully dyed wools.

But for the electric lamps and their jewellike shades, the small stereo tucked into a stack of books on a shelf, he might have convinced himself he'd stepped into another century.

Absently he crouched to pet the cat, which was rubbing seductively against his legs. The fur was warm and damp. Real. He hadn't walked into another century, Cal assured himself. Or into a dream. He was going to ask his hostess some very pointed questions, he decided. And he wasn't going anywhere until he was satisfied with the answers.

As she carried the tray back down the short hallway, she berated herself for losing her sense in the storm of emotion, for moving too quickly, saying too much. Expecting too much.

He didn't know her. Oh, that cut through the heart into the soul. But it had been foolish of her to expect him to, when he had blocked out her thoughts, her need for him for more than fifteen years.

She had continued to steal into his dreams when he was unaware, to watch him grow from boy to man as she herself blossomed into womanhood. But pride, and hurt, and love had stopped her from calling to him.

Until there had been no choice.

She'd known it the moment he stepped onto the ground of her own country. And her heart had leaped. Had it been so wrong, and so foolish, to prepare for him? To fill the house with flowers, the kitchen with baking? To bathe herself in oils of her own making, anointing her skin as a bride would on her wedding night?

No. She took a deep breath at the doorway. She had needed to prepare herself for him. Now she must find the right way to prepare him for her—and what they must soon face together.

He was so beautiful, she thought as she watched him stroke

the cat into ecstasy. How many nights had she tossed restlessly in sleep, longing for those long, narrow hands on her?

Oh, just once to feel him touch her.

How many nights had she burned to see his eyes, gray as
storm clouds, focused on her as he buried himself deep inside
her and gave her his seed?

Oh, just once to join with him, to make those soft, secret
sounds in the night.

They were meant to be lovers. This much she believed he
would accept. For a man had needs, she knew, and this one
was already linked with her physically—no matter that he
refused to remember.

But without the love in the act of mating, there would be
no joy. And no hope.

She braced herself and stepped into the room. "You've
made friends with Hecate, I see." His gaze whipped up to
hers, and her hands trembled lightly. Whatever power she
still held was nothing compared with one long look from
him. "She's shameless around attractive men." She set the
tray down. "Won't you sit, Calin, and have some tea?"

"How do you know who I am?"

"I'll explain what I can." Her eyes went dark and turbu-
lent with emotions as they scanned his face. "Do you have
no memory of me then? None at all?"

A tumble of red hair that shined like wet fire, a body that
moved in perfect harmony with his, a laugh like fog. "I don't
know you." He said it sharply, defensively. "I don't know
your name."

Her eyes remained dark, but her chin lifted. Here was
pride, and power still. "I am Bryna Torrence, descendant of
Bryna the Wise and guardian of this place. You're welcome
in my home, Calin Farrell, as long as you choose to stay."

She bent to the tray, her movements graceful. She wore a
long dress, the color of the mists curling outside the window.
It draped her body, flirted with her ankles. Columns of carved
silver danced from her ears.

"Why?" He laid a hand on her arm as she lifted the first
cup. "Why am I welcome in your home?"

"Perhaps I'm lonely." Her lips curved again, wistfully. "I

am lonely, and it's glad I am for your company." She sat, gestured for him to do the same. "You need a bit of food, Calin, a bit of rest. I can offer you that."

"What I want is an explanation." But he did sit, and because the hot liquid in his cup smelled glorious, he drank. "You said you knew I would come, you knew my name. I want to know how either of those things is possible."

It wasn't permitted to lie to him. Honesty was part of the pledge. But she could evade. "I might have recognized your face. You're a successful and famous man, Calin. Your art has found its way even into my corner of the world. You have such talent," she murmured. "Such vision." She arranged scones on a small plate, offered it. "Such power inside you."

He lifted a brow. There were women who were willing, eager to rock onto their backs for a man who had a hold on fame. He shook his head. "You're no groupie, Bryna. You didn't open the door to me so that you could have a quick bout of sex with a name."

"But others have."

There was a sting of jealousy in her voice. He couldn't have said why, but under the circumstances it amused him. "Which is how I know that's not what this is, not what you are. In any case, you didn't have the time to recognize my face from some magazine or talk show. The light was bad, the rain pouring down."

His brows drew together. He couldn't be dreaming again, hallucinating. The teacup was warm in his hand, the taste of the sweet, whiskey-laced brew in his mouth. "Damn it, you were waiting for me, and I don't understand how."

"I've waited for you all my life." She said it quietly, setting her cup down untouched. "And a millennium before it began." Raising her hands, she laid them on his face. "Your face is the first I remember, before even my own mother's. The ghost of your touch has haunted me every night of my life."

"That's nonsense." He brought a hand up, curled his fingers around her wrist.

"I can't lie to you. It's not in my power. Whatever I say

to you will be truth, whatever you see in me will be real.''
She tried to touch that part of his mind, or his heart, that
might still be open to her. But it was locked away, fiercely
guarded. She took one long breath and accepted. For now.
''You're not ready to know, to hear, to believe.'' Her eyes
softened a little, her fingertips stroking his temples. ''Ah,
Calin, you're tired, and confused. It's rest you're needing
now and ease for your mind. I can help you.''

His vision grayed, and the room swam. He could see nothing but her eyes, dark blue, utterly focused. Her scent swam
into his senses like a drug. ''Stop it.''

''Rest now, love. My love.''

He felt her lips brush his before he slid blissfully into the
dark.

Cal awoke to silence. His mind circled for a moment, like a
bird looking for a place to perch. Something in the tea, he
thought. God, the woman had drugged him. He felt a quick
panic as the theme from Stephen King's *Misery* played in his
head.

Obsessed fan. Kidnapping.

With a jolt, he sat straight up, terrified, reaching for his
foot. Still attached. The black cat, which had been curled on
the edge of the bed, stretched lazily and seemed to snicker.

''Yeah, funny,'' Cal muttered. He let out a long breath
that trailed into a weak laugh. Letting your imagination turn
cartwheels again, Calin, he told himself. Always been a bad
habit of yours.

He ordered himself to calm down, take stock of the situation. And realized he was buck naked.

Surprise ran a swift race with embarrassment as he imagined Bryna undressing him with those lovely tea-serving
hands. And getting him into bed. How in the hell had the
woman carted him into a bedroom?

For that was where he was. It was a small and charming
room with a tiny stone hearth, a glossy bureau. Flowers and
candles again, books tucked into a recessed nook. A doll-size
chair sat near a window that was framed in white lace cur-

tains. Sunlight slipped through them and made lovely and intricate patterns on the dark wood floor.

At the foot of the bed was an old chest with brass fittings. His clothes, clean and dry, were folded neatly on it. At least she didn't expect him to run around in his skin, he decided, and with some relief reached quickly for his jeans.

He felt immediately better once they were zipped, then realized that he felt not just better. He felt wonderful.

Alert, rested, energized. Whatever she'd given him, he concluded, had rocked him into the solid, restful sleep he hadn't experienced in weeks. But he wasn't going to thank her for it, Cal thought grimly as he tugged on his shirt. The woman went way past eccentric—he didn't mind a little eccentricity. But this lady was deluded, and possibly dangerous.

He was going to see to it that she gave him some satisfactory answers, then he was going to leave her to her fairy-tale cottage and ruined castle and put some miles between them.

He looked in the mirror over the bureau, half expecting to see a beard trailing down to his chest like Rip Van Winkle. But the man who stared back at him hadn't aged. He looked perplexed, annoyed, and, again, rested. The damnedest thing, Cal mused, scooping his hair back.

He found his shoes neatly tucked beside the chest. Putting them on, he found himself studying the patterns the sunlight traced on the floor.

Light. It struck him all at once, had him jumping to his feet again. The rain had stopped. For Christ's sake, how long had he been sleeping?

In two strides he was at the window, yanking back those delicate curtains. Then he stood, spellbound.

The view was stunning. He could see the rugged ground where the ruined castle climbed, make out the glints of mica in the stone where the sun struck. The ground tumbled away toward the road, then the road gave way to wave after rolling wave of green fields, bisected with stone walls, dotted with lolling cattle. Houses were tucked into valleys and on rises, clothes flapped cheerfully on lines. Trees twisted up, bent by the years of resisting the relentless wind off the sea and glossy green with spring.

He saw quite clearly a young boy pedaling his blue bike along one of the narrow trenches of road, a spotted black-and-white dog racing beside him through thick hedgerows.

Home, Cal thought. Home for supper. Ma doesn't like you to be late.

He found himself smiling, and reached down without thinking to raise the window and let in the cool, moist air.

The light. It swelled his artist's heart. No one could have described the light of Ireland to him. It had to be seen, experienced. Like the sheen of a fine pearl, he thought, that makes the air glimmer, go luminous and silky. The sun filtering through layers of clouds had a softness, a majesty he'd never seen anywhere else.

He had to capture it. Now. Immediately. Surely such magic couldn't last. He bolted out of the room, clattered down the short flight of steps, and burst out into the gentle sun with the cat scampering at his heels.

He grabbed the Nikon off the front seat of his car. His hands were quick and competent as he changed lenses. Then swinging his case over his shoulder, he picked his position.

The fairy-tale cottage, he thought, the abundance of flowers. The light. Oh, that light. He framed, calculated and framed again.

CHAPTER 3

Bryna stepped through the arched doorway of the ruin and watched him. Such energy, such concentration. Her lips bowed up. He was happy in his work, in his art. He needed this time, she thought, just as he'd needed those hours of deep, dreamless sleep.

Soon he would have questions again, and she would have to answer. She stepped back inside, wanting to give him his privacy. Alone with her thoughts, she walked to the center of the castle, where flowers grew out of the dirt in a circle thick with blooms. Lifting her face to the light, raising her arms to the sky, she began her chant.

Power tingled in her fingertips, but it was weak. So weak that she wanted to weep in frustration. Once she had known its full strength; now she knew the pain of its decline.

It was ordained, this I know. But here on ground where flowers grow, I call the wind, I call the sun. What was done can be undone. No harm to him shall come through me. As I will, so mote it be.

The wind came, fluttering her hair like gentle fingers. The sun beat warm on her upturned face.

I call the faeries, I call the wise. Use what power you can devise. Hear me speak, though my charms are weak. Cast the circle for my own true love, guard him fast from below, from above. Harm to none, my vow is free. As I will, so mote it be.

The power shimmered, brighter, warmer. She fought to hold it, to absorb what gift was given. She thrust up a hand, the silver of the ring she wore exploding with light as a single narrow beam shot through the layering clouds and struck. The heat of it flowed up her arm, made her want to weep again. This time in gratitude.

She was not yet defenseless.

Cal clicked the shutter again and again. He took nearly a dozen pictures of her. She stood, still as a statue in a perfect circle of flowers. Some odd trick of the wind made it blow her hair away from her glowing face. Some odd trick of the light made it beam down on her in a single perfect diagonal shaft.

She was beautiful, unearthly. Though his heart stumbled when her fingers appeared to explode with light, he continued to circle her and capture her on film.

Then she began to move. Just a sway of her body, rhythmic, sensual. The wind whipped the thin fabric of her dress, then had it clinging to those slim curves. The language she spoke now was familiar from his dreams. With unsteady hands, Cal lowered the camera. It was unsettling enough that he somehow understood the ancient tongue. But he would see beyond the words and into her thoughts as clearly as if they were written on a page.

Protect. Defend. The battle is nearly upon us. Help me. Help him.

There was desperation in her thoughts. And fear. The fear made him want to reach out, soothe her, shield her. He stepped forward and into the circle.

The moment he did, her body jerked. Her eyes opened, fixed on his. She held up a hand quickly before he could touch her. "Not here." Her voice was raw and thick. "Not now. It waits for the moon to fill."

Flowers brushed her knees as she walked out of the circle. The wind that had poured through her hair gentled, died.

"You rested well?" she asked him.

"What the hell is going on here?" His eyes narrowed. "What the hell did you put in my tea?"

"A dollop of Irish. Nothing more." She smiled at his camera. "You've been working. I wondered what you would see here, and need to show."

"Why did you strip me?"

"Your clothes were damp." She blinked once, as she saw his thoughts in his eyes. Then she laughed, low and long with a female richness that stirred his blood. "Oh, Cal, you have a most attractive body. I'll not deny I looked. But in truth, I'm after preferring a man awake and participating when it comes to the matters you're thinking of."

Though furious, he only angled his head. "And would you find it so funny if you'd awakened naked in a strange bed after taking tea with a strange man?"

Her lips pursed, then she let out a breath. "Your point's taken, well taken. I'm sorry for it. I promise you I was thinking only of giving you your ease." Then the humor twinkled again. "Or mostly only of that." She spread her arms. "Would you like to strip me, pay me back in kind?"

He could imagine it, very well. Peeling that long, thin dress away from her, finding her beneath. "I want answers." His voice was sharp, abrupt. "I want them now."

"You do, I know. But are you ready, I wonder?" She turned a slow circle. "Here, I suppose, is the place for it. I'll tell you a story, Calin Farrell. A story of great love, great betrayal. One of passion and greed, of power and lust. One of magic, gained and lost."

"I don't want a story. I want answers."

"It's the same they are. One and the other." She turned back to him, and her voice flowed musically. "Once, long ago, this castle guarded the coast, and its secrets. It rose silver and shining above the sea. Its walls were thick, its fires burned bright. Servants raced up and down the stairways, into chambers. The rushes were clean and sweet on the floor. Magic sang in the air."

She walked toward curving steps, lifted her hem and began to climb. Too curious to argue, Cal followed her.

He could see where the floors had been, the lintels and stone bracings. Carved into the walls were small openings. Too shallow for chambers, he imagined. Storage, perhaps. He saw, too, that some of the stones were blackened, as if from a great fire. Laying a hand on one, he swore he could still feel heat.

"Those who lived here," she continued, "practiced their art and harmed none. When someone from the village came here with ails or worries, help was offered. Babies were born here," she said as she stepped through a doorway and into the sun again. "The old died."

She walked across a wide parapet to a stone rail that stood over the lashing sea.

"Years passed in just this way, season to season, birth to death. It came to be that some who lived here went out into the land. To make new places. Over the hills, into the forests, up into the mountains, where the faeries have always lived."

The view left him thunderstruck, awed, thrilled. But he turned to her, cocked a brow. "Faeries."

She smiled, turned and leaned back against the rail.

"One remained. A woman who knew her fate was here, in this place. She gathered her herbs, cast her spells, spun her wool. And waited. One day he came, riding over the hills on a fine black horse. The man she'd waited for. He was a warrior, brave and strong and true of heart. Standing here, just here, she saw the sun glint off his armor. She prepared for him, lighting the candles and torches to show him the way until the castle burned bright as a flame. He was wounded."

Gently she traced a fingertip on Cal's thigh. He forced himself not to step back, not to think about the hallucination he'd had while driving through the hills toward this place.

"The battle he had fought was fierce. He was weary in body and heart and in mind. She gave him food and ease and the warmth of her fire. And her love. He took the love she gave, offered back his own. They were all to each other from that moment. His name was Caelan, Caelan of Farrell, and hers Bryna. Their hearts were linked."

He stepped back now, dipping his hands into his pockets. "You expect me to buy that?"

"What I offer is free. And there's more of the story yet." The frustration at having him pull back flickered over her face. "Will you hear it, or not?"

"Fine." He moved a shoulder. "Go ahead."

She turned, clamped her hands on the stone balustrade, let

the thunder of the sea pound in her head. She stared down at that endless war of water and rock that fought at the base of the cliff.

"They loved each other, and pledged one to the other. But he was a warrior, and there were more battles to fight. Whenever he would leave her, she watched in the fire she made, saw him wheel his horse through smoke and death, lift his sword for freedom. And always he came back to her, riding over the hills on a fine black horse. She wove him a cloak out of dark gray wool, to match his eyes. And a charm she put on it, for protection in battle."

"So you're saying she was a witch?"

"A witch she was, yes, with the power and art that came down through the blood. And the vow she'd taken to her heart, as close as she'd taken the man she loved, to harm none. Her powers she used only to help and to heal. But not all with power are true. There was one who had chosen a different path. One who used his power for gain and found joy in wielding it like a bloody sword."

She shuddered once, violently, then continued. "This man, Alasdair, lusted for her—for her body, her heart, her soul. For her power as well—for she was strong, was Bryna the Wise. He came into her dreams, creeping like a thief, trying to steal from her what belonged to another. Trying to take what she refused to give. He came into her home, but she would not have him. He was fair of face, his hair gold and his eyes black as the path he'd chosen. He thought to seduce her, but she spurned him."

Her fingers tightened on the stone, and her heart began to trip. "His anger was huge, his vanity deep. He set to kill the man she loved, casting spells, weaving charms of the dark. But the cloak she had woven and the love she had given protected him from harm. But there are more devious ways to destroy. Alasdair used them. Again in dreams he planted seeds of doubt, hints of betrayal in Caelan's sleeping mind. Alasdair gave him visions of Bryna with another, painted pictures of her wrapped in another man's arms, filled with another man's seed. And with these images tormenting his mind, Caelan rode his fine black horse over the hills to this place. And finding her he accused her.

"She was proud," Bryna said after a moment. "She would not deny such lies. They argued bitterly, tempers ruling over hearts. It was then that he struck—Alasdair. He'd waited only for the moment, laughing in the shadows while the lovers hurled pain at each other. When Caelan tore off his cloak, hurled it to the ground at her feet, Alasdair struck him down so that his blood ran through the stones and into the ground."

Tears glinted into her eyes, but went unshed as she faced Calin. "Her grief blinded her, but she cast the circle quickly, fighting to save the man she loved. His wound was mortal and there was no answer for him but death. She knew but refused to accept, and turned to meet Alasdair."

She lifted her voice over the roar of the sea. It came stronger now, this story through her. "Then the walls of this place rang with fury, with magic loosed. She shielded her love and fought like a warrior gone wild. And the sky thundered, clouds dark and thick covered the full white moon and blotted out the stars. The sea thrashed like men pitched in battle and the ground trembled and heaved.

"In the circle, weak and dying, Caelan reached for his sword. But such weapons are useless against witchcraft, light and dark, unless wielded with strength. In his heart he called for her, understanding now his betrayal and his own foolish pride. Her name was on his lips as he died. And when he died, her heart split in two halves and left her defenseless."

She sighed, closed her eyes briefly. "She was lost without him, you see. Alasdair's power spread like vultures' wings. He would have her then, willing or not. But with the last of her strength, she stumbled into the circle where her lover's blood stained the ground. There a vow she made, and a spell she cast. There, while the walls rang and the torches burned, she swore her abiding love for Caelan. For a thousand years she would wait, she would bide. She sent the fire roaring through her home, for she would not let Alasdair have it. And the spell she cast was this."

She drew a deep breath now, kept her eyes on his. "A thousand years to the night, they would come back and face

Alasdair as one. If their hearts were strong, they would defeat him in this place. But such spells have a price, and hers was to vow that if Caelan did not believe, did not stand with her that night as one, her power would wink out. And she would belong to Alasdair. Pledging this, she knelt beside her love, embraced him. And vanished them both.''

He waited a moment, surprised that he'd found her story and the telling of it hypnotic. Studying her, he rocked back on his heels. ''A pretty tale, Bryna.''

''Do you still see it as such?'' She shook her head, her eyes pleading. ''Can you look at me, hear me, and remember nothing?''

''You want me to believe I'm some sort of reincarnation of a Celtic warrior and you're the reincarnation of a witch.'' He let out a short laugh. ''We've waited a millennium and now we're going to do battle with the bad witch of the west? Come on, honey, do I look that gullible?''

She closed her eyes. The telling of the tale, the reliving of it had tired her. She needed all her resources now. ''He has to believe,'' she murmured, pacing away from the wall. ''There's no time for subtle persuading.'' She whirled back to face him. ''You had a vivid imagination as a child,'' she said angrily. ''It's a pity you tossed it aside. Tossed me aside—''

''Listen, sweetheart—''

''Oh, don't use those terms with me. Haven't I heard you croon them to other women as you guided them into bed? I didn't expect you to be a monk waiting for this day, but did you have to enjoy it so damn much?''

''Excuse me?''

''Oh, never mind. Just never mind.'' She gestured impatiently as she paced. '' 'A pretty tale,' he says. Did it take a millennium to make him so stubborn, so blind? Well, we'll see, Calin Farrell, what we'll see.''

She stopped directly in front of him, her eyes burning with temper, her face flushed with it. ''A reincarnation of a witch? Perhaps that's true. But you'll see for yourself one simple fact. I am a witch, and not without power yet.''

''Crazy is what you are.'' He started to turn.

"Hold!" She drew in a breath, and the wind whipped again, wild and wailing. His feet were cemented to the spot. "See," she ordered and flung a hand down toward the ground between them.

It was the first charm learned, the last lost. Though her hand trembled with the effort, the fire erupted, burning cold and bright.

He swore and would have leaped back if he'd been able. There was no wood, there was no match, just that golden ball of flame shimmering at his feet. "What the hell is this?"

"Proof, if you'll take it." Over the flames, she reached out a hand. "I've called to you in the night, Calin, but you wouldn't hear me. But you know me—you know my face, my mind, my heart. Can you look at me and deny it?"

"No." His throat was dust-dry, his temples throbbing. "No, I can't. But I don't want this."

Her hand fell to her side. The fire vanished. "I can't make you want. I can only make you see." She swayed suddenly, surprising them both.

"Hey!" He caught her as her legs buckled.

"I'm just tired." She struggled to find her pride at least, to pull back from him. "Just tired, that's all."

She'd gone deathly pale, he noted, and she felt as limp as if every bone in her body had melted. "This is crazy. This whole thing is insane. I'm probably just having another hallucination."

But he swept her up into his arms and carried her down the circle of stone steps and away from the Castle of Secrets.

CHAPTER 4

"Brandy," **he muttered,** shouldering open the door to the cottage. The cat slipped in like smoke and led the way down the short hall. "Whiskey. Something."

"No." Though the weakness still fluttered through her, she shook her head. "I'm better now, truly."

"The hell you are." She felt fragile enough to dissolve in his arms. "Have you got a doctor around here?"

"I don't need a doctor." The idea of it made her chuckle a little. "I have what I need in the kitchen."

He turned his head, met her eyes. "Potions? Witch's brews?"

"If you like." Unable to resist, she wound her arms around his neck. "Will you carry me in, Calin? Though I'd prefer it if you carried me upstairs, took me to bed."

Her mouth was close to his, already softly parted in invitation. He felt his muscles quiver. If he was caught in a dream, he mused, it involved all of the senses and was more vivid than any he'd had in childhood.

"I didn't know Irish women were so aggressive. I might have visited here sooner."

"I've waited a long time. I have needs, as anyone."

Deliberately he turned away from the steps and started down the hall. "So, witches like sex."

That chuckle came again, throaty and rich. "Oh, aye, we're fond of it. I could give you more than an ordinary woman. More than you could dream."

He remembered the jolt of that staggering kiss of welcome.

And didn't doubt her word. He made a point of dropping her, abruptly, on one of the two ladder-back chairs at a scrubbed wooden table in the tiny kitchen.

"I dream real good," he said, and she smiled silkily.

"That I know." The air hummed between them before she eased back, tidily folded her hands on the table. "There's a blue bottle in the cupboard there, over the stove. Would you mind fetching it for me, and a glass as well?"

He opened the door she indicated, found the cupboard neatly lined with bottles of all colors and shapes. All were filled with liquids and powders, and none were labeled. "Which one of these did you put in my tea?"

Now she sighed, heavily. "Cal, I put nothing in your tea but the whiskey. I gave you sleep—a small spell, and a harmless one—because you needed it. Two hours only, and did you not wake feeling well and rested?"

He scowled at the bottles, refusing to argue the point. "Which blue one?"

"The cobalt bottle with the long neck."

He set the bottle and a short glass on the table. "Drugs are dangerous."

She poured a careful two fingers of liquid as blue as the bottle that held it. " 'Tis herbs." Her eyes flickered up to his, laughed. "And a touch or two of magic. This is for energy and strength." She sipped with apparent enjoyment. "Will you be sitting down, Calin? You could use a meal, and it should be ready by now."

He'd already felt his stomach yearn at the scents filling the room, puffing out of the steam from a pot on the stove.

"What is it?"

"Craibechan." She smiled as his brows drew together. "A kind of soup," she explained. "It's hearty, and your appetite's been off. You've lost more than a pound or two in recent weeks, and I feel the blame for that."

Wanting to see just what craibechan consisted off—and make sure there was no eye of newt or tongue of frog in the mix, he had started to reach for the lid on the pot. Now he drew back, faced her. He was going to make one vital point perfectly clear.

"I don't believe in witches."

A glint of amusement was in her eyes as she pushed back from the table. "We'll set to working on that soon enough."

"But I'm willing to consider some sort of . . . I don't know . . . psychic connection."

"That's a beginning, then." She took out a loaf of brown bread, set it in the oven to warm. "Would you have wine with your meal? There's a bottle you could open. I've chilled it a bit." She opened the refrigerator, took out a bottle.

He accepted it, studied the label. It was his favorite Bourdeax—a wine that he preferred chilled just a bit. Considering, he took the corkscrew she offered.

The obsessed-fan theory just didn't hold, he decided, as he set the open bottle on the slate-gray counter to breathe. No matter how much information she might have dug up about him, she couldn't have predicted he would come to Ireland—and certainly not to this place.

He would accept the oddity of a connection. What else could he call it? It had been her voice echoing through his dreams, her face floating through the mists of his memory. And it had been his hands on the wheel of the car he'd driven up to this place. To her.

It was time, he thought, to discover more about her.

"Bryna."

She paused in the act of spooning stew into thick white bowls. "Aye?"

"How long have you lived here, alone like this?"

"The last five years I've been alone. It was part of the pattern. The wineglasses are to the right of you there."

"How old are you?" He took down two crystal glasses, poured blood-red wine.

"Twenty-six. Four years less than you." She set the bowls on the table, took one of the glasses. "My first memory of you, this time, was of you riding a horse made out of a broom around a parlor with blue curtains. A little black dog chased you. You called him Hero."

She took a sip from her glass, set it down, then turned to take the warmed bread from the oven. "And when he died, fifteen years later on a hot summer day, you buried him in the backyard, and your parents helped you plant a rosebush over his grave. All of you wept, for he'd been very dear. Neither you nor your parents have had a pet since. You don't think you have the heart to lose one again.''

He let out a long, uneasy breath, took a deep gulp of wine. None of that information, none of it, was in his official bio. And certainly none of the emotions were public fare. "Where is your family?"

"Oh, here and there." She bent to give Hecate an affectionate scratch between the ears. "It's difficult for them just now. There's nothing they can do to help. But I feel them close, and that's comfort enough."

"So . . . your parents are witches too?"

She heard the amusement in his voice and bristled. "I'm a hereditary witch. My power and my gift runs through the blood, generation to generation. It's not an avocation I have, Calin, nor is it a hobby or a game. It is my destiny, my legacy and my pride. And don't be insulting me when you're about to eat my food." She tossed her head and sat down.

He scratched his chin. "Yes, ma'am." He sat across from her, sniffed at the bowl. "Smells great." He spooned up some, sampled, felt the spicy warmth of it spread through his system. "Tastes even better."

"Don't flatter me, either. You're hungry enough to eat a plate of raw horsemeat."

"Got me there." He dug in with relish. "So, any eye of newt in here?"

Her eyes kindled. "Very funny."

"I thought so." It was either take the situation with humor or run screaming, he decided. "Anyway, what do you do up here alone?" No, he realized, he wasn't sure he wanted to know that. "I mean, what do you do for a living?"

It was no use being annoyed with him, she told herself. No use at all. "You're meaning to make money? Well, that's a necessary thing." She passed him the bread and salt butter. "I weave, and sell my wares. Sweaters, rugs, blankets, throws, and the like. It's a soothing art, and a solitary one. It gives me independence."

"The rugs in the other room? Your work?"

"They are, yes."

"They're beautiful—color, texture, workmanship." Remembering the spinning wheel, he blinked. "Are you telling me you spin your own wool?"

"It's an old and venerable art. One I enjoy."

Most of the women he knew couldn't even sew on a button. He'd never held the lack of domesticity against anyone, but he found the surplus of it intriguing in Bryna. "I wouldn't think a witch would . . . well, I'd think she'd just— you know—*poof.*"

"Proof?" Her brows arched high. "Saying if I wanted a pot of gold I'd just whistle up the wind and coins would drop into my hands?" She leaned forward. Annoyance spiked her voice. "Tell me why you use that camera with all the buttons and business when they make those tidy little things that all but think for you and snap the picture themselves?"

"It's hardly worthwhile if you automate the whole process. If it's to mean anything I have to be involved, in control, do the planning out, see the picture . . ." He trailed off, catching her slow, and smug, smile. "Okay, I get it. If you could just snap your fingers it wouldn't be art."

"It wouldn't. And more, it's a pledge, you see. Not to abuse a gift or take it for granted. And most vital, never to use power to harm. You nearly believe me, Calin."

Stunned that she was right, he jerked back. "Just making conversation," he muttered, then rose to refill his empty bowl, the cat trailing him like a hopeful shadow. "When's the last time you were in the States?"

"I've never been to America." She picked up her wine after he topped it off. "It wasn't permitted for me to contact you, face-to-face, until you came here. It wasn't permitted for you to come until one month before the millennium passed."

Cal drummed his fingers on the table. She sure knew how to stick to a story. "So it's a month to the anniversary of . . . the spell casting."

"No, it's on the solstice. Tomorrow night." She picked up her wine again, but only turned the stem around and around in her fingers.

"Cutting it close, aren't you?"

"You didn't want to hear me—and I waited too long. It was pride. I was wanting you to call to me, just once." Defeated by her own heart, she closed her eyes. "Like some foolish teenage girl waiting by the phone for her boy to call her. You'd hurt me when you turned away from me." Her eyes opened again, pinned him with the sharp edge of her unhappiness. "Why did you turn from me, Calin? Why did you stop answering, stop hearing?"

He couldn't deny it. He was here, and so was she. He'd been pulled to her, and no matter how he struggled to refuse it, he could remember—the soft voice, the plea in it. And those eyes, so incredibly blue, with that same deep hurt glowing in them.

It was, he realized, accept this or accept insanity. "Because I didn't want to answer, and I didn't want to be here." His voice roughened as he shoved the bowl aside. "I wanted to be normal."

"So you rejected me, and the gift you'd been given, for what you see as normality?"

"Do you know what it's like to be different, to be odd?" he tossed back furiously. Then he hissed through his teeth. "I suppose you do," he muttered. "But I hated it, hated seeing how it worried my parents."

"It wasn't meant to be a burden but a joy. It was part of her, part of me that was passed to you, Calin, that small gift of sight. To protect you, not to threaten."

"I didn't want it!" He shoved back from the table. "Where are my rights in all this? Where's my choice?"

She wanted to weep for him, for the small boy who hadn't understood that his uniqueness had been a loving gift. And for the man who would reject it still. "The choice has always been yours."

"Fine. I don't want any of this."

"And me, Calin." She rose as well, slowly, pride in the set of her shoulders, the set of her head. "Do you not want me as well?"

"No." It was a lie, and it burned on his tongue. "I don't want you."

He heard the laughter, a nasty buzz on the air. Hecate hissed, arched her back, then growled out a warning. Cal saw fear leap into Bryna's eyes even as she whirled and flung herself in front of him like a shield.

"No!" Her voice boomed, power and authority. "You are not welcome here. You have no right here."

The shadows in the doorway swirled, coalesced, formed into a man. He wore sorcerer's black, piped with silver, on a slender frame. A face as handsome as a fairy-tale prince was framed with golden hair and accented with eyes as black as midnight.

"Bryna, your time is short." His voice was smooth, laced with dark amusement. "There is no need for this war between us. I offer you such power, such a world. You've only to take my hand, accept."

"Do you think I would? That a thousand years, or ten thousand, would change my heart? Doomed you are, Alasdair, and the choice was your own."

"The wait's nearly at an end." Alasdair lifted a hand, and thunder crashed overhead like swords meeting. "Send him away and I will allow it. My word to you, Bryna. Send him away and he goes unharmed by me. If he stays, his end will be as it was before, and I will have you, Bryna, unbound or in chains. That choice is your own."

She lifted a hand, and light glinted off her ring of carved silver. "Come into my circle now, Alasdair." Her lips curved in a sultry dare, though her heart was pounding in terror, for she was not ready to meet him power to power. "Do you risk it?"

His lips thinned in a sneer, his dark eyes glittering with malicious promise. "On the solstice, Bryna." His gaze flickered to Cal, amusement shining dark. "You, warrior, remember death."

There was pain, bright and sharp and sudden, stabbing into Cal's belly. It burned through him like acid, cutting off his breath, weakening his knees, even as he gripped Bryna's shoulders and shoved her behind him.

"Touch her and die." He felt the words rise in his throat,

heard them come through his lips. He felt the sweat pearl cold and clammy on his brow as he faced down the image.

And so it faded, leaving only a dark glint like a smudge, and an echo of taunting laughter.

CHAPTER 5

Cal pressed a hand to his stomach, half expecting to find blood, and worse, dripping through his fingers. The pain had dulled to numbness, with a slick echo of agony.

"He can't harm you." Bryna's voice registered dimly, made him aware that he was still gripping her arm. "He can only make you remember, deceive you with the pain. It's all tricks and lies with him."

"I saw him." Dazed, Cal studied his own fingers. "I saw it."

"Aye. He's stronger than I'd believed, and more rash, to come here like this." Gently she put a hand over the one bruising her arm. "Alasdair is sly and full of lies. You must remember that, Calin. You must never forget it."

"I saw him," Cal repeated, struggling to absorb the impossible into reality. "I could see through him, the table in the hall, the flowers on it."

"He wouldn't dare risk coming here in full form. Not as yet. Calin, you're hurting my arm."

His fingers jerked, dropped. "Sorry. I lost my head. Seeing ghosts does that to me."

"A ghost he isn't. But a witch, one who embraced the dark and closed out the light. One who broke every oath."

"Is he a man?" He whirled on her so abruptly that she caught her breath, then winced as his hands gripped her arms again. "He looked at you as a man would, with desire."

"We're not spirits. We have our needs, our weaknesses. He wants me, yes. He has broken into my dreams and shown

me just what he wants from me. And rape in dreams is no
less a rape.'' She trembled and her eyes went blind. For a
moment she was only a woman, with a woman's fears. "He
frightens me. Is that enough for you? Is it enough that I'd
rather die than have his hands on me? He frightens me," she
said again and pressed her face into Cal's shoulder. "Oh,
Calin, his hands are cold, so cold."

"He won't touch you." The need to protect was too strong
to deny. His arms tightened, brought her close. "He won't
touch you. Bryna." His lips brushed over her hair, down her
temple. Found hers. "Bryna," he said again. "Sweet God."

She melted into him, yielding like wax, giving like glory.
All the confusion, the doubt, the fear slid away from him.
Here was the woman, the only, the ever. His hands dived
into her hair, fisted in those soft ropes of red silk, pulled her
head back so that he could drive the kiss deeper.

Whatever had brought him here he would face. Whatever
else he might continue to deny, there was no denying this.
Need could be stronger than reason.

The sounds humming in her throat were both plea and
seduction. Her heart hammered fast and hard against his, and
her body shuddered lightly. She nipped at his lip, urging him
on. He heard her sigh his name, moan it, then whisper words
ripe with longing.

The words were in Gaelic, and that was what stopped him.
He understood them as if he'd been speaking the language
all his life.

"Love," she had said. "My love."

"Is this the answer?" The fury returned as he pushed her
back against the wall. "Is this what you want?" Now his
kiss tasted of violence, of desperation, nearly of punishment.

Her own fears sprang hot to her throat, taunting her to fight
him, to reject the anger. But she offered no struggle, took the
heat, the rough hands until he drew back and stared at her
out of stormy eyes.

She took a steadying breath, waited until she was sure her
voice would be strong and sure. "It's one answer. Yes, I
want you." Slowly she unfastened the buttons running down
the front of her dress. "I want you to touch me, to take me."

Parted the material, let it slide to the floor so that she stood before him defenseless and naked. "Where you like, when you like, how you like."

He kept his eyes on hers. "You said that to me before, once before."

Emotions swirling, she closed her eyes, then opened them again. And smiled. "I did. A thousand years ago. More or less."

He remembered. She had stood facing him, flowers blooming at her feet. And she had undraped herself so that the pearly light had gleamed on her skin. She had offered herself without restrictions. He'd lost himself in her, flowers crushed and fragrant under their eager bodies.

He shook his head, and the image faded away. Memory or imagination, it no longer mattered. He knew only one vital thing. "This is now. This is you and me. Nothing else touches it. Whatever happened or didn't happen before, this is for us."

He scooped her into his arms. "That's the way I want it," he stated.

She stared at him, for she was spellbound now. She'd thought he would simply take her where they stood, seeking release, even oblivion. She'd tasted the sharp edge of his passion, felt the violence simmering under his skin. Instead, he carried her in his arms as if she were something he could cherish.

And when he laid her on the bed, stepped back to look at her, she felt a flush warm her cheeks. She managed a quick smile. "You'll be needing your clothes off," she said, tried to laugh and sit up, but he touched a hand to her shoulder.

"I'll do it. Lie back, Bryna. I want to see you with your hair burning over the pillows, and the sun on your skin." He would photograph her like this, he realized. Would be compelled to see if he could capture the magic of it, of her—long limbs, slender curves, eyes full of needs and nerves.

He watched her as he undressed, and his voice was quiet and serious when he spoke. "Are you afraid of me?"

"I wasn't. I didn't expect to be." But her heart was fluttering like bird's wings. "I suppose I am, yes. A little. Because it means . . . everything."

He tossed his clothes toward the little chair, never taking his eyes from hers. "I don't know what I believe, what I can accept. Except one thing." He lowered himself to her, kept his mouth a whisper from hers. "This matters. Here. Now. You. It matters."

"Love me." She drew his mouth down to hers. "I've ached for you so long."

It was slow and testing and sweet. Sighs and secrets, tastes and textures. He knew how her mouth would fit against his, knew the erotic slide of her tongue, the suggestive arch of her hips. He swallowed each catchy breath as he took his hands slowly, so slowly over her. Skimming curves, warming flesh. He filled his hands with her breasts, then his mouth, teasing her nipples with tongue and teeth until she groaned out his name like a prayer.

She took her hands over him, testing those muscles, tracing the small scars. Not a warrior's body, but a man's, she thought. And for now; hers. Her heart beat slow and thick as he used his mouth on her with a patience and concentration she knew now she'd been foolish not to expect.

Her heart beat thickly, the sun warmed her closed lids as pleasure swamped her. And love held so long in her heart bloomed like wild roses.

"Calin."

His name shuddered through her lips when he cupped her. He watched her eyes fly open, saw the deep-blue irises go glassy and blind in speechless arousal. He sent her over the edge, viciously delighted when she cried out, shuddered, when her hands fell weakly.

His, was all he could think as he blazed a hot trail down her thigh. His. His.

Blood thundered in his head as he slipped inside her, as she moaned in pleasure, arched in welcome. Now her eyes were open, vivid blue and intense. Now her arms were around him, a circle of possession. She mated with him, their rhythm ancient and sure.

His strokes went deep, deeper, and his mouth crushed

down on hers in breathless, mutual pleasure. She flew, as she had waited a lifetime to fly, as he emptied himself into her.

She held him close as the tension drained from his body. Stroked his hair as he rested his head between her breasts. "It's new," she said quietly. "Ours. I didn't know it could be. Knowing so much, yet this I never knew."

He shifted, lifted his head so that he could see her face. Her skin was soft, dewy, her eyes slumberous, her mouth rosy and swollen. "None of this should be possible." He cupped a hand under her chin, turned her profile just slightly, already seeing it in frame, in just that light. Black and white. And he would title it *Aftermath*. "I'm probably having a breakdown."

Her laugh was a quick, silly snort. Carefree, careless. "Well, your engine seemed to be running fine, Calin, if you're after asking me."

His mouth twitched in response. "We're pushing into the twenty-first century. I have a fax built into my car phone, a computer in my office that does everything but make my bed, and I'm supposed to believe I've just made love to a witch. A witch who makes fire burn out of thin air, calls up winds where there isn't a breeze in sight."

She combed her fingers through his hair as she'd dreamed of doing countless times. "Magic and technology aren't mutually exclusive. It's only that the second so rarely takes the first into account. Normality is only in the perspective." She watched his eyes cloud at that. "You had visions, Calin. As a child you had them."

"And I put away childish things."

"Visions? Childish?" Her eyes snapped once, then she closed them on a sigh. "Why must you think so? A child's mind and heart are perhaps more open to such matters. But you saw and you felt and you knew things that others didn't. It was a gift you were given."

"I'm no witch."

"No, that only makes the gift more special. Calin—"

"No." He sat up, shaking his head. "It's too much. Let it be for a while. I don't know what I feel." He scrubbed his hands over his face, into his hair. "All I know is that here was where I had to be—and you're who I had to be with. Let the rest alone for a while.''

They had so little time. She nearly said it before she stopped herself. If time was so short, then what they had was precious. If she was damned for taking it for only the two of them, then she was damned.

''Then let it rest we will.'' She lay back, stretched out a hand for his. ''Come kiss me again. Come lie with me.''

He skimmed a hand up her thigh, watched her smile bloom slow. And the light. Oh, the light. ''Stay right there.'' He bounded out of bed, grabbing his jeans on the run.

She blinked. ''What? Where are you going?''

''Be right back. Don't move. Stay right there.''

She huffed out a breath at the ceiling. Then her face softened again and she stretched her arms high. Oh, she felt well loved. Like a cat thoroughly stroked. Chuckling, she glanced over at Hecate, curled in front of the hearth and watching her.

''Aye, you know the feeling, don't you? Well, I like it.'' The cat only stared, unblinking. Ten seconds. Twenty. Bryna closed her eyes. ''I need the time. Damn it, we need it. A few hours after so many years. Why should we be denied it? Why must there be a price for every joy? Go then, leave me be. If the fare comes due, I'll pay it freely.''

With a swish of her tail, the cat rose and padded out of the room. Calin's footsteps sounded on the steps seconds later. Prepared to smile, Bryna widened her eyes instead. He'd snapped two quick pictures before she could push herself up and cross her arms over her breast.

''What do you think you're about? Taking photographs of me without my clothes. Put it away. You won't be hanging me on some art gallery wall.''

''You're beautiful.'' He circled the bed, changing angles. ''A masterpiece. Drop your left shoulder just a little.''

''I'll do no such thing. It's outrageous.'' Shocked to the core, she tugged at the rumpled spread, pulled it up—and to Cal's mind succeeded only in looking more alluring and rumpled.

But he lowered the camera. ''I thought witches were supposed to like to dance naked under the full moon."

"Going skyclad isn't an exhibition. And there's a time and place for such things. No one snaps pictures of private matters nor of rituals."

"Bryna." Using all his charm, he stepped closer, tugged gently at the sheet she'd pulled over her breasts. "You have a beautiful body, your coloring is exquisite, and the light in here is perfect. Unbelievable." He skimmed the back of his fingers over her nipple, felt her tremble. "I'll show them to you first."

She barely felt the sheet slip to her waist. "I know what I look like."

"You don't know how I see you. But I'll show you. Lie back for me. Relax." Murmuring, he spread her hair over the pillows as he wanted it. "No, don't cover yourself. Just look at me." He shot straight down, then moved back. "Turn your head, just a little. I'm touching you. Imagine my hands on you, moving over you. There. And there." He braced a knee on the foot of the bed, working quickly. "If I had a darkroom handy, I'd develop these tonight and you'd see what I see."

"I have one." Her voice was breathless, aroused.

"What?"

"I had one put in for you, off the kitchen." Her smile was hesitant when he lowered the camera and stared at her. "I knew you would come, and I wanted you to have what you needed, what would make you comfortable."

So you would stay with me, she thought, but didn't say it.

"You put in a darkroom? Here?"

"Aye, I did."

With a laugh, he shook his head. "Amazing. Absolutely amazing." Rising, he set the camera down on the bureau. "I think you need to be a little more . . . mussed before I shoot the rest of that roll." He climbed onto the bed. "The things I do for my art," he murmured and covered her laughing mouth with his.

CHAPTER 6

Later, in the breezy evening when the sun gilded the sky and polished the air, he walked with her toward the cliffs. Both his mind and his body were relaxed, limber.

Logically he knew he should be racing to the nearest psychiatric ward for a full workup. But a lonely cliffside, a ruined castle, a beautiful woman who claimed to be a witch—visions and sex and legends. It was a time and place to set logic aside, at least for a while.

"It's a beautiful country," he commented. "I'm still trying to adjust that I've only been here since this morning. Barely twelve hours."

"Your heart's been here longer." It was so simple to walk with him, fingers linked. So simple. So ordinary. So miraculous. "Tell me about New York. All the movies, the pictures I've seen have only made me wonder more. Is it like that, really? So fast and crowded and exciting?"

"It can be." And at that moment it seemed a world away. A thousand years away.

"And your house?"

"It's an apartment. It looks out over the park. I wanted a big space so I could have my studio right there. It's got good light."

"You like to stand on the balcony," she began, then rolled her eyes when he shot her a quick look. "I've peeked now and then."

"Peeked." He caught her chin in his hand before she could turn away. "At what? Exactly?"

"I wanted to see how you lived, how you worked."

She eased away and walked along the rocks, where the water spewed up, showered like diamonds in the sunlight. Then she turned her head, tilting it in an eerily feline movement.

"You've had a lot of women, Calin Farrell—coming and going at all hours in all manner of dress. And undress."

He hunched his shoulders as if he had an itch he couldn't scratch. "You watched me with other women?"

"I peeked," she corrected primly. "And never watched for long in any case. But it seemed to me that you often chose women who were lacking in the area of intelligence."

He ran his tongue around his teeth. "Did it?"

"Well . . ." A shrug, dismissing. "Well, so it seemed." Bending, she plucked a wildflower that had forced its way through a split in the rock. Twirled it gaily under her nose. "Is it worrying you that I know of them?"

He hooked his thumbs in his pockets. "Not particularly."

"That's fine, then. Now, if I were the vindictive sort, I might turn you into an ass. Just for a short time."

"An ass?"

"Just for a short time."

"Can you do that sort of thing?" He realized when he asked it that he was ready to believe anything.

She laughed, the sound carrying rich music over wind and sea. "If I were the vindictive sort." She walked to him, handed him the flower, then smiled when he tucked it into her hair. "But I think you'd look darling with long ears and a tail."

"I'd just as soon keep my anatomy as it is. What else did you . . . peek at?"

"Oh, this and that, here and there." She linked her fingers with his and walked again. "I watched you work in your darkroom—the little one in the house where you grew up. Your parents were so proud of you. Startled by your talent, but very proud. I saw your first exhibition, at that odd wee gallery where everyone wore black—like at a wake."

"SoHo," he murmured. "Christ, that was nearly ten years ago."

"You've done brilliant things since. I could look through your eyes when I looked at your pictures. And felt close to you."

The thought came abruptly, stunning him. He turned her quickly to face him, stared hard into her eyes. "You didn't have anything to do with . . . you haven't made what I can do?"

"Oh, Calin, no." She lifted her hands to cover the ones on her shoulders. "No, I promise you. It's yours. From you. You mustn't doubt it," she said, sensing that he did. "I can tell you nothing that isn't true. I'm bound by that. On my oath, everything you've accomplished is yours alone."

"All right." He rubbed his hands up and down her arms absently. "You're shivering. Are you cold?"

"I was for a moment." Bone-deep, harrowing. Alasdair. She cast it out, gripped his hand tightly and led him over the gentle slope of the hill. "Even as a child I would come here and stand and look out." Content again, she leaned her head against his shoulder, scanning hill and valley, the bright flash of river, the dark shadows cast by twisted trees. "To Ireland spread out before me, green and gold. A dreaming place."

"Ireland, or this spot?"

"Both. We're proud of our dreamers here. I would show you Ireland, Calin. The bank where the columbine grows, the pub where a story is always waiting to be told, the narrow lane flanked close with hedges that bloom with red fuchsia. The simple Ireland."

Tossing her hair back, she turned to him. "And more. I would show you more. The circle of stones where power sleeps, the quiet hillock where the faeries dance of an evening, the high cliff where a wizard once ruled. I would give it to you, if you'd take it."

"And what would you take in return, Bryna?"

"That's for you to say." She felt the chill again. The warning. "Now I have something else to show you, Calin." She glanced uneasily over her shoulder, toward the ruins. Shivered. "He's close," she whispered. "And watching. Come into the house."

He held her back. He was beginning to see that he had run

from a good many things in his life. Too many things. "Isn't it better to face him now, be done with it?"

"You can't choose the time. It's already set." She gripped his hand, pulled. "Please. Into the house."

Reluctantly, Cal went with her. "Look, Bryna, it seems to me that a bully's a bully whatever else he might be. The longer you duck a bully, the worse he gets. Believe me, I've dealt with my share."

"Oh, aye, and had a fine bloody nose, as I remember, from one. The two of you, pounding on each other on the street corner. Like hoodlums."

"Hey, he started it. He tried to shake me down once too often, so I . . ." Cal trailed off, blew out a long breath. "Whoa. Too weird. I haven't thought about Henry Belinski in twenty years. Anyway, he may have bloodied my nose, but I broke his."

"Oh, and you're proud of that, are you now? Breaking the nose of an eight-year-old boy."

"*I* was eight too." He realized that she had maneuvered him neatly into the house, turned the subject, and gotten her own way. "Very clever, Bryna. I don't see that you need magic when you can twist a conversation around like that."

"Just a small talent." She smiled and touched his cheek. "I was glad you broke his nose. I wanted to turn him into a toad—I had already started the charm when you dealt with it yourself."

"A toad?" He couldn't help it, the grin just popped out. "Really?"

"It would have been wrong. But I was only four, and such things are forgiven in the child." Then her smile faded, and her eyes went dark. "Alasdair is no child, Calin. He wants more than to wound your pride, skin your knees. Don't take him lightly."

Then she stepped back, lifting both hands. *I call the wind around my house to swirl.* She twisted a wrist and brought the wind howling against the windows. *Fists of fog against my windows curl. Deafen his ears and blind his eyes. Come aid me with this disguise. Help me guard what was trusted to me. As I will, so mote it be.*

He'd stepped back from her, gaping. Fog crawled over the windows, the wind howled like wolves. The woman before him glowed like a candle, shimmering with a power he couldn't understand. The fire she'd made out of air was nothing compared with this.

"How much am I supposed to believe? Accept?"

She lowered her hands slowly. "Only what you will. The choice will always be yours, Calin. Will you come with me and see what I would show you?"

"Fine." He blew out a breath. "And after, if you don't mind, I'd like a glass of that Irish of yours. Straight up."

She managed a small smile. "Then you'll have it. Come." As she started toward the stairs, she chose her words carefully. "We have little time. He'll work to break the spell. His pride will demand it, and my powers are more . . . limited than they were."

"Why?"

"It's part of it," was all she would say. "And so is what I have to show you. It isn't just me he wants, you see. He wants everything I have. And he wants the most precious treasure of the Castle of Secrets."

She stopped in front of a door, thick with carving. There was no knob, no lock, just glossy wood and that ornate pattern on it that resembled ancient writing. "This room is barred to him by power greater than mine." She passed a hand over the wood, and slowly, soundlessly, the door crept open.

" 'Open locks,' " Cal murmured, " 'whoever knocks.' "

"No, only I. And now you." She stepped inside, and after a brief hesitation, he crossed the threshold behind her.

Instantly the room filled with the light of a hundred candles. Their flames burned straight and true, illuminating a small, windowless chamber. The walls were wood, thickly carved like the door, the ceiling low, nearly brushing the top of his head.

"A humble place for such a thing," Bryna murmured.

He saw nothing but a simple wooden pedestal standing in a white circle in the center of the room. Atop the column was a globe, clear as glass.

"A crystal ball?"

Saying nothing, she crossed the room. "Come closer." She waited, kept her hands at her side until he'd walked up and put the globe between them.

"Alasdair lusts for me, envies you, and covets this. For all his power, for all his trickery, he has never gained what he craves the most. This has been guarded by a member of my blood since before time. Believe me, Calin, wizards walked this land while men without vision still huddled in caves, fearing the night. And this ancient ball was conjured by one of my blood and passed down generation to generation. Bryna the Wise held this in her hands a thousand years past and through her power, and her love, concealed it from Alasdair at the last. And so it remained hidden. No one outside my blood has cast eyes on it since."

Gently, she lifted the globe from its perch, raised it high above her head. Candlelight flickered over it, into it, seemed to trap itself inside until the ball burned bright. When she lowered it, it glowed still, colors dazzling, pulsing, beating.

"Look, my love." Bryna opened her hand so that the globe rolled to her fingertips, clung there in defiance of gravity. "Look, and see."

He couldn't stop his hands from reaching out, cupping it. Its surface was smooth, almost silky, and warmed in his hands like flesh. The pulse of it, the life of it, seemed to swim up his arms.

Colors shifted. The bright clouds they formed parted, a magic sea. He saw dragons spewing fire and a silver sword cleaving through scales. A man bedding a woman in a flower-strewn meadow under a bright white sun. A farmer plowing a rocky field behind swaybacked horses. A babe suckling at his mother's breast.

On and on it went, image after image in a blur of life. Dark oceans, wild stars, a quiet village as still as a photograph. An old woman's face, ravaged with tears. A small boy sleeping under the shade of a chestnut tree.

And even when the images faded into color and light, the power sang. It flooded him, a river of wine. Cool and clean.

It hummed still when the globe was clear again, tossing the flames of the candles into his eyes.

"It's the world." Cal's voice was soft and thick. "Here in my hands."

"The heart of it. The hope for it. Power gleams there. In your hands now."

"Why?" He lifted his gaze to hers. "Why in my hands, Bryna?"

"I am the guardian of this place. My heart is in there as well." She took a slow breath. "I am in your hands, Calin Farrell."

"I can refuse?"

"Aye. The choice is yours."

"And if he—Alasdair—claims this?"

She would stop him. It would cost her life, but she would stop him. "Power can be twisted, abused—but what is used will turn on the abuser, ten times ten."

"And if he claims you?"

"I will be bound to him, a thousand years of bondage. A spell that cannot be broken." But with death, she thought. Only with death. "He is wicked, but not without weaknesses." She laid her hand on the globe so that they held it together. "He will not have this, Calin. Nor will he bring harm to you. That is my oath."

She stared hard into his eyes, murmuring. His vision blurred, his head spun. He lifted a hand as if to push back what he couldn't see. "No."

"To protect." She laid a hand on his cheek as she cast the charm. "My love."

He blinked, shook his head. For a moment his mind remained blank with some faint echo of words. "I'm sorry. What?"

Her lips curved. He would remember nothing, she knew. It was all she could do for him. "I said we need to go." She placed the globe back on the pedestal. "We're not to speak of this outside this room." She walked toward the door, held out a hand. "Come. I'll pour you that whiskey."

CHAPTER 7

That night his dreams were restful, lovely. Bryna had seen to that.

There was a man astride a gleaming black horse, riding hard over hills, splashing through a bright slash of river, his gray cape billowing in a brisk and icy wind.

There was the witch who waited for him in a silver castle atop a spearing cliff where candles and torches burned gold.

There was a globe of crystal, clear as water, where the world swam from decade to decade, century past century.

There was love sweet as honey and need sharp as honed steel.

And when he turned to her in the night, lost in dreams, she opened for him, took him in.

Bryna didn't sleep, nor did she dream. She lay in the circle of his arms while the white moon rose and the shudders his hands had caused quieted.

Who had loved her? she wondered. Cal, or Caelan? She turned her face into his shoulder, seeking comfort, a harbor from fear on this last night before she would face her fate.

He would be safe, she thought, laying a hand over his heart. She had taken great pains, at great risk, to assure it. And her safety depended on the heart that beat quietly under her palm. If he did not choose to give it freely, to stand with her linked by love, she was lost.

So it had been ordained in fire and in blood, on that terrible night a millennium before.

For a thousand years we sleep, a hundred years times ten.

*But blood stays true and hearts are strong when we are born
again. And in this place we meet, with love our lifted shield.
In the shortest night the battle will rage and our destiny be
revealed. My warrior's heart his gift to me, his sword bright
as the moon. If he brings both here of his own free will, we
will bring to Alasdair his doom. When the dawn breaks that
longest day and his love has found a way, our lives will then
be free of thee. As I will, so mote it be.*

The words of Bryna the Wise, lifted high the blazing castle
walls, echoed in her head, beat in her heart. When the moon
rose again, it would be settled.

Bryna lay in the circle of Cal's arms, listened to the wind
whisper, and slept not at all.

When Cal woke, he was alone, and the sun was streaming.
For a moment, he thought it had all been a dream. The
woman—the witch—the ruined castle and tiny cottage. The
globe that held the world. A hallucination brought on, he
thought, by fatigue and stress and the breakdown he'd secretly worried about.

But he recognized the room—the flowers still fresh in the
vases, the scent of them, and Bryna, on the air. True, then.
He pressed his fingers to his eyes to rub away sleep. All true,
and all unbelievable. And all somehow wonderful.

He got out of bed, walked into the charming little bathroom, stepped into the clawfoot tub, and twitched the circling
curtain into place. He adjusted the shower for hot and let the
steam rise.

He hadn't showered with her yet, Cal thought, grinning as
he turned his face into the spray. Hadn't soaped that long,
lovely body of hers until it was slick and slippery, hadn't
seen the water run through that glorious mane of flame-red
hair. Had yet to ease inside her while the water ran hot and
the steam rose in clouds.

His grin winked off, replaced by a look of puzzlement.
Had he turned to her in the night, in his dreams, seeking that
tangle of tongues and limbs, that slow, satiny slide of bodies?

Why couldn't he remember? Why couldn't he be sure?

What did it matter? Annoyed with himself, he flicked off

the water, snatched a towel from the heating rack. Whether it had been real or a dream, she was there for him as he'd wanted no one to be before.

Was it you, or another, she moved under in the night?

Cal's eyes went dark as the voice whispered slyly in his head. He toweled off roughly.

She uses you. Uses you to gain her own ends. Spellbinds you until she has what she seeks.

The room was suddenly airless, the steam thick and clogging his lungs. He reached blindly for the door, found only swirling air.

She brought you here, drew you into her web. Other men have been trapped in it. She seeks to possess you, body and soul. Who will you be when she's done with you?

Cal all but fell into the door, panicked for a shuddering instant when he thought it locked. But his slippery hands yanked it open and he stumbled into the cool, sun-washed air of the bedroom. Behind him the mists swirled dark, shimmered greedily, then vanished.

What the hell? He found himself trembling all over, like a schoolboy rushing out of a haunted house. It had seemed as if there had been . . . something, something cold and slick and smelling of death crowded into that room with him, hiding in the mists.

But when Cal turned and stepped back to the door, he saw only a charming room, a fogged mirror, and the thinning steam from his shower.

Imagination working overtime, he thought, then let out half a laugh. Whose wouldn't, under the circumstances? But he shut the bathroom door firmly before he dressed and went down to find her.

She was spinning wool. Humming along with the quiet, rhythmic clacking of spindle and wheel. Her hands were as graceful as a harpist's on strings and her wool was as white as innocence.

Her dress was blue this morning, deep as her eyes. A thick silver chain carrying an ornately carved pendant hung between her breasts. Her hair was pinned up, leaving that porcelain face unframed.

Cal's hands itched for his camera. And for her.

She looked up, her hands never faltering, and smiled. "Well, did you decide to join the living, then?"

"My body clock's still in the States. Is it late?"

"Hmm, nearly half-ten. You'll be hungry, I'll wager. Come, have your coffee. I'll fix your breakfast."

He caught her hand as she rose. "You don't have to cook for me."

She laughed, kissed him lightly. "Oh, we'd have trouble soon enough if you thought I did. As it happens, it's my pleasure to cook for you this morning."

His eyes gleamed as he nibbled on her knuckles. "A full Irish breakfast? The works."

"If you like."

"Now that you mention it . . ." His voice trailed off as he took a long, thorough study of her face. Her eyes were shadowed, her skin paler than it should have been. "You look tired. You didn't sleep well."

She only smiled and led him into the kitchen. "Maybe you snore."

"I do not." He nipped her at the waist, spun her around and kissed her. "Take it back."

"I only said maybe." Her brows shot up when his hands roamed around, cupped her bottom. "Are you always so frisky of a morning?"

"Maybe. I'll be friskier after I've had that coffee." He gave her a quick kiss before turning to pour himself a cup. "You know I noticed things this morning that I was too . . . distracted to take in yesterday. You don't have a phone."

She put a cast-iron skillet on a burner. "I have ways of calling those I need to call."

"Ah." He rubbed the chin he had neglected to shave. "Your kitchen's equipped with very modern appliances."

"If I choose to cook why would I use a campfire?" She sliced thick Irish bacon and put it on to sizzle and snap.

"Good point. You're out of sugar," he said absently when he lifted the lid on the bowl. "You spin your own wool, but you have a state-of-the-art stereo."

"Music is a comfort," she murmured, watching him go

unerringly to the pantry and fetch the unmarked tin that held her sugar supply.

"You make your own potions, but you buy your staples at the market." With quick efficiency, he filled her sugar bowl. "The contrast is fascinating. I wonder . . ." He stopped, stood with the sugar scoop in his hand, staring. "I knew where to find this," he said quietly. "I knew the sugar was on the second shelf in the white tin. The flour's in the blue one beside it. I knew that."

" 'Tis a gift. You've only forgotten to block it out. It shouldn't disturb you."

"Shouldn't disturb me." He neglected to add the sugar and drank his coffee black and bitter.

"It's yours to control, Cal, or to abjure."

"So if I don't want it, I can reject it."

"You've done so for half your life already."

It was her tone, bitter as the coffee, that had his eyes narrowing. "That annoys you."

She cut potatoes into quick slices, slid them into hot oil. "It's your choice."

"But it annoys you."

"All right, it does. You turn your back on it because you find it uncomfortable. Because it disturbs your sense of normality. As I do." She kept her back to him as she took the bacon out of the pan, set it to drain, picked up eggs. "You shut out your gift and me along with it because we didn't fit into your world. A tidy world where magic is only an illusion done with smoke and mirrors, where witches wear black hats, ride broomsticks, and cackle on All Hallows' Eve."

As the eggs cooked, she spooned up porridge, plopped the bowl on the table, and went back to slice bread. "A world where I have no place."

"I'm here, aren't I?" Cal said evenly. "Did I choose to be, Bryna, or did you will it?"

She uses you. She's drawn you into her web.

"Will it?" Insulted, struck to the bone, she whirled around to face him. "Is that what you think? After all I've told you, after all we've shared?"

"If I accept even half of what you've told me, if I put

aside logic and my own sense of reality and accept that I'm
standing in the kitchen with a witch, a stone's throw away
from an enchanted castle, about to do battle of some kind
with an evil wizard in a war that has lasted a millennium, I
think it's a remarkably reasonable question.''

"Reasonable?" With clenched teeth she swept back to the
stove and shoveled eggs onto a platter. " 'It's reasonable,'
says he. Have I pulled him in like a spider does a fly, lured
him across an ocean and into my lair?'' She thumped the
laden platter down and glared at him. "For what, might I ask
you, Calin Farrell? For a fine bout of sex, for the amusement
of having a man for a night or two. Well, I needn't have
gone to such trouble for that. There's men enough in Ireland.
Eat your breakfast or you'll be wearing it on your head like
a hat.''

Another time he might have smiled, but that sly voice was
muttering in his ear. Still he sat, picked up his fork, tapped
it idly against the plate. "You didn't answer the question. If
I'm to believe you can't lie to me, isn't it odd that you've
circled around the question and avoided a direct answer? Yes
or no, Bryna. Did you will me here?''

"Yes or no?''

Her eyes were burning-dry, though her heart was weeping.
Did he know he was looking at her with such doubt, such
suspicion, such cool dispassion? There was no faith in the
look, and none of the love she needed.

One night, she thought on a stab of despair, had not been
enough.

"No, Calin, will you here I did not. If that had been my
purpose, or in my power, would I have waited so long and
so lonely for you? I asked you to come, begged without
pride, for I needed you. But the choice to come or not was
yours.''

She turned away, gripping the counter as she looked out
the window toward the sea. "I'll give you more," she said
quietly, "as time is short." She inhaled deeply. "You broke
my heart when you shut me out of yours. Broke it to pieces,
and it's taken me years to mend it as best I could. That choice
was yours as well, for the knowledge was there in your head,

and again in your heart if you chose to see it. All the answers are there, and you have only to look.''

''I want to hear them from you.''

She squeezed her eyes tightly shut. ''There are some I can't tell you, that you must find for yourself.'' She opened her eyes again, lifted her chin and turned back to him.

Her face was still pale, he noted, her eyes too dark. The hair she'd bundled up was slipping its pins, and her shoulders were stiff and straight.

''But there's something that's mine to tell, and I'll give you that. I was born loving you. There's been no other in my heart, even when you turned from me. Everything I am, or was, or will be, is yours. I cannot change my heart. I was born loving you,'' she said again. ''And I will die loving you. There is no choice for me.''

Turning, she bolted from the room.

CHAPTER 8

She'd vanished. Cal went after her almost immediately but found no trace. He rushed through the house, flinging open doors, calling her. Then cursing her.

Damn temperamental female, he decided. The fury spread through him. That she would tell him she loved him, then leave him before he had even a moment to examine his own heart!

She expected too much, he thought angrily. Wanted too much. Assumed too much.

He hurried out of the house, raced for the cliffs. But he didn't find her standing out on the rocks, staring out to sea with the wind billowing her hair. His voice echoed back to him emptily, infuriating him.

Then he turned, stared at the scarred stone walls of the castle. And knew. "All right, damn it," he muttered as he strode toward the ruins. "We're going to talk this through, straight. No magic, no legends, no bullshit. Just you and me."

He stepped toward the arch and bumped into air that had gone solid. Stunned, he reached out, felt the shield he couldn't see. He could see through it to the stony ground, the fire-scored walls, the tumble of rock, but the clear wall that blocked him was cold and solid.

"What kind of game is this?" Eyes narrowed, he drove his shoulder against it, yielded nothing. Snarling, he circled the walls, testing each opening, finding each blocked.

"Bryna!" He pounded the solidified air with his fists until

they ached. "Let me in. Goddamn it, let me pass!"

From the topmost turret, Bryna faced the sea. She heard him call for her, curse her. And oh, she wanted to answer. But her pride was scored, her power teetering.

And her decision made.

Perhaps she had made it during the sleepless night, curled against him, listening to him dream. Perhaps it had been made for her, eons before. She had been given only one single day with him, one single night. She knew, accepted, that if she'd been given more she might have broken her faith, let her fears and needs tumble out into his hands.

She couldn't tell him that her life, even her soul, was lost if by the hour of midnight his heart remained unsettled toward her. Unless he vowed his love, accepted it without question, there was no hope.

She had done all she could. Bryna turned her face to the wind, let it dry the tears that she was ashamed to have shed. Her charge would be protected, her lover spared, and the secrets of this place would die with her.

For Alasdair didn't know how strong was her will. Didn't know that in the amulet she wore around her neck was a powder of poison. If she should fail, and her love not triumph, then she would end her life before she faced one of bondage.

With Cal's voice battering the air, she closed her eyes, lifted her arms. She had only hours now to gather her forces.

She began the chant.

Hundreds of feet below, Cal backed away, panting. What the hell was he doing? he asked himself. Beating his head against a magic wall to get to a witch.

How had his life become a fairy tale?

Fairy tale or not, one thing was solid fact. Tick a woman off, and she sulks.

"Go on and sulk, then," he shouted. "When you're ready to talk like civilized people, let me know." His mood black, he stalked back to the house. He needed to get out, he told himself. To lose himself in work for a while, to let both of them cool off.

One day, he fumed. He'd had one day and she expected him to turn his life around. Pledge his undying love. The hell with that. She wasn't pushing him into anything he wasn't ready for. She could take her thousand-year-old spell and stuff it. He was a normal human being, and normal human beings didn't go riding off into the sunset with witches at the drop of a hat.

He shoved open the bedroom door, reached for his camera. Under it, folded neatly, was a gray sweater. He pulled his hand back and stared.

"That wasn't there an hour ago," he muttered. "Damn it, that wasn't there."

Gingerly he rubbed the material. Soft as a cloud, the color of storms. He remembered vaguely something about a cloak and a charm and wondered if this was Bryna's modern-day equivalent.

With a shrug, he peeled off his shirt and tried the sweater on. It fit as though it had been made for him. Of course it had, he realized. She'd spun the wool, dyed it, woven it. She'd known the length of his arms, the width of his chest.

She'd known everything about him.

He was tempted to yank it off, toss it aside. He was tired of his life and his mind being open to her when so much of hers was closed to him.

But as he started to remove the sweater, he thought he heard her voice, whispering.

A gift. Only a gift.

He lifted his head, looked into the mirror. His face was unshaven, his hair wild, his eyes reflecting the storm-cloud color of the sweater.

"The hell with it," he muttered, and snatching up his camera and case, he left the house.

He wandered the hills for an hour, ran through roll after roll of film. Mockingbirds sang as he clambered over stone walls into fields where cows grazed on grass as green as emeralds. He saw farmers on tractors, tending their land under a cloud-thickened sky. Clothes flapping with whip snaps on the line, cats dozing in dooryards and sunbeams.

He wandered down a narrow dirt road where the hedgerows grew tall and thick. Through small breaks he spotted sumptuous gardens with flowers in rainbows of achingly beautiful colors. A woman with a straw hat over her red hair knelt by a flower bed, tugging up weeds and singing of a soldier gone to war. She smiled at him, lifted her hand in a wave as he passed by.

He wandered near a small wood, where leaves unfurled to welcome summer and a brook bubbled busily. The sun was straight up, the shadows short. Spending the morning in normal pursuits had settled his mood. He thought it was time to go back, see if Bryna had cooled down—perhaps try out the darkroom she had equipped.

A flash of white caught his eye, and he turned, then stared awestruck. A huge white stag stood at the edge of the leafy shadows, its blue eyes proud and wise.

Keeping his movements slow, controlled, Cal raised his camera, then swore lightly when the stag lifted his massive head, whirled with impossible speed and grace, and bounded into the trees.

"No, uh-uh, I'm not missing that." With a quick glance at the ruins, which he had kept always just in sight, Cal dived into the woods.

He had hunted wildlife with his camera before, knew how to move quietly and swiftly. He followed the sounds of the stag crashing through brush. A bird darted by, a black bullet with a ringed neck, as Cal leaped over the narrow brook, skidded on the damp bank, and dug in for the chase.

Sun dappled through the leaves, dazzling his eyes, and sweat rolled down his back. Annoyed, he pushed the arms of the sweater up to his elbows and strained to listen.

Now there was silence, complete and absolute. No breeze stirred, no bird sang. Frustrated, he shoved the hair out of his eyes, his breath becoming labored in the sudden stifling heat. His throat was parchment-dry, and thinking of the cold, clear water of the brook, he backtracked.

The sun burned like a furnace through the sheltering leaves now. It surprised him that they didn't singe and curl under the onslaught. Desperate for relief, he pulled off the sweater, laid it on the ground beside him as he knelt by the brook.

He reached down to cup water in his hand. And pulled back a cup of coffee.

"Do you good to get away for a few days, change of scene."

"What?" He stared down at the mug in his hand, then looked up into his mother's concerned face.

"Honey, are you all right? You've gone pale. Come sit down."

"I . . . Mom?"

"Here, now, he needs some water, not caffeine." Cal saw his father set down his fishing flies and rise quickly. Water ran out of the kitchen faucet into a glass. "Too much caffeine, if you ask me. Too many late nights in the darkroom. You're wearing yourself out, Cal."

He sipped water, tasted it. Shuddered. "I—I had a dream."

"That's all right." Sylvia rubbed his shoulders. "Everybody has dreams. Don't worry. Don't think about them. We don't want you to think about them."

"No—I thought it was, it wasn't . . ." Wasn't like before? he thought. It was more than before. "I went to Ireland." He took a deep breath, tried to clear his hazy brain. Desperately, he wanted to turn, rest his head against his mother's breast like a child. "Did I go to Ireland?"

"You haven't been out of New York in the last two months, slaving to get that exhibition ready." His father's brow creased. Cal saw the worry in his eyes, that old baffled look of concern. "You need a rest, boy."

"I'm not going crazy."

"Of course you're not." Sylvia murmured it, but Cal caught the faint uncertainty in her voice. "You're just imagining things."

"No, it's too real." He took his mother's hand, gripped it hard. He needed her to believe him, to trust him. "There's a woman. Bryna."

"You've got a new girl and didn't tell us." Sylvia clucked her tongue. "That's what this is about?"

Was that relief in her voice, Cal wondered, or doubt?

"Bryna—that's an odd name, isn't it, John? Pretty, though, and old-fashioned."

"She's a witch."

John chuckled heartily. "They all are, son. Each and every one." John picked up one of his fishing lures. The black fly fluttered in his fingers, its wings desperate for freedom. "Don't you worry now."

"I—I need to get back."

"You need to sleep," John said, toying with the fly. "Sleep and don't give her a thought. One woman's the same as another. She's only trying to trap you. Remember?"

"No." The fly, alive in his father's fingers. No, no, not his father's hand. Too narrow, too long. His father had workingman's hands, calloused, honest. "No," Cal said again, and as he scraped back his chair, he saw cold fury light his father's eyes.

"Sit down."

"The hell with you."

"Calin! Don't you speak to your father in that tone."

His mother's voice was a shriek—a hawk's call to prey—cutting through his head. "You're not real." He was suddenly calm, deadly calm. "I reject you."

He was running down a narrow road where the hedgerows towered and pressed close. He was breathless, his heart hammering. His eyes were focused on the ruined walls of the castle high on the cliff—and too far away.

"Bryna."

"She waits for you." The woman with the straw hat over her red hair looked up from her weeding and smiled sadly. "She always has, and always will."

His side burned from cramping muscles. Gasping for air, Cal pressed a hand against the pain. "Who are you?"

"She has a mother who loves her, a father who fears for her. Do you think that those who hold magic need family less than you? Have hearts less fragile? Needs less great?"

With a weary sigh, she rose, walked toward him and stepped into the break in the hedge. Her eyes were green, he saw, and filled with worry, but the mouth with its serious smile was Bryna's.

"You question what she is—and what she is bars you from giving your heart freely. Knowing this, and loving you, she has sent you away from danger and faces the night alone."

"Sent me where? How? Who are you?"

"She's my child," the woman said, "and I am helpless." The smile curved a little wider. "Almost helpless. Look to the clearing, Calin Farrell, and take what is offered to you. My daughter waits. Without you, she dies this night."

"Dies?" Terror gripped his belly. "Am I too late?"

She only shook her head and faded back into air.

He awoke, drenched with sweat, stretched out on the cool, damp grass of the bank. And the moon was rising in a dark sky.

"No." He stumbled to his feet, found the sweater clutched in his hand. "I won't be too late. I can't be too late." He dragged the sweater over his head as he ran.

Now the trees lashed, whipped by a wind that came from nowhere and howled like a man gone mad. They slashed at him, twined together like mesh to block his path with gnarled branches armed with thorns. He fought his way through, ignored the gash that sliced through denim into flesh.

Overhead, lighting cut like a broadsword and dimmed the glow of the full white moon.

Alasdair. Hate roiled up inside him, fighting against the love he'd only just discovered. Alasdair would not win, if he had to die to prevent it.

"Bryna." He lifted his head to the sky as it exploded with wild, furious rain. "Wait for me. I love you."

The stag stood before him, white as bone, its patient eyes focused. Cal rushed forward as it turned and leaped into the shadows. With only instinct to trust, he plunged into the dark to follow the trail. The ground trembled under his feet, thorns ripped his clothes to tatters as he raced to keep that flash of white in sight.

Then it was gone as he fell bleeding into a clearing where moonlight fought through the clouds to beam on a jet-black horse.

Without hesitation, Calin accepted the impossible. Taking

the reins, he vaulted into the saddle, his knees vising as the stallion reared and trumpeted a battle cry. As he rode, he heard the snap of a cloak flying and felt the hilt of a sword gripped in his own hand.

CHAPTER 9

The Castle of Secrets glimmered with the light of a thousand torches. Its walls glinted silver and speared up toward the moon. The stone floor of the great hall was smooth as marble. In the center of the charmed circle cast by the ancients, Bryna stood in a robe of white, her hair a fall of fire, her eyes the blue of heated steel.

Here she would make her stand.

"Do you call the thunder and whistle up the winds, Alasdair? Such showmanship."

In a swirl of smoke, a sting of sulphur, he appeared before her. Solid now, his flesh as real as hers. He wore the robes of crimson, of blood and power. His golden looks were beautiful, an angel's face but for the contrast of those dark, damning eyes.

"And an impressive, if overdone entrance," Bryna said lightly, though her pulse shuddered.

"Your trouble, my darling, is that you fail to appreciate the true delights of power. Contenting yourself with your woman's charms and potions when worlds are at your mercy."

"I take my oath, and my gifts, to heart, Alasdair. Unlike you."

"My only oath is to myself. You'll belong to me, Bryna, body and soul. And you will give me what I want the most." He flung up a hand so that the walls shook. "Where is the globe?"

"Beyond you, Alasdair, where it will remain. As I will."

She gestured sharply, shot a bolt of white light into the air to land and burn at his feet. A foolish gesture, she knew, but she needed to impress him.

He angled his head, smiled indulgently. "Pretty tricks. The moon is rising to midnight, Bryna. The time of waiting is ending. Your warrior has deserted you once again."

He stepped closer, careful not to test the edge of the circle and his voice became soft, seductive. "Why not accept—even embrace—what I offer you? Lifetimes of power and pleasure. Riches beyond imagination. You have only to accept, to take my hand, and we will rule together."

"I want no part of your kingdom, and I would rather be bedded by a snake than have your hands on me."

Murky blue fire gleamed at his fingertips, his anger taking form. "You've felt them on you in your dreams. And you'll feel them again. Gentle I can be, or punishing, but you'll never feel another's hand but mine. He's lost to you, Bryna. And you are lost to me."

"He's safe from you." She threw up her head. "So I have already won." Lifting her hands, she loosed a whip of power, sent him flying back. "Be gone from this place." Her voice filled the great hall, rang like bells. "Or face the death of mortals."

He wiped a hand over his mouth, furious that she'd drawn first blood. "A battle, then."

At his vicious cry, a shadow formed at his feet, and the shadow took the shape of a wolf, black-pelted, red-eyed, fangs bared. With a snarl, it sprang, leaping toward Bryna's throat.

Cal pounded up the cliff, driving his mount furiously. The castle glowed brilliant with light, its walls tall and solid again, its turrets shafts of silver that nicked the cloud-chased moon. With a burst of knowledge, he thrust a hand inside the cloak and drew out the globe that waited there.

It swam red as blood, fire sparks of light piercing the clouds. He willed them to clear, willed himself to see as he thundered higher toward the crest of the cliff.

Visions came quickly, overlapping, rushing. Bryna weeping as she watched him sleep. The dark chamber with the globe held between them and her whispering her spell.

You will be safe, you will be free. There is nothing, my love, you cannot ask of me. Follow the stag whose pelt is white, if your heart is not open come not back in the night. This gift and this duty I trust unto you. The globe of hope and visions true. Live, and be well, and remember me not. What cannot be held is best forgot. What I do I do free. As I will, so mote it be.

And terror struck like a snake, its fangs plunging deep into the heart. For he knew what she meant to do.

She meant to die.

She wanted to live, and fought fiercely. She sliced the wolf, cleaving its head from its body with one stroke of will. And its blood was black.

She sent her lights blazing, the burning cold that would scorch the flesh and freeze the bone.

And knew she would lose when midnight rang.

Alasdair's robes smoked from the violence of her power. And still he could not break the circle and claim her.

He sent the ground heaving under her feet, watched her sway, then fall to her knees. And his smile bloomed dark when her head fell weakly and that fiery curtain of hair rained over the shuddering stones.

"Will you ask for pain, Bryna?" He stepped closer, felt the hot licks when his soft boots skimmed the verge of the circle. Not yet, he warned himself, inching back. But soon. Her spell was waning. "Just take my hand, spare yourself. We will forget this battle and rule. Give me your hand, and give me the globe."

Her breath was short and shallow. She whispered words in the old tongue, the secrets of magic, incantations that flickered weakly as her power slipped like water through her fingers.

"I will not yield."

"You will." He inched closer again, pleased when he met with only faint resistance. "You have no choice. The charm was cast, the time has come. You belong to me now."

He reached down, and her shoulder burned where his fingers brushed. "I belong to Calin." She gripped the amulet, steeling herself, then flipped its poison chamber open with her thumb. She whipped her head up and, with a last show of defiance, smiled. "You will never have what is his."

She brought the amulet to her lips, prepared to take the powder.

The horse and rider burst into the torchlight in a flurry of black, storm-gray, and bright steel.

"Would you rather die than trust me?" Cal demanded furiously.

The amulet slipped through her fingers, the powder sifted onto the stones. "Calin."

"Touch her, Alasdair"—Cal controlled the restless horse as if he'd been born astride one—"and I'll cut off your hands at the wrists."

Though there was alarm, and there was shock, Alasdair straightened slowly. He would not lose now. The woman was already defeated, he calculated, and the man was, after all, only a foolish mortal. "You were a warrior a thousand years ago, Caelan of Farrell. You are no warrior tonight."

Cal vaulted from the horse, and his sword sang as he pulled it from its scabbard. "Try me."

Unexpected little flicks of fear twisted in Alasdair's belly. But he circled his opponent, already plotting. "I will bring such fury raining down on your head . . ." He crossed his arms over his chest, then flung them to the side. Black balls of lightning shot out, hissing trails of snaking sparks.

Instinctively Cal raised the sword. Pain and power shot up his arm as the charges struck, careened away, and crashed smoking into stone.

"Do you think such pitiful weapons can defend against a power such as mine?" Arrogance and rage rang in Alasdair's voice as he hurled arrows of flame. His cry echoed monstrously as the arrows struck Cal's cloak and melted into water.

"Your power is nothing here."

Bryna was on her feet again, her white robe swirling like

foam. And her face so glowed with beauty that both men stared in wonder.

"I am the guardian of this place." Her voice was deeper, fuller, as if a thousand voices joined it. "I am a witch whose power flows clean. I am a woman whose heart is bespoken. I am the keeper of all you will never own. Fear me, Alasdair. And fear the warrior who stands with me."

"He will not stand with you. And what you guard, I will destroy." With fists clenched, he called the flames, shot the torches from their homes to wheel and burn and scorch the air. "You will bow yet to my will."

With lifted arms, Bryna brought the rain, streaming pure and cool through the flames to douse them. And felt as the damp air swirled, the power pour through her, from her, as rich and potent as any she'd known.

"Save this place," Alasdair warned, "and lose the man." He whirled on Cal, sneered at the lifted sword. "Remember · death."

Like a blade sliced through the belly, the agony struck. Blood flowed through his numbed fingers, and the sword clattered onto the wet stone. He saw his death, leaping like a beast, and heard Bryna's scream of fear and rage.

"You will not harm him. It's trickery only, Calin, hear me." But her terror for him was so blinding that she ran to him, leaving the charm of the circle.

The bolt of energy slapped her like a jagged fist, sent her reeling, crumbling. Paralyzed, she fought for her strength but found the power that had flowed so pure and true now only an ebbing flicker.

"Calin." The hand she'd flung out to shield him refused to move. She could only watch as he knelt on the stones, unarmed, bleeding, beyond her reach. "You must believe," she whispered. "Trust. Believe or all is lost."

"He loses faith, you lose your power." Robes singed and smoking, Alasdair stood over her. "He is weak and blind, and you have proven yourself more woman than witch to trade your power for his life."

Reaching down, he grabbed her hair and dragged her roughly to her knees. "You have nothing left," he said to her. "Give me the globe, come to me freely, and I will spare you from pain."

"You will have neither." She gripped the amulet, despairing that its chamber was empty. She bit off a cry as icy fingers squeezed viciously around her heart.

"From this time and this place, you are in bondage to me for a hundred years times ten. And this pain you feel will be yours to keep until you bend your will to mine."

He lowered his gaze to her mouth. "A kiss," he said, "to seal the spell."

She was wrenched out of his arms, her fingers locked with Cal's. Even as she whispered his name, he stepped in front of her, raised the sword in both hands so that it shimmered silver and sharp.

"Your day is done." Cal's eyes burned and the pain swirling through him only added to his strength. "Can you bleed, wizard?" he demanded and brought the sword down like fury.

There was a cry, ululating, inhuman, a stench of sulphur, a blinding flash. The ground heaved, the stones shook, and lightning, cold and blue, speared out of the air and struck.

The explosion lifted him off his feet. Even as he grabbed for Bryna, Cal felt the hot, greedy hand of it hurl him into the whirling air, into the dark.

CHAPTER 10

Visions played through his head. Too many to count. Voices hummed and murmured. Women wept. Charms were chanted. He swam through them, weighed down with weariness.

Someone told him to sleep, to be easy, but he shook off the words and the phantom hands that stroked his brow.

He had slept long enough.

He came to, groggy, aching in every bone. The thin light of pre-dawn filtered the air. He thought he heard whispering, but decided it was just the beat of the sea and the flow of the wind through grass.

He could see the last of the stars just winking out. And with a moan, he turned his head and tried to shake off the dream.

The cat was watching him, sitting patiently, her eyes unblinking. Dazed, he pushed himself up on his elbows, wincing from the pain, and saw that he was lying on the ground outside the ruins.

Gone were the tall silver spears, the glowing torches that had lighted the great hall. It was, as it had been when he'd first seen it, a remnant of what it once had been, a place where the wind wound about and the grass and wildflowers forced their way through stony ground.

But the scent of smoke and blood still stung the air.

"Bryna." Panicked, he heaved himself to his feet. And nearly stumbled over her.

She was sprawled on the ground, one arm outflung. Her

face was pale, bruised, her white robe torn and scorched. He fell to his knees, terrified that he would find no pulse, no spark of life. But he found it, beating in her throat, and shuddering with relief, he lowered his lips to hers.

"Bryna," he said again. "Bryna."

She stirred, her lashes fluttering, her lips moving against his. "Calin. You came back. You fought for me."

"You should have known I would." He lifted her so that he could cradle her against him, resting a cheek on her hair. "How could you have kept it from me? How could you have sent me away?"

"I did what I thought best. When it came to facing it, I couldn't risk you."

"He hurt you." He squeezed his eyes tight as he remembered how she'd leaped from safety and been struck down.

"Small hurts, soon over." She turned, laid her hands on his face. There were bruises there as well, cuts and burns. "Here." Gently, she passed her hands over them, took them away. Her face knit in concentration, she knelt and stroked her fingers over his body, skimming where the cloak hadn't shielded until every wound was gone. "There. No pain," she murmured. "No more."

"You're hurt." He lifted her as he rose.

"It's a different matter to heal oneself. I have what I need in the cupboard, in the kitchen."

"We weren't alone here. After?"

"No." Oh, she was so weary, so very weary. "Family watches over. The white bottle," she told him as he carried her through the kitchen door and sat her at the table. "The square one, and the small green one with the round stopper."

"You have explaining to do, Bryna." He set the bottles on the table, fetched her a glass. "When you're stronger."

"Yes, we've things to discuss." With an expert hand, an experienced eye, she mixed the potions into the glass, let them swirl and merge until the liquid went clear as plain water. "But would you mind, Calin, I'd like a bath and a change of clothes first."

"Conjure it," he snapped. "I want this settled."

"I would do that, but I prefer the indulgence. I'll ask you

for an hour.'' She rose, cupping the glass in both hands. "It's only an hour, Calin, after all.''

"One thing.'' He put a hand on her arm. "You told me you couldn't lie to me, that it was forbidden.''

"And never did I lie to you. But I came close to the line with omission. One hour,'' she said on a sigh that weakened him. "Please.''

He let her go and tried to soothe his impatience by brewing tea. His cloak was gone, he noted, and the sweater she'd woven for him stank of smoke and blood. He stripped it off, tossed it over the back of a chair, then glanced down as the cat came slinking into the room.

"So how do I handle her now?'' Cal cocked his head, studied those bland blue eyes. "Any suggestions? You'd be her familiar, wouldn't you? Just how familiar are you?''

Content with the cat for company, he crouched down and stroked the silky black fur. "Are you a shape-shifter too?'' He tilted the cat's head up with a finger under the chin. "Those eyes looked at me from out of the face of a white stag.''

Letting out a breath, he simply sat on the floor, let the cat step into his lap and knead. "Let me tell you something, Hecate. If a two-headed dragon walked up and knocked on the kitchen door, I wouldn't blink an eye. Nothing is ever going to surprise me again.''

But he was wrong about that. He was stunned with surprise when Bryna came downstairs again. She was as he'd seen her the night before, when her power had glowed in her face, striking it with impossible beauty.

"You were beautiful before,'' he managed, "but now . . . Is this real?''

"Everything's real.'' She smiled, took his hand. "Would you walk with me, Cal? I'm wanting the air and the sun.''

"I have questions, Bryna.''

"I know it,'' she said as they stepped outside. Her body felt light again, free of aches. Her mind was clear. "You're angry because you feel I deceived you, but it wasn't deception.''

"You sent the white stag to lure me into the woods, away from you."

"I did, yes. I see now that Alasdair knew, and he used it against me. I wanted you safe. Knowing you now—the man you are now—that became more important than . . ." She looked at the castle. "Than the rest. But he tricked you into removing the protection I'd given you, then sent you into dreams to cloud your mind and make you doubt your reason."

"There was a woman . . . she said she was your mother."

"My mother." Bryna blinked once, then her lips curved. "Was she in her garden, wearing a foolish hat of straw?"

"Yes, and she had your mouth and hair."

Clucking her tongue, Bryna strolled toward the ruins. "She wasn't meant to interfere. But perhaps it was permitted, as I bent the rules a bit myself. The air's clearing of him," she added as she stepped under the arch. "The flowers still bloom here."

He saw the circle of flowers, untouched, unscarred. "It's over, then. Completely?"

Completely, she thought and fought to keep her smile in place. "He's destroyed. Even at the moment of his destruction he tried to take us with him. He might have done it if you hadn't been quick, if you hadn't been willing to risk."

"Where's the globe now?"

"You know where it is. And there it stays. Safe."

"You trusted me with that, but you didn't trust me with you."

"No." She looked down at the hands she'd linked together. "That was wrong of me."

"You were going to take poison."

She bit her lip at the raw accusation in his voice. "I couldn't face what he had in mind for me. I couldn't bear it, however weak it makes me. I couldn't bear it."

"If I'd been a moment later, you would have done it. Killed yourself. Killed yourself," he repeated, jerking her head up. "You couldn't trust me to help you."

"No, I was afraid to. I was afraid and hurt and desperate.

Have I not the right to feelings? Do you think what I am strips me of them?''

Her mother had asked almost the same of him, he remembered. ''No.'' He said it very calmly, very clearly. ''I don't. Do you think what I'm not makes me less?''

Stunned, she shook her head, and pressing a hand to her lips, turned away. It wasn't only he who had questioned, she realized. Not only he who had lacked faith.

''I've been unfair to you, and I'm sorry for it. You came here for me and learned to accept the impossible in only one day.''

''Because part of me accepted it all along. Burying something doesn't mean it ceases to exist. We were born for what happened here.'' He let out an impatient breath. Why were her shoulders slumped, he wondered, when the worse of any life was behind them? ''We've done what we were meant to do, and maybe it was done as it was meant to be.''

''You're right, of course.'' Her shoulders straightened as she turned, and her smile was bright. And false, he realized as he looked into her eyes.

''He can't come back and touch you now.''

''No.'' She shook her head, laid a hand briefly on his. ''Nor you. He was swallowed by his own. His kind are always here, but Alasdair is no more.''

Then with a laugh she brought his hand to her cheek. ''Oh, Cal, if I could give you a picture, as fine and bold as any of your own. How you looked when you hefted that sword over your head, the light in your eyes, the strength rippling in waves around you. I'll carry that with me, always.''

She turned then, walked regally to the circle of flowers. In the center she turned, faced him, held out her hands. ''Calin Farrell, you met your fate. You came to me when my need was great, when my life was imperiled. In this place you stood between me and the unbearable, fought against magic dark and deadly, wielded sword for me. You've saved my life and in so doing saved this place and all I guard in it.''

''Quite a speech,'' he murmured and stepped closer.

She only smiled. ''You're brave and true of heart. And from this hour, from this place you are free.''

"Free?" Understanding was dawning, and he angled his head. "Free from you, Bryna?"

"Free from all and ever. The spell is broken, and you have no debt to pay. But a debt is owed. Whatever you ask that is in my power you shall have. Whatever boon you wish will be yours."

"A boon, is it?" He tucked his tongue in his cheek. "Oh, let's say, like immortality?"

Her eyes flickered—disappointment quickly masked. "Such things aren't within the power I hold."

"Too tough for you, huh?" With a nod, he circled around her as if considering. "But if I decided on, say, unlimited wealth or incredible sexual powers, you could handle that."

Her chin shot up another inch, went rigid. "I could, if it's what you will. But a warning before you choose. Be wary and sure of what you wish for. Every gift, even given freely, has a price."

"Yeah, yeah. I've heard that. Let's think about it. Money? Sex? Power, maybe. Power's good. I could have a nice island in the Caribbean, be a benign despot. I could get into that."

"This offer was not made for your amusement," she said stiffly.

"No? Well, it tickles the hell out of me." Rocking back on his heels, he tucked his hands into his pockets. "All I had to do was knock off an evil wizard and save the girl, and I can have whatever I want. Not a bad deal, all in all. So, just what do I want?"

He narrowed his eyes in consideration, then stepped into the circle. "You."

Eyes widening, she jerked back. "What?"

"You. I want you."

"To—to do what?" she said stupidly, then blinked when he roared with laughter. "Oh, you've no need to waste a boon there." She lifted her hands to unfasten her dress, and found them caught in his.

"That, too," he said, walking her backward out of the circle, keeping her arms up, her hands locked behind her head. "Yeah, in fact, I look forward to quite a bit of that."

The warrior was back, she thought dizzily. There, the glint

of battle and triumph in his eyes. "What are you doing?"

"I'm holding you to your boon. You, Bryna, all of you, no restrictions. For better or worse," he continued until he had her backed against the wall. "For richer or poorer. That's the deal."

She couldn't get her breath, couldn't keep her balance. "You want . . . me?"

"I'm not getting down on one knee when it's my boon."

"But you're free. The spell is broken. I have no hold on you."

"Don't you?" He lowered his mouth, buckling her knees with his kiss. "You can't lie to me." He crushed his lips to hers again, pulling her closer. "You were born loving me." He swallowed her moan and dived deeper. "You'll die loving me."

"Yes." Powerless, she flexed the hands he held above her head.

"Look at me," he murmured, easing back as she trembled. "And see." He gentled his hands, lowered them to stoke her shoulders. "Beautiful Bryna. Mine. Only mine."

"Calin." Her heart wheeled when his lips brushed tenderly over hers. "You love me. After it's done, after it's only you and only me. You love me."

"I was born loving you." The kiss was deep and sweet. "I'll die loving you." He sipped the tears from her cheeks.

"This is real," she said in a whisper. "This is true magic."

"It's real. Whatever came before, this is what's real. I love you, Bryna. You," he repeated. "The woman who puts whiskey in my tea, and the witch who weaves me magic sweaters. Believe that."

"I do." Her breath released on a shudder of joy. She felt it. Love. Trust. Acceptance. "I do believe it."

"It's time we made a home together, Bryna. We've waited long enough."

"Calin Farrell." She wound her arms around his neck, pressed her cheek against his. "Your boon is granted."

CASTLE DOOM

JILL GREGORY

To Marianne, Nora, and Ruth—with love

CHAPTER 1

Danger rode the moonless night like a witch as the slender, cloaked figure made her way through the gloom-shrouded countryside. The dark road was deserted, the woods flanking it silent but for the rustling tree branches and the moaning winter wind. Yet the gray night was fraught with peril. Arianne felt it in her bones. Fear prickled down her spine as she hurried along the road toward the Briar Knoll Inn. She glanced this way and that and tightened the snood that hid her fiery hair, but she never slowed her pace.

Once her fingers brushed the jeweled dagger hidden within her cloak, and the fear subsided a little. But her breath came in short, rapid bursts, and her skin beneath the dark woolen cloak felt clammy.

The fear was not for herself but for her brother, Marcus, the imprisoned Count of Galeron. And for the kingdom she'd left behind and the shattered lives of her people. All depended on her now, on what happened this night.

If she failed to free Marcus from the dungeon of Castle Doom this eve, all would be lost. He would be hanged in three days' time, and their distant cousin Julian would then have succeeded in cruelly subduing both his own lands of Dinadan and those of her beloved Galeron. Whatever these neighboring kingdoms had once known of peace and prosperity would be lost from that time forward. If she failed . . .

You shall not fail, Arianne told herself, quickening her pace as the shadowy outline of the inn's stables came into view. Her soft lips pressed together in determination. *Duke*

Julian will find that Marcus and I are not to be betrayed and bested so easily. He will discover that despite his treachery he has not yet won.

A sudden pounding of hooves sent her dashing for cover behind an oak tree, her heart skittering as she scrambled to conceal herself.

A pair of destriers ridden by Julian's black-masked knights came up the road, less than a stone's throw from her hiding place. Arianne crouched, scarcely daring to breathe, as deep voices reached her straining ears.

'' 'Tis a night for sleeping in a soft bed with a pretty maid,'' one of the soldiers grumbled, "not for patrolling when the whole damned countryside's asleep."

"Me, I'd rather be here than inside the walls of the castle." His companion's voice rumbled through the woods. "The duke heard a report earlier that Lady Arianne of Galeron had been found at the border. It proved false, but that, taken with the gypsy's prediction in the square yesterday about Lord Nicholas returning to wrest the kingdom away, put the duke in the devil's own black rage. Word is he struck down the minstrels playing at his supper and had the gypsy woman whipped and locked in the dungeon."

The soldier beside him gave a snort of laughter. His companion joined in and then continued, "Heard tell he imprisoned the messenger bearing the false report as well. He ordered that none of the prisoners in the dungeon are to be fed for three days."

"He needn't be so nervous. Lady Arianne will be found," the other soldier said with comfortable assurance, his voice fading as the horses moved off. "She can't stay in hiding forever."

The other man's reply was drowned out by the clatter of hooves as the horses turned onto the paved road to the inn.

Arianne drew in her breath. She found that she was trembling with rage. No food for the prisoners for three days!

Marcus, she thought, choking back a cry of despair for her brother. So Julian planned to starve him right up until his hanging.

Fury rose in a bitter tempest within her. At that moment

she wanted nothing more than to drive her dagger through Julian's heart herself, plunge it deep until his life's blood spilled across the castle floors.

But she quickly gained control of her emotions. If all went as planned tonight, Marcus would be freed within the next few hours. They would flee together, hide, and make their way to the secret camp where Felix, the captain of Galeron's troops, was gathering Marcus's scattered knights. Then they would plan how best to recapture Castle Galeron from Julian's marauders—

Arianne's thoughts broke off suddenly as black wings beat the sky above her head. She glanced up to see the crow wheeling, cawing harshly, toward the looming towers of the castle.

Arianne shivered. For a moment she feared that the crow was spying on her, carrying tales of her presence just outside the castle walls to Julian himself. But she shook off that absurd idea. Julian knew nothing, not even that she was here in Dinadan, for she'd been in disguise. No one, perhaps not even Morgana, her own lady-in-waiting, would recognize Lady Arianne of Galeron in the plain-gowned tavern wench who served ale and mopped floors at the Jug and Spoon Inn near the river road.

Standing in the windy darkness, the trees bending and sighing about her, Arianne stared for a moment at the castle that the villagers had of late dubbed Castle Doom. Even through the gloom, the outline of the towers and turrets seemed to glimmer with a cold white mist that chilled her to the bone. How strange that as children she and Marcus and Julian and Nicholas had all played and hidden and frolicked there, that once the gleaming stone fortress had been a place of rich beauty and gaiety, where minstrels performed and banquets were held and the people came and went in peace and harmony. Under Archduke Armand—Julian's father and a distant cousin to Arianne and Marcus—it had been a shimmering place where the duke ruled with wisdom and tolerance and an eye toward the welfare of his people.

But the good Duke Armand was dead now, and Julian, his son by his second wife, had succeeded him upon the throne.

Julian was a very different sort of man than his father had
been. A lying, cunning villain who even as a child had
cheated at games in order to win, Arianne remembered scorn-
fully.

If only Marcus had not left Galeron to try to forge a peace
treaty with Julian. If only Nicholas had not been banished . . .
Nicholas.

No use thinking of *him*, Arianne told herself angrily as she
spun away from the castle and headed swiftly toward the
stables behind the Briar Knoll Inn. *Lord Nicholas of Dinadan
has chosen not to return to Dinadan in its time of need,
ignoring the plight of your brother, whom he claimed as his
closest friend, she reminded herself. Do not think of him. He
is not what you imagined him all those years ago, when you
were naught but a silly child.*

A month ago, Marcus had come on his peacemaking mission to Duke Julian, to negotiate a treaty that would end the
border raids into Galeron. Instead, he found himself imprisoned and his lands viciously attacked. Since then Arianne
had been able to think of little else besides Nicholas, Duke
Armand's oldest son. As boys, Marcus and Nicholas had
been the best of friends. They'd sworn allegiance to one another, pledged to stand by one another through fire and famine. But now, though she'd had Marcus's captain send
messages far and wide, Nicholas had not returned or responded.

He'd disappeared ten years earlier, after Duke Armand
banished him, and no one had heard from him since.

I don't need him, Arianne assured herself as she unlatched
the stable door. *My plan will succeed, and Marcus will be
safe. I will get him out this very night.*

Her throat tightened as she stepped into the dim stable.
One torch flickered feeble amber light against the wall, revealing that he was here already, the dungeon guard she had
met at the Jug and Spoon, the one she'd been discreetly ques-
tioning for bits of information, the one who had let it be
known that he was not above accepting bribes.

"There you are, wench. Bretta, is it not?"

"Yes," she replied, her voice low and only a little trem-

ulous. As her eyes adjusted to the dark, she walked toward
him with what she hoped was a confident stride. "You are
ready to strike a bargain, Galdain?"

"Not so quick, eh? The night is young. Sit yourself down,
lass, and share a tankard with me."

He'd been drinking already, Arianne noted with disgust as
he tilted the tankard to his fat, moist lips and took a swig.
The man was hairy as a goat and smelled like one too. She
wrinkled her nose in distaste, trying to focus on the scent of
the hay instead. The woolen tunic covering Galdain's broad
form was frayed and grease-stained, and blood spattered the
front of it. Who had the man been beating tonight? She
fought her revulsion and forced herself to meet his oily black
eyes with outward equanimity.

"I have little time," she continued briskly. "They're expecting me back at the inn. Quickly now, tell me—your keys
will open all of the cells in the dungeon?"

"That they will, wench." His crude laughter rang out as
he dug in his pocket and produced a large silver ring of keys.
He dangled it before her, the keys clanging together discor-
dantly. "See—I'm a very important man in the duke's service."

"If you weren't, we wouldn't be here at this moment,"
she snapped, then quickly switched to a sweeter, more coaxing tone as she saw his eyes widen. She needed this brute,
whether she liked it or not. Scalding him with her tongue
wouldn't bring him to heel, but gold and a honeyed smile
would.

"I can meet your price, Galdain." She withdrew three gold
coins from the pocket of her cloak. "I'll give you one now
and the other two when Count Marcus is freed."

"Count Marcus! Eh, what's this? You never said he was
the one you wanted me to let go." Galdain frowned and took
another deep swig of his ale, then wiped his sleeve across
his dripping lips. "I don't know about that. I'd be risking
my neck. The archduke might well hang me in the count's
stead if that one gets away."

"Five coins," Arianne said, producing the additional coins

like a magician and waving them under his nose. "Three now and two later—"

"Ten."

Tension ripped through Arianne's stomach. She didn't have ten. If she gave this man five pieces of gold, it would leave her with only one—one that she might need to smuggle herself and Marcus across the border.

"I don't have ten. You had agreed to three."

"That was before you wanted Count Marcus. What's he to you, eh?" he asked suddenly, suspicion darkening his beefy features. "Why are you trying to help that foreigner anyway?"

"That's not your concern." She heard the royal haughtiness in her voice and hastened to amend her tone. She opened her eyes very wide and reached out to touch his arm. "Galdain, please. Five coins is all I have. They're yours if you will only keep your end of the bargain. Open the cell door and look the other way. Count Marcus will make his own way out of the castle."

"The duke will have my head if I'm caught," he growled. Sharp eyes studied the fine bones of her face, the beautiful violet eyes that shone from beneath slim auburn brows, the soft, full mouth, parted now as she stared at him. "You'll have to make it worth my while," he said slowly. "Five coins won't free a rat, much less Count Marcus."

Arianne drew in her breath. She wanted to strike this scoundrel, to draw her dagger and hold it to his throat and force him to agree, but that wouldn't serve. Once he went back to the castle, there was no guarantee that he would comply with the plan. What could she do? She had precious little money, for she'd had to flee Castle Galeron quickly when Julian's men had sprung their attack. There'd been no time to gather gold or jewels or even a parcel of her belongings.

All she had was the amethyst necklace and ring that had once belonged to her mother, both of which she'd been wearing the night of the attack. They were hidden now, deep in the pocket of her cloak. Should she give them over to this greedy, disgusting oaf?

Tears stung her eyes. "I have this ring. Here." She produced it, her hands shaking. "You may have it when Count Marcus is freed."

"How'd the likes of you get a beauty like this?" Galdain studied the warm, dark flash of the amethyst in the dim stable. His eyes glinted.

"Never you mind. It was lost, and I found it. That's all you need to know." She shoved the ring back inside her pocket. "Now, will you go back to the castle and keep your end of the bargain or not?"

"By the saints, I will. And I'll take the coins with me. All of 'em. And the ring. I don't believe for a minute it's real, but it's a pretty bauble and could fetch a fair price in the village. I'll also take you, sweet lady," he sneered, licking his lips. "Come and persuade me, wench. Show me why I should let the damned count go free, and just maybe I'll risk my neck to oblige you."

He lunged toward her, but Arianne jumped nimbly out of reach. "Don't you touch me!" she cried.

"You're too pretty not to touch. Come, the hay is warm." He sprang toward her again, and this time he was too quick for her. Arianne felt heavy arms imprison her, smelled the liquor and garlic on his breath, the stench of sweat permeating his thick body.

She kicked his shin, and her hand slid toward her dagger. "Let me go or pay with your life," she warned breathlessly, her fingers closing over the hilt.

Then the dagger was free, and as Galdain groped for her breast beneath the cloak, she stabbed at him with all her might.

But the guard was lucky. He wrenched aside just in time, and the blade missed his heart. It slashed through his shoulder, and he drew back with a grunt of pain, glaring at her.

"I'll teach you to try to murder me!" he bellowed, and with brute strength struck her full across the face. Arianne went spinning onto the stable floor, and while she lay there, dizzy, he kicked the dagger out of her hand.

"Now you'll see how unwise it is to cross Galdain," he muttered and fell upon her.

Arianne, still dizzy, tried to roll aside, but he was upon

her before she could move. Heavy and foul-breathed, he pinned her to the floor. She fought and kicked, clawing furiously at his face, but could not get free.

"No! Damn your soul, no! Let me go!"

Fear and rage gave her strength, but not enough to throw him off her. She bucked futilely, and her nails grazed his cheek. "Damn you, get off me!"

"I'll have you—and the gold—and the ring." The guard's voice grunted in her ear as he tore open her cloak. "Rich pickings, wench. Neither of us will soon forget this night."

Suddenly a deeper shadow moved through the gloom of the stable, and Galdain, perhaps with a sixth sense of impending disaster, glanced up.

Arianne saw a shadow, nothing more. Then a huge hand appeared, seized the guard's tunic, and hurled him across the stable.

"The lady said to let her up. It appears that a lesson in manners is in order."

"Argggghhhh!" With a wordless roar, the enraged dungeon guard hurled himself at his attacker.

Arianne struggled to her knees and watched the fight through wide eyes. The man who had come to her aid was tall, wide-shouldered, and far more heavily muscled than the burly guard. His short-cropped hair and plain cloak, tunic, and breeches were dark, unadorned in any way that marked him as a noble or a knight, yet he fought with the smooth, fierce skill of one trained in battle.

When he deftly struck a series of powerful blows, Galdain staggered back. But as the stranger started toward him again, the guard clanged out his sword.

The breath whistled out of Arianne. "No!" she cried.

In the next instant she saw the answering gleam of metal. Quick as lightning, the stranger had drawn his rapier. She heard his mocking, confident laugh as he faced the other man.

"Come, ruffian. Let us see how you meet an opponent of equal strength and skill."

Arianne scrambled in the darkness for her own fallen dagger and held it tightly in trembling fingers, watching the thrust and parry. The tall stranger fought magnificently, with a quickness, strength, and ruthless skill that won admiration even through her fear. It was clear at once that the dungeon guard was no match for him.

Just as she was beginning to think that Galdain would cry for mercy at any moment and her protector would send him running, from outside the stable came the thunder of hooves, shouting and the sound of boots thumping on the frozen earth.

The stranger heard the commotion too. For just an instant his keen gaze flicked toward the door. It was all the opening Galdain needed. He lunged with his sword straight at the stranger's heart, but the tall man swung his blade just in time and turned aside the fatal thrust. An instant later, he ran Galdain through, and the guard's blood spilled in a crimson gush as he cursed, trembled, and fell dead.

Horror filling her throat, Arianne shrank from the sight. The din outside roared in her ears. She darted to the door and peered out.

Soldiers. At least a dozen of them, Julian's own hand-picked men in black masks and hauberks, with drawn swords. No doubt they were searching for the phantom Lord Nicholas or for Lady Arianne of Galeron, whichever they could get their hands on first.

They were fanning out—to search the inn, she realized, the stables, the grounds. They were everywhere.

She was trapped.

CHAPTER 2

"Duke's men, are they? Seems he's sent enough of them."

The stranger's deep voice spoke wryly in her ear.

"Quick, there's not much time." Scarcely thinking, Arianne grabbed his powerful arm and tugged him outside into the misty darkness.

As one, they melted through the night and edged around the stables into the brush. Suddenly he seized her and dragged her down behind a tangled thicket.

One big gauntleted hand covered her mouth, while the other held her helpless against a lean male torso that was as strong as an oak. Arianne had never been held in any fashion by a man before. She'd had suitors, but none she cared for, and she'd kept them all at arm's length. A rush of heat spiraled through her at this stranger's intimate nearness, the pressure of his large, strong body against hers.

But there was little time to ponder her reaction, for the next moment a trio of guards stomped by, holding blazing torches aloft.

"Since yesterday sunset we've searched from the seacoast to the forest, and all the main roads, and there's been not one sign of Lord Nicholas," one man grumbled, his boots crunching less than five paces from where she and the stranger crouched.

"The duke's own astrologer claims he's dead." The soldier beside him spat in the dirt.

"Well, I saw the gypsy woman's eyes when she prophesied,'' the third soldier muttered, glancing left and right, his eyes shining warily in the wildly flickering torchlight. "She knows more than you or I . . . something strange is afoot.''

They hurried on.

It was several seconds more before the stranger eased his hand away from Arianne's lips.

"Don't you dare touch me again," she whispered furiously in the darkness. "How dare you . . ."

"Quiet. Do you want them to find us?" There was steel in his voice and in his sudden grip on her arm. Arianne was certain that later there would be a bruise. He yanked her up as abruptly as he had tugged her down, then pulled her after him through the woods, ducking beneath the low-hanging branches.

She kept up with him as best she could. There was nothing else to do at this point but continue fleeing through the darkness. Despite the stranger's rough, even arrogant, conduct, she felt safer with him than she would if she were surrounded by Duke Julian's soldiers.

For such a large man he moved with uncommon stealth, and they made little noise as they tore through the night, leaping past rocks and twigs and fallen logs, scrambling down ravines, plunging along twisting paths beneath overhanging boughs. The frigid wind bit through Arianne's cloak like the teeth of a wild beast, and her hair came loose from its snood, streaming freely behind her, bright as copper coins.

Still they ran. On and on through the Great Forest.

At last, when they were deep within the black heart of the forest, the stranger slowed his pace. Glancing down, he noted Arianne's flushed face and tortured breathing, loud in the hushed quiet of the wood.

"This way," he told her curtly, drawing her past a trickling stream. "There's a place I used to go as a boy. If it's still deserted, we'll be safe for now. We can spend the night there. I wish to talk with you."

Arianne was almost too weary to hear his quietly spoken words. Her chest hurt, and the muscles in her legs throbbed as if they were on fire. Her one thought now was of the dead guard, Galdain.

Her plan was ruined.

Her despair showed in her drooping shoulders. How would she ever free Marcus from Castle Doom before Julian had him hanged?

She did notice, though, when the cottage came into view. It huddled, nearly hidden, at the bottom of a shallow valley, not far from the stream. Sheltered by great oaks and a thick stand of silver birches, it was a crude but sturdy little box, built of stone and mud, with a chimney and a door, but no window.

It was dark as a cave inside.

The stranger at last let go of her arm as they entered. In silence, he set about striking tinder. When a weak yellow glow beamed out across the shadows, revealing no occupants, human or otherwise, he kicked the door shut.

"What we need is a fire," he remarked almost cheerfully and went to the hearth.

While he busied himself stacking and lighting the remains of several split and scarred logs and then lit a tallow candle set in a holder on a small table in the center of the room, Arianne shivered in her cloak and watched him, trying to gather her scattered thoughts.

There was something about him. He moved with great decisiveness, with authority and a quick, hard grace that was somehow familiar. There was something familiar, too, in the dark hair, the broad build . . .

And then, as the fire roared to life, he turned and looked her full in the face, and her heart stood still.

It was him. Dear God, it was him.

After all this time, after the frantic messages sent by Marcus's captain, after the searches, the inquiries, the sweep of neighboring and distant lands, he was here.

The gypsy spoke true, she thought dazedly, but as she was about to murmur the words, shock rippling through her, she somehow bit them back.

You can't be sure. Wait and see . . .

But it was him. *Nicholas.* Ten years had passed since she'd seen him, her brother's friend, Duke Armand's son, but she knew him. He had been a young man of twenty years the last time he'd come to Galeron—a dark, wild, impossibly handsome young man who took scant notice of the small, freckled girl of no more than ten years who had watched openmouthed beside her father's head groom as Lord Nicholas of Dinadan galloped grandly across the drawbridge with his company of men, his fine horses, his banner.

She had known from that moment that she would never forget him.

His eyes as he studied her now in the light of the fire were the dark gray of a winter sea, chill and harsh. The lean planes of his face were harsh, too, but handsome—still ruggedly, wildly handsome, though now there was a scar, white and wicked, cutting across one lean cheek. The straight slash of a nose, the downward slanting brows as fiercely dark as his hair, as dark as night, and the long, hard jaw that now looked more weathered, more weary than when she had last laid eyes on him. But yet it was the same.

His mouth, straight and thin, appeared to be set in a permanent state of anger. Yet she had in earlier days seen him laugh, had seen those arrogant lips kiss a maid as if he would devour her . . .

Arianne's thoughts flew back. As a child and a girl, she'd been excluded from the feasts in his honor, as well as the hunting expeditions that he and Marcus and her father, along with the nobles, had set out on each bright, sparkling morn. How agonized she'd been, forced to sit in the tower room spinning with her mother and the other women each day, confined to the solar or her own chambers by night, always with fat old Gerta watching her like a hawk.

But she'd glimpsed him now and then all the same. Just as she'd done when she was even younger, four or five, and visited Archduke Armand at Castle Dinadan with her family, she tagged after him and Marcus as they climbed and raced and wrestled. When they rode at breakneck speed across the lush, rolling lands of Dinadan, she ran after them demanding that they wait for her, but they only laughed and galloped faster.

She'd managed to creep downstairs on the final night of his visit the last time he'd come to Galeron. He'd been twenty then and she only ten. She waited until old Gerta was snoring soundly, then in her nightgown she slipped through the solar, and down the winding back staircase to the alcove behind the great hall. There, hiding behind a velvet curtain, she gazed eagerly out at the dancers.

She saw him dancing with one of her mother's lovely young cousins. Marta the fair, with her pale, gleaming locks and sideways smiles, seemed to enchant him. As Arianne watched from her hiding place, her palms cold and damp, Nicholas led Marta toward the very alcove where she had hidden herself.

She dashed around a corner in the nick of time and peeked out. He pulled Marta to him and kissed her in a way that Arianne in all the years since that night had never been able to forget.

"You're cold." He spoke to her roughly now, interrupting her thoughts. "Go and warm yourself before the fire. Then we must talk."

"What makes you think I have anything to say to you, my lord?" Arianne spit out angrily. Then she saw the surprise that darkened those gray eyes that missed nothing. They narrowed, and his lip curled.

"Insolent child, I've just saved you from a fate worse than any other, unless I mistook the intent of your friend back there in the stables. I thought you might wish to thank me by providing me with some useful information."

"I am not a child." Arianne surprised him again by focusing on the first portion of his speech. She saw his eyebrows go up, then his features quickly took on an iron impassivity, and she could read nothing more there but a hint of harshness and of anger kept rigidly in check.

"Very well, my lady," he responded coolly, his tone flirting with mockery. She remembered with a shock that he had no idea who she was. No doubt from her dull brown homespun gown and thin, plain cloak he thought her only what she had been pretending all these months to be: a simple tavern wench who had hidden from the soldiers out of fear, who was no doubt eager to go home to her own family and bed.

"So you are not a child, but you are behaving like one." He advanced on her and gripped her by the arms so firmly that she gasped.

"Now, I have done you a good turn, my girl. It is incumbent upon you to do one for me." He scowled suddenly, noting how her delicate cheeks were still red from the cold, how thoroughly she was shivering.

"You'll sit before the fire and have a sip of wine. When you have answered my questions—and it shall not take long—you will be free to go. But," he continued, his eyes piercing her in warning, "you will tell no one of this place. Or that you have seen me. Do not speak of it. Is that clear?"

"Perfectly clear, my lord Nicholas." She spoke slowly, clearly, almost sweetly. But anger flashed in her eyes as he stared down at her in shock upon hearing his name.

"As clear as your own cowardice in having stayed away for lo these many months while your people were enslaved!" she rushed on, her voice throbbing now with growing fury. "As clear as your indifference to the suffering of one you professed to love as a brother!"

His grip tightened. The look he gave her could have sliced through a stone. "What nonsense is this?"

"Nonsense? I speak the truth. Can you deny it—*Nicholas*?"

He let her go. His expression turned so cold, so darkly dangerous, that Arianne involuntarily stepped back a pace.

"I don't deny who I am," he muttered. "But, by God, it's high time you did me the honor of gracing me with *your* name, my lady—and with how you know of me."

Quickly, with shaking fingers, she reached up and yanked the strings of her cloak. As the hood fell back and the cloak slid from her shoulders, she stared fixedly into Nicholas's swarthy face.

"I am Arianne of Galeron," she said with contempt. "I am the one who summoned you to the aid of your friend—my brother. Behold, my lord. At last, when it is nearly too late, you have come."

For a moment there was dead silence in the cottage, except for the hiss and crackle of the logs. The sound of the moaning wind soughing through the trees of the Great Forest faintly reached her ears, as if from far, far away. Fingers of heat, of rich amber light, flickered across the faces of the tall, dark man and the slender, flame-haired woman who confronted one another with anger and distrust in that small space lit by fire and shadow.

Nicholas spoke first. "*You* . . . are Arianne? That little mouse who scurried after Marcus and me . . . that pest who would not cease annoying us?"

He looked so amazed that she flushed. Deep rose color burned her cheeks, turning them nearly the hue of her lips.

"How you flatter me, my lord. Take care you don't turn my head."

He smiled suddenly, a smile that broke through the grimness of his face and momentarily softened his features. "If it's flattery you want, Arianne, I can give it to you. Heartily and sincerely." His gaze contemplated her lush, sweet mouth, then shifted lower to appraise the slender form and feminine curves revealed by her simple gown. "You've grown into a lovely woman now, an entrancing woman . . ."

She stepped forward and slapped him. "I don't want your damned flattery!"

Dark fury blazed in his eyes. He caught her wrist, and Arianne felt mortal fear flood through her. She'd gone too far. With a man like this, the type of man Nicholas of Dinadan had clearly become, one did not risk anger. It was not only his size and strength that were daunting, it was something in his bearing, in the swift, sure way he moved, in the coldness that lurked behind those fascinating eyes. He was not a man to cross. A dangerous man, much different from the laughing boy who had kissed Marta in the alcove, fenced with Marcus in the courtyard, and ridden her father's prize destrier as if born in the saddle.

She wondered suddenly if the rumors about him were true, that he had become a warrior in the years of his banishment, a mercenary who spent his life fighting on behalf of those who would pay him for his service. Looking into that ruthless and icy gaze, she knew in a flash of insight that it was true.

He was a man who thought nothing of killing another, who lived for hunting and war.

How many times had Marcus warned her that she needed to learn to control her temper? Somehow she could not. Especially with this man, who had once claimed to be her brother's friend, then had callously left him to rot all this time in the hellhole of Castle Doom.

She had expected so much more from him. Based on her early memories, her foolish, girlish imaginings, she had envisioned him a hero, someone bound to aid her brother, as well as his own people, freeing them from the tyrant who had taken his father's place. But he had stayed away. Damn him, he was not worthy of Marcus's love or respect. Or of hers.

"Let me go," she commanded, fighting back the tears that threatened. "You have no right . . ."

"I have every right. I rescued you, and now you will make yourself useful to me. Before this night is over, Lady Arianne, you are going to explain your hatred of me. And much else besides. Don't even think of sleep for many hours, for we have much to discuss," he told her roughly.

"Oh? Do you plan to help me, then?" she inquired, her wrist burning from the touch of his fingers. And for some reason the heat still had not left her face.

"My plans are my concern. You will answer my questions and do as you are told."

"You mistake the matter. I am in charge of this rescue, my lord. I am working closely with Felix, my brother's captain, who is even now assembling Marcus's men to retake Galeron as soon as Marcus is freed. At this late date, if you wish to throw in with us, it is necessary for *you* to answer to *me*."

Her violet eyes locked on his gray ones. There was no wavering in them, no uncertainty.

So, Nicholas thought, taking in not only the wide violet gaze but also the delicate line of her jaw, her blazing cheeks, and thick, spiraling curls that shimmered like a red-gold sunset in the firelight. *The child with the braids and freckles and soiled tunic has grown into a slender, heart-stoppingly lovely warrior-woman*. He fought a smile.

"The freckles," he said musingly.

"I beg your pardon?"

He released her wrist, and his hand went to her chin. Very gently, he tilted it up so that he could better examine her.

"You've lost nearly all your freckles, Arianne. Save for a mere dusting across your nose. And a most comely little nose it is, may I add."

She jerked back. Her face felt hot where he had touched it. "If you think to soften me with flattery, you're sadly mistaken. I told you already, you will not turn my head with words, my lord. I am not a stupid maid who will come all undone because you have directed your attentions to me."

His brows rose again. He looked puzzled.

"There are serious matters afoot," she rushed on, lest she indeed become distracted by his touch, by the admiration in his words. Foolish first loves died hard. But hers was dead now, she told herself. Completely dead. The only thing she wanted from Nicholas was aid in freeing Marcus.

"We must plan. However much we may dislike one another, if you are interested in helping me to rescue Marcus, we must work together."

"Very well. But my friend would never forgive me if I were to let his little sister freeze to death. For the last time, Arianne, go and sit before that fire, and then we'll talk."

"Don't tell me what to do."

He cursed under his breath in exasperation and grasped her arm. He hauled her to the low stool near the fire and pushed her roughly down upon it. "Stay there. And drink this."

The flask he pulled from his pocket was silver, she noted, glaring at it and at him. There were rich carvings upon it and small encrusted jewels. A contrast to his peasant clothes.

"If you argue with me, *Lady* Arianne, I will pour this wine down your throat. The entire flask. Now *drink*!"

Arianne drank. She did not doubt that he would carry out his threat. Everything about him suggested barely leashed violence and deep, cold anger. The truth was, it did feel good to sit here before the fire. She was frozen to the bone. As she stretched her hands toward the flames, she felt the warmth returning to her limbs, flowing through her in lovely golden waves. And the wine . . . the wine burned her throat with its own sweet fire.

Spirits always made her drowsy, and she didn't want to be drowsy. She needed to be alert, to keep her eye on Nicholas lest he vanish again before she could wrest from him a promise to help her. She needed to be on guard against any soldiers who might find the cottage and seek to question her. She needed to plan, to think, to come up with a new course of action—and quickly.

Yet, as the wine and the fire warmed her, a relaxed weariness stole over her, despite her best efforts to resist it.

She yawned. She couldn't help it, it just happened, a small, delicate, catlike yawn, but Nicholas saw it and scowled.

"You look half dead."

"More flattery," she mumbled.

"You need rest."

"No. I need . . ." Another yawn, quickly stifled. ". . . to talk to you."

"You always were troublesome as a gnat, even as a child, Arianne. I never gave it much thought, but I suppose it stands to reason you'd turn into a stubborn, troublesome woman." He stripped off his heavy cloak and draped it over her shoulders, then took back the flask still clutched in her fingers.

He tilted it up and enjoyed a long drink.

"If you wish to talk, then we'll talk," he told her curtly. "I have a great many questions, and I consider it a stroke of good fortune that I came upon you tonight—because you can answer them for me."

"If I do, will you help me free Marcus?"

Ice glinted in his eyes. "What in hell's name do you think I am doing here, Arianne? Julian's men will have my head on a platter if they find me. Yet I'm here. You ought to be clever enough to figure out why."

"I'll have your word on it before I speak."

Mockery curled his lip. "Since when does the word of a banished scoundrel mean anything?" he asked sardonically.

"Marcus believes in you," she replied stiffly. "I suppose I must do the same."

He turned away from her. He began to pace back and forth around the small confines of the cottage, looking far too large and strong for such a feeble dwelling. At length he turned back to her, and suddenly Arianne felt a vise tightening around her heart as she saw his face.

Bitterness filled it, a resigned and hopeless bitterness imprinted so clearly upon the strong, handsome features that it tore at her soul.

"You have my word," he told her grimly. "My solemn oath. I will free Marcus from the castle dungeon or die. Is that good enough for you, Lady Arianne?"

She nodded, too stunned by the bleak emotions that she read in him to speak.

"Then we must act quickly. I know only bits and pieces. Tell me all that has happened in Dinadan and Galeron since my father's death." His tone was heavy. "By tomorrow we must devise a plan and begin at once, for if my information is correct, Marcus is to be hanged in three days' time."

"That is correct," she whispered.

He heard the catch in her voice and fixed those implacable gray eyes upon her. "By all that is holy, my girl, it will not happen."

There was no tenderness in his tone, no concern or kindness. Only flint. The hard, fine-edged flint of a man not to be swayed from his purpose.

"Lord Nicholas, thank you." She spoke formally, suddenly overcome with relief, and with a whole range of emotions, among them, finally, the faint stirrings of hope. "I . . . I believe in you."

"Then you and Marcus are the only two souls on this earth who do," he muttered with a quick, harsh smile. "So talk, Arianne. Quickly. There is no time to lose."

CHAPTER 3

The wind roared like a wild beast all through the night. With their cloaks spread on the dirt floor beneath them, Nicholas and Arianne huddled before the fire, and she told him of all that had happened since Archduke Armand had died.

"At first there were murmurings in Dinadan over Marcus being crowned archduke. He was never popular with the people, you know. Many prayed for your return—some even dared to call for it."

This remark was greeted by silence. She bit her lip, knowing that when Armand had banished his son, he'd decreed that Nicholas should never succeed him as ruler of Dinadan. She'd never discovered what had transpired between the archduke and Nicholas to cause his banishment, and if her father or Marcus had known the reason, neither had shared it with her. It must have been something horrible indeed for Armand to turn against his firstborn son with such finality.

"Continue," Nicholas ordered, his eyes hard as agates as she hesitated.

She inched closer to the fire, her hair drifting forward across her cheeks. "Immediately after the coronation, Julian had all the nobles who'd spoken publicly against him locked away. Then rumors reached us in Galeron that he was preparing for war, making plans to overrun his neighbors' lands."

"Didn't wait long, did he?"

"Scarcely a sennight." Arianne shivered despite the lovely blaze of heat from the fire. She was no longer drowsy; the story stirred her blood with fresh zeal against the man who had imprisoned Marcus.

"It started with border raids to the south, in Ruanwald," she told him with a quick, flashing glance. "Duke Edmund realized that he didn't stand a chance against Dinadan's army, so he quickly offered his daughter, Katerine, in marriage as a means of securing peace with Julian."

She frowned into the fire, remembering how shocked she had been by this event, for it had seemed to her, the last time she'd seen Katerine of Ruanwald at Midwinter Festival last year, that she and Marcus had been quite taken with one another. Indeed, when Marcus had heard of Katerine's being bartered off to Dinadan in order to keep the peace, he'd gone white as a bone.

"Marcus saw then that if he didn't face Julian directly and at once, our own land would be next under attack," she told Nicholas with a sigh.

"What of your father?" Turning to look at her, Nicholas saw the glisten of sadness in her brilliant eyes.

Arianne steadied herself and explained how first her mother had died four years earlier of a fever and then scarcely a year later her father's heart had given out after a hard day of hunting and riding.

"I am sorry to hear of it."

"Thank you. So you see, Marcus is the Count of Galeron now."

"Let me guess." He shook his head. "My trusting friend went straight off to his 'cousin' Julian to propose a treaty of peace." At her nod, he brought his fist down in frustration on the hard-packed floor. "By all that's holy, from the time we were boys, Marcus was always so honest and upright he could scarcely conceive of villainy in others. The fool . . ."

"Marcus is no fool!"

"No? I'd wager a storehouse full of gold that it was during this visit that Julian took Count Gullible prisoner," he added caustically.

Furious, Arianne scrambled up on her knees to face him. "Marcus couldn't possibly have known that Julian would engage in such treachery!" she cried, her face hot and flushed. Though she might rail at Marcus for not allowing her to sit in on his strategy sessions and meetings with the nobles, she would brook no criticism of him from another. "Marcus went to Dinadan in peace! He did take a company of knights with him, a small contingent, but they were overpowered. How was he to guess that Julian would stoop to attacking him when his mission was to reach an accord?"

Nicholas leaned back, gazing at her lazily, his hands braced on the floor behind him. He studied the proud, delicate curve of her chin, the fire-flash of her eyes, the rich, bright hair that poured around her shoulders like molten copper. She was exquisite. So brave, so intense, and so innocent of the harsh realities of the world. Or at least she had been, he reminded himself, until Marcus had been thrown into prison.

"Julian is a knave, Arianne," he told her coolly, "a scoundrel. As evil a creature as ever walked this earth. I suspected it when we were children together, but by the time of my twentieth year, I knew it to be true." He paused, and as the firelight flickered across his face, Arianne saw once again the bitterness there, etched deep into his very soul. She saw anger, too, an icy, dangerous anger that made her shiver despite the blaze of the fire.

"What did he do to you?" The words spilled out before she could catch them.

Nicholas turned his head and stared at her.

"I can see that there is something . . . something beyond what he has done since your father's death . . . something beyond taking Marcus prisoner," she went on quickly. She searched his face. "He did something to you. Long ago."

"Are you a witch?" he asked abruptly, his eyes steady upon her.

"No. But I can see things sometimes—things that are beneath the surface. I can sense anger, fear, and, often, falsehoods." She shrugged. "It is just something that is clear to me even when others are blind. If that be witchcraft, then I am a witch. I have no powers other than those. But with you, I sense . . . here."

Without thinking, she reached out and touched her fingers to his chest. A jolt of heat zigzagged through her. She nearly gasped. She could have sworn that he felt it, too, that light-ning current racing between them. The hard muscles of his chest tensed beneath his tunic, and her fingers trembled and fell away, burning.

She stared helpless into his eyes. They had turned the color of scorched silver.

"Go on," he said tautly, gripping her hand before she could pull away.

"There is a pain," she whispered, not knowing from where this sudden insight came but knowing it was the truth, "a pain deep inside you that goes beyond all else."

He dropped her hand and pushed himself to his feet. Abruptly he turned away and picked up a stick to poke savagely at the fire. "Let us just say it was a sad day for Dinadan when my father wed the Countess Viviane. The son she bore him could well be the devil's spawn."

The fire blazed under his prodding. Still gripping the stick, he glanced back at her, looking suddenly so fierce, so deadly, that she recoiled in fear even though it was clear that his anger was not directed at her.

"Tell me what happened after Marcus was taken prisoner."

"Before news had even reached us, before any warning could be given, Julian's troops attacked Galeron. The castle was stormed, the village was burned, children were slaughtered."

It was the first time she had spoken of it since that awful, unforgettable day when she'd seen horrors she hoped never to see again. The smoke, the blood, the running and screaming people, her own dear old Gerta slain in the melee.

She swallowed back tears and sobs, staring down at her hands.

Suddenly Nicholas knelt and threw the stick aside. He captured both of her small hands in his own large ones. His fingers were calloused and heavily scarred. They were very strong, very warm. Arianne felt the warmth of life flowing between them as he gripped her hands in his. When she lifted her eyes to his face, she read ironclad determination there.

"He will pay, Arianne. Never fear, he will pay."

She nodded, that small flicker of hope again flaring within her.

The heat had left his eyes; they were now cool and calm and gray as the sea. She felt a quiver as she gazed into their keen, appraising depths. What had this man seen during all those years when he was estranged from his father? What had he done? His eyes held a grimness that was not there in his youth.

Strain showed, too, around the corners of his hard, sensuous mouth. He was weary, she realized suddenly, as he slowly let go of her hands. Every bit as exhausted as she. Yet his tone remained steady and alert.

"Tell me, Arianne, how did you escape? Surely Julian's men wanted you too. The Lady of Galeron would be a war prize indeed."

She nodded, folding her hands. To be considered a trophy of war irked her, but it was a fact of her station. She had not grown up in a castle without learning her worth as a noblewoman.

"His men did try to capture me, but I escaped." She took a breath and told him of how she had fled with two of her ladies through the secret tunnel that led beneath the bailey, how they had been attacked and her ladies captured just outside the walls, how Marcus's knights had come to her aid, wrenching her out of the arms of the huge soldier who had grabbed her up onto his destrier. She told him of how, surrounded by knights, she'd been riding pell-mell for the shelter of Sir Elven's manor, when they'd been overtaken by another company of enemy soldiers. In the ensuing battle, she had killed one of them herself before Felix, Marcus's captain, had shouted an order for her to flee.

"He was right, of course. I wanted to stay and help in the fight, but I knew, as Felix did, that if I were captured, it would only strengthen Julian that much more. So I rode as far and as fast as I could. The manor house had fallen—it was burning as I went past. Some peasants took me in at nightfall and hid me in their cottage. They gave me clothes, food. They offered to hide me until help came. I stayed for a few days, but it was dangerous for them. Julian's men were searching the countryside for me. I insisted on leaving and slowly, carefully, made my way to Dinadan.''

''Alone?'' he asked sharply. ''All this way?''

''Yes.'' With pride, she smoothed back her hair. So he thought her too fragile a creature to survive on her own, outside the walls and courtyards of the castle. She felt pride in showing him his mistake.

''Since coming here, I've made contact with my brother's men, who have in turn borne missives to Felix for me. One of the things I requested of him was that he send messages near and far searching for you.''

''One reached me . . . only days ago. So now I am here.''

Arianne was not fooled by the calm simplicity with which he spoke. There was more to his story than he was telling. She remembered how she had accused him of not caring for Marcus because he had not come sooner. Now, looking into the lean, harsh face before her, she realized that she had misjudged him. There was something more here, something he wasn't telling her. Nicholas had once been a wild daredevil of a boy, perhaps even irresponsible—after all, his father had banished him, had he not?

But no longer. She would have staked her life that this man took his responsibilities seriously. They—or *something*— seemed to weigh on him, to be a burden upon those great, wide shoulders. He bore it well, but it was there all the same, now that she had taken care to look.

Suddenly she could have bitten off her tongue. ''I said some things earlier, my lord, that I regret. I was upset, angry. I shouldn't have judged you or spoken to you thus.''

A slow smile smoothed the harsh line of his lips. His grave face lightened. ''Don't think of it, Ari.''

Ari. The nickname he and Marcus had tagged her with all those years ago, when she'd tried in vain to keep up with them.

''But I believe my words have wounded you, my lord . . .''

This time his smile was so quick and unexpectedly warm that it pierced straight to her heart. ''You're a strange woman, Arianne. One moment you despise me, and the next you worry over having hurt me with words. What am I to do with you?''

Flustered by the light, musing way he was gazing into her eyes, and fighting weariness and the temptation to succumb to his very potent and thoroughly male charm, Arianne spoke the first words that popped into her head.

"Take me to bed, my lord."

His dark, slanting brows rose and laughter sprang into those cool gray eyes.

Too late, Arianne realized what she had said.

"I mean, lead me to bed . . . to *my* bed . . . er, *a* bed. I am weary beyond belief . . . I must sleep . . . I only meant . . ."

"No, my girl. Don't say any more. I won't pretend to mistake your meaning. You've gone through much today."

He helped her to rise, then scooped her cloak from the floor and spread it on the thin straw pallet by the far wall, the only bedding in the cottage.

"Sleep now. By the morrow, I'll have concocted a plan to free Marcus. So you may rest easy. He will not be in the dungeons much longer."

"Where will you sleep, my lord?"

"Before the fire, upon the floor."

"You will scarcely be comfortable!"

"I have slept in far worse places, Ari," he said with some amusement. He put his hands on her shoulders and pushed her gently down on the pallet as if she were a stubborn child resisting her bed. "Sleep," he said firmly. "In the morning you will tell me just what you thought you were doing with that ruffian in the stable."

Her limbs seemed to melt as she eased her tired body onto the pallet. In a twinkling she was curled on her side, struggling to keep her eyes open. "I can tell you . . . now." She yawned. "I was bribing him to let Marcus go. He is a guard stationed in the dungeon. I've been . . . getting to know him at the inn where I work for some time now . . ." Another yawn. "And . . . finally reached the point where it seemed . . . he was greedy enough to take the risk. . . . I offered him gold . . ."

Her voice trailed off.

Staring down at her, Nicholas saw with an odd tightening in his gut that she had fallen asleep in midsentence.

He lifted his own cloak from the floor and carefully draped it across her. Little Ari, Marcus's small, impossible sister.

The troublesome brat had somehow become an incredibly sumptuous woman. Her beauty was not of the classical wan and ladylike fashion, however. No, it was far more potent and spellbinding than that. This girl with the clear violet eyes and the sensuous kitten's face, the rich cascade of hair every bit as glorious as fire, had an intoxicating beauty that reached to his core and shook him like an oak in a windstorm. Her body was slim and delicate yet lushly curved. There was grace in the way she moved and elegance in the way she held her head. But her high cheekbones and full, soft lips hinted at a passion running not so far beneath that proper surface, a passion that sprang from her very soul.

Nicholas forced his glance away from her slender form. The last thing he needed now was to get distracted by Marcus's exquisite and headstrong little sister. In fact, now that she was here, his job was doubly complicated. He had to rescue Marcus, ultimately find a way to overthrow Julian, and all the while keep Arianne safely out of the fray.

He suspected that would not be easy to do. But tomorrow he would send her packing—willingly or in chains, if need be.

Marcus would not be pleased if anything were to happen to her. *Neither would I be*, Nicholas thought, turning back for one last glance at her. The firelight gilded her creamy skin. One hand was curled beneath a cheek. She looked like a woman but slept the deep, innocent sleep of a child.

Nicholas stalked away. *You'd fall in love with a sow tonight,* he told himself, and Marcus's charmingly delicate sister was anything but that. Still, he had gone a long while without a woman until just recently.

When he'd escaped that place he never wanted to think of again and made his way back toward Dinadan, he'd had a few tavern whores along the way. They provided a quick, animal slaking of his needs. But something inside of him had been left unsatisfied, craving something more.

He raked a hand through his hair and decided that weariness was making him sentimental—and foolish. This was a time to rest and prepare for the battle ahead. Because a battle it would be. He would need all of his wits and his gradually returning strength to rescue Marcus and to retake the castle.

By tomorrow this time, I'll have breached the castle walls, he vowed as he lowered himself to the floor before the fire. *There will be no time for thoughts of a woman, even one as lovely as Arianne—no space in my mind for anything but the fighting and killing and dying that the sunrise will bring.*

CHAPTER 4

"I'll do no such thing!'' Arianne exclaimed indignantly, staring at Nicholas the next morning as if he'd just suggested she strip off all her clothing and run naked through the town. ''It's a grave insult, one I warn you I won't soon forget. How could you even contemplate it?'' she flashed.

It was shortly past dawn. She had awakened to find him gone, the cottage silent and deserted, the fire burnt low. But outside, the dawn had brought an unexpected mildness to the air. A lark sang. The fierce wind had fled with the night, and a fanciful breeze raced through the brush and teased the branches of trees, where tiny spring buds struggled to burst free.

Beneath a sapphire sky, Arianne had made her way to the river and washed, and by the time Nicholas showed up a short while later, she had smoothed and braided her hair with a thong she'd discovered in a box in the cottage. She'd also found some tin cups and old rag shoes, and, on a shelf, a moldy wedge of cheese.

He brought food from the village. There was a thick loaf of rye, still warm and fragrant, a slab of ham, and some cheese. It stood on the table between them, and though she'd been half starved when he came in, she now forgot all about eating.

''I will not stay behind while you enter the castle and free Marcus. You might well need my help, and I refuse to sit idle while that *murderer* counts the hours until he can hang my brother.''

"I'll make arrangements for your stay at a safe place. The matter is settled."

"It is settled that I'm going into the castle with you. I've made up my mind. If you knew me better, my lord, you would know that once I make up my mind I *never* change it."

Nicholas shoved the stool up to the table and yanked her down atop it. "Sit. Eat."

"My lord is confused. Let me assure you that I'm not a pet dog who performs tricks and obeys commands!"

He sighed, regarding her in irritation as he broke the rye loaf in half and handed her a chunk. "Arianne, do you always make things difficult? I pity Marcus and, worse, the man who weds you."

Crimson color flooded her cheeks. She jumped up from the stool. "I refuse to sit here and be insulted by a man who—"

She broke off, the flush now spreading to her ears and down her neck.

"Go ahead. Say it." Nicholas's eyes glinted like shards of ice as he took out his knife and began slicing the ham onto a chunk of bread. "A man who left his home in disgrace, who deserted his father, his people . . ."

"You didn't desert them. You were banished. You couldn't stay and couldn't return. Everyone knows that."

"Make up your mind, Arianne. Are you attacking me or defending me?"

She bit her lip, scowling. "Neither," she said defiantly. "I am joining forces with you."

Their eyes met and held. There was no give in his, she saw. She tightened her scowl.

But Nicholas shook his head. "Too dangerous."

"You forget to whom you speak. While Marcus is imprisoned, I am charged with the leadership of Galeron's troops. Felix and the knights under his command will do my bidding. You may well need them behind you if you are to succeed."

He said smoothly, "Your offer does me honor, but I have my own men to stand behind me."

"What men?"

"When you're finished with your meal, I'll show you."

She lowered herself with regal dignity onto the stool and broke off a hunk of the cheese.

She did not speak to Nicholas during that brief, quick repast, but she felt his gaze on her; and each time as she met it, her countenance and bearing grew more determined.

Here she sits, Nicholas thought in grudging admiration as he swallowed the last of the ham, *in a serving woman's homespun, within as poor and humble a cottage as any in the land, and she moves and speaks and looks every inch a noblewoman.*

A beautiful noblewoman.

The last thing he intended to do was allow her to put herself in danger, and setting foot inside Castle Doom would be perilous indeed.

It was with great doubt that Arianne accompanied him shortly thereafter to the manor house of one of Dinadan's nobles.

"I hope you know what you're doing," she murmured as they traversed the hilly ground leading to the gates.

"Sir Castor was the one person who believed in me when my father banished me, the only one who came forward and told me that he suspected what I knew to be true: that Julian had somehow conspired to ruin me in the eyes of my father, to turn him against me. I sent a message ahead to him before embarking on my journey to Dinadan. He's expecting me."

Sir Castor was a bowlegged, hawk-nosed, robust old knight whose black mustache and whiskers matched his deepset eyes. As he came striding into the hall, he looked as if he would be far more at home on the fighting field than here in his richly embroidered tunic and fur-lined surcoat. At sight of Nicholas, he froze.

"By all that is holy, it *is* you!" Joy suffused his fierce pink face. "Lord Nicholas, at last. Ah, my boy, at last!"

Arianne had no doubt of his loyalty when she saw the way he greeted Nicholas and ushered him through the great hall, then called for food and wine.

She was introduced and warmly greeted. Then the two men talked long and hard.

But Sir Castor frowned when Nicholas informed him he intended to enter the castle as soon as possible.

"Why not wait until you can be sure of a stronger force behind you, my lord? My men, of course, will follow you. I will assign them as you say, but alone they're no match for those black-masked troops of Julian's. Now if Lady Arianne could summon forth her brother's knights to join with mine, then we would have a real army. But they may not come in time . . ."

"We'll send word to Galeron's captain this day," Nicholas replied curtly, "but we cannot wait. We cannot wait even for my men, those I have attempted to summon during my journey."

Sir Castor gazed at him inquiringly. "Your men?"

"Those soldiers for hire that I trained and led into battle during my years away from home. My lieutenants are assembling the men-at-arms even as we speak." His tone was grim, and he flicked a glance at Arianne before continuing quietly, "Count Marcus is being starved and has probably been beaten. In a matter of mere days he is scheduled to hang. It's possible that my men and Galeron's will arrive by then, perhaps even sooner—but I'm taking no chances. I want him out."

"As do I," Arianne said tautly, rising from the gilded bench near the window and approaching them.

Sir Castor smiled at her when Nicholas told him he wished Lady Arianne to be hidden here at the manor and given every protection and comfort until the business was ended.

"Of course. My lady, you are most welcome. My wife will be pleased to—"

"You are all consideration, my lord. But I am going into the castle this very day, with or without Lord Nicholas. I have as much right to protect my brother's life as he does—no, *more*."

Sir Castor appeared astonished. He turned toward Nicholas, waiting for him to contradict her.

But Nicholas was watching Arianne closely. The strength

of her resolve was not lost on him. He made a sudden decision.

He knew something of injustice, and it struck him suddenly and forcibly that it would be injustice indeed to confine her to this house while matters so important and so close to her heart were being decided.

Besides, it was true that she could prove helpful to him. Two heads were better than one. Two of them working together within the castle might move things along with the speed that was needed.

"The lady speaks with courage—and conviction." He gave her a curt, unsmiling nod, hoping he wasn't making a terrible mistake. "You may come."

Arianne's relief nearly made her dizzy. She quickly recovered and with grave dignity held out her hand to Nicholas.

He raised it to his lips and kissed her fingers lightly. All the while, he held her gaze. It was suddenly all Arianne could do not to tremble as his lips brushed along her skin.

"You have made a wise decision, my lord." Arianne struggled to concentrate as he continued to hold her hand in his. "It's apparent that you will govern sagaciously when Julian is overthrown and you take your rightful place as Archduke of Dinadan," she added with a smile.

But then she saw the ready, answering smile freeze upon his lips. Sir Castor made a coughing sound.

"I will never rule in Julian's stead."

Nicholas's tone was calm and level, yet Arianne heard the quiet pain beneath it and felt her heart constrict.

"But why not? You're Archduke Armand's firstborn son. It is your right . . ."

Her voice faded away as too late she remembered Archduke Armand's terrible pronouncement—that Nicholas was never to succeed him upon the throne.

"Surely the pronouncement was unjust," she hurried on. "Especially if, as you believe, Julian did indeed conspire to turn your father against you. If your quarrel was due to that and not to your own misdeeds, surely your father's edict need not stand."

"I will honor it." The grim finality of his tone sliced

through her like a knife's blade. "As I never properly honored him in his lifetime."

He spun away from her and strode to the window, staring past the rich velvet curtains at the rolling, fertile land beyond.

Suddenly she wanted to go to him. She didn't know why. She only knew that she wanted to touch his cheek, his hair, to smooth that hard jaw, as if by doing so she could smooth away the pain he tried to hide.

But her feet were rooted to the floor. He looked so unapproachable. So strong and resolute. As if he would never need the soothing word or touch of a girl he could only regard as a nuisance.

"My lord, perhaps you could reconsider . . . for Dinadan . . ." Sir Castor began, but Nicholas interrupted.

"My father died without my ever having reconciled with him." He spoke with a harsh matter-of-factness, but in his eyes she saw the dark flash of grief for just a moment. Then it was gone, hidden, and the cool, light grayness was back, revealing nothing of his soul. "For that I will never forgive myself. Or Julian."

He turned toward them again. "The edict cannot be overturned. I won't allow it. That would be the ultimate disrespect for my father's wishes. Enough." He held up a hand as Sir Castor started to argue. "It's done with. Let's talk of strategy."

Nicholas gazed from one to the other of them. "I've been mulling the matter all morning and now have the seedlings of a plan."

Late that afternoon, four of Duke Julian's feared blackmasked soldiers rode through the tip of the Great Forest, just east of the castle walls.

Suddenly a log fell across the road. Their horses reared up in alarm. Before the soldiers could even draw their swords, they were surrounded.

It was a brief and bloody battle.

Nicholas killed the two brawniest with two sweeps of his sword. Sir Castor's men-at-arms slew the others.

Arianne watched from beneath an oak tree at the edge of

the forest, her heart in her throat. In this battle there was little for her to do. But she would soon play a part.

Once inside the castle, she would get her chance to be of use. She could finally strike back at Julian, could finally get Marcus out of that cell. No longer would she have to rush around the inn discreetly gathering information, trying to concoct a workable plan. Now she would be inside Castle Doom itself, where she could act.

And Nicholas would be working with her. His presence inspired confidence. Yet, she acknowledged as she somberly watched the battle in the road, they were only two.

Somehow they must thwart Duke Julian, who had all the power of Dinadan at his command. His Captain of Arms, a man known as Baylor, was feared by all who encountered him, and his knights were known for their ruthlessness and efficiency.

Capture would mean imprisonment and almost certain death.

What lay before them would be more dangerous than any-thing Arianne had ever imagined back in Castle Galeron, be-fore Marcus had been taken prisoner. But she refused to let her thoughts dwell on that.

When one of Sir Castor's men brought her the garments of the smallest knight who had been killed, she retreated into the forest and donned them quickly. A short time later, Duke Julian's company was again seen making its way toward the castle.

Over the drawbridge and beneath the portcullis they went. Leaving their horses for the royal groomsmen, they entered the great hall. The largest and the smallest of the four ducked without incident into a small, little-used chamber branching off the corridor that led to the solar.

"Quickly," Nicholas growled as Arianne tore off her mask and guard's cloak.

"I'm moving as quickly as I can," she snapped. Her fin-gers flung off the heavy tunic.

Beneath the guard's uniform she wore the sedate green-gold gown of a lady-in-waiting, provided by Sir Castor's wife.

"Do you remember how to reach the duchess's apartments?" Nicholas asked as he rolled the discarded garments into a bundle, then draped his cloak over them.

"Down this hall and through the first chamber on the left. Nicholas . . ." She touched his arm as he reached forward to ease open the door.

"Take care," she blurted out, suddenly shy as she met his cool gaze. He stared down at her, and Arianne tried to slow the thumping of her heart. It suddenly occurred to her that if something went awry, this might be the last time she ever saw him.

Fear for him more than for herself made her tremble.

"You take care, Arianne. Take very good care. Stay with the duchess's ladies and avoid the duke at all costs."

Was that something more than ordinary concern in his voice? Arianne wondered in amazement, lifting her gaze to his intent face. With great gentleness he traced a finger along her cheek. "Don't try to find me or Sir Castor's men," he warned. "When it's time to act, I'll come to you."

His expression changed, softened, as he stared down at her. *He's going to kiss me*, she thought on a rush of wild joy, certain that she had not misread the expression in his eyes. But abruptly, almost savagely, he pushed her away.

"Go. Now, Ari. Don't pause and don't look back."

The next thing she knew, he had pushed her out into the corridor and she was hurrying along, glancing neither to the left nor to the right.

She reached the apartment where the duchess and her ladies resided. There was only one woman inside when she slipped through the door—a small, slim figure standing at the window, her light brown hair coiled in a braid so tight that not even a wisp escaped.

The figure stiffened as Arianne shut the door behind her. "I asked you to please wait in the garden. I wish to be alone—"

The small, weary voice broke off when the young woman saw Arianne swiftly crossing the room toward her.

"You ... You're not one of my ... who ... *Lady Arianne*?"

"You remember." Arianne beamed hopefully at her and took her hands. "Oh, Katerine, I beg of you—do not give me away."

CHAPTER 5

Incredulity and shock mingled on the young duchess's heart-shaped face. Then bone-thin fingers clenched Arianne's with surprising strength.

"You're here for Marcus," she whispered. "I'm so glad!"

She cares for him still, Adrianne thought on a breath of hope. Despite the richness of her sky-blue gown and the jewels at her throat and upon her fingers, the Duchess of Dinadan looked poorly indeed—pale, thin, and drawn, with obvious shadows beneath her soft brown eyes.

"Yes," Arianne replied, squeezing her hands. "That's exactly why I'm here. Tell me, have you seen Marcus? Is he all right? Have they hurt him?"

"He's weak, and Julian had him beaten by that dreadful Baylor only a few days ago—but he has been brave, so brave. Oh, Arianne, it is terrible. Julian is a monster!"

Beaten! Arianne choked back her rage. "It's clear you're not happy in your marriage, Katerine—"

"I hate it—and Julian!" Katerine shuddered. "Arianne, being married to Julian is a nightmare."

"Will you help me rescue Marcus?"

The girl's eyes shone. She spoke simply. "I'll do anything to help him."

"It's dangerous," Arianne warned. "If you were to be caught, Julian would be furious."

"He would not hesitate to have me put to death. I am sure of it," the duchess whispered. "As for the treaty with my father, he would forgo it and invade Ruanwald in a twinkling.'' She took a deep breath, her shoulders trembling. ''But I have to risk it—I can't let him murder Marcus.''

''Don't worry. If we're careful, you won't be caught and neither will I,'' Arianne said, turning on her heel and beginning to pace around the pretty chamber with its tapestries and rush-strewn floor. ''It is Julian who's going to suffer, Katerine, not you, not Marcus. Not any longer.''

''I have been smuggling food to him when I go for my daily visits,'' Katerine said brokenly. ''Some bread and cheese. One of the guards looks the other way—I think he believes it cannot do any harm.''

''Daily visits?''

''Yes. Julian comes to my chamber each afternoon and insists that I accompany him and whatever visitors are in the castle on a tour of the dungeon. He is no doubt on his way here at this very moment, Arianne. By all that is holy, you must hide . . .''

''No—take me with you.''

''But none of my ladies has ever come. They hate going there. They have begged me not to force them. Julian will notice if one of them changes her custom.''

''We'll have to risk it,'' Arianne decided, biting her lip. ''I must see Marcus so he will know that rescue is at hand.''

She had only just finished speaking when they heard the sound of heavy footsteps in the hall. A knot tightened in her stomach. She had not seen Julian since she was a child. On his last visits to Castle Dinadan, her father had not brought Arianne along, and when Julian had accompanied Duke Armand on a royal visit to Galeron a few years ago, Arianne had been away, visiting at the court of Count Paxton. So Julian ought not to recognize her. Especially if . . .

Her gaze fell on a wimple atop a wooden chest in the corner. No doubt it belonged to Katerine or one of her ladies-in-waiting. She dashed toward it and slipped it over her braided hair, in one smooth movement fastening the linen band beneath her chin and adjusting the stiff white cap so that it completely hid her hair.

Katerine let out a small gasp as the door swung open without warning. Arianne turned calmly toward it.

"My lord," the duchess murmured, a slight quaver in her voice.

Julian surveyed her from the doorway. Behind him stood an entourage of noblemen, soldiers, and courtiers, among them, Arianne noted in a swift glance, one who wore the starred black-and-white robes and pointed black-velvet hat of a Dinadaian astrologer. But Arianne paid scant attention to any of them—she was interested only in the tall, slim man whose sea-blue eyes chilled her even from across the room.

Julian was handsome in the same way a beautiful marble statue is handsome. There was a cold perfection in the way his wavy golden hair fell to his shoulders, in the arrogance of his chin and of his long, thin nose. His hands flashed with the fire of numerous rings, and his richly embroidered robes and velvet shoes bespoke royalty as much as did the golden emerald-studded crown upon his head. But there was no spark of warmth, no trace of humanity in that finely chiseled face. His narrow mouth revealed cruelty, and his movements were sweeping and precise as he stepped forward into the chamber and offered his arm to his wife.

"Come, my dear, it is time for our tour."

Katerine hurried toward him. As Arianne, head bowed, went to follow, she heard his voice bark out, "What's this? You never take your ladies into the dungeon. They are too weak and sniveling to face the enemies of this land."

"I am feeling ill today, my lord," Katerine answered at once. "Lady . . . Lucinda offered to accompany me should I have need of her."

"Lady Lucinda." Heedless of the group waiting in the hall, Julian turned his head to inspect Arianne, studying her with curiosity. "You are braver than the rest of my wife's serving women," he sneered. "Your devotion is touching."

"Thank you, my lord."

"Look at me when I speak to you, insolent woman!"

She snapped her head up. Her heart was hammering. Julian was staring at her, scrutinizing her every feature with heart-stopping shrewdness. "Have I seen you before?"

"Of course, my lord." Arianne was thankful that her voice

did not quaver. But beneath her gown her knees were shaking.

"It seems I would remember such a pretty face." There was a different tone to his voice now, a considering, almost admiring tone. *Right in front of his wife,* Arianne thought, her contempt mounting.

Thank God Katerine didn't care for him. She risked a small smile.

"Thank you, my lord."

If you dare to touch me, I'll kill you, my lord.

To her relief, he turned then, his robes sweeping behind him. "Let us delay no longer. The miserable scum in the dungeons await our inspection."

Julian led the way down a dim stair. The dungeon master bowed low as the duke approached him at the head of the dank corridor of cells. *You must be brave,* Arianne told herself, feeling sweat on her palms. *You mustn't cry out or give any sign when you see Marcus, no matter how awful he looks.*

They passed gaunt, miserable men and women, chained and bruised, some whose eyes were filled with hate, others with pleading, or dull hopelessness. When they reached Marcus's cell, the duke paused to consider him.

"My fine traitor of a cousin has little time left to ponder his betrayal of Dinadan," he taunted. "Only think what your treachery has cost you, Marcus of Galeron. All of your lands are under my control—or will be soon. Your riffraff soldiers cannot escape my men for long. And there is no leader in your land. Even your sister has deserted her people. When I find her, she will take your place in this cell for daring to defy me."

"There is only one treacherous soul here, Julian, and that is yours. And it is your days that are numbered." The brown-haired man spoke with calm dignity through bruised lips. "Nicholas will never allow you to steal the throne or to continue to tyrannize Dinadan. He'll be back and he'll have your black heart on a stick for his supper."

"Nicholas is dead," the astrologer crowed. "He walks no more on this earth."

"And the last of your line will soon join him," Julian mocked. "When you're dead, and then your sister after you, I will become the rightful heir to Galeron as well, and then none of your nobles will dare to oppose me, even in secret."

Beneath the bruises on his square, handsome face, Marcus paled and his deepset eyes glistened with anger at his enemy, but he held his tongue.

Arianne's heart went out to him, yet she sensed that even Julian's entourage was struck by his dignity and courage. Pride swelled within her.

"He is to have *no* food or drink—not a morsel or a sip— until he hangs!" Julian barked at the dungeon keeper, whose keys rattled on a ring at his belt. The man bowed low.

As Julian and the entourage moved past, Arianne saw Katerine linger at the rear of the crowd. She brushed past the cell, and only Arianne saw her thrust a parcel through the bars into the prisoner's hands. Only Arianne saw the longing glances the two exchanged.

Then the group moved past, Katerine hurrying after them. Arianne followed slowly, her gaze fixed upon the man in the cell. At last, after tearing his eyes away from Katerine's slight form, Marcus turned and saw her.

She saw his gaze widen. His deep, weary eyes glittered. For a moment their gazes locked as they reached out to each other in silent love, in fear, in desperate, blind hope. Marcus's hand trembled as he reached toward her instinctively.

Without breaking stride, Arianne stuffed a linen-wrapped parcel through the bars. "Nicholas is in the castle," she whispered with almost no sound.

The instant Marcus grasped the parcel, she hurried on. Julian had turned back to survey the group, and she reached the others just as his glance fell on her.

"Behold the gypsy who spoke treason in the streets." He gestured contemptuously toward the stoop-shouldered woman in the cell. "She will be hanged alongside Count Marcus of Galeron to pay for her perfidy."

Arianne's stomach clenched as the entourage swept on. She was in so much turmoil over what had transpired with Marcus, she didn't even spare a glance for the scrawny, haggard creature in the cell—until a bony hand grabbed her sleeve as she passed by.

"The tower room," the gypsy whispered.

Arianne froze, staring at her. Through black wisps of strawlike hair, glowing midnight eyes pierced hers. She saw the flash of large white teeth in a saggy, sallow face shining with perspiration.

"Yes—the *blue panel*. That's the one." The gypsy nodded wildly. "You must find the tower room."

The group ahead of Arianne disappeared around the corner. She would be missed if she didn't hurry. "What tower room?" she asked, her own hand clamping around the gypsy's for a brief instant. "Please tell me . . ."

"Is this old one bothering you?" The dungeon master had returned without Arianne's noticing him. She paled as she gazed up into his long, cruel face.

"No, no—she said she was thirsty, that's all."

"Ha! She'll be worse than thirsty before the duke has finished with her," he snorted. "Be off with you. Only the duke is allowed to speak with the prisoners."

"I didn't know," Arianne mumbled, trying to look suitably cowed. She threw the gypsy one last glance before hurrying after Katerine and the others. The woman's glowing eyes seemed to burn a hole in her brain.

As did the image of Marcus's weary ones.

Where was Nicholas right now? she wondered. She didn't recall a tower room from her previous visits to Dinadan. She would have to ask him about it. It was impossible to know whether the gypsy was speaking truth or rambling like a madwoman, but Arianne felt in the old woman's words an import that she couldn't dismiss.

She prayed that Nicholas was safe. Somehow the thought of his being captured, the image of him at Julian's mercy, twisted through her even more painfully than the thought of her own capture.

Nicholas, she thought, her mind scanning the great height and scope of the castle, searching for him as if she could visualize him somewhere on the grounds. *Where are you? Please be safe. Stay safe. You are my hope.*

And my heart. It was the first time she had admitted this even to herself.

When the visitors had left, Marcus set aside the smuggled food from Katerine. He unwrapped the parcel from his sister and smiled for the first time in a long while. Inside the linen was Arianne's sharp-edged, jeweled dagger.

Nicholas swept a keen glance around Julian's apartments. They were the same ones his father had inhabited when Nicholas had last been in the castle. Julian had changed a few things here and there, but most of the rich tapestries, the carved bedposts adorned with circlets of emeralds and rubies, hung with purple satin and gold tassels—were the same. He closed his eyes, almost imagining that he could feel his father's presence. He saw the archduke's eyes on the day he'd banished his son. Filled with rage they'd been—rage and something more. Disappointment, pain. So much pain.

He shook off the heaviness in his heart. The past was dead. He could not change or revive it now. Never would he have the chance to reconcile with his father, to make things right between them, to see love and acceptance once again in his father's eyes.

It was too late for that.

But it was not too late to save others from Julian's machinations. The fate of many hung in the balance—in particular, and weighing most on Nicholas's mind, the fate of Arianne.

She was in dire danger every moment Julian held command of this castle, and Nicholas vowed to himself as he searched through the duke's private chambers that not another sun would set before his enemy was overthrown.

He moved swiftly through the antechambers and the bed-chamber. His father had kept the dungeon keys in a small chest near the window. When Nicholas looked there today, however, he found not the keys but another treasure.

The royal medallion of Dinadan.

The ancient gold gleamed warmly in his hands as he lifted the square medallion out of the chest. Something wrenched inside him as he stared at it.

The medallion was the symbol of Dinadan peace and unity.

It was worn on all state occasions, whenever the archduke appeared before his people—at coronations, celebrations, executions, feasts, and during battle. Nicholas had received it from his father when he turned eighteen, as a sign that he was the one chosen to rule Dinadan when Armand stepped down.

But he'd been commanded to return it before he left Castle Dinadan and his homeland ten long years ago.

It scalded his palm. Somehow the medallion felt heavier now than he remembered. Its inscription read, *Long Live Dinadan.*

The sound of footsteps in the corridor galvanized him. Quick as a blink he dropped the medallion into his pocket and slipped into the anteroom just as the door opened and Duke Julian strolled in, accompanied by several nobles, Cren the Astrologer, and Baylor, the Captain of Arms.

"I've been pondering the executions of Count Marcus and that gypsy," Julian informed his captain. Nicholas listened from the anteroom, his fingers clenched around his sword.

"The stench of their perfidy is rising from the dungeons to pervade the castle. I want them gone, a warning to my people that any opposition to the crown will not be tolerated. I have decided to move up their executions. Baylor, proclaim to all that the traitors will die tomorrow. I expect every noble and merchant and peasant to attend."

"My lord, it will be done. When?" Baylor inquired.

"My subjects are commanded to gather in the courtyard at the stroke of dawn. When first light comes, the prisoners will be brought to the scaffold in chains for all to see, and they will be paraded and then hanged before all of Dinadan."

Nicholas could hear the smile in Julian's smug, velvety voice. In the shadows of the anteroom, Nicholas's eyes narrowed, and tension gripped him like iron chains.

This was too soon, much too soon. No reinforcements could be expected yet, unless fortune was strongly on his side—and it had not been on his side for a long while now.

But he couldn't wait. With or without the soldiers, he needed to retake the castle, and he had to act before dawn.

CHAPTER 6

Arianne never heard even a footfall behind her before she was roughly grabbed.

She gasped, but before the scream could form in her throat, Nicholas's hand clamped over her mouth.

"Easy—keep quiet," he warned and pulled her through the door of the duchess's anteroom and out into the cold stone corridor, up a short flight of stairs, to a low narrow hall. She wasn't familiar with this part of the castle, but Nicholas yanked her through a door and into a darkened chamber without hesitation. Only when he'd kicked the door shut did he release her.

Nearly everyone in the castle was at supper in the great hall, dining on eggs in jelly and quince pie. It was the first chance Nicholas had found to catch her alone.

"We need to talk, and I couldn't take the chance of being interrupted in the solar," he informed Arianne curtly, trying not to notice how beautiful she looked tonight, in that flowing sea-green gown, her face flushed, her eyes huge and brilliant in the dusk. He longed to remove that damned wimple and cap and watch her lovely hair float free, cascading down her back like a river of fire. Longed to twine his fingers through the silk of it . . .

He snapped his attention back to the business at hand, frowning. This was no time for distractions.

"What is it?" Arianne asked, her heart still hammering in her throat as he turned away from her and lit candles atop a low chest. The room shimmered with a warm, pale light that flickered eerily across his darkly somber face.

"Ill news. We must act quickly. There's no time to wait for your troops to arrive—or mine."

Swiftly he explained what he'd overheard in Julian's chambers.

"He's planning to hang Marcus at *dawn*?" Arianne felt the color draining from her face. Suddenly she sprang forward and grasped his arm. "Let's go. Right now, Nicholas. We must free him tonight, even if we have to kill all the guards—I'll need a sword."

"Arianne, calm yourself." He grabbed her by the shoulders and gave her a shake. "You've no need of a sword, for you're staying far from the fray. The situation is under control."

"Under control?" she flashed, her chin flying up. "How can you say that?"

"Do you want to hear my plan or not?"

She took a deep breath, summoning calm, and then nodded. Her violet eyes flashed thoughtfully as she listened to him outline how he had already arranged with Sir Castor's knights—the ones who had entered the castle with them— that they and Nicholas would enter the dungeon shortly before dawn and demand that the prisoners be given over to them. They would say that Julian had ordered them to bring Count Marcus and the gypsy before him for a private exchange before the public hanging.

"Yes, oh, yes, that's good." A smile bloomed across her face. "And once you get him out?"

"Sir Castor's men will have horses ready. They'll make for the drawbridge with him and stop for nothing. I'll remain here, still in disguise."

"No, you must go, too," Arianne cried, fear bright in her eyes as she stared up at him. "Nicholas, they'll be hunting for you . . ."

"I'm not leaving without you. Or without bringing Julian to his knees," he replied quietly. His eyes lit with ruthless anticipation. "I'll wait until Marcus and the others have marshaled our combined forces. When the signal for the attack is given, I'll be well positioned to draw my sword against Duke Julian.''

She was silent. The immense danger looming before them lay like a rock upon her heart. Through the flickering candlelight, she studied Nicholas's face, the fierce scar, the harsh readiness in his gray hawk's eyes.

''What can I do?'' she asked steadily, suddenly realizing that after this night she might never see him again. Anything might happen once their plan was set in motion. Anything at all . . . Death could come swiftly to him, to Marcus, even to herself.

''Keep close to Duchess Katerine. If fighting breaks out, lock yourselves in her rooms and stay there—'' He broke off, frowning. ''I recognize that look, Arianne. You don't intend to follow a word of my instructions, do you?''

Her chin lifted higher. Violet eyes locked with his gray ones, reflecting back an implacability every bit as firm as his. ''I promise to look after Katerine as best I can, but if fighting breaks out, I will not hide in a corner. If I have a chance to run Duke Julian through, I'll seize it!''

''All hell you will!'' Nicholas dragged her to him with a roughness born of alarm. ''You stay away from Julian. He's ruthless and he would cut you down, woman or no, without a second glance.''

''Not if I drove a blade through his evil heart first!''

Fury swept across his face and smoldered in his eyes. His fingers tightened around her wrists painfully, but Nicholas didn't notice how fierce his grip was until she winced. He let her go and stepped back, studying her with a darkening expression that had been known to strike terror into the hearts of armed and helmeted men. But she met his gaze unflinchingly.

''Arianne, if you don't give me your word, I'll have to lock you in the tower room. There's no way in hell I'll leave you to get yourself killed while I'm busy breaking Marcus out of the dungeon—''

''Tower room? What tower room?''

''Don't change the subject,'' he told her impatiently.

''I'm not, but . . . the gypsy said something to me about

the tower room today. I'd forgotten about it until just now.''

"What did she say?"

"She just whispered something about the tower room. Oh, and something about the blue panel."

Nicholas's mouth tightened. "Now how would she know that? There is a secret door, opened by pressing on the blue panel near the stairway. Few know of the tower room. It is a sort of royal dungeon. My great-grandfather kept his enemy, the Earl of Axwith, a prisoner there for nearly three years until a kingly ransom was paid. One hundred years ago, a royal prisoner went mad after being confined there and threw himself out of the tower window onto the stone courtyard below. I thought at first that perhaps Julian would have kept Marcus there instead of in the dungeon."

"He is not so thoughtful." Arianne paced up and down the length of the small chamber, her feet whispering over the rushes. Candlelight gilded her hair, and the shadows thrown by her delicate strides played across her daintily elegant features. "I wonder why the gypsy told me of it," she mused.

"Perhaps she knew that it was your destiny to be shut away there for the duration of this siege, if you will not give me your solemn oath to keep away from the danger."

He gripped her around the waist, and without thinking his other hand tangled in her hair, tilting her head back. "This is not a game, Arianne, and I won't be put off. Your word."

"I'll try," she told him, her voice quavering despite herself. Damn him, the very touch of his hand upon her waist, the sensation of his fingers in her hair, were sending her senses spinning. She fought to regain her equilibrium, but his nearness, the size and power and dark, wild ferocity of him had a dizzying effect that slurred her tongue even as she tried to fire back a sharp retort.

I'll try? What kind of a weak, blathering response was that?

"But I shan't run from an opportunity to repay Julian for all the suffering he's brought . . ."

Nicholas made a sound like a growl deep in his throat and hauled her closer, holding her so tightly that she thought her ribs would crack.

"What am I going to do with you, woman?" he snarled, and Arianne, to steady herself from the thunderous emotions whirling through her, grasped his massive shoulders and spoke the first silly words that sprang to her lips.

"Kiss me as you did Marta!"

Dead silence shook the chamber. The candles hissed and sputtered. Shadows danced.

"Do . . . what? Like I did . . . *who*?"

Now a blush as fiery as a rose swept across her cheeks. "Marta . . . my mother's c-cousin. I saw you kiss her at a banquet that last time in Galeron . . . in the alcove. I was hiding."

His eyes darkened, turning the color of night. "And?"

Staring into those eyes, held in those arms, Arianne felt a compulsion to speak the yearning in her heart, a foolish, idiotic yearning that had been hidden there for ten long years.

"I always wondered what it would be like were you to kiss me in that way," she whispered.

She saw the astonishment cross his face, then a flicker of laughter, immediately followed by an indefinable gleam in those keen eyes. She saw a muscle pulse in his jaw.

"It is a knight's duty to oblige a lady." He shifted her up against him so that her mouth was only a breath away from his.

She wanted to run. Couldn't. Wanted to tell him she'd changed her mind. Didn't dare to. She found herself held in an iron grip, pinned against his towering and hard-muscled body.

She wanted this kiss. Oh, dear Lord, she wanted this kiss. Yet she feared appearing foolish, young, far too innocent. She didn't know how to kiss him back. Where to put her hands, how to form her lips.

No one like Nicholas had ever kissed her before.

Breathless, she watched his face lower toward hers, felt herself drowning in those cool, oddly intense eyes that seemed to read her very soul.

"One kiss, Lady Arianne. One."

Then his mouth descended upon hers, claiming it as a knight would claim a battlefield.

A shock like lightning quivering through a birch tree ran through her. A shimmering fire caught and held.

The kiss was gentle. But not so gentle that she didn't feel the ripple of power from him, the control he was exercising, the deliberation. She wanted suddenly to startle him out of that control, to make him want her as she wanted him.

Her lips clung to his, parted, heat flaring from her to him, her arms circling his neck and tightening.

Nicholas knew he should stop after that one kiss. He'd meant to, but she tasted like summer honey and autumn spice. Shock ran through him—and something else. Desire. With an oath, Nicholas twisted his hands in her hair and deepened the kiss. He heard her soft gasp, knew a swift, grim satisfaction, and then he felt her entire body quiver as his mouth explored the curve of her lips with rough, demanding thoroughness. He took his time, tasting and savoring.

"Arianne," he muttered at last, lifting his head, letting her breathe, but before she could speak, he backed her against the hard stone wall, held her there helpless, and kissed her yet again.

He didn't want to stop. Was damned if he would stop . . .

Unless she wanted him to . . .

Her full, soft breasts were pressed against him, straining, yearning. He felt her tremble in his arms like a wild creature.

Careful, he warned himself, even as he claimed her mouth still, ruthless with the wanting of it. A voice inside shouted that it was nearly too late for caution.

Then, suddenly, without warning, he pulled back. Her eyes were shining, her lips bruised. She stared at him in dazed wonder and rising joy.

His sanity flooded back.

"Arianne, go."

"No." She flung her arms around his neck.

He disengaged them, his blood beating hotly in his temples.

"Go!"

"I am staying. I . . ."

He wheeled away from her, then immediately sprang back. He gripped her by the arms, not gently, his lean face dangerous in that dim and silent chamber. "If you stay, I can't answer for what will happen. I'm a strong man." He gave a bitter half laugh. "I've survived worse dungeons than the one far beneath us in the bowels of this castle. I've survived whippings and beatings, starvation, bitter cold, and war—but I cannot survive you. The wanting of you . . . needing of you . . . not being able to have you . . ."

"Have me. Take me. I'm yours," she whispered and threw her arms around his neck again, rising up on tiptoe to kiss him.

A sweet kiss. An innocent, giving, yearning kiss that stirred something previously untouched inside him and sent the fire raging even more intensely until, abruptly, Nicholas knew he had to pull away.

He held her at arm's length, reining in with a supreme act of will the tattered remnants of his self-control.

"This is wrong, Ari." His voice was thick, yet dogged. "Wrong. You know nothing of men, of the world. You're in love with some boy you knew long ago, some wild, heedless daredevil you admired from afar . . ."

"Yes—and no! I loved you then, loved *him* then—but you're not that boy anymore. I know that. He's gone forever. You're not that boy, and I'm not that skinny, freckled child who followed after you. Look at me, Nicholas." She raised her chin, her eyes bright as stars, defiant, compelling. "I'm a woman, a grown woman."

He groaned and raked a hand through his hair. That she was. A beautiful woman. With her lush, pouting lips, her brilliant eyes, her creamy, flawless skin. And hair softer than velvet and sweeter-smelling than the wildest of forest flowers.

"And I love the man I see before me," she went on in a whisper that tore at his heart. "I would trust my life to you, give my life for you. I love you, Nicholas of Dinadan. I always have. And now, now more than ever, I always will."

Firm and stubborn she stood there, a slender, incredibly lovely woman reaching out to him. Giving, loving, hoping.

"I was wrong about you before . . . in the cottage. Those things I said. You are a true friend to my brother. You're risking everything for Marcus. For me. I beg forgiveness for misjudging you.''

"Arianne, if I stay, if I kiss you again . . . I won't stop . . . not until I've had you, taken you . . .''

"Please." She laughed shakily, reaching up to drag her fingers through his hair, to stroke his face. "Take me. I want you to . . .''

"By God, you'll wed me when this is over. If we live we'll take our vows. It will be forever. Answer me now, yes or no.''

Arianne tugged his head down toward hers. "You make it sound like a threat." Her laughter was soft, spilling over him like sun-warmed honey as she traced her finger gently, teasingly, around his lips.

"It's a vow. A vow of honor.''

Nicholas pulled her against him. As his hand closed over her breast, Arianne's eyes widened with newly discovered pleasure.

"Forever," she squeaked.

"You won't change your mind." It was a statement as his thumb found her nipple.

"I . . . never change my mind . . . Nicholas,'' she managed and then closed her eyes in pure pleasure as his mouth devoured hers again.

When they sank down on the corner pallet, it was as one. Her body was aflame everywhere he touched, and he touched everywhere. With furious, exquisite passion they clung together, shedding tunics and hauberk and breeches and chemises and hose, their bodies hot and feverish despite the chill easing off the stone walls.

By candlelight they kissed and touched and tasted. Neither knew what the morrow would bring. They might have only this one night.

Arianne's hands slid down his powerful back, and her fingers paused as she discovered the many scars embedded in his flesh.

"Nicholas!''

"It's nothing, sweet. It doesn't matter.''

"But these are whip scars . . .''

"From when I was imprisoned . . . by men who did Julian's bidding." He was trailing kisses down her throat. "They fell upon me after I was wounded in a battle in Chessperon. They brought me to a dungeon in the far marshy reaches of the land. I was thrown in prison, beaten . . ."

Her mouth and eyes were wide with horror.

Nicholas brushed a kiss on the top of her nose. He spoke gently. "Ari, don't think about it."

"That's why you weren't here sooner," she murmured brokenly, clutching his shoulders.

"I only recently escaped. I came as soon as I got word of your pleas."

"Nicholas, forgive me, forgive me. I wronged you . . . my poor dear."

"Don't pity me, Arianne." He caught her against him and cupped a warm, strong hand under her breast. The kisses he pressed against her throat, and then lower, to the swell of her breasts, heated her flesh. "At this moment I am the luckiest of men."

This time when he claimed her mouth with his, the kiss nearly blocked the horrid images from her mind. It swept through her, wild and possessive and demanding, and she gave herself up to it, but far beneath the sheer ardent passion of the moment, love and need and tenderness burned. As her mouth parted beneath the onslaught of his, as she slipped her arms around him and drew him close, closer still, love poured from her heart, open and free and giving. It wrapped them both in a cloak that no wind or breath of coldness could penetrate.

As they drew together on the pallet, he gave to her his strength, his courage, his love, and she gave tenderness and warmth and healing. They rocked together in that cold, uncertain night, while the candle sputtered and the wind sighed at the window, and destiny waited beyond the walls of the chamber.

CHAPTER 7

"We've come for the prisoner from Galeron. Archduke Julian commands his presence in the great hall prior to the execution."

Nicholas and his black-masked companions waited with feet planted apart as the dungeon master fumbled for his key ring. "Does he want the gypsy, too?" the man grunted.

"Both of them." Nicholas's hand was on his sword hilt. "Quick, you fool. If you keep the archduke waiting, he'll see you locked here in their stead!"

Another guard ambled along the corridor of miserable prisoners. His feral eyes inspected the tall, masked knight with suspicion. He halted before Count Marcus's cell, his back to the bars, and folded his arms across his chest.

"Nees told me at supper last evening *he* was the one selected to lead the escort for the prisoners today."

"There's been a change in plans," Nicholas snarled, gesturing impatiently at the dungeon master, who had frozen at the other guard's words. "Now hurry, or the archduke will have our heads. The prisoners—quickly, fool, or by all that is holy . . ."

At that moment one of Sir Castor's knights, unnerved by the complication, made a move toward his sword.

" 'Tis a trick!" the second guard shouted suddenly, drawing his own sword.

But he never had a chance to use it, for Marcus's arm shot through the bars and grabbed him by the throat, and the next instant the Count of Galeron had plunged Arianne's jeweled dagger into the guard's neck.

Fighting erupted in a furious tempest as Nicholas and the knights whipped out their swords and a dozen of Julian's men-at-arms, hearing the cries from the dungeon guards, came swarming down the stairs.

"Kill them! They're imposters! 'Tis a trick, a trick!"

The dungeon master slashed his sword at Nicholas, who leaped aside only just in time. He sliced his own blade forward, then leveled it sideways in a wicked thrust that tore through the dungeon master's chest. Blood poured, the man sank to his knees with a death groan, and then Nicholas had the keys from him.

He tossed them through the bars to Marcus as he advanced upon the next shouting, slashing onslaught of Julian's men.

Marcus fitted the key in the lock and swung the door wide. An instant later he was out, grabbing up the sword of the guard he'd stabbed and hefting it even as the gypsy shouted out in glee from her cell.

At that moment the soldier blocking Nicholas's path drove his great shining sword past Nicholas's guard and thrust straight for his heart.

"What have you done with my medallion?"

Glaring, Julian bore down upon his wife with deadly rage and grabbed her by the throat. Cren the Astrologer paused three paces from them and folded his arms, watching the duchess's terrified eyes with satisfaction.

"Tell me, you conniving whore, or I'll throttle you here and now!"

"Nothing, my lord. I . . . never . . . saw . . ."

"Only you and Cren have access to my chambers and know where it is kept. I need the medallion for the execution today—do you think to save your scum lover Marcus by hiding from me the royal medallion of Dinadan?"

"Stop . . . stop . . . I beg of you . . ."

Arianne, who had just a moment before entered the adjoining anteroom, heard the duchess's strangled cries and darted forward. Without hesitation, she threw herself at Julian, wrenching his arm to free Katerine from his death grip.

Cren half turned, gesturing to the guards at the outer door. "Subdue this woman."

"No!" Arianne cried desperately as she was dragged back. "My lord, let her go . . . I beg you, don't harm her!"

At that moment there was a thunderous pounding in the corridors of the castle. She heard shouting, boots stomping, and from a distance came the clash of swords.

"To arms! To arms! The castle is besieged!"

The shout reached their ears, and Julian froze even as Cren gave a hoarse cry of fear.

"You did not foretell this!" Julian cried, releasing Katerine's throat with a growl as he spun furiously toward the astrologer.

"My lord, the stars do not lie. But they did not show me . . ."

"Do you know what this means? What I must do now? Quick, the tower!"

Then Julian was gone, the guards whipping aside to let him pass. "Go! Fight! Drive them back!" he screamed as he ran up the corridor, the astrologer striding after him, pale as frost.

Arianne helped the bruised and weeping Katerine to a bench as the other ladies emerged fearfully from the anteroom. "Tend to her," she ordered, then raced out into the hall.

Which way? Which way had he gone?

It was then that she saw the sweep of a starred black-and-white robe just disappearing around a corner. Cren!

She rushed after him, dashing up the corner stair on slippered feet.

Over the bare hills and through the Great Forest galloped a seemingly endless stream of soldiers. The portcullis had been raised for the nobles and peasants and townsfolk to enter the bailey and witness the executions, and the encroaching armies crashed across the drawbridge in a thundering charge that echoed through the hills and mountains surrounding the south end of the kingdom.

Some troops carried the banner of Galeron—they were led by Count Marcus's captain of arms. Others waved a strange banner—green with black letters that spelled "Nicholas the Hawk." These warriors were fierce-looking men astride powerful destriers.

Sir Castor's men, bearing his own banner, led another charge, tearing through the courtyard and hacking at the black-masked guards who were loyal to Duke Julian.

The fighting was furious and bloody. The crowd shoved and ran and fought and fell. Julian's troops attacked from above with arrows and from below with swords. They swarmed from the castle like a frenzy of locusts.

All of Dinadan roared with battle.

Blood flowed down the stairway of Castle Doom behind them as Nicholas and Marcus fought their way up. They'd hacked through dozens of men thus far, and their swords were bloodied, their clothes torn, but they fought on with a ferocity that terrified all those who opposed them. A dozen soldiers surrounded the two of them as they reached the head of the stairs, and the clang and hiss of swords rang out in frenzied chorus as back to back they fought.

As Nicholas shoved a soldier down the stairs and sent him crashing into three others who were clambering up, he spotted Katerine watching in terror from the doorway of her chambers.

"Where's Arianne?" he shouted, blocking the thrust of his opponent.

"The tower room—she followed Julian and Cren— ahhh!" she screamed as one of Julian's men seized her from behind.

"Traitor," the man snarled. "I'll teach you to give aid to the enemy . . ."

With a vicious thrust, Marcus dispatched the soldier who had just bloodied his arm. He swerved toward Katerine and the soldier who held her, rage suffusing his handsome face.

"Release her!" In that instant he recognized the soldier: Baylor, the Captain of Arms, who had delighted in beat-

ing the prisoners of the dungeon, who had beaten Marcus
only a week earlier.

With an evil smirk, Baylor moved his blade toward Katerine's heart.

"You've been lusting after the duke's honored wife, and
she after you. Now you can watch the whore die."

At that moment, Katerine tried to wrench free, and Marcus
sprang forward. His sword flashed with cold fire as he shoved
Baylor's blade aside only just in time.

Baylor hurled Katerine into the wall and rounded on the
count.

Time froze. Katerine stared at the two men in horror, fear
for Marcus shining in her eyes. But he didn't glance at her;
his gaze was locked on Baylor, who was grinning mali-
ciously, circling.

"Get inside, Katerine!" Marcus ordered, remarkably calm.
"Lock the door!"

She stayed where she was, and without warning, Marcus
lunged toward the soldier again.

Fear tore at Nicholas even as he fought off two more of
Julian's men. Something terrible was about to happen. He
didn't know how he knew—he just did. Years on the battlefield had given him a sixth sense where death was concerned.
True, it was all around him now, but he sensed that it was
bearing down like a wild, panting wolf on someone he loved.

Arianne, he thought in raw terror for her, even as he
brought his sword down on the last man in his path. With a
quick glance he saw that Marcus had slain the man who had
dared threaten Katerine; he was now holding the trembling
young woman in his arms.

In a flash Nicholas remembered the secret passageway
leading into the tower room itself, and the door that opened
only from the outside.

He ducked down the corridor, following several twists and
turns. He had to get to Arianne before she confronted Julian
and Cren. In the secret passage no soldiers would impede
him.

He found the hidden panel, pressed it, and entered dank

darkness. With swift, practiced movements he tindered a light, then ran through the close-walled gloom, his boots scraping over the stones as he sprinted toward the secret stair.

When Arianne arrived at the top of the landing, she peered about in dismay. The landing led nowhere. There was nothing here but another short corridor, ending in a wall. No windows, no doors. Just a single light overhead and an arced multicolored panel painted beside a low bench.

Julian and Cren had disappeared.

From below came the distant sounds of fighting. Where were Nicholas and Marcus in all of this pandemonium? At this moment they were most likely battling for their very lives. She closed her eyes, overcome by the horrible images crowding into her brain.

It would do no good to sob or even to search for them. Instinct told her to follow Julian. If she got the chance to rid the earth of him, she would. She had no weapon but her wits, and she was afraid, but she was more afraid of what would happen should he remain archduke of this subjugated land.

She turned her thoughts from the awful din of battle belowstairs and focused on the gypsy's words. The blue panel.

That blue panel? she wondered, staring at the colorful design beside the bench. She reached up and pressed the oblong that was blue.

Nothing happened. She pressed again, harder.

The wall with the panel swung partly open, making no sound in the silent hallway.

Instantly Arianne stepped forward. She slid through the gap—and froze.

Julian and Cren had their backs to her. They were facing a huge bed in a well-appointed chamber, with green silk bed hangings and draperies, a gold-and-green-threaded tapestry upon the wall, a carved chest of drawers, rugs and rushes upon the stone floors, and a fire in the hearth.

"Quick, my lord, there is no time to be lost. Kill him now!" Cren hissed.

Sword drawn, Julian stared at the white-haired figure lying in the bed.

Arianne recognized him at once. It was Archduke Armand. Nicholas's father was *alive*.

CHAPTER 8

Shock flooded Arianne. She almost started forward, but the old duke, who had not seen her, began to speak, and she stayed rooted where she was, surveying the tableau as if it were a scene from some bizarre dream.

"Yes, kill me now, Julian. End this. I've suffered enough. I should have been struck dead the day I sent my son away. I believed you . . . your lies . . . over Nicholas."

"I don't want to kill you, Father," Julian said in the quietest, most reserved tone Arianne had ever heard him use. Yet he sounded resigned. He was going to follow through!

"But there is no choice," Julian continued. "A rebellion is under way. I must marshal my men and fight those who would cast out the rightful heir to Dinadan."

"You're not the rightful heir. Nicholas is."

"You disowned him. Banished him. And Cren here claims he is dead. So it is left to me—once you are gone. And so now, lest someone find that the old duke lives still, you must needs be truly gone."

"Then do it!" the old duke rasped, contempt in his sagging, lined face, as well as grief, a grief so great that Arianne's heart ached for him, because she knew it was not himself he grieved for but the son he had wronged.

"At least admit to me, before I die, that you were the architect of my feud with Nicholas. You drove the wedge between us with your lies . . . You paid those peasants to swear they saw him attack that girl . . ."

"And I paid her to swear to it," Julian said softly.

The duke groaned.

"What would you have had me do?" Julian demanded, his voice rising, shrill with hatred. "I knew that with him here in this court, I would never have a chance to succeed you. He was the firstborn, and you favored him over me in every way besides. Outright murder would have been too risky. So I found another way."

"Evil . . . boy," the duke whispered, and despite his frailty, his eyes glinted with rage.

"Yes, it's true. It was wicked of me, wasn't it?" Julian sneered. "But brilliant, too, you must admit. For that little incident never happened, my lord, none of it—nor any of the other rumors of Nicholas's wrongdoing that I whispered in your ear." Julian gave a laugh so low and spiteful that it filled Arianne with horror. "Your precious Nicholas was innocent of it all. Now at last you know the whole truth."

"I suspected . . ."

"Ah, yes, you became suspicious, and that's what forced me to arrange your death. You would have summoned Nicholas some time ago, searched for him and heard him out. You were ready to doubt me and welcome him home, so therefore you left me no choice!"

"You have no choice now, my lord," Cren spat. "Kill him and let us go down to the fray. You must rally your soldiers and your supporters among the people. There isn't a moment to spare!"

"You do it!" Julian shoved his sword back into its scabbard. "I cannot. He is my own father—you kill him, quickly, and then we will go . . ."

"No!" Arianne rushed forward as Cren drew out his sword with a billowing motion of his sleeve. She braced herself between the two men and the duke's sickbed.

They stared at her in stupefaction, then wrath lit Julian's face. His eyes glittered like sword points.

"What the devil are you doing here? My wife's servant dares . . ."

"You mistake the matter, *cousin*." With shaking fingers, Arianne tugged off her wimple, letting her hair tumble free. "I am Arianne come from Galeron to free my brother. He is free even as we speak, Julian. He is fighting alongside Nicholas, driving back your men.'' She prayed it was true as she continued imperiously. "Killing the duke will do no good. You have lost. Your reign is over!"

"Nicholas is alive, you say?" Julian sprang forward and grasped her arm, his fingers digging into her flesh so painfully that Arianne nearly whimpered, but she forced herself to remain silent.

"You lie, it cannot be! Cren has announced that he is dead!" Suddenly he struck her across the face. "You would say anything to try to spare your brother!"

The ringing pain from his blow made Arianne blink in fury, but she faced Julian with head held high. "This is the truth! Do you truly wish to continue fighting here, with me— or are you man enough to face the battle raging all through Castle Dinadan? The choice, my brave lord, is yours!"

Arianne flung these words at him with the utmost contempt. She reached out and gripped the weak, trembling fingers of Archduke Armand, who was breathing shallowly beside her.

Cren rushed to the tiny window carved into the stone and peered down at the melee in the courtyard. The air was filled with shouts, screams, groans, and the clanging of swords. Arrows rained down from the watchtowers. Even as he stared at the gallows where the executions were to have taken place this day, he saw a small, dark figure scrambling to ascend the structure.

To his chagrin, he saw it was the gypsy.

"Lord Nicholas lives! He lives! He is within the castle walls, fighting in the name of Dinadan!"

Her rallying shriek echoed even up to that high, secret chamber.

Cren spun away from the window and met Julian's livid gaze.

"We must kill them both now, my lord, and go down to lead the knights! Our soldiers will win, and the duke's proclamation that you are to succeed him will still carry weight."

Julian was literally shaking with anger. "Quickly, then," he snarled, and, having made up his mind, the utter ruthlessness of his darkest side swiftly consumed him. His sword scraped out of its scabbard.

"Dearest Arianne, you never could learn a woman's place—you were forever trying to join in the war games of boys. Now you'll pay the price of death for it."

But as he advanced on her, Arianne dodged around the small table near the window, keeping him at bay on the far side of it. Breathing hard, she saw Cren rushing toward the duke, and in desperation snatched up the ceramic jug on the table before her. She hurled it at him.

It struck the back of his head, and he groaned, turning a monstrous, glaring face at her.

But the blow had only slowed him down.

"If I had a sword, I would slay you both!" she shouted as Julian started toward her again, but at that instant a hidden panel beside the bed slid open, and Nicholas stepped through.

His garments were tattered and bloody, but he looked splendid and fierce and invincible. His face was flushed, his dark hair slick with sweat, but there was an iron calm in his bearing and in his eyes that bespoke a man in control of his destiny.

Through the rent leather of his tunic, the royal medallion of Dinadan gleamed gloriously against his swarthy chest.

"I have a sword, my sweet love, and I will gladly perform that service for you."

He seemed to have summed up the situation at a glance, but when his quick hawklike gaze spied his father lying in the bed, all color drained from Nicholas's face.

Arianne stood frozen, terrified for what he was feeling and thinking at this moment, her heart pounding as she realized that his shock would leave him distracted and vulnerable to Julian and Cren.

"Archduke Armand is not hurt ..." she began, but the words died in her throat as she caught the expression on Julian's face.

He, too, was in shock. Shock at seeing his hated half brother alive and *here*. But beneath the shock was hatred, a hatred as raw and ugly as an open sore. Then the terrible rage lashed through Julian as his gaze centered on the royal medallion of Dinadan around Nicholas's neck.

"The medallion!" he croaked. "You!" He swung his sword in a glittering, deadly arc.

"Kill him!" Julian screamed to Cren and lunged forward. Cren obediently joined the attack against the banished heir.

Arianne flung herself back to the opposite side of the duke's bed. There was nothing in the chamber that could be used as a weapon, there was nothing she could do but grasp the archduke's shriveled hand.

"Nicholas will prevail," she tried to reassure him, but her lips felt numb, and her gaze was fixed in terror on the battle where Nicholas coolly faced two enemies who wielded their swords with deadly intent. It was clear that Julian and Cren had learned their swordsmanship from a master. There was sweat on Nicholas's upper lip, and he was forced to thrust and dodge and parry at a furious pace as they both came at him at once.

"Julian . . . you cannot shed . . . your brother's blood," the archduke rasped out feebly.

Arianne would have told him to save his breath. Cren and Julian were attacking as ruthlessly as mongrel dogs fighting over a rabbit. Except that Nicholas was no rabbit.

He was a magnificent warrior, larger and stronger than both of them, and far more agile. Though they had been well trained, he had honed his formidable skills on countless fields of battle. His sword swept and plunged. Deftly he turned aside each vicious thrust. Then, with one mighty blow, he sent Cren's sword clattering across the floor.

When the astrologer scrambled to retrieve it, Arianne sprang forward. This time she lifted the chamber pot and struck him over the top of the head.

He toppled to the floor, limp as an eel.

"Throw down your sword, Julian." Nicholas's eyes were alight with a cold fury that sent shivers up and down Arianne's spine. "Else I will kill you now."

"Hah!" Julian sneered and lunged forward then, with a quickness born of hate and desperation. "You may have escaped from that prison, but you will not escape from Castle Dinadan or from me. I will smear your blood across every wall in this chamber! Die, my hated brother. Die!'' The sword point glided past Nicholas's defense and slid toward his chest.

But Nicholas leaped aside just in time and followed up with a vicious thrust of his own. With grim strength he plunged the tip of his sword into Julian's throat.

Arianne shut her eyes against the gush of blood. She heard a single strangling gurgle, then the thud as Julian's body hit the floor.

A racking shiver went through her.

When she saw Nicholas next, he was on his knees beside the bed, clasping the old duke's hand between both of his. His face ashen, he kissed his father's withered fingers.

"I never thought to see you alive again," he whispered hoarsely.

"My son. I never thought to have the chance to ask your . . . forgiveness." Tears shone in the duke's sunken but still lucid eyes. "I condemned you wrongly, banished you, trusted that jackal and would not listen to your pleas . . ."

"Father, there's no need . . ." Nicholas tried to interrupt.

But the duke continued without heeding him. "Julian made it appear . . . that you had committed those heinous offenses against that girl. He has admitted it. Arianne is my witness."

"It's true," she put in softly, kneeling beside Nicholas. "It was all his doing, just as you suspected. When your father had second thoughts, when he would have called you back, Julian had him declared dead and locked away in this chamber." She touched Nicholas's arm. An array of emotions must be besetting him at this moment—love, shock, disbelief, and staggering joy to find his father alive. Not to mention a stunned realization of his own vindication. He looked like a man who'd been struck on the head by an iron beam.

She yearned to embrace him, to kiss away that glazed icy shock, and hold him close against her heart, but he turned swiftly back toward Duke Armand.

"You're ill. He has harmed you," Nicholas said sharply, but the old duke shook his head.

"No, a sickness came over me just before he brought me

to this place. A . . . fever. A doctor cared for me here—then Julian had him killed so he would tell no one that I still lived.'' His voice broke. A great sigh ran through his thin body as he met his son's sorrowful gaze.

''I'll never forgive myself . . . for being such a fool,'' Duke Armand whispered.

Before Nicholas could reply, two figures burst through the narrow opening that Arianne had entered a short time before.

Nicholas sprang to his feet, sword in hand, but it was Marcus and Katerine on the threshold.

''My captain, Felix, and the troops of Galeron are driving Julian's men from the bailey,'' Marcus panted. ''Sir Castor and other nobles are fighting beside us. And soldiers bearing your hawk banner are fighting madly, cutting off those trying to flee . . . *My lord!*'' he exclaimed, astonishment crossing his flushed and battered face as he saw the duke.

''What miracle is this?'' Katerine cried, her hands fluttering to her throat.

''It is time . . . for the fighting to stop.'' Duke Armand tried to sit up. Nicholas leaned down to help him. ''Julian has caused enough bloodshed, enough division in my kingdom.''

''Then I'll stop it.'' Nicholas spoke with quiet purpose. His gaze softened briefly as Arianne flew toward Marcus and they embraced, their heads touching. He wanted to get down on his knees and thank God that she was safe; he wanted to hold her and inhale the sweetness of her being and thereby banish the stench of death from his soul.

But there was no time yet for gentle thoughts or loving words, or for the healing that only she could give him. The battle still raged below.

As a reminder of this, Katerine suddenly spied Julian's body and wrenched away, gasping, from the sight.

More were dying even as he stood here, Nicholas reflected, his glance hardening once again.

His father was right. It was time for the violence and strife to end. He knew exactly what he had to do.

• • •

The scene below was a panorama of chaos. After Nicholas settled Duke Armand upon the gold-backed chair that Marcus had carried out to the balcony directly beneath the secret tower room, he paused a moment to survey the destruction and ongoing bloodshed below.

Grim-mouthed, he stepped forward and gripped the balcony wall.

"Halt! Lay down your arms! In the name of the archduke, I command you!"

People glanced up, pointed, gasped. The cry was taken up, swelling through the crowd. "Halt! Halt in the name of the archduke!" the people echoed, the chant growing louder as the fighting stopped, and the multitude of the throng took up the cry.

Duke Armand, having been carried down to this balcony where traditionally he had stood countless times to speak to his people, summoned the strength to rise, with Nicholas's and Marcus's help, and wave at the stunned watchers below.

A joyous shout went up from the crowd.

"Duke Armand lives! Duke Armand lives!"

"And Julian the usurper is dead!" Nicholas called down, standing sword in hand at the rail. "All men loyal to the true duke, throw down your arms. The false and evil reign of Julian is over!"

Arianne's heart thundered as she watched what happened next. The will to fight seemed to drain out of Julian's soldiers like tidewater receding. Some ran—and under Nicholas's orders, the men bearing the hawk banner reluctantly permitted them to flee the gates. But most of the people in the courtyard cheered and then stared up at the balcony in awe, as Duke Armand, with Nicholas on one side and Marcus on the other, began to speak.

Hushed silence fell. The duke spoke in a raspy voice that yet carried down to his people.

"I hereby proclaim that my firstborn son, Nicholas, is empowered to act on my behalf as your new archduke—to unite the land of Dinadan once more!"

A roar rose up from the multitude. The people were cheering. Tears pricked Arianne's eyes, and her heart swelled with happiness as she watched Nicholas ease the old duke back into his chair.

"Fealty to Archduke Nicholas!" Sir Castor shouted from the bailey and dropped to one knee.

"Fealty to Nicholas!" went round the cry, and then, as Arianne watched in mounting relief and joy, the whole assembled throng knelt, lifting their faces to Nicholas and the old duke.

Even the gypsy on the scaffold knelt. Arianne saw the smile of satisfaction flash across her face.

A short time later, Duke Armand rested upon his own bed, in the grandness of his own former chambers. Outside, the cheers could still be heard. "Long live Archduke Armand! Long live Duke Nicholas!"

Arianne and Marcus and Katerine retreated to an anteroom to allow father and son a few moments of privacy for their reunion. But they returned when a steady stream of soldiers and courtiers presented themselves to Nicholas, awaiting his orders.

A doctor was summoned for the old duke, and then Nicholas announced that he and Marcus were needed below. Men of both their kingdoms awaited instructions.

Marcus stared at Nicholas, then at Arianne, and grinned.

"Not a bad day's work," he said. "Little sister, you have done well. If not for your efforts to find him, this rapscallion might not have arrived to free me from the dungeon—I'd have missed all this day's festivities . . ."

"Festivities!" Katerine exclaimed with a shudder.

Marcus grinned at her and kissed her hand.

"If I hadn't arrived, your sister would have found a way to free you." Nicholas's gray gaze was fixed intently upon Arianne's sparkling face. "She is the most determined woman I've ever met."

Marcus chuckled. "Aye, she is determined."

"And the most courageous."

"Well . . ."

"And the most beautiful."

Marcus suddenly glanced back and forth between his sister

and his friend. There was no mistaking either of their expressions. They might have been the only occupants of the castle.

He flashed a surprised grin at Armand, who raised his eyebrows.

"Well, then . . ." Marcus began, but Nicholas cut him off.

"We'll have the wedding at the same time as the coronation," he announced.

"Wedding!" Marcus and Katerine burst out together.

Arianne had not taken her eyes from Nicholas's intent face, but a smile gently curved her lips. She nodded almost imperceptibly.

"Well done, my son!" From the handsomely appointed feather bed, the old duke beamed up at his son. "I see you've learned wisdom during these past years."

"I trust so, my lord." Nicholas's eyes still held Arianne's. She looked so beautiful, even with her torn and crumpled gown, her wildly flowing hair, and the pale lavender shadows of weariness from the events of the day beneath her eyes. "We shall be married at the earliest time possible—if Lady Arianne has not changed her mind."

"When you know me better, my lord duke, you will know that I never change my mind," Arianne said sweetly, and now laughter and love shone from her eyes, banishing the weariness as she went into his arms.

"A woman who never changes her mind," the archduke chuckled dryly. "You have a challenge before you indeed, my son."

"I pledge to meet the challenge—and to surmount it." Nicholas's quick, flashing grin lit his face as he tilted her chin up with a gentle finger. "We will be wed and we will be happy until the end of our days," he promised so quietly that she alone heard the words. "I will devote my life to your happiness, safety, and well-being."

"And I to yours," she whispered back.

"It is customary in Galeron to seal such agreements with a kiss," Marcus pointed out gravely.

"In Dinadan as well." Nicholas's eyes held a distinct gleam as he pulled Arianne close.

"Far be it from me to defy custom, my lord," she murmured with such unaccustomed meekness that he grinned and then kissed her so thoroughly, so deeply, so hungrily that Arianne forgot completely where she was and who was watching, and imagined herself on the very brink of heaven.

CHAPTER 9

The bedchamber was redolent with fresh, sweet-smelling rushes, with wine and candlelight. Arianne brushed her hair before the fire, impatient as she waited for her bridegroom. Growing more and more annoyed as the moments passed, she began to pace back and forth from window to door.

She glanced once or twice, fuming, at the magnificent feather bed with its rich scarlet hangings and fur coverlets. This was her wedding night—and it appeared that she was doomed to spend it alone.

The day had been a blur of noise, color, confusion, of ceremony, laughter, and feasting. First the coronation and wedding ceremony held in the Grand Cathedral, brilliant with candlelight and torches and all the lords and ladies in their richest finery. The knights of Dinadan, Galeron, and Nicholas's own loyal legion of mercenaries had all been in attendance, as had the gypsy, smiling as she watched the royal procession from the very rear of the cathedral.

When Nicholas had watched her glide down the aisle in her gown of pale cream velvet trimmed with mulberry satin, her slender throat and dainty hand adorned with her mother's amethyst necklace and ring, he'd looked appropriately dazzled and proud. Arianne had never felt happier.

The feast had been all anyone could want—succulent venison cooked in a spicy corn stew, capons and pheasants, a pike stuffed with almonds, fruit pies and marzipan sweetmeats . . . and there had been wine and ale and dancing and

speeches. Endless speeches! Of course, it was wonderful that
peace had returned to the land, that Marcus and his troops
had driven off the last of Julian's soldiers from Galeron, that
her homeland was being rebuilt, that alliances between all
the neighboring kingdoms, including that of Katerine's father, were now stronger than ever before.

And Castle Dinadan had been restored to its place as a
stronghold of peace and beauty. The aura of evil no longer
clung to its stone walls—they glistened now in daylight and
starlight with a silver-white luminosity that served as a bea-
con of glory to all who saw it.

Castle Doom was no more. Archduke Armand's beautiful
castle was once again a symbol of safety and pride for his
people, a place of joy and festivity.

Arianne was thrilled to know that after a decent interval
of mourning, Katerine would wed her brother. She wished
them as much happiness as she had found with Nicholas.

But after the feast and the speeches and the dancing—that
was when the trouble had begun.

Nicholas's men had come for him, had claimed it was tra-
dition to get the bridegroom drunk on his wedding night.

He had gone with them, laughing, bowing to her, disappearing and leaving her to be escorted to their chamber by
Katerine and her waiting women.

That had been eons ago, and now as she brushed her hair
before the crackling fire, attired in her daintily embroidered
silk shift, with the candles burning low, and anger sparking
her brilliant eyes, she found herself fuming. If he thought he
could leave her on their wedding night and then return whenever he pleased, expecting her to be waiting for him like a
dish of figs, he was sadly mistaken.

She bounded forward, grabbed her sable wrapper from its
hook, and sprang toward the door.

There were many, many places to hide in this castle. If
Nicholas wanted her when he returned—if he was not so
drunk that he forgot he even had a wife—let him find her.
Let him turn the castle upside down and *try* to find her.

She flung open the heavy door and hurled herself through
it—staight into the iron chest of her husband.

"Going somewhere, Arianne?" He chuckled, his strong arms encircling her.

"No! Yes! Let me go at once!" she ordered as he drew her into the room and kicked the door closed behind them, his tight embrace never loosening.

"Let you go? What a thing is that to say to your husband on your wedding night, my sweet love?" He chuckled again, and his eyes glanced approvingly at the fiery ripple of her hair, at her creamy shoulders, and the thin, clinging silk of her shift.

"You left me—to get drunk with that motley crew of barbarians!"

He shook his head at her and ran a hand slowly, teasingly through her hair. "Do I appear drunk, Arianne?"

He didn't. She studied his keen, clear gray eyes, the healthy but not high color in his handsome face. There was no slurring of his words and, she realized, relaxing slightly in his arms as the rush of anger ebbed, his step was as sure and strong as ever.

"N-no," she replied cautiously, searching his face.

"In truth, it would take much more than the time I spent with those ruffians to make me forget that I have such a sweet and lovely bride waiting for me. A bride whose charms I wish to admire all night long—unhindered by the numbing effects of spirits."

He suddenly scooped her up without warning and carried her to the bed. By the time he set her down, their kisses were deep and more intoxicating than any wine or ale.

"But I'm angry with you," Arianne said, trying not to laugh as they drew apart only by inches. "I've resolved to leave this room—to make you regret that you left me for even a moment."

"Then I'll have to change your mind, won't I?" Nicholas grinned, pushing her back against the pillows and pressing a trail of slow kisses down her throat, making her quiver and burn.

"But I . . . never change my mind," she whispered, her arms already snaked around his neck. She drank kisses from the warmth of his lips.

"This time you will."

He reached out and grasped the satin ribbons adorning the bodice of her shift, tugging until they parted and revealed the sweet nakedness of her form. "I am an expert in many kinds of persuasion."

Arianne gulped a deep breath as his gleaming eyes gazed into hers. "Show me," she whispered on a breath of laughter and drew him down to her.

As Nicholas clasped her close and rained kisses down upon her eyelids, he spoke again. This time his voice was hoarse with emotion. "My sweet, I'll spend the rest of my life persuading you to love me always as you do tonight. I never thought to have a home, my title, my father's respect, or a wife. Now I have them all."

She held him close to her, and her fingers stroked lovingly across the hard, scarred planes of his face.

"And I have you, my beloved Nicholas," she whispered on a crest of love so rich and powerful it brought tears to her eyes. "Surely no woman was ever so fortunate, or ever loved her husband as much as I love you. And will for all time."

"For all time," he repeated, catching her close again and claiming her mouth in a fierce and tender kiss.

As the night sky beyond the window bloomed with purple darkness and starlight, the duke and duchess in their castle chamber celebrated their wedding night and all the days and nights to come.

FALCON'S LAIR
RUTH RYAN LANGAN

For Tom—my free spirit

PROLOGUE

"He's summoned the American." The voice was little more than a whisper.

The tower room was illuminated by a single candle. The two who met there in secret dared not light a fire, for fear of being discovered. With each word, their breath plumed on the frosty air.

"Why?"

"He suspects something and thinks his brilliant friend will come to his aid."

"Then we must stop him."

There was a momentary pause. "Are you suggesting . . . ?"

The hooded head nodded. The silence seemed to stretch out until it was broken by an ominous murmur. "One more makes no difference. We must do whatever is necessary. No one will be allowed to alter our plans."

A chilling gust of wind snuffed the candle, leaving the two in darkness.

"Did you feel that? It seemed . . . unnatural."

Cold hands clasped cold hands. A voice said soothingly, "Just a draft in the tower. It changes nothing. The American must be eliminated."

CHAPTER 1

It was raining again. Felicity Andrews shivered inside her heavy cloak. Ever since she'd boarded the ship in Boston Harbor, the skies had been weeping. But here in England it seemed an icy, bitter downpour that seeped through to her very bones.

The journey had been long and difficult, and she felt weary beyond belief. But the letter from Lord Falcon, her father's oldest and dearest friend, had left her little choice. Though it had been an invitation, it seemed more a summons. He bade his friend Rob to come quickly—before it was too late.

She mulled over the carefully worded letter, as she had many times since its arrival. Oliver, Lord Falcon, had hinted at something dark and mysterious. Something too painful for him to put into words.

Felicity wondered what the old man would think when he discovered that his friend's daughter had come in his stead.

Her head was still spinning from all the details she'd been forced to see to. Selling her furniture. Cataloging all her father's books and letters. By far the most difficult had been letting go of the flat she'd shared with her father before his death. A flat that held a lifetime of memories.

What now, she wondered, now that she'd cut herself adrift from the only life she'd ever known, in Boston, and was about to embark on a life of uncertainty in a foreign land? She wouldn't think of that. She would think only about the end of this tedious journey. The thought of a hot meal and a cozy bed lifted her spirits.

Despite her best intentions, her lids fluttered while she fantasized about the things she would see while she was here in England. The wild, rocky countryside. The small, picturesque villages. The lovely people her father had always spoken so kindly about . . .

The coach, racing across the windswept moors, suddenly rocked and swayed, jolting her into wakefulness, causing her to reach out a hand to steady herself. Felicity glanced out the small window. Her heart almost stopped.

Through the swirling mist she could make out a horse and a cloaked rider, on a collision course with her coach. As she watched, a jagged flash of lightning sliced the darkness, illuminating the rider's handsome, brooding features. Though it was but a single moment, Felicity felt as though the face had been seared into her soul. He had coal-black hair, tossed wildly by wind and rain; dark eyes, deep and fathomless, filled with an eternity of pain; a mouth twisted in anger, as though cursing the heavens. Then darkness closed around him once more. Thunder rumbled across the heavens with all the force of a cannon.

Jolted into action, Felicity rapped on the roof of the carriage, crying out a warning to the driver. But the sounds of the storm and the clatter of the coach's wheels drowned out her voice.

She felt a moment of panic as she braced herself for impact. Instead, the coach continued along its perilous course. And in the next flash of lightning, she blinked in astonishment. The rider had vanished as mysteriously as he had appeared. The only sign of life was a falcon, its wings beating furiously against the buffeting winds.

She covered her mouth with her hand to stifle her little cry of alarm. She must be more weary than she realized. Her mind was playing tricks. Annoyed at herself, she huddled in the corner of the coach until she heard a shout from the driver.

The pace of the carriage slowed perceptibly. As she peered out the window, the ancient towers of Falcon's Lair loomed in the mist. Most of the castle was in darkness. Only a few candles, outlined in windows, flickered in welcome.

The coach halted at the foot of wide stone steps. The driver tossed Felicity's trunks down to a waiting servant, then helped her to alight.

"Welcome to Falcon's Lair, m'lady," he called.

"Thank you."

"And beware." His voice lowered conspiratorially. " 'Tis said there are things here . . ." He looked up as the scowling servant stepped between them.

There was no time to ask what he'd meant to say. With wind and rain pummeling her, Felicity followed the servant up the stairs and inside the open double doors.

The doors clanged hollowly as they were pulled shut behind her. The servant disappeared without a word, and Felicity was left standing alone and shivering.

She had a quick impression of towering walls hung with ancient tapestries and a stone floor gleaming in the light of masses of candles. The scent of beeswax and a faint fragrance of woodsmoke lingered in the air.

At the sound of footsteps drawing near, she turned expectantly. The woman coming toward her was tall, broad of shoulder, and thick in the middle. She wore a shapeless dark gown and heavy shoes. Dark, graying hair was pulled back into a tidy knot.

The woman peered at her, apparently annoyed at this untimely distraction and said accusingly, "The master is asleep."

"I'm sorry it's so late. My name is Felicity Andrews. My father, Robert, was a dear friend to Lord Falcon."

Felicity saw the slight widening of the woman's eyes, the only indication that she recognized the name. "I am Maud Atherton, housekeeper at Falcon's Lair."

"How do you do?" Felicity offered her hand, but the woman merely stared at her in disdain. She realized that only an American would make such a gesture to a servant. Embarrassed, she lowered her hand and clenched it into a fist at her side.

"I was not told to expect you." The woman made no attempt to smile. Her eyes, small and dark, peered from behind thick spectacles.

"There was no time to write Lord Falcon of the news of my father's death. I simply booked passage, trusting that Lord Falcon's friendship would extend to Robert Andrews' daughter as well."

The housekeeper's eyes narrowed in distrust. She turned to a hovering servant. "It is too late to wake the mistress. Take the lady's bags to the east room and see that a fire is laid quickly." To Felicity she said sternly, "Follow me."

They passed through a long, dimly lit hallway where candles sputtered in pools of wax, casting grotesque shadows on the walls and ceilings. Felicity glanced up at the gargoyles glaring down from their perches along the gallery and found herself wondering at the prickly feeling along her spine. She felt as if she were being watched.

After climbing wide, curving stairs to the second floor, the housekeeper continued on to the third floor, holding her candle aloft as she led the way along a narrow, darkened hallway.

"This will have to do." She entered a small, cramped room and set the candle on a chest beside a bed.

Across the room a servant huddled before a fireplace, coaxing a thin flame to life on the hearth. Felicity's trunk and valise had been deposited beneath a window.

"Have you eaten?" the housekeeper asked.

"Not for many hours."

Maud Atherton seemed annoyed at having to attend to one more chore. "I'll see that a meal is sent up. But it will have to be a cold one. Most of the servants have retired for the night."

"If it's too much bother . . ."

Without waiting for her to finish, the woman strode across the room and signaled for the servant to follow.

When the door closed behind them, Felicity dragged a chair close to the fire and sank down wearily. Drawing her cloak around her for warmth, she struggled to hold back her simmering temper.

Fool, she berated herself. Why had she jumped at Lord Falcon's invitation without first weighing the consequences?

Because, another part of her mind replied, she had seen it

as a chance to recover from the shock of her father's death. She'd leaped at this opportunity to withdraw to a place of safety and nurse her wounds. But she hadn't anticipated such a cold reception.

Oh, what in the world had she gotten herself into?

Felicity dozed until a loud knock on the door snapped her awake. For one dizzying moment she had no idea where she was. Then it all came rushing back to her. Falcon's Lair. The drafty room. The surly servant.

"Supper, ma'am." The girl was young, no more than twelve or thirteen, and looked as though she'd been yanked out of her bed. Hair flying. Clothes in disarray. Eyes heavy with sleep.

Felicity could sympathize. She'd been awakened as well, from a dream that was sweet and soothing. Now she was forced back to stark, unwelcome reality.

"My name is Felicity Andrews," she said. "What's yours?"

"Bean, ma'am."

"Bean?"

The little waif shot her a beguiling smile. "My real name's Beatrice Nim. Bea Nim, you see. But everybody calls me Bean."

Felicity couldn't help but grin. "Hello, Bean. I'm sorry you had to miss your sleep."

"No matter, ma'am. With all the chores I do here at Falcon's Lair, I'll be asleep again quick as a fox."

Felicity rubbed her stiff neck and watched as the maid placed a tray on the table before crossing the room to pile more logs on the fire. That finished, she bowed her way from the room and hurried away, presumably to her bed.

It was simple fare. Simple but satisfying. Several thick slices of hard-crusted bread. Slabs of cold roast beef. A hunk of cheese. A mug of tea. And a tankard of ale.

Felicity ate the first slice of bread smothered with meat and cheese quickly and washed it down with ale. At once her spirits improved. Feeling warmer now, she removed her cloak and spread it before the fire to dry. Then she ate the rest of the meal slowly, while she removed her shoes and stockings and wiggled her toes in contentment.

As the ale and food slowly built a layer of warmth in her stomach, she felt her fears evaporating. A good night's sleep was what she needed. She sipped her tea. By morning the worst would be behind her, and she could begin to enjoy this adventure for what it was. A chance to meet her father's old friend. An opportunity to see England. A glimpse of her father's past and perhaps her own future.

She rummaged through her valise and withdrew a nightshift, then undressed quickly and pulled the simple gown over her head. As she crossed to the dressing table, she removed the pins from her hair. Freed of the restraint, it tumbled in wild disarray to below her waist. She sat down and picked up a brush. But as she began to smooth the tangles, she caught sight of something in the mirror that stopped her hand in midair.

"Sweet heaven!" She covered her mouth with her palm to keep from crying out.

A man stood in front of the window, his hands on his hips, his legs apart, in a menacing pose. He was dressed all in black, from his highly polished boots to the cloak tossed rakishly over his shoulders. He would have been fashionably dressed several centuries ago. But it was his scowling face that almost stilled her heart and caused her breath to catch in her throat. It was the face she had seen outside the window of the coach. The face of the horseman who had mysteriously disappeared.

"You!" She dropped the brush with a clatter and whirled to face him. "Who are you? What are you doing in my room?"

"Yours, is it?" His voice was a low, deep growl of anger. "You arrive a nameless stranger on these shores, and already you're laying claim to Falcon's Lair?"

"No. I didn't mean . . ." She caught herself before she could apologize. Her tone sharpened. "How did you get in here without being seen?"

"I'll ask the questions, wench. Who are you, and what are you doing at Falcon's Lair?"

"You don't think I'd bother to answer a madman, a . . . lecher." While she spoke she darted a look around for an escape route.

Reading her intentions, he moved so quickly that it seemed no more than a blink of the eye. One moment he was at the window, the next he stood barring the door.

Now her panic deepened, constricting her throat until she could barely speak. What sort of evil monster was this? She stared around the room in search of a weapon with which to defend herself. "Are you telling me you've been here since I arrived? That you stood there and watched me undress?"

Seeing her fear, he gave a dangerous, chilling smile. "Aye. A most charming sight it was, too. Though I'm sorry you managed the feat so quickly. I would have enjoyed it more if you had taken a bit of time. The sight of all that flesh was most erotic."

"How dare—" Suddenly she'd had enough. It was the final straw in a crushing day. Racing across the room, she lifted a hand to the bellpull. She would have this madman taken away to an infirmary or an asylum where he belonged.

Before she could summon a servant, he stood beside her. Though he didn't physically touch her, she found she could not lift her hand.

"Don't be a fool. That would do you no good. The others can't see me."

At the nearness of him she felt a wave of heat, stronger and more intense than any fire.

"Where is this heat coming from?"

"Heat?" He went very still. "It is cold you should be feeling."

She tried to free herself, but his strength was too great. With only the power of his mind, he was able to restrain her. All she could do was stare at him in stunned silence.

She was not the only one shocked. Standing so near, it was obvious that he had experienced something as well. Something that caused him to take a step back as though he'd been burned.

"What in the name of . . . ?" He stared at her as if really seeing her for the first time. His gaze skimmed the small oval

face, the full lips pursed in a little pout. She was breathtaking.
Lips made for kissing. Skin like porcelain. Eyes more green
than blue. And a mass of tangled curls the color of autumn
foliage. An altogether appealing picture. But it was more than
her beauty that attracted him. There was something else.
Some . . . inner strength that he found utterly fascinating.

The scent of her filled his lungs, and he breathed her in,
feeling almost intoxicated. It was a soft, subtle fragrance, like
a meadow of wildflowers after a spring rain. He would not
soon forget the scent of this woman or the look in those eyes.
Fear shimmered in them, but there was an underlying edge
of anger. Though she was frightened, she didn't faint, as
many of her gender would have. Instead—to her credit—she
stood her ground.

What a rare, magnificent creature. He knew in that moment
that despite the cost to him, he would one day touch her.

When she found her voice she managed to say, ''Are you
asking me to believe that I am the only person who can see
you?''

''Oh, there are a few others.'' He saw the fear begin to
dissolve and a trace of defiance take over. *Aye,* he thought.
Magnificent. What he would give to have her. Almost at once
he rejected that idea as nothing more than an impossible
dream. Still, the thought tantalized, softening his rough tone.
''It's up to me to decide who'll see me and who won't.''

Her voice frosted over. He was, indeed, a madman. ''How
was I chosen for this dubious honor?''

A grin touched his lips, quick and easy, causing a hitch in
her heart. When he smiled he was the most handsome man
she'd ever seen. Handsome and arrogant, a potent combina-
tion. And extremely dangerous.

For a moment he lifted a hand and tempted himself with
the thought of touching her. His fingers actually tingled at
the suggestion. Not yet, he cautioned himself. Not just yet.
He closed his hand into a fist and lowered it to his side.
''Because I wanted it.''

''Do you get everything you want?''

''It's my right as lord of the manor.''

''Lord of . . .'' Disgusted, she turned away and caught

sight of her reflection in the mirror. She was shocked to see that she was alone.

Turning back, she saw a falcon perched on the windowsill. As she watched, it spread its wings in flight. Over the whisper of wings, she could have sworn she heard a low, deep moan.

Or was it the keening of the wind?

CHAPTER 2

Felicity was up before the servants. Her sleep had been disturbed by dreams and visions, though now that she was awake she couldn't recall them. She knew only that she'd been unsettled by the images that flitted through her mind.

She couldn't stop thinking about the strange events of the previous night. The only explanation she could accept was the fact that she had been completely exhausted.

Ghosts, indeed! She was an educated, intelligent woman and, as her father had often said, too sensible for her own good. Hardly the type to indulge in flights of fancy.

A good strong cup of tea, she thought, would clear her head and put a shine on the day. Still, she glanced carefully around the room before removing her nightshift. Annoyed at her thoughts, she buttoned the simple white blouse and dark skirt that skimmed the tops of her kid boots, then ran a brush through her hair and secured it with combs.

She crossed the room and drew open the draperies, allowing shimmering morning sunbeams to filter into the room. For long minutes she stood at the window, transfixed by her first glimpse of Falcon's Lair by daylight. The land below seemed to roll and fold into itself like a well-kept secret. Heavily wooded valleys opened unexpectedly into gorse-covered stretches of moor that climbed steeply toward the clouds. Perhaps a mile away to the east lay a village, with a row of shops and houses, and a church steeple catching the first rays of morning sunlight.

Her heartbeat quickened. How she would love to paint the

scene in just this light. Tomorrow, if she awakened early enough, she would carry her sketchbook to the moors and try to capture it.

"Lovely, isn't it?"

At the deep voice she whirled. "You again. But how— What—"

He was standing directly behind her, and though he didn't touch her, she felt the tingling warmth radiate through her veins.

"I thought . . ." She moistened her lips and forced herself to go on. "I thought I'd dreamed you."

It was she who looked like a dream. So fresh, so lovely in the light of morning, she nearly took his breath away. "Oh, I'm real enough," he said. "To those who believe."

She took a step back until she felt the cold window at her back. "Last night I thought you were a . . ." She couldn't bring herself to say the word. Besides, this was no ghostly specter. This was a man. Tall, menacing, and very much alive. He was toying with her. Trying to make her believe the impossible. She would not be coerced into playing his game.

"How did you do that trick?"

"Trick?"

"Appearing. Disappearing. Is it a parlor game?"

He didn't want to answer. Not yet. So he simply changed the subject. "You never told me your name."

"Felicity Andrews."

"Andrews. But you were supposed to be . . ." He paused, unwilling to reveal more. Changing tactics, he muttered, "Felicity. That is Latin for happiness. It suits you. You have a happy face." He bowed slightly. "My name is Gareth, First Lord of Falcon's Lair."

"Gareth. My father never mentioned you." She searched her mind but could not recall having heard the name before. "You're not one of Lord Falcon's sons."

"Nay." He studied her lips, pursed into a little pout. The desire to crush those lips with his own was so tempting that he had to clench his hands at his sides to keep from pulling her to him. He cautioned himself to tread carefully with this prim little American. Instead of touching her, he pressed a hand to the window casing above her head and leaned close to her, inhaling the delicate woman scent. "There are things you should know about Falcon's Lair."

"What things?"

He shook his head. "It is not in my power to reveal them. You must learn these things on your own. But be warned. You will be in grave peril while you are here."

"From you?"

"I will not bring you harm."

There was absolutely no reason to believe this madman. And yet, for some unknown reason, she did. Another lapse of intelligence. With a sigh she muttered, "I just don't understand."

If he couldn't touch her, he would at least allow himself to skim her hair. He caught a strand and watched it sift through his fingers. The heat surrounding him grew until it was an inferno. His voice was little more than a whisper. "Understand this, little happy face. Since you have been sent to us, you must hold the key."

"The key to what?"

When he didn't respond, she turned away and pressed her forehead to the cool windowpane, eager to escape the heat that seemed to envelop her whenever he was near. "Why must you speak in riddles?"

Again he didn't reply, and she turned. The room was empty. The heat had died as quickly as it had begun.

For long minutes she stood at the window, her mind brimming with all the questions she needed answered. Who was this Gareth? Why had he singled her out? What had he meant by the key? She shrugged and touched a hand to her throbbing temple. Perhaps she wasn't nearly as rested as she'd thought. Her mind, which had always been so keen, now betrayed her. She was seeing people who weren't here and hearing words that made no sense.

Needing to escape, she slipped out the door and hurried down the stairs in search of the kitchen.

The hallways were steeped in gloom, the candles having long ago burned out. A few still sputtered in pools of melted wax, but their light was barely enough to show the way. Felicity took her time, peering into darkened rooms, hearing the echo of her footsteps along the stone floors.

Like all castles, this one was cold and drafty, with large, cheerless rooms that begged for fires to be stoked and people to fill the empty spaces. Instead there was only darkness and a chill dampness that added to its somber atmosphere.

There was no mistaking the kitchen. Though the rest of the household lay abed, a roaring fire already burned on the hearth. A pig roasted on a spit. The air was perfumed with the fragrance of freshly baked biscuits.

At a long trestle table sat a row of servants spooning gruel into their mouths while struggling to dispel the last vestiges of sleep. They looked up, curious at the presence of this stranger, and began a low murmur among themselves. Most of them could never recall having seen a family member or a guest of Lord Falcon set foot in this room. At a furious command from the cook, they lowered their heads and continued to eat. All except young Bean, who shot a quick smile at Felicity before returning her attention to her meal.

Across the room Maud Atherton was engaged in a whispered conversation with a tall man in a spotless dark suit. Seeing Felicity, they fell silent. The man set something on a silver tray and hurried forward.

"Miss Felicity." He bowed stiffly. "I am Simmons, butler to Lord Falcon. I bid you welcome."

"Thank you, Simmons. Does Lord Falcon know I'm here?"

At her eager question he shook his head. "I shall deliver the news at once." He gave a glance toward the staff, who were studying her with keen interest. "It is rare for anyone except the servants to be about this early. Mrs. Atherton assures me that a morning meal can be prepared for you in short order and will be served in the dining room. Perhaps, in the meantime, you would like a walk in the gardens. Though they are not yet in bloom, there are some lovely fountains and stone benches for your comfort."

"Will Lord Falcon be joining me?"

The butler shook his head. "These days the old lord rarely leaves his bed."

"Then perhaps I could join Lord Falcon in his room for a morning meal."

Though his expression never altered, Simmons stood even straighter. His tone was stern, revealing his outrage. "I'm afraid that would be highly improper. Lord Falcon does not entertain guests in his private chambers."

Felicity blushed clear to her toes, knowing that she must appear bold indeed. "There was a time when Lord Falcon was my father's oldest and dearest friend. Though I've never met him, I feel as though I've known him for a lifetime. I'm eager to see if the impressions I have of him are correct."

Simmons seemed to consider for a moment, his frown deepening. "It is an unusual request, one I feel certain Lord Falcon will deny. But I shall ask him at once. If he gives his approval, what shall I fetch you to eat, Miss Felicity?"

"Tea and a biscuit will be fine."

If he was surprised at the simplicity of her needs, he gave no indication. He strode away and returned a few minutes later carrying a silver tray covered with a linen cloth. "Follow me," he said as he led the way from the kitchen.

Felicity followed him up the wide, curving staircase and along the upper hallway to a set of double doors. Except for a few candles in sconces, the sitting room was in darkness. They crossed the room, and he signaled her to wait in the doorway as he entered an even larger room, where a fire blazed on the hearth. By the light of the fire Felicity could make out the figure in the bed.

"Good morning, my lord," the butler said softly.

"Simmons." The voice was rough and scratchy but still carried the roar of an old lion. "Who is that in the shadows?"

"Miss Felicity Andrews, from America." The butler set the tray on a table and hurried toward the bed. "She wishes to take her morning meal with you here in your room."

There was a moment of stunned silence. Then the figure struggled to a sitting position. At once Simmons was beside him, propping mounds of pillows around him, smoothing the coverlet until not a wrinkle remained.

"Open the drapes," the old lord commanded.

Simmons moved around the room, pulling open the heavy draperies. Morning sunlight streamed in, filling the room with light and warmth. It was a large room, comfortably furnished, with a huge bed hung with linens. Over the bed were crossed swords, their jeweled hilts and finely honed blades glinting in the sun's rays.

"Come closer," the old man commanded imperiously.

Felicity strode to the foot of the bed, and she and Lord Falcon had their first look at one another.

"So." It seemed more a sigh than a word. A sigh that welled up from deep within the old man's soul. Lord Falcon cleared his throat and tried again. "You have the look of your father. About the eyes mostly. And the hair, though his was more red, as I recall."

Felicity smiled. She had heard such comments all her life.

"Where is Rob?"

"I buried him almost a month ago." The pain was so unexpected she nearly swayed. But pride and propriety would not allow it. She merely clasped her hands together until the knuckles were white.

"Dead." Lord Falcon looked stricken. "This cannot be," he said more to himself than to her. "I needed him. Was counting on him to . . ." He looked up. "Why have you come?"

"When Father received your letter, he was already too weak to leave his bed. But it cheered him to hear from his old friend. He spent hours afterward, whenever he was strong enough, talking about you and the adventures the two of you shared in your youth. I thought . . . I thought I might find a friend in you as well."

Nodding, Lord Falcon patted the chair that Simmons had positioned beside the bed. "Come and sit a while, my dear. Tell me about your father's work. Did he ever write the book he'd planned, about his study of herbs and plants in the Dark Continent?"

Felicity sat and folded her hands primly in her lap. "I'm afraid not. I helped him with voluminous notes on the subject. He dreamed of the day his writings would be published.

But Father was more a dreamer than a doer, I'm afraid. He often said he never would have left the comfort of home and hearth had he not been prodded by his old friend. He claimed that though he was as timid as a churchmouse, you were absolutely fearless."

Lord Falcon gave a snort of derision. "Fearless? I thought so at the time. Now I wonder if I wasn't simply foolish. It's a family curse, I'm afraid. Every male in my family has this need to explore the unknown. And all, with the exception of me, have died young. My father helped chart the Nile and drowned when his boat overturned. His father before him traveled to the Orient and never returned. I grew up accepting this restlessness, this need for adventure, as my fate. When your father and I fell into a cave deep in the heart of the jungle, I feared I was under the family curse as well. Ironic, isn't it? We emerged unscathed and lived to be old men." His voice lowered with passion. "But I would willingly give up every year that I have lived if it would remove the curse from my own sons."

Felicity heard the pain in his voice. "What has happened to your sons, Lord Falcon?"

He looked away, but not before she saw the haunted look in his eyes. "My oldest, Chandler, has been lost in the Amazon and is presumed dead."

She reached a hand to his. "I'm so sorry."

He studied the long, tapered fingers, so like another he'd known. "William, my younger son, was thrown from his horse while racing across the moors. He now lies broken and lost to us in body and mind. He is trapped in the bed of his youth, which he may never leave."

"How terrible." She glanced at Simmons, who stood stiffly beside the table, waiting to serve their breakfast. "Can nothing be done for him?"

The old man shook his head. "The doctor has done all he can. The rest is up to the fates. But if the Falcon curse is to be believed, the fates will not be kind, and William's wife will soon be a widow."

"His wife?"

"You did not meet Honora?" the old man asked.

"It was very late when I arrived last night." The thought of another young woman was most appealing. Perhaps they could find common ground. Oh, it would be wonderful to have someone she could call friend.

"I fear Honora's life at Falcon's Lair is not what she'd hoped. Instead of hosting lavish parties and teas, she must nurse a dying husband and spend long days dispensing medicine with a doctor."

Lord Falcon signaled for his tray, and Simmons obliged, tucking a napkin into the front of the old man's nightshirt before pouring tea.

Felicity sipped her tea and studied the man in the bed. It wasn't only his voice that reminded her of a lion. A mane of silver hair, in need of a trim, fell to his shoulders. His face, though etched with the lines of age, was still handsome. And his eyes. So like the ones she had seen in the darkened moors and again in her room. Shadowy, watchful, they seemed to see more than they cared to reveal. They were watching her now, over the rim of his cup.

"How long can you stay in England, my dear?"

She gave a negligent shrug of her shoulders. "I haven't really set a time. But I thought a few weeks."

"Nonsense. That's not nearly long enough. You'll need at least a few months to get to know this lovely land and its people."

"Lord Falcon, I couldn't possibly stay a few months."

"Why not?" he demanded.

"Because . . ." She set the cup down and busied herself sprinkling sugar and cinnamon on a warm biscuit. "Because I do not wish to be a burden. I will accept your kind hospitality, but only for a short while."

As she lifted the biscuit to her lips, she gave a little sigh. "Oh, this is the best I've ever tasted."

Lord Falcon's breakfast lay forgotten. His voice warmed. "Rob always said that about Cook's biscuits."

"Did he?"

Lord Falcon nodded. "He was more like a brother than a friend. When I look at you, my dear, I see him. Even the inflection in your voice is the same."

It gave Felicity a strange, comforting feeling to know that she shared something with the father who was now gone.

"Simmons," the old man suddenly called, "tell Maud Atherton that I desire a special feast for tonight, in honor of our guest."

"Yes, my lord." The butler freshened their tea. "I believe Cook has already begun. She ordered a pig slaughtered."

"Fine. And tell her to bake her special tarts. The ones Rob always liked."

"Now, my lord?"

"Now. And Simmons—"

The butler paused with his hand on the door.

"Tell her I will be eating in the dining room tonight."

The elderly servant showed no emotion, but Felicity thought she'd seen a flicker of something in his eyes. "Yes, my lord." He walked stiffly away.

When the door closed behind him, Lord Falcon leaned closer. "I must tell you that I had a reason for asking Rob to make the arduous journey. But now that he is gone and you are here . . ." He shook his head. "I can only hope that you will prove to be your father's daughter."

"I'll certainly try." She gave him a wide smile and patted his hand. "I'm so pleased that you aren't angry at my unexpected arrival."

"Angry?" He grasped her hand, suddenly as eager as a child. "You will stay? You . . . won't leave, will you? No matter what?"

"Now why would you ask such a thing?"

"There are few who would have the courage to remain at Falcon's Lair. For there are things here . . ."

When he didn't elaborate, she prodded, "Things?"

He looked up. "I will not hide the truth from you. I sent for Rob because I needed a friend. One I could trust completely."

"I don't under—"

He held a finger to his lips. "I no longer know who is friend and who is foe. Nor will you. You must learn to trust your instincts. But know this. You are never alone. There are many here at Falcon's Lair who sense . . . someone or something. A blast of cold air when no window or door has been opened. A chill that raises gooseflesh or causes the hair at the back of one's neck to rise. Sometimes a sound, like a sob or a moan.'' He glanced up sheepishly. "Forgive me, my dear. You must think me an addled old fool for believing that Falcon's Lair is haunted.''

"Not at all.'' She patted his hand. "As a matter of fact, I almost had myself believing that I'd encountered a spirit.''

Blackbird eyes met hers. One bushy white brow lifted slightly.

Felicity blushed furiously and cursed herself for revealing such a thing. "I was very tired when I arrived last night. I thought . . . he was in my room upstairs. And this morning I thought he stood behind me as I looked out over the land.''

Lord Falcon folded her hand between both of his and lay back against the pillows with a sigh. "I should have known he would seek you out.''

"Who?''

Ignoring her question, he sighed, "Oh, this is indeed a memorable day.'' His eyes suddenly snapped open. His tone sharpened. "Did you say 'bedroom upstairs'? Is that where you slept last night?''

She nodded, puzzled by his sudden agitation. "It has a lovely view of the village in the distance.''

"No. Oh, no. That will not do at all.'' He tugged on the bellpull. Almost at once Maud Atherton appeared.

"Yes, m'lord?''

Lord Falcon's voice frosted over. "Why did you put Miss Andrews on the upper floor?''

The housekeeper shot a stinging glance at Felicity, then lowered her gaze. "It was quite late, and I wasn't prepared for the young lady's arrival. I thought . . . that is, I did not wish to anger Lady Honora . . .''

"I want her in the suite beside mine,'' he said sternly.

"Yes, m'lord. I'll see to it at once.''

"See that you do. And Mrs. Atherton,'' he called as she started out. "You will instruct the servants to assist Cook in making tonight's dinner a feast fit for royalty.''

She kept her back ramrod straight as she turned to face

him. "Yes, m'lord. We are roasting a succulent young pig. There will be mutton and beef as well. Will you require anything else?"

"Not at the moment." He returned his attention to Felicity and missed the angry look that darted into the housekeeper's eyes. But it wasn't lost on his young guest. She found herself wondering if so much resentment was the result of the additional work the servants were forced to do. Or was there something else?

Whatever the reason, she vowed to give the housekeeper a wide berth and to try to be as light a burden as possible while she sorted out all these strange, unsettling events.

CHAPTER 3

Felicity remained beside Lord Falcon's bed, hoping he would tell her more about the things he feared. But the old lord's eyes closed. His head sank deeper into the pillows, and soon his breathing became slow and rhythmic.

When Simmons entered the bedroom and saw that his master was asleep, he picked up the tray and whispered, "Lord Falcon may sleep for several hours, miss. Since Mrs. Atherton has said it may take some time to prepare your suite of rooms, you may want to explore the gardens."

"Thank you, Simmons." Felicity stood and followed him out of the room. "I believe I'd like to see some of your lovely countryside. I'll just get my cloak."

She hurried to her room and stopped in her tracks. Her trunks had been opened and her belongings scattered everywhere. Gowns, undergarments, books and papers. All had been shuffled.

A servant perhaps hungry for valuables? Or . . . something more sinister? Hadn't Lord Falcon warned her?

She whirled as the door opened. Bean, the young serving girl, looked around in stunned surprise. "Oh, ma'am. What have ye done?"

Felicity quickly gathered her wits. "Made quite a mess, I'm afraid. I was . . . looking for my cloak." She crossed the room and rifled through her gowns until she located it. "Here it is." She turned. "I'll just clean up this mess."

The little maid held out a hand. "Mrs. Atherton would

have my head if I let you clean your own room. No, ma'am. I'll have it set to rights in no time.''

With a sinking heart Felicity turned away. As she strode down the steps of the ancient castle, she felt an icy thread of fear snake along her spine. Once again she had the feeling that she was being watched. But though she turned and studied the windows, she could see no one looking out.

She shook off the dread and moved out at a fast pace until she had passed through the gates marking the entrance to Falcon's Lair. She would save the garden for another time. Today she needed to put some distance between herself and this strange castle.

Though the sun had broken free of the clouds, there was a bite to the air, and Felicity gathered her cloak around her as she walked. She had gone some distance when a cart came clattering along the lane. As it drew abreast, a boy of about ten years studied her with interest.

''Goin' to Falcon's Way, ma'am?'' he asked.

''Is that the village in the distance?''

He nodded. ''Would you like to ride wi' me?''

''Thank you.'' She climbed in beside him and said, ''My name is Felicity Andrews. I'm from America, visiting Lord Falcon.''

''Ye're stayin' at Falcon's Lair?'' He shot her a look of astonishment before flicking the reins. The swaybacked mare leaned into the harness, and they started off at a slow, plodding gait.

''Haven't you ever met a guest of Falcon's Lair before?'' she asked.

He shook his head. ''Me mum says there's evil up there and a curse on all who dwell within.''

''You can't believe that,'' she said with a smile.

But her smile faded when the boy said solemnly, ''Can't argue wi' truth. Lord Chandler is gone and Lord William more dead than alive. There's those who say old Lord Falcon will be next. It's the Falcon curse.'' He pulled up beside a row of shops. ''I'll leave ye' here, miss.''

''Thank you.'' Felicity stepped down and walked slowly through the village, smiling at the young mothers who hur-

ried by with babes in their arms and the older women who
swept their stoops or sat in the late-morning sunshine, gos-
siping with their neighbors. She passed by the bakery, the
milliner, the apothecary. Though the people nodded as she
walked by, she felt their curious stares as well. No one
stopped to speak with her. She had the feeling that they already knew where she was staying and had decided to keep
their distance, in case she had been tainted by the Falcon
curse.

Felicity kept up a brisk pace as she returned to the castle.
The sun had taken refuge behind the clouds, and the air had
grown colder. Despite the warmth of the hooded cloak, she
shivered and wished she hadn't gone so far.

As she passed through the gates, her footsteps faltered.
Though she could see no one, she had the strange feeling
that she was not alone.

"What did you think of our village?"

She halted, recognizing Gareth's voice directly behind her.
She would not spin around and let him see her fear. Lifting
her chin at a haughty angle, she challenged, "Why didn't
you come along and see for yourself?"

"I cannot go beyond these gates. I am bound to this land,"
he said simply.

She did turn then, and the look of pain in his eyes caused
her breath to catch in her throat. She instinctively lifted a
hand. But before she could touch his arm, he stepped back
out of reach.

So, he didn't like to be touched. She filed the knowledge
away in her mind.

"The villagers are fearful," she said softly.

"It isn't you they fear." He gave a shallow laugh. "They
have heard of the ghost that haunts Falcon's Lair. It is only
natural for them to fear what they cannot understand." He
studied her a moment, then said, "What about you, little
happy face? Why don't you fear the ghost of Falcon's Lair?"

"Perhaps I do. Or perhaps I don't believe in ghosts."

He studied the glowing cheeks, the wind-tousled hair, and
felt a wave of pure desire that left him shaken. It pulsed

through him, adding to the aura of heat that seemed to shimmer around him.

His voice lowered. "Oh, I'm real enough. But you needn't fear me. I will never harm you."

"What keeps you here?" she asked softly.

"Unfinished business." His eyes narrowed as he glanced toward the castle.

She followed his gaze but could see nothing out of the ordinary. When she turned back, she saw that he was watching her with a look that made her heart race. It was a hungry, wolfish look that nearly devoured her.

She caught up her skirts, determined to get away from him. But before she could take a step, his hand shot out. Though he didn't actually touch her, she could have sworn that she felt the curl of his fingers around her wrist, stopping her in midstride. The heat was shocking in its intensity. It raced along her arm and sent the blood pulsing like liquid lava through her veins.

He saw the widening of her eyes. Just a flicker. His admiration for her went up a notch. Though she was afraid, she didn't panic. And though she stiffened, she didn't struggle. Didn't fight. She merely stood toe-to-toe with him and shot him a look that dared him to step over the line.

He'd always loved a dare. It was his weakness—and his downfall. After all, it was a dare all those centuries ago that sent him into this limbo.

He shifted his gaze to her mouth. What would it be like to kiss her? To brush those soft lips with his? It could be an experiment. To see just how far he could push the boundaries. Of course, it was forbidden by the Fates. But then, hadn't he always broken the rules?

Hers was a mouth made for kissing. A dangerous temptation. Would she yield or would she fight? Either way, it would prove very satisfying.

Felicity had never felt like this before. Though he made no move to touch her, she was completely helpless to move. She was quite certain that she didn't want him to kiss her. And yet she knew that if he did, she would not fight him. In fact, she would be lost.

Feelings, strange, compelling feelings, churned through her, leaving her dazed and reeling.

Gareth was annoyed with himself. The power of his mind wasn't enough. He desired a physical touch. But that would mean losing control. And strength.

With extraordinary effort, he managed to break off the thought, releasing her.

"You must beware, little happy face." He took a step back and then another, until the rush of heat subsided.

"Of what?" She blinked.

She suddenly found herself alone.

The walk back to the castle required only a few minutes, but to Felicity it seemed an eternity. She was unaware of the wind that sighed through the trees and the clouds that scudded across the sky, blotting out the sun. In her mind she was still looking into Gareth's eyes, seeing a tormented soul.

As she climbed the steps, she shivered against a sudden chill. Before she could reach for the front door it was opened by a servant.

"Thank you," she said absently.

The girl nodded and bowed.

Felicity turned, throwing back the hood of her cloak as she did, and collided with a solid wall of chest. The man had to be well over six feet, with strong hands that caught roughly at her shoulders to keep her from tumbling backward.

"I say. Not quite the way I'd hoped to welcome a guest to Falcon's Lair," he muttered.

She looked up to see dark eyes glinting with amusement.

"Sorry." She took several deep breaths to compose herself. "I didn't see you."

"Obviously." He allowed his hands to linger a moment longer before lowering them to his sides. "I'm Ian St. John, nephew to Lord Falcon, as well as his physician."

"I'm—"

"Felicity Andrews," he finished. "Everyone here is talking about you."

He turned as a beautiful blonde in a billowing gown descended the stairs and paused beside him. "Miss Felicity Andrews, this is William's wife, Honora."

"Honora, Lord Falcon spoke of you." Felicity extended her hand. "How nice to meet you."

The woman's mouth curved into an imitation of a smile, but there was no answering warmth in her eyes or in the limp handshake she offered.

"I expect you're hungry." She studied Felicity thoroughly from head to toe. What she saw apparently alarmed her, for her frown grew more pronounced.

Felicity nodded. "I must admit it's been a good many hours since my morning meal with Lord Falcon."

Honora's tone was frigid. "He said you'd been in to see him."

Felicity unfastened her cloak. "Yes. We had a lovely time. He couldn't have been more charming."

"I must warn you, Miss Andrews. Such things tire him. From now on, I hope you will check with me before you intrude on his privacy."

Felicity's fingers paused in their work. She could feel her cheeks growing pink. "I'm sorry. I had no idea . . ."

Honora turned to the housekeeper. "Maud, I'll show Miss Andrews to her new suite of rooms while you see about something to eat."

The dour woman hesitated for just a moment, but it was enough to let Felicity know that she considered this additional chore a burden.

"Come, Miss Andrews. I'm sure you'd like to freshen up."

"Yes. Well . . ." Felicity offered her hand, and Ian St. John accepted it. "I suppose I'll see you here again, Doctor."

"Oh, indeed. I'm on daily call."

Honora paused on the stair and turned. "I was hoping you might join us for some refreshment, Ian."

"I'd like that." He nodded toward a closed door. "I'll just wait in the library." He turned away with the ease of someone comfortable with his surroundings.

"Come along, then, Miss Andrews." Honora led the way along a column of wide stairs that led to the second floor.

The wood of the balustrade was polished to a high sheen. Overhead the crystal chandeliers, filled with hundreds of candles, rivaled the glitter of a sky filled with stars. To Felicity, who had lived her entire life amid the simple pleasures of a Boston flat, this was luxury beyond belief.

"Your home is lovely, Honora."

"Thank you. Though I must confess I much prefer life in London to this dreary little countryside. But I fear it will be a long time before I see London again."

"Lord Falcon told me about William's accident."

"Ian has prepared me for the fact that he will never leave his bed."

Felicity stopped in midstride. "I don't know how you can bear it."

The young woman shrugged, then continued walking. "William has been an adventurer since his youth. Like all the Falcons, I'm afraid. You heard about his older brother, Chandler?"

Felicity nodded.

"Broke the old man's heart. And now William. Ian says it will be too much for Lord Falcon's delicate health."

Felicity rounded a corner and followed her hostess through wide double doors into a beautifully appointed sitting room. A cozy fire burned on the hearth, filling the suite with heat and light. A sofa and a pair of claret-colored chairs were positioned to take advantage of the warmth. The floors were covered with exotic rugs in lush jewel tones. On a sideboard a silver tray held an assortment of crystal decanters and goblets.

In the adjoining room was a huge bed hung with fine linen. Two chattering maids were unpacking Felicity's trunks, hanging her gowns in a lovely carved armoire. The minute she and Honora entered, the conversation ceased. The servants finished their work efficiently, then bowed their way out of the room.

Felicity wondered if either of them had been responsible for the earlier chaos. But then, she reminded herself, it could have been anyone at Falcon's Lair.

When they were alone, Honora walked to the sideboard

and watched as Felicity made a slow turn around each room. "Wine or ale?" she asked.

"Whatever you're having." Felicity was astonished by such luxury. She couldn't resist touching a hand to the bed. Soft. The mattress was as soft as down, and the bed linens were as fine as silk, all delicately embroidered with Lord Falcon's crest. It was everywhere—on the heavy damask quilt, the draperies, even on the crossed swords that hung over the mantel, like the ones over his bed.

Honora handed her a goblet of clear, pale wine. "This will revive you."

"Thank you." Felicity followed the young woman across the room and took a seat in front of the fire. "I'm already feeling better. After the confinement of the ship and then the long coach ride, it felt good to walk in a bracing wind." She took a sip of wine and felt the warmth radiate through her veins.

"I prefer a carriage. I find our English winters and brief springs tedious." Honora sipped her wine, watching her guest carefully. "Especially here on the moors. Thankfully these seasons don't last long. Perhaps by summer I'll be back in London." She seemed to mentally shake herself. "Are you satisfied with your accommodations?"

"Satisfied?" Felicity gave a little laugh. "Oh, Honora, I couldn't be more pleased."

There was a tap on the door, and Bean stepped timidly into the room. "Mrs. Atherton says there's a light meal ready."

"Thank you, Bean. Come along," said Honora, setting her goblet aside. "We'll join Dr. St. John in the library."

She led the way down the stairs and into a room that smelled of leather and woodsmoke. One wall was dominated by a massive stone fireplace. Close by was a table covered with crisp linens and set with an assortment of fine china and silver.

Felicity gazed in awe at the floor-to-ceiling shelves filled with books. Ian St. John hastily returned a book he'd been perusing and hurried to join the two ladies.

"I've never seen so many books in one place in my life,"

Felicity said with a sigh of disbelief. "How my father would have loved this."

"A man of letters?" The doctor held a chair for Honora, then Felicity, before taking his own place.

"Yes. He was a physician who lectured at Harvard."

"A physician?" Ian's head came up sharply.

"His field was exotic medicines." She glanced toward the doorway, missing the look that passed between the doctor and Honora. "Will Lord Falcon be joining us?"

"I thought you knew. The old man never leaves his bed."

"But he told me he'd be joining me tonight for dinner in the dining room."

Ian's tone was sympathetic. "Just an old man's ravings."

"Ravings? I don't understand."

Several servants entered and began to serve the meal. The doctor and Honora sipped their soup. "Excellent," Ian murmured before continuing in that same matter-of-fact tone. "Most days my uncle doesn't even know who he is. In his weakened state, I doubt the old lord will live past spring."

Felicity's gasp of alarm was the only sound in the room. She watched as the two continued eating. With a sigh she pushed aside her plate and concentrated instead on sipping strong, hot tea.

Her appetite had fled along with the happiness she'd felt only moments before.

CHAPTER 4

Felicity was just slipping into her gown in preparation for dinner when there was a knock on the door.

"Bean, come in." She stepped aside, genuinely pleased to see the young serving girl.

"Mrs. Atherton sent me to help you." The girl's wispy blond hair was hidden beneath a hat that resembled a lace doily. Her black dress was two sizes too big, nipped at the waist by a starched white apron.

"How kind. But I can manage by myself."

"Well, then, I'll just make myself useful." The girl added another log to the fire, then glanced around the room, searching for any chore that might keep her here a while longer. "Here now," she called, crossing to where Felicity sat in front of a dressing table. "Why don't I do up your hair for you?"

"All right." Felicity relinquished the brush.

"Ah, you've lovely hair."

"Thank you. Tell me about yourself, Bean. Have you worked here long?" Felicity's eyes closed after just a couple of smooth, long strokes of the brush.

"Since I was eight, ma'am."

"That's very young."

"Not so young. My brother was apprenticed at seven. He works in the stables. Lord Falcon himself arranged for us to work here when our parents died."

"That was kind of him."

"Aye, ma'am. He's a good man. I don't know what would

have happened to us if he hadn't taken us in.''

"Then you've grown up here. You knew Chandler, and William before the accident?''

"Oh, yes. They made all the young ladies' hearts flutter. Handsome they were. And charming. But that was before they were cursed.''

"Come now. Do you really believe in the Falcon curse?'' Felicity's lips curved in a teasing smile.

The servant gave a solemn nod of her head and lowered her voice. "You've not seen Lord William yet, ma'am. When you do, you'll swear he's possessed by the devil himself. Stares off into space. Mumbles to himself. Doesn't seem to see or know anything anymore.''

She twisted a clump of curls and began to anchor it with a jeweled comb. Just then the comb slipped from her fingers and dropped to the floor. Felicity bent over to retrieve it. As she straightened, she caught sight of the servant in the mirror. The poor child was cringing, and all the color had drained from her face.

"I'm sorry,'' Bean said with a catch in her voice. "Truly I am, ma'am.''

"No damage done,'' Felicity said gently. Seeing the way the girl flinched at her outstretched hand, she asked, "What's wrong, Bean? Why are you so afraid?''

"Nothing. It's just . . .'' She accepted the comb and tried again, her hand trembling. "Lady Honora would strike me if I did such a clumsy thing in her presence. Then she would order Mrs. Atherton to have me punished as well.''

Felicity struggled with a sense of outrage. "What sort of punishment?''

"I'd be sent to the scullery and made to work without food for a day or two.''

Felicity could hardly contain her fury. "That's despicable.''

"But she's the mistress of Falcon's Lair, ma'am. It's her right to do as she wishes. She's vowed to dismiss all of us unless our work pleases her.''

"Does Lord Falcon know how his new daughter-in-law

treats the servants?'' Felicity twisted in her chair to face the young girl.

''Oh, ma'am, what could the old lord do about it?'' Bean looked away, her voice dropping to a whisper. ''There are some days he hardly knows his own name. Like now.''

''Now?'' Felicity was on her feet, nearly knocking over the stool in her agitation.

''Yes, ma'am. I was in there not half an hour ago. With Simmons and Mrs. Atherton. Lord Falcon's skin was the color of those bed linens, and I swear he didn't even recognize us.''

''Then we must cancel dinner.'' Felicity headed toward the door.

''Oh, no, ma'am. That isn't possible,'' Bean cried.

Felicity turned. ''Why not?''

''Lady Honora has invited guests.''

''Guests? Knowing her father-in-law is so ill?''

The girl nodded and began twisting her apron in her hands.

''Who is coming to dinner?'' Felicity demanded.

''Dr. St. John, of course. He has dinner here most nights. And Lord and Lady Summerville and their daughter, Diana.''

''Who are these people?''

''Old friends of Lord Falcon's.'' The girl lowered her voice. ''They live in the lovely manor house just a carriage ride away.''

''Friends or no . . .'' Without finishing, Felicity pulled open the door.

''Where are you going, m'lady?'' Bean replaced the brush and hurried across the room to follow her.

''To pay a visit to Lord Falcon. I need see for myself whether or not he's strong enough to accompany me to dinner.''

The sight that greeted Felicity made her gasp in shock. As Bean had said, Lord Falcon's skin was pasty and his breathing labored.

This was not the man she had seen just this morning. In the space of several hours, he had aged beyond recognition.

Drawing a chair to the side of the bed, she sat down and

took his hand in hers. ''Lord Falcon, can you hear me?''

The eyelids fluttered for a moment, then closed.

Felicity touched a hand to his forehead. The skin was damp. Clammy. It had the feel of death to it.

She leaned close and said firmly, ''Lord Falcon, it is Felicity Andrews. Robert's daughter. Don't you remember your old friend Rob?''

At that his eyes opened, and he stared vacantly at the face swimming in his line of vision. ''Rob, is it truly you? Oh, praise heaven. I knew you'd come. You're the only one who can save me.''

Felicity stiffened as his big hand closed over hers.

''See how I must pay for my sins,'' the old man managed between wheezing breaths.

''Hush, now,'' Felicity crooned. ''You've nothing to atone for.''

''But I do.'' His voice grew feeble, and for long moments he lay, eyes closed, breathing shallowly. After a long pause he opened his eyes and fixed his gaze on Felicity. His hand gave a gentle squeeze. ''You knew. You've always known, haven't you, Rob?''

When she said nothing, he closed his eyes, as if to shield himself from another wave of pain. ''Of course you knew. You could always see through my little charades.'' He sighed, long and deep, as if relieved that he was finally about to unburden himself. ''It wasn't just a love of adventure that caused me to lure you to Africa. I knew you couldn't resist a chance to see firsthand how the witch doctors did their healing. But I had . . . other reasons.''

At her little gasp of surprise, he added quickly, ''Ah, I'll not deny the rest of it. I needed to flee my brother's wife as well. You could tell that I'd . . . dallied with her, and I was so ashamed. I thought that if I went far away she would be able to forget me and repair her marriage to my brother. But it was a foolish, selfish ploy, and one that nearly cost us our lives. When you and I fell into that cave, I made a promise. If we survived, I would do the honorable thing and mend my ways.''

Moved by his confession, Felicity touched a hand to his

cheek in a gesture of tenderness. "You didn't need to tell me all this."

He covered her hand with his. "Oh, but I did, Rob. You deserve the truth. I feel as though a burden has been lifted from my soul. Now promise me that you'll find the cure. You see, they are . . ."

Suddenly he gazed around the room with a look of sheer terror. "You'd better leave before they find you here . . ."

"They?"

Instead of replying, he put a finger to his lips and shook his head.

"But I can't leave you," she whispered. "You need someone to be with you."

"I have an angel watching out for me."

"An angel?"

He gave her a sly wink. "You and I know. Now go, Rob. And kiss your lovely wife for me."

As she made her way to the door, Felicity felt the sting of tears and had to swallow the lump that threatened to choke her. She found herself hoping that her father was indeed kissing her mother and that both had found a measure of peace.

Lost in thought, she didn't hear the light footfall behind her as she paused at the top of the stairs. She was jolted as hands shoved roughly against her back. With a cry she tangled her foot in the hem of her skirt and pitched forward.

The stairs were steep, the distance to the landing far too perilous. Though the fall might not be fatal, it would surely result in some broken bones and a great deal of pain. With those thoughts rushing through her mind, Felicity struggled to bring her hands up to her face to cushion the blow. But just before she would have fallen on the landing below, she felt strong hands wrap around her waist. Heat enveloped her. She was set gently on her feet. Then, as quickly as it came, the heat was gone.

Felicity followed along the hallway toward the hum of voices. When she paused at the doorway to the parlor, the babble ceased. All heads turned toward her.

"Here she is now." Ian St. John was standing beside the

fireplace, one hand on the mantel, a crystal goblet of ale in the other. He looked relaxed, content. The words Gareth had spoken earlier came to mind: "Lord of the manor." The doctor looked perfectly at home here at Falcon's Lair.

"You've kept us waiting. Come and meet our guests." Honora crossed the room in a swirl of petticoats and studied Felicity.

Thanks to a stop at her room, Felicity showed no trace of nerves. She had carefully brushed her hair and calmed her racing heartbeat before facing the others. Now, as she looked around, she wondered if someone present was the guilty party.

"Miss Felicity Andrews, may I present Lord and Lady Summerville and their daughter, Diana."

Felicity offered her hand, which Lord Summerville gallantly kissed. His neatly trimmed hair and mustache were shot with silver. Though his middle had begun to thicken, he still had the proud bearing of a military man.

His plump wife wore a pink confection that was far too girlish for her figure. The neckline was enhanced by a diamond-and-pearl necklace that was worth a king's ransom. Her smile was warm and genuine. "Welcome to England, my dear."

"Thank you." Felicity turned to the Summervilles' daughter. "Diana, I'm delighted to meet you. I do hope we can be friends."

"I'd like that." Diana clasped her hand. Like her mother, she gave Felicity a welcoming smile.

"I understand you are old friends of Lord Falcon," Felicity remarked.

"Oh, yes." Lord Summerville nodded vigorously. "Oliver and I grew up on neighboring estates and went off to Oxford together. Muriel and I were in India and stood up at his wedding. We grieved with him when his beloved Catherine passed away two years ago."

"He's had a great deal of grief in his life, hasn't he?" Felicity asked.

She saw Diana's eyes fill as she looked away.

"Enough of this maudlin talk." Honora signaled for a

serving girl and helped herself to a glass of wine. Her tone left little doubt that she was annoyed at the direction of the conversation. "What kept you, Felicity? Did Bean do something clumsy again?"

Again? Was she being spied upon? "Bean was most helpful. I'm late because I stopped by Lord Falcon's room for a visit."

"How is my old friend?" Lord Summerville accepted a drink from the servant's tray.

"He seems quite frail tonight. But he did manage to talk for a while. I think it brought him a measure of comfort."

"Talk? You encouraged him to talk?" Honora's eyes flashed. "I simply must insist that you refrain from visiting my father-in-law unless you first check with me." Seeing the look of surprise on the faces of her guests, Honora added quickly, "As mistress of Falcon's Lair, I am responsible for William's father." She shot a glance at the doctor. "Don't you agree, Ian?"

"Quite." He set his empty goblet on the tray with a clatter. "The old man is too ill to have visitors dropping by at all hours. It's far too draining. I've suggested to Honora that even Simmons should be restricted to one or two visits a day."

"That seems heartless," Diana cried.

Everyone turned to look at her.

With her cheeks burning, she added, "It would tear Simmons apart to be denied access to Lord Falcon. You said yourself, Father, that the two have been inseparable since they were lads."

"Indeed. Simmons was groomed for the position by his own father, who was butler to Oliver's father. I've never known a time when Simmons wasn't tending to Oliver's needs. Except, of course, when Oliver was traipsing off to some godforsaken corner of the world. The Falcons have always been an adventuresome lot," he added with a sigh.

Maud paused in the doorway to announce, "Supper is ready, m'lady."

With a satisfied nod, Honora linked her arm through Lord Summerville's and led the way to the dining room, with Ian

St. John escorting Lady Summerville, and Diana and Felicity trailing behind.

"Did you happen to look in on William?" Diana asked softly.

Felicity shook her head. "I'm afraid not. I haven't even met him yet."

"Perhaps it's just as well." Diana's voice trembled for just a moment before she added, "He seems to grow weaker with each passing day."

"Perhaps an infirmary could be of some help. Or a sanitorium, where he could rest and recover his health."

The young woman shook her head. "Honora won't hear of it. She wants William by her side. And why not? They were barely wed when this happened. Who can blame her for wanting to spend as much time as possible with her new husband before . . ."

Her voice trailed off, and she bit her lip to keep it from trembling.

"Here we are." Lord Summerville held a chair as Honora took her place at the head of a long table, with Ian St. John at her right and Lady Summerville at her left. Diana sat beside her father, and Felicity took the seat beside the doctor.

The meal was long, consisting of eight courses. At some other time Felicity would have found it a marvelous experience. The roasted pork, the beef and mutton, were done to perfection. As promised, Cook's tarts were the best she'd ever tasted. But she found the evening tedious. The endless chatter grated on her nerves. All she could think of was the fact that someone wanted her harmed, or worse, dead. And upstairs, an old man, alone in his bed, was hoping for a magic cure. But why had he summoned her father? Robert Andrews' experiences in the field of health and science were limited to exotic medicines.

"I know you long for the excitement of London," Lady Summerville was saying to her hostess, "but I do hope you're beginning to look more kindly on our little bit of England."

"It has its moments." Honora pushed aside her tart and picked up a goblet of wine.

"And you, Ian," Lord Summerville put in. "I should think it's a relief to be home after so many months away."

Felicity looked up. "Where were you, Dr. St. John?"

"Africa." He twirled the stem of his goblet, staring into the clear, pale liquid. "A fascinating place."

Felicity felt a curl of ice along her spine. "What were you doing in that far-off land?"

He lifted his head and met her gaze. His smile was chillingly bland. "Studying exotic medicines."

CHAPTER 5

Felicity's nerves felt stretched to the breaking point. She could no longer concentrate on the others around the table. All her thoughts centered on one inescapable fact. Out of desperation, Lord Falcon had sent for her father, and not merely because he needed a friend. It was much more than that. He needed her father's expertise.

Could it be that the old man's illness had been induced? But if that were so, it would have to mean that the handsome, charming man beside her—

She pushed away from the table.

The conversation abruptly ceased.

"What is it, my dear?" Lord Summerville touched a napkin to his lips and started to rise. A touch of Honora's hand on his sleeve stopped him.

"Nothing. Perhaps I am more tired than I thought." Felicity took several halting steps and prayed her trembling legs wouldn't fail her. "Please don't let me spoil your meal. I believe I'll just catch a breath of air."

"When you're feeling better," Honora said with a trace of impatience, "we'll be taking our brandy in the parlor."

"Thank you. I'll join you there." Catching up her skirts, Felicity hurried from the room.

Once in the hallway she leaned against the cold stone wall and touched a hand to her chest, as if to still her pounding heart. If her fears were confirmed, it would mean that she had stumbled into a den of evil. She felt touched by icy fingers. Whoever had rifled her bags and pushed her down the stairs had meant it as a warning. Someone wanted to frighten her off. But if she stayed? Her life, like that of Lord Falcon, was in grave peril. Hadn't Gareth said as much?

She took several long, calming breaths, then charted a course of action. Right now it was not fear for herself that mattered. The more pressing danger lay with Lord Falcon. And perhaps his son, the bedridden William. The first thing she needed to do was to find out where William's rooms were and then confirm or dismiss her fears.

Lifting a candle from a sconce on the wall, she made her way along the dimly lit hallway, poking her head into doorways. After more than a dozen false starts, she located a gloomy sitting room. The only illumination came from the fire on the grate. Beyond, she could see a thin stream of light beneath a closed door. Crossing the room, she shoved open the door. A single taper burned in a wall sconce, casting much of the room in shadow.

A man lay on the bed. The twisted covers signaled a tortured sleep. He moaned and flung an arm wide, then writhed and turned onto his back.

Felicity waited for the space of several heartbeats. When he made no further move, she inched closer, holding her light aloft. At the sight of him she had to stifle a gasp of recognition. He bore a striking resemblance to Gareth. He had dark hair badly in need of a trim, broad shoulders, narrow waist and hips. All in all a strong, muscular body, despite the time spent in the confines of his bed.

"So you are William," she muttered.

At once his eyes opened, and she felt another shock. He had the same dark, tormented eyes of another.

"Who are . . . ?" His gaze fastened on the flame of the candle, and he shrank back, as though expecting her to inflict pain.

Did others come here, tapers in hand, to do harm? It would explain his reaction. Or was she seeing evil where none existed?

"I'm a friend," she whispered.

He seemed not to hear as he began muttering curses. He tried to rise but fell back weakly. Then, while he stared at her with a look that haunted her, he continued to mumble incoherent words.

She heard the door to the sitting room open and close. Sweet heaven. Someone was coming. Determined to hide, she looked frantically around the room, then ducked into a wardrobe and blew out the candle. A moment later she peered out and watched as a shadowy figure made its way to the bedside.

"Oh, my beloved," came the sound of a woman's fierce whisper.

Felicity was riddled with guilt at witnessing this tender moment between husband and wife.

"My poor, dear William. I feel so helpless. It tears my heart out to see you like this."

As Felicity's eyes adjusted to the darkness, she realized that the figure beside the bed was not Honora. The gown was not the daring low-cut confection that Honora had worn at dinner. This was a more subdued, elegant sheath of pale silk.

Felicity stared in disbelief.

The woman beside the bed, whispering words of love, was Diana Summerville.

Felicity was too stunned to confront the distraught young woman. Instead she waited until Diana had soothed the savage William with gentle hands and barely audible phrases. As he slipped into blessed sleep, Diana smoothed the covers over him and let herself out.

Only then did Felicity step out of her place of concealment and cross the room. As she made her way to her own suite, she tried to digest all that she had seen and heard.

Could it be that Diana and the doctor were working together to bring down Falcon's Lair? But why? What possible motive could she have? Felicity paused. Diana's actions had not been that of a conspirator or a woman scorned. Rather, they had been the actions of a lover. But if not Diana, there had to be someone else assisting the doctor. He could not accomplish such a conspiracy alone. One name came to mind: Honora. But for what purpose? She was already mistress of Falcon's Lair. What could she possibly gain by bringing harm to her husband and his father?

Felicity sighed in distress. She needed a friend here at Falcon's Lair, one who could help her through this labyrinth. But whom could she trust?

"Ah, here you are, ma'am." Bean looked up from the cozy fire she had built on the hearth. "There's a real chill in the air tonight. Thought you might enjoy a bit of warmth after your meal with Lady Honora and Dr. St. John."

Felicity stepped close to the fire and perched on the edge of the sofa, choosing her words carefully. "What do you know about the mistress of Falcon's Lair, Bean?"

The little maid shrugged. "Not much, ma'am. Lady Honora's a mystery. The last thing Lord William's father expected was for his son to return from abroad with a wife. Especially since . . ." She stopped herself in midsentence and glanced away.

"Go on, Bean. Especially since what?"

The little maid lowered her voice and settled herself on a footstool at Felicity's feet. "Begging your pardon, ma'am. Everyone knew that Lord William and Diana Summerville loved each other. And had since they were children. Why, it near broke Diana's heart when she heard the news of his marriage. But she has tried in every way to be a friend to William's new wife."

"Tell me about William's accident. Do you know how it came about?"

Bean nodded. "Lord William's horse stumbled during a race across the moors."

"Who was he racing against?"

"Dr. St. John." The little maid hugged her knees. "The doctor boasted that his gelding could beat any horse in England and dared his cousin to prove him wrong. Everyone knew Lord William could never refuse a dare, and he was overly proud of Titan, his black stallion."

"How did Lord William's new bride react to the news that her husband was going to attempt a dangerous race?"

Bean thought for a moment. "I'd say she was quite eager about it, ma'am. Encouraged him. You see, she often complained that there was no excitement here at Falcon's Lair.''

Felicity stared into the flames, her mind awhirl with chilling thoughts. "It looks as if she got more excitement than she bargained for." At length she said, "Please send my regrets to Lady Honora. Tell her I am indisposed and will not be joining the others in the parlor tonight."

A crescent moon hung suspended in a midnight sky. Starlight filtered through the tall, narrow windows as Felicity made her way along the upper gallery. Candles flickering in sconces along the walls sent the gargoyles' shadows into an eerie dance.

Bean had told her about this gallery, hung with portraits of every lord of the manor, from the first Lord Falcon to the present. Since all in the castle were sleeping, Felicity thought it the perfect time to investigate.

She lifted her candle high, studying the faces in the portraits. Though the manner of dress changed dramatically through the ages, the faces of the men were strangely similar and hauntingly familiar. The same dark hair and eyes. The same full, sculpted lips, firm and unsmiling. The same eyes. Piercing. Knowing.

She moved slowly past the shadowed faces, pausing now and then to read a name, a date of birth or death. When she reached the far end of the gallery, she stopped in front of a portrait and, with pounding heart, lifted her candle to study the face of the first Lord Falcon.

"What are you doing here? And at such a late hour?"

Felicity spun around and brought a hand to her throat. "Maud—Mrs. Atherton. You . . . gave me quite a start."

The housekeeper glowered at her. "Lady Honora said you were indisposed."

"Just a bit weary, I'm afraid. But now I find I can't sleep. I thought I'd explore some of the castle." She knew she was babbling and turned away to avoid the woman's pointed look. But when the light from her candle illuminated Gareth's face staring down at her from its ornamental frame, she let out a gasp of surprise.

Following her gaze, the old woman misunderstood her reaction. "A fearsome countenance, is it not?" She paused beside Felicity and stared at the portrait. "But handsome and charming as well. He is Gareth, the first Lord Falcon. A dashing nobleman and close friend to Henry VIII."

At Felicity's look of surprise, she continued. "Falcon's Lair was a gift from the king. It is said he often came here to hunt with his friend and to play tennis. And, of course, to be entertained by the ladies. Falcon's Lair has a fascinating history. I've made it my life's work to study it."

"How did the first Lord Falcon . . . ?" Felicity couldn't bring herself to say the word.

"Die?" Before waiting for an assent from the young woman beside her, Maud Atherton went on. "He accepted the offer of a duel with his brother, Adrian."

"His own brother?"

"Half brother, actually. Adrian was a bastard. He coveted Falcon's Lair and complained to all who would listen that had he not been born on the wrong side of the blanket, Falcon's Lair would have been his."

"He was willing to kill for it?"

"He wanted much more than Falcon's Lair. It is rumored that Gareth loved Cara, a maiden from the village, and she in turn loved him. To taunt his brother, Adrian boasted that he would kill Gareth and force Cara to marry him instead. Falcon's Lair would pass to Adrian's descendants, since Gareth had none of his own."

"Couldn't Gareth save his ladylove from Adrian?"

"He desperately wanted to. He was an excellent swordsman and a fierce warrior. But instead of a fight between the two of them, Adrian sent an army to do his fighting for him. Gareth was forced to remain at Falcon's Lair to protect the lives of his retainers and tenant farmers. That is, after all, the duty of the lord of the manor. It caused Gareth even greater sadness, knowing his honor and duty had to come before love. So he stayed, even though he knew that he would lose forever the woman who owned his heart."

Felicity held her candle higher, to see the sad, tormented eyes of the man in the portrait.

"It is rumored that Gareth roams these halls still. Though

the betrayal occurred centuries ago, he refuses to accept his eternal reward because he is haunted by the thought of his beloved bearing another man's son.''

"You mean Adrian made good his threat?''

"Aye.'' Maud pointed to the next portrait. "Alexander, son of Adrian and Cara. Thus, all who rule Falcon's Lair are descended from Adrian instead of Gareth.''

For long minutes the two women fell silent, each caught up in the drama that, after all these centuries, still held them in its thrall.

As the housekeeper started to turn away, Felicity touched a hand to her sleeve.

"Mrs. Atherton, I know you must be tired after the full day you've put in here at Falcon's Lair. Thank you for taking so much time with me.''

The woman glanced down at her hand, then up into Felicity's eyes, all the while pursing her lips in a tight, thoughtful line. "I am never too weary to talk to anyone who truly cares about those who dwell at Falcon's Lair.'' She seemed to consider for a moment, then gave voice to her thoughts. "If you wish to learn more, there is a book. 'Tis old and dusty and difficult to read, since it is handwritten. It is the history of Falcon's Lair, and it resides on the highest shelf in the library, beside the family Bible. Few save me know of its existence.''

Was that a spark of . . . friendship in the older woman's eyes? Felicity could have hugged her. Maud Atherton turned away, and within minutes Felicity was alone, with the portraits of all the lords of Falcon's Lair staring down at her.

It was that rare hour between darkness and dawn. A soft pearl mist seemed to cover the land. The world was at rest.

Felicity sat on a stone bench in the garden, poring over the pages of the Falcon family history. Just as Maud Atherton had promised, it was all here. Births, deaths, wars. Those who had loved. Those who had lost. Recorded by those who had lived here and had witnessed it all firsthand.

As she turned another page she felt the heat. It seemed to shimmer in waves, until she was forced to lower her shawl.

She knew, without looking around, that Gareth had approached.

Setting the book aside, she turned to him. "Why didn't you tell me that someone was trying to harm Lord Falcon?"

"By all that is holy, woman," he said, his voice betraying his inner rage, "I warned you. Even that is more than I am permitted."

"Permitted?"

"I am forbidden by the Fates to interfere in the affairs of this world."

She could hear the emotion in his voice, could see the pain in his eyes. At last she understood. "Your powers are limited?"

"Powers." He spoke the word with venom. "My . . . powers, such as they are, are useless to help those I love."

"But you are permitted to love?"

"Love is not a favor granted." His eyes narrowed with feeling. "Love is an emotion so strong, so powerful, it transcends time and place. Love . . ." He turned away, but not before she saw the raw passion in his eyes. "Love is pain as well as pleasure."

"I'm sorry, Gareth. I know about Cara and the fact that you were forced to choose duty and honor over love."

"Forced?" He whirled to face her. "Nay. In life, one makes choices. I chose to consider the lives of many over the life of one, even though that one life meant more to me than anything in this world."

"Oh, Gareth." Seeing his bleak look, she reached out to touch his arm. At once he stepped back.

Instead of drawing away, she took a step closer and boldly curled her fingers into his flesh. "You've suffered far too much for your choice."

He stared down at her hand, and for a moment she thought he would draw away from her. She was startled when he gently lifted her hand to his lips. Against her knuckles, he murmured, "Did you know, little happy face, that you are the first woman since Cara that I have touched? Or permitted to touch me?"

"I knew it was you who caught me on the stairs."

"Aye, and the touch of you was my undoing." With a tenderness she would not have believed possible, he lifted her hand to his cheek. "You not only touch me, you touch my heart."

"Gareth . . ."

"Shhh." Though he didn't move or alter his position, she felt hands on her shoulders drawing her fractionally closer, until their lips were inches apart. Heat shimmered and pulsed around them, but neither seemed to notice. "Since we have already broken the rules, I must break another. I need to taste your lips."

She thought about protesting. Even as the thought formed, she dismissed it. She wanted what he wanted. She leaned into him, and, though he didn't move, his lips skimmed over hers.

The hunger was so sharp, so painful, that they both stepped back from it. Those dark, piercing eyes looked into hers, as though reading her soul. She was lost. With a sigh she offered her lips for another intoxicating kiss. This time the press of his hands was rougher as he pulled her against him. On a moan he seemed to devour her as his mouth crushed hers.

This was more than hunger. More than passion. The need was so powerful, so compelling, it could not be satisfied. No kiss or touch could quench this thirst. The heat was so intense now, they could feel sparks igniting wherever they touched.

And oh! They touched. His hands molded her hips to his, then slid along her back, kneading her waist, the slope of her shoulders, the soft curve of her neck. He touched with a hunger that spoke of centuries of loneliness.

Her arms encircled his waist, clinging as if to life itself. Her hands moved up his chest, her fingers curling into the folds of his shirt. Finally, with a sigh, she wound her arms around his neck and gave herself up to the pleasure.

It was a pleasure akin to pain. He wanted her. Wanted her with a desperation that bordered on madness. Here. Now.

He knew he had crossed a line. Knew, also, that it no longer mattered. He could no more stop than he could call down the thunder. There was a limit to his powers. And right now, all his powers were concentrated on the woman in his arms. A flesh-and-blood woman. Warm. Willing. Lovely. Innocent.

That knowledge, and that alone, stopped him. Calling on all his willpower, he lifted his head and took a step back. At once he felt bereft. His heart ached with need.

What was worse, he felt all his strength draining from him. It was the price he would have to pay for his indulgence. After all, he knew the rules that governed the spirit world. And had just recklessly broken them.

Felicity felt a moment of confusion. How could she have given in so easily to this man's charms? What had happened to her cool, carefully controlled logic?

"Beware, my little happy face." He was surprised at how difficult it was to speak. He gave in to the need to touch her one last time, by tracing his index finger across the curve of her brow, along her cheek, to the fullness of her lips. Even that small act further drained him. "I would not like anything to happen to you."

"I can . . . take care of myself." She stepped back, breaking contact.

At once she felt a cooling breath of air. She glanced up to see a falcon lifting into the sky. When she looked around, she found herself alone.

CHAPTER 6

Felicity slipped quietly into Lord Falcon's suite and took a seat beside his bed. So many questions danced in her mind. She felt a sense of urgency. She needed to speak with him as soon as he awoke. Before Dr. St. John paid his daily visit.

"Ah. My dear." The old man's lids fluttered open, and he greeted her with a smile. "I just had the loveliest dream. Rob and I were off on another adventure. He, of course, was seeking knowledge. And I, as always, sought a different sort of treasure."

"Did you find it?" she asked gently.

He gave her a sly smile. "I told you it was a lovely dream. That means it had a happy ending. That's the best kind." He struggled to sit up, and she helped him, heaping pillows behind him until he settled back comfortably. "Tell me what brings my delightful houseguest to an old man's room at dawn?"

"I find myself wondering why you are so lucid each morning and so . . . confused by midafternoon."

"Am I? Confused?"

She nodded.

He gave a sigh. "It's as I feared, then."

"That's why you sent for my father, isn't it?"

It was Oliver's turn to nod. He kept his voice to a whisper. "Whatever I am being given, it could not come from the apothecary in our small village. There would be too many questions." He caught her hand. "I have placed a terrible burden upon you, my dear. You must realize by now that your life is in grave peril.''

"No more than yours, Lord Falcon. But the question is why? Why would Ian St. John, your own nephew, want to bring you harm?"

"Perhaps he learned of my youthful transgressions and is seeking revenge. I did, after all, nearly come between his father and mother. But I assure you I repented my sins. And it happened so many years ago. Or perhaps it is simply jealousy because I, as the elder brother, inherited Falcon's Lair and the title, while his father was given a smaller estate nearby."

Felicity pressed his cold hands between both of hers. "I looked in on William last night."

"How is my son? I have not seen him in such a long time. Oh, my dear." He clutched her hands tightly in his, and she could feel his fevered pulse beating through the fragile flesh. "I fear for William more than I fear for myself."

"I intend to pay him a visit this morning as well," she whispered, "and if my hunch is correct, I will find him as I found you. Now I must go, before Honora awakens and has me barred from your room."

"She would do such a thing?"

"She . . . is very protective of you and William." Felicity was reluctant to accuse until she had more proof. At the door she turned. "One question, Lord Falcon. Can you refuse your medicine?"

"Dr. St. John remains with me until it is swallowed."

The jealous nephew was taking no chances, she thought. Her look was grim as she walked away.

The fire in William's sitting room had long ago burned to embers. In his bedchamber, the candle had sputtered out. The room was cold and damp. But the face of the man asleep in the bed was bathed in perspiration. Even in a drug-induced sleep, it seemed, he waged a fierce battle with his enemies.

Felicity pulled a chair close to the bed and sat down. As she smoothed her skirts she was surprised to find his eyes, wide and unblinking, fixed on her.

"You're a new one. Haven't seen you before. Have you come with another foul-tasting potion?"

She shook her head. "I came at your father's request. From America. My name is Felicity Andrews. Daughter of your father's old friend Rob."

He visibly relaxed. "How is Father? Honora told me he's at death's door."

"Not quite. Nor are you," she added.

"I might as well be. Condemned to this bed for the rest of my life. To a Falcon, being a cripple is worse than death."

She glanced at the covers that hid his legs. "Have you tried to walk?"

"Right after the accident. I went down like a stone."

"And since?" she prodded.

He shrugged. "I seem to recall walking. But then I wake up in bed and realize it's all just a foolish dream."

"What else do you dream?"

"More foolishness." He looked away, ashamed to meet her eyes. "I dream of an old love, looking as young and beautiful as when we were children, whispering . . ." He stopped, embarrassed at having revealed so much. "The dreams are cruel. But not as cruel as reality. Reality, Miss Andrews, is the knowledge that I shall never again leave this bed."

"What if I told you that was untrue? That your dreams weren't dreams at all?"

He held up a hand to stop her. "If you've come to add to my misery . . ."

"Take my hand, William." She held it out to him. "See if I speak the truth."

For long moments he stared at her outstretched hand, and she could see the warring of emotions. Doubt. Fear. A slowly darkening anger at the cruelty of her suggestion. But in the end, determined to settle the issue once and for all, he reached for her hand. A true Falcon, and adventurer to the end.

He flung back the covers and swung his legs to the floor. For several seconds he sat still as his head swam. Then, taking a deep breath, he gripped her hand firmly and prepared to stand.

Just then they heard the opening of the sitting room door. Felicity let out a groan of disgust. "You must lie down, William. And whatever you do, don't mention my visit. They musn't know I was here."

She pressed him into the pillows and pulled the blanket over him, then replaced the chair at its original position before slipping into the wardrobe.

Through a crack in the door she watched as Dr. St. John sailed into the room, followed by Honora.

"I've brought your medicine, William," the doctor said, holding a vial of dark fluid aloft.

"No. No more," came the muffled voice.

"In a bit of a temper this morning, are we?" It was Honora, her tone shrill and sarcastic.

While Felicity watched helplessly, Honora lifted William's head off the pillow. Ian St. John brought the vial to his lips and forced the liquid down his throat. William made a choking, gasping sound, then fell silent.

A short time later, after they'd gone, Felicity stepped from her place of concealment. The man in the bed lay in a stupor, his eyes blank, his body limp.

Outside William's room she felt the shimmer of heat that always accompanied Gareth. She paused, waiting for him to reveal himself.

"You play with fire. If you're not careful, you'll get burned. They nearly caught you in William's room."

"I had to see if my hunch was correct. But now that I know that Ian and Honora are drugging William and his father, I need to know why they wish them dead."

Gareth shook his head. "You are more innocent than I thought, little happy face. Can you not see? Ian covets not only Falcon's Lair but William's wife as well."

"Does Honora feel the same way about Ian?"

"Aye. She only married William for his money and title. With him out of the way, Ian, as the only other living heir, will inherit. That has always been the true curse of the Falcons. It is not our love of adventure or the fact that most

have died young. The curse is that those who least deserve
to inherit desire it most—and will do whatever is necessary
to achieve their evil goals.'' He motioned for her to follow.
''Come. You must see for yourself.''

She followed him along the hall until he paused outside
Honora's lavish suite. The door to the sitting room was ajar.
Inside, they could see the silhouettes of a man and woman
locked in an embrace.

''Soon,'' the man said as his lips claimed the woman's,
''Falcon's Lair and all its treasure will be ours.''

''Ours,'' the woman echoed as she pulled him down to
the bed.

With her hand to her mouth to stifle her outrage, Felicity
turned away. And found herself once again alone.

''What is all the excitement, Bean?'' Felicity looked up from
her father's journal. All morning she'd remained locked away
in her room reading, until her eyes ached from the exertion.
But she'd found nothing in her father's notes that sounded
even remotely like the medicine Dr. St. John had used.

She'd heard the servants bustling about and the furious
commands from Maud Atherton to have Falcon's Lair sparkling. But until now, when she'd set aside her reading, she
hadn't really paid any attention.

''Tonight's the charity ball,'' the little maid explained.
''All the gentry will be here. Lady Honora has even invited
friends from as far away as London.'' Bean lowered her
voice. ''She's in quite a snit, she is. Says if she finds so much
as a smudge on the crystal, we'll all pay tomorrow.''

Felicity felt her temper rising. ''A charity ball, when her
husband and father-in-law lie abed?''

''Lady Honora says life must go on, and she intends to
put a brave face on her unhappiness.''

''A brave face.''

At Felicity's outraged tone, Bean turned to look at her.
''Do you think it is wrong of Lord and Lady Summerville
and their daughter to betray old friendships by coming tonight?''

''Oh, no, Bean,'' Felicity assured her. ''In fact, I believe

they may be the only true friends Lord Falcon and William
have.'' She felt a sudden sense of foreboding. ''If anything
should happen here, I want you to go to them. Do you understand?''

For long moments the girl stared at her. Then she meekly
nodded. ''Yes, ma'am.'' She crossed the room and opened a
wardrobe before laying out an assortment of undergarments.

''What are you doing, Bean?''

''Why, preparing for your toilette, ma'am.''

''I'll not be attending Honora's ball.''

''Oh, but you must, ma'am.''

''And why must I?''

''Because . . .'' The little waif thought long and hard. ''Because Lady Honora would take out her temper on all of us
if you don't.''

Felicity relented. The maid had just said the one thing that
could change her mind. Felicity was far too tenderhearted.
She simply couldn't be the cause of someone else's misery.

''I believe this is my dance, Miss Andrews.'' Lord Summerville bowed grandly and swept Felicity into the maze of
circling couples.

The women were a kaleidoscope of color in their elegant
gowns and opulent jewels that caught and reflected the glow
from hundreds of candles. A cloud of rich perfume seemed
to envelop them.

The men were preening peacocks, bowing and strutting,
hoping to attract the attention of their elegant hostess, who
had, it seemed to Felicity, made a valiant effort to put aside
her unhappiness.

Honora was, in fact, the life of the party; and though she
danced with many men, she saved the most dances for Ian
St. John. Felicity watched as they swayed to the music, their
bodies touching, their faces bent in intimate conversation.
They made no effort to hide their passion. Ian said something
that amused Honora. She laughed, then looked up into his
eyes and whispered to him. His arms tightened around her,
and as he and Honora swept past Felicity, the sound of their
laughter trailed behind.

Felicity was relieved when the dance ended. With a slight bow to Lord Summerville, she slipped past the crowds and opened the door to a brick-paved courtyard. She stepped into the cool shadows, closing the door behind her. After the raucous laughter and raised voices, the silence was a welcome relief.

She felt overwhelmed by so many emotions. Disgust at Honora and Ian, for they would sacrifice anyone to have what they wanted; fear of the coming confrontation, for she knew that she would fight them, to the death if necessary, to save Lord Falcon and his son; and exhaustion, because she stood alone against such evil.

But, she reminded herself, she wasn't completely alone.

"Tired of dancing?"

At Gareth's deep tone, she turned. As always, the heat surrounded him like a shimmering cloud.

"There is no one in there I care to dance with."

He paused and arched a brow. "And out here? Is there no one out here you care to dance with?"

Felicity had never flirted in her life, but there was something about this man that brought out an imp in her. Suddenly all emotions were swept away except one: a sense of pure joy in his presence. "There might be."

With a smile he glanced around, then brought his gaze back to her. "I don't see anyone else. Could it be me, Miss Andrews?"

When she didn't respond, he made a gallant bow and said, "Miss Andrews, may I have the honor of this dance?"

She steeled herself for his touch, and for the warmth she knew would follow. But instead of drawing near, he stood apart from her. Amazingly, even from that distance, she felt his arms encircle her. Nothing could have prepared her for the potent feelings that raced like wildfire through her. At the touch, she saw the haze of heat around him begin to shimmer and vibrate and knew that he felt it too.

Music filtered through the closed doors. Soft, muted, it seemed to play only for them. She closed her eyes, imagining him holding her close. As one they moved, their bodies swaying, touching. His warm breath feathered the hair at her temple, and he drew her even closer, until she could feel his heartbeat in her own chest.

How safe she felt here in his arms. How right.

She glanced up at him and saw that he wasn't smiling now. As he looked down at her, the look on his face was so fierce, so intense, she felt her breath catch in her throat.

"What is it, Gareth? What's wrong?"

"I must leave you soon."

"Leave? But why? Why now, when I know who is causing all the evil at Falcon's Lair? It's only a matter of time until I find a way to stop them. And what about us, Gareth? We've only just discovered each other."

"Oh, my sweet Felicity. How the gods must laugh at their creations. We mortals are such foolish creatures." The look on his face grew pensive. "I wish . . ."

"What?" she demanded. "What do you wish?"

He shook his head. "I was thinking that, just for tonight, I would give anything if . . ."

When his words trailed off, she clutched at him, desperate to know his thoughts. "If what?"

His voice was rough with feeling. "If only you could go back in time. Or if I could go forward. But it's impossible. The dice were tossed long before either of us was born."

She sighed and drew her arms around his waist, pressing her lips to his throat. "But we have now. We have this time. Isn't it enough?"

He held her at a little distance, wondering if he should tell her that each time he allowed himself to touch her, he lost a little more of himself, a little more of his power.

"Do you know how desperately I want you?" he whispered.

Felicity's heart nearly stopped. Never before had she wanted to be with a man. She'd never even been tempted. But with Gareth everything was different. With this man she had no rules, no guidelines. The mere touch of him left her trembling, wanting things—wanting them, yet fearing them. But, despite her fear, she found herself speaking boldly.

Her voice trembled, as did her body. "Is it possible?"

"What are you saying?" He couldn't hide his astonishment. "Would you let me love you? Truly love you, as a man loves a woman?"

Slowly, shyly, she nodded.

He cupped her face in his big hands and stared deeply into her eyes. His lips brushed her mouth, his breath mingling with hers as he murmured, "Oh, my little happy face. With love anything is possible."

CHAPTER 7

They stood apart, not touching. Yet as soon as Felicity closed her eyes, she could feel Gareth lifting her in his arms. In quick strides he crossed the brick paving and halted in a circular stand of trees that bordered the gardens. Setting her on her feet, he tossed his cloak to the ground. She opened her eyes. He seemed to be several paces away, yet that was impossible, for in that instant she was crushed roughly against him, her mouth savaged with kisses until she was breathless.

She sensed the change in him, an urgency and a barely controlled tension. Was this anger? she wondered. Or a darker side of passion she didn't understand?

"Wait. I . . ." She took a step back.

As if regretting his earlier lapse, his touch gentled. When she closed her eyes, he kissed her again, lingering over her lips. His voice, when at last he spoke, was rough. "There is still time to change your mind, Felicity. I'll understand if you walk away. I won't hold you." A lie, he knew. He would beg, even crawl, to have her. But he would not hold her against her will. He was determined to fight the needs that cried for release, if she but said a single word of refusal.

She took a deep breath. "I won't go, Gareth." Standing on tiptoe, she pressed a kiss to his lips. "I can't. I've tried to deny what I feel. But I know now that we were fated to meet and to love. Oh, Gareth, hold me. Love me."

The shimmering haze of heat seemed to envelop them until she was blinded by it. They came together in a blaze of passion, mouth meeting mouth, bodies pressed so closely together that each could feel the wildly beating pulse of the other.

He brushed soft, nibbling kisses across her forehead, her eyelids, her cheek, the tip of her nose. With each gentle touch, she gave herself up to his ministrations and relaxed in his arms. His mouth moved over hers, and her lips parted for him, allowing his tongue to tangle with hers.

"Soft," he murmured. "You're so soft. I'd nearly forgotten . . ."

His lips traced her jaw, across her cheek to her ear, where he tugged on her lobe before darting his tongue inside, causing her heart to beat faster still. All the while his hands moved over her, igniting little fires of their own.

His hands closed around her waist, and he lifted her effortlessly off her feet. Suddenly reminded of another time he'd caught and held her like this, the touch of his lips stilled on hers. He lifted his head, and his eyes narrowed in furious remembrance. "When I think of what almost happened on the stairs . . ."

"Hush, Gareth. We won't think about it now, love." She touched a finger to his lips.

Love. At her unexpected endearment, he caught her hand and pressed a kiss to the palm. "Aye, we'll not speak. I'll show you without words how I love you."

How I love you. His words brought a rush of feeling unlike anything she'd ever known. He loved her. The truth was, she loved him too. Desperately.

With exquisite tenderness he brought his lips to her throat and ran hot, moist kisses across her shoulder, then lower, to her collarbone, then lower still, until he encountered the swell of her breast. The bodice of her gown grew wet with his kisses until, consumed with heat, they dropped to their knees in the damp grass. But nothing would cool the blazing heat between them.

"God in heaven, Felicity. What have you done to me?" He caught her hand and placed it over his heart. It was beating as wildly as her own.

The darkened sky was awash with millions of twinkling

diamonds. The high, clear notes of a muted violin were carried on the breeze. The air was perfumed with the first blooms of early spring blossoms, though a day before there had been only a hint of buds. It was as though the whole world had burst into bloom because of their feelings for each other.

With great care he undressed her, watching as the silk gown fell away, revealing a delicate chemise. His fingers were strong and sure as he reached for the ribbons, and then it, too, was discarded.

"Oh, my love, how beautiful you are." His fingers skimmed her skin, and he watched as her eyes darkened with passion before he bent his head to taste her.

That first glimpse on the night she'd arrived at Falcon's Lair hadn't prepared him for this. She was the most perfect creature he'd ever seen. With mouth and fingertips he began to explore, lingering over her mouth, her jaw, the sensitive hollow between her neck and shoulder.

He was leading her to new places where she had never been. But though she felt shy and awkward and would have resisted any other, she knew she could trust Gareth. She gave herself up to the pleasure as she sighed and moved in his arms.

His lips and fingertips moved lower. He felt her body grow tense, her breathing shallow. He wouldn't allow himself to think about tomorrow and the price that would be exacted for this thing they shared. Nor would he dwell on all the centuries of loneliness and pain that he had endured. For now, there was no past or future. There was only now, this moment. He would think only about the pleasure he could give this woman in his arms, for it was his only gift to her. He prayed it would be enough to last for all the tomorrows they would be denied.

As her blood heated and her body pulsed, Felicity experienced needs she'd never even known existed. This, then, was why she'd been born. For this man. This moment. Nothing else mattered.

She needed to touch him as he was touching her. With quick, hurried movements she slid his shirt from his shoulders and bent to him, brushing her lips across his chest. She heard his little gasp of surprise and thrilled to it. It excited her to please him as he was pleasing her. Drunk with power, she reached for the fasteners at his waist. When her fingers fumbled, he closed his hands over hers, helping her, until his clothes lay discarded alongside hers.

He was magnificent. Muscles rippled along his chest and arms. He had the contoured body of a warrior. She traced a finger over the flat planes of his stomach and was rewarded by his sudden intake of breath.

Desire smoldered in his eyes as he pulled her against him and devoured her mouth with his. All the while his fingers worked their magic, until her body was a mass of nerve endings.

How could he be otherworldly, when his heart beat the same as hers? When his body fit so perfectly to hers? When his hands, his lips, could weave such magic?

This was no ghost, she told herself. He was a man, and he was hers.

Ensnared by her newly awakened passion, she felt her hands clutching the cloak beneath her as she reached the first unexpected crest. It rippled through her, leaving her gasping.

He saw the way her eyes widened, then darkened with desire.

"Please, Gareth. Now. I want you now."

Instead, his hands tangled in her hair, and he savaged her mouth with bruising kisses. All the tenderness, the gentleness, the patience he'd demonstrated earlier were gone. In their place was a primitive darkness, a relentlessness, that left her stunned.

So this was why he'd resisted. This was why he'd tried to warn her.

Instead of being afraid, she found this dark side of passion deeply arousing, secretly exciting. Following his lead, she began, with lips and tongue and fingertips, to explore him as he had explored her.

Gareth's body hummed with need, but still he held back. There was so much more he wanted to give her, to show her, and he knew that after tonight it would be too late.

He feasted on her breasts, nibbling, suckling, until she moaned with pleasure. But though she arched toward him, he refused to offer her the release she sought. Instead, he brought his lips lower, drawing out every sensual pleasure.

A breeze rippled through the branches of the trees, but it couldn't cool their overheated flesh. The heat rose between them, shimmering like a cloud, filming their bodies with a fine sheen.

Felicity was beyond thought now. There was only Gareth and the pleasure he could bring. A pleasure that was close to pain.

She writhed and trembled as he slid along her body. He took her higher, then higher still, keeping release just out of reach.

Her hands clutched at him as she felt herself reaching another peak. He gave her no time to catch her breath as he brought his lips back to hers. She cried out his name as he entered her.

Her body sensitized, completely aroused, she wrapped herself around him as he began a slow descent into madness. He filled himself with the taste of her, the fresh, clean scent that would always be her. And he knew that for an eternity to come, he would hold this memory of paradise in his heart and be warmed by it.

The need for release clawed at him until he felt himself exploding. The madness was complete. He no longer existed, and neither did she. Now they were one. Joined. Forever changed.

Then she soared with him, climbing to some distant place just out of reach. Their bodies trembled and shuddered. They reached the bright distant star together and shattered into a million blinding pieces.

"God in heaven, what have we done?" They lay, still joined. Gareth's cheek rested against hers. He could feel the warmth of her tears. Could taste the salt on his lips. His heart forgot to beat. "I knew you were a maiden. A virgin. And I took you like some wild . . ."

She put a hand over his mouth to still his words. "You said in life we all make choices. In case you haven't noticed, I'm a grown woman, able to make my own decisions. This was my choice."

"But now those tears tell me you regret that choice."

She shook her head. "They're happy tears. I've never known anything quite so . . . stunning."

His fears dissipated. His heart began to beat once more. "Truly, my little happy face? You have no regrets?"

"None."

With a deep sigh of relief he rolled to one side, drawing her firmly into the circle of his arms and wrapping them both in his cloak.

It felt so good here. So right. She reached a finger to his mouth and traced the outline of his strong lower lip, laughing when he caught it lightly between his teeth and nipped.

Suddenly avoiding his eyes, she ran her fingers through the hair on his chest. "How is it that I can taste you, feel you, experience all that I did just now, if you are . . . what you say you are?"

He put his hand beneath her chin and forced her to look at him. His words were spoken with a rare gentleness, though his eyes remained solemn. "Don't question the fates, love. Just be grateful for the miracle. Savor it, for all too soon a price will be named. And we will have to pay."

"Oh, Gareth." She closed her eyes against the pain and drew his head down for a long, lingering kiss.

Hearing his little moan of pleasure, she thrilled to her newly discovered power. Even now she could feel the passion rise in him again, could feel the strain of his muscles as he dragged her almost savagely against him. Her man. Her love. The knowledge made her heart soar. "I don't care about the price. I'll gladly pay, as long as we have this night."

"Then let's not waste a minute of it," he murmured against her throat as he took her again.

The light of dawn streaked the eastern sky. A chorus of birds sang in the nearby gardens. The sharp tang of meat roasting, and the sweeter scent of bread baking, attested to the cook's diligence. A light in the scullery windows signaled the beginning of a new day for the servants.

Still Gareth and Felicity lay in their secret bower, sheltered from view, locked in a fierce embrace.

All night they had loved, then slept, only to awaken and love again. Their lovemaking was by turns tender then savage. At times they lay calm and cozy as old lovers. At other times, sensing that their time together was all too brief, they came together in a wild frenzy, until, sated, they would doze once more.

Now, with morning upon them, there was no more time to waste. Every moment was precious to them. There was still so much to say, so much that each wanted to tell the other.

"Why did you let me see you, when you kept yourself hidden from everyone else?"

Gareth smiled at her question. "You're a beautiful woman. Isn't that enough?"

She shook her head. "You're keeping something from me. What is it?"

He caught a strand of her hair and, avoiding her eyes, watched it sift through his fingers. "You looked like another."

"Cara. Did she have red hair?" The words escaped her lips before she could stop them.

She saw the sudden clenching of his jaw before he nodded. "Aye. And green eyes. But it was more than the physical resemblance. There's a goodness in you, love, that was so like her." He caught her by the shoulder and stared deeply into her eyes. "Love, true love, is never only physical. Love is the mating of one soul to another. And it was your soul that touched mine."

His words warmed her, yet she was surprised to feel only a faint pulse of heat at his touch. Alarmed, she sat up and brushed his lips with hers. The heat grew, and she sighed with satisfaction.

"You once said that you stay here at Falcon's Lair because there is something you haven't done. What is it, Gareth?"

She felt him begin to withdraw from her. Laying a hand

on his arm, she said, "If you share it with me, maybe I can help you."

He shook his head. "No one can help me, love. The choices I made were my own. They in turn led to my fate. I must live an eternity knowing I cannot save the ones I most love. And the hell of it is, I must spend that eternity alone, without heirs, because I chose honor over love."

"I made a choice last night." She wound her arms around his neck and offered her lips to him. "What will be my fate?"

Instead of kissing her, he touched a finger to her mouth in the gentlest of caresses. His eyes wore the same haunted look she'd seen that first night, crossing the moors. "You wear your heart on your sleeve, little happy face. But that heart is destined to be pierced by a sword."

She caught her breath at the pain. He dipped his head and brushed his lips over hers. She waited for the heat, but none came. Instead, the man beside her began to blur and fade.

She felt a piercing wave of panic. "Don't leave me. Hold me, Gareth. I'm so afraid."

"Close your eyes, love, and hold tightly to me."

She did as she was told. She heard a sound like rushing wind, and the trees overhead dipped and sighed. Then a strange silence settled over the land.

Thoroughly chilled, Felicity opened her eyes. She was alone, kneeling in the dew-dampened grass. She was wearing the gown she'd worn the night before, thoroughly wrinkled and thoroughly soaked.

Was it possible that she'd fallen asleep, that all of this had been nothing more than a dream?

It was no dream. Gareth had been here with her. He'd touched her. Loved her. The things she'd experienced had been beyond her imagination. Weren't they?

And yet . . . and yet she could still feel the imprint of those strong fingers tingling along her body. And those lips. Had they brushed hers? She pressed a finger to her mouth. It wasn't just her imagination. Was it?

Sweet heaven. What was happening to her? Could the

sane, sensible daughter of Robert Andrews really believe she'd been loved by a ghost?

In the morning silence she looked up to see a falcon passing overhead as swiftly and as soundlessly as a shadow. At the sight of it her heart soared.

Then she glanced at the grass beside her. It still bore the imprint of a man's body. She touched it. It was still warm.

Tears sprang to her eyes. Logic be damned. All that mattered was that she loved and was loved by Gareth, the first Lord of Falcon's Lair.

CHAPTER 8

Felicity rubbed her fists over her tired eyes, hoping to ease the strain. All day she had remained in her room, poring over her father's notes, hoping to uncover the source of Ian's drugs. After the public display Ian and Honora had made of their affection for one another at the ball, she felt a sense of urgency. Besides, another visit to Lord Falcon and William had confirmed her worst fears. The conspirators had grown bolder. Both William and his father had been given much stronger doses and had fallen into a deep sleep. If she did not find a way to save them soon, it would be too late.

Suddenly she paused to read a notation in the margin written in her father's barely legible script. She blinked, carried the paper to the window for a better view, and read again.

Praise heaven for her father's meticulous documentation. He had written down not only the poison and its effects but the antidote as well.

She snatched up her cloak and hurried down the stairs. Now, if only the apothecary in the village had what she needed.

Felicity stood at the window and watched as evening shadows gathered over the land. There was a majestic beauty to this part of the world. A softness, a stillness, that spoke of peace and tranquillity. How ironic that she should be locked in a life-and-death struggle in such a place.

She glanced at the vials of murky liquid on her night table. If her father's notes were correct, they would render Ian's

potions useless. If her father had made but a single error in
his calculations, however, his dearest friends would pay with
their lives. As would she. For she was certain that Ian and
Honora had no intention of allowing her to leave this place
alive to reveal what she knew.

To pass the time, Felicity picked up the dusty family history of the Falcons and began to read. Hours passed. Suddenly she glanced up in astonishment. The book fell from
her nerveless fingers. She raced to the window. Where was
Gareth? Why had he not come to her? It was essential that
she share this news with him. What she had just read changed
everything here at Falcon's Lair.

She was shocked to see that darkness covered the land. It
had to be past midnight. All of the household had retired for
the night. She would share her news with Gareth later. Right
now, it was time to put her plan into motion.

Peering cautiously around her door, she slipped down the
hall and into Lord Falcon's room. The old man lay deep in
sleep. It took her several minutes to rouse him. Even when
his eyes finally opened, she couldn't be certain that her words
were reaching his consciousness.

"Lord Falcon, I've found the antidote to Ian's drug. It was
in my father's notes." She struggled to lift his head. "You
must drink this."

In his confusion he tried to wave her away and nearly
spilled the contents of the vial. With her heart thudding, she
held it to the old man's lips. At the first taste he made a face
and tried to turn away.

"I know it tastes vile, but you must drink all of it," she
urged. "Do it for your old friend Rob."

When he emptied the vial, she lowered his head to the
pillow. "I wish I could stay by your side," she whispered
as she smoothed the blanket over him, "but there's no time
to waste. I must get the antidote to William."

She hesitated for a moment, wishing he would say something that would set her mind at ease. But he stared mutely,
then closed his eyes.

She struggled against a growing feeling of dread as she
hurried along the darkened hallway toward William's suite.

Inside, she found him tossing and turning, fighting the demons that came to him in sleep.

"William," she whispered fiercely, touching a hand to his shoulder.

At once he swung out a fist, barely missing her.

"William," she said again in a louder voice, "I bring you word from Diana."

At the mention of that name he went very still.

Felicity took a deep breath and reminded herself that the lie was for his own good. "Diana has said that if you love her you will drink this. All of it," she added as she lifted the vial to his lips.

Without a word of protest he did as he was told.

Felicity dropped the empty vial into her pocket and touched a hand to his cheek in a gesture of tenderness. "Rest now, William. I pray you are soon removed from this nightmare and reunited with your true love."

As she turned, she was shocked to see two menacing figures in the doorway.

"So. It's as you suspected, Ian. Our houseguest refused to heed my warning." Honora advanced on Felicity. "We'd hoped your absence today meant that you were packing to return to America. But that was too much to hope for. Now you'll have to pay for your meddling."

"What . . . do you think you can do to me?" Felicity took a step backward and found herself trapped against the wall.

"What can we do?" Ian laughed, and Honora followed suit. "Miss Andrews, you're going to disappear. Never to be seen again."

In the glow of candlelight, Felicity saw a cloth in his hand. Too late, she realized what he intended. He pinned her and held the cloth to her face until she breathed deeply. The sickly odor made her head swim. Though she was not unconscious, she no longer had the will to fight.

Felicity could feel the drug taking effect. Her mind seemed separated from her body. When Ian lifted her in his arms and descended the stairs, she felt herself drifting. She heard the door to the castle being opened and closed. A cold, dark mist

swirled before her eyes, and she wondered why she was being carried outside. She felt the wet brush of tree branches
as she was being carried through the gardens. There was a
loud scraping sound, as of a heavy door being forced open.
They descended more steps, and the air reeked of damp earth
and mold.

Honora's voice seemed to roll in waves over Felicity, loud,
then soft, then loud again. "You can scream as much as you
please in this place, and no one will ever hear. How apt. The
Falcon family mausoleum. In a few weeks, when we return,
it will be a simple matter to dispose of your body in one of
the crypts."

Felicity tried to speak, to implore them not to leave her.
But her throat was so constricted, she couldn't manage more
than a small moan. She heard the sound of their footsteps,
and the scrape of the heavy door. Shared laughter trilled.
Then there was only silence.

The blackness was impenetrable, like a shroud. Holding her
hand in front of her face, Felicity bit back a cry when she
couldn't see it. So this, then, was her fate. She would die,
alone, in the Falcon mausoleum. No one would mourn her.
Nor would anyone ever find her. She would disappear without a trace. Tears welled up in her eyes, but she blinked them
away. She must not allow herself to give in to grief. Until
her last breath was drawn, she would fight. Somehow.

She groped blindly, in search of any means of escape. She
shuddered when her hands tangled in a spiderweb and she
felt the rush of insects across her arms. It took several
minutes before she could stop the trembling. Then, forcing
herself to move on, she scraped her knuckles over the sharp
edges of stone and realized she was standing before a crypt.

As she stood there, a soft glow seemed to radiate from the
stone. She watched in fascination as the glow became a halo
of light shimmering around the figure of a man.

"Gareth. Oh, Gareth, thank heaven."

He gathered her into an embrace and she hugged him
fiercely, pressing her lips to his throat. He could hear the
tears in her voice as she whispered fiercely, "Honora and Ian

left me here to die. I thought . . . I thought this time they'd
won.''

Against a tangle of hair at her temple he muttered, ''You
may be right, love.''

She lifted her head to peer at him. His image blurred and
faded. And then it struck her. There was no heat in his touch.
No strength in his embrace.

''Oh, Gareth. What are you saying?''

''My powers . . . are diminished. That is the price exacted.''

She touched a hand to his cheek and felt the chill. ''You
knew. Before we loved.''

He nodded.

''Then why . . . ?''

''Loving you was worth any price.''

''But why are you here?'' Even as she spoke, she knew
the answer with chilling clarity. Over his shoulder she could
read the inscription on the crypt. *Gareth, First Lord of Falcon's Lair.* ''Oh, my love. You were here, all alone in the
darkness, waiting to . . .''

They stood together, their breathing shallow, their thoughts
scattered.

When she finally spoke, Felicity's tone was resigned. ''At
least you won't be alone now. Nor will I. We'll face our fate
together.''

''No.'' He held her a little away, his eyes hot and fierce.
''This is not to be your fate. I won't allow you to give up.''

''But you said yourself that your powers have diminished,
and I have none at all.''

''You forget the power of love.'' He turned away, con-
centrating all his energy on the heavy door that barred their
way.

As Felicity watched in amazement, a sound, like that of a
terrible rushing wind, sent the door scraping open. Gareth
caught her hand and led her up the steps and into the chill
night air. Jagged slashes of lightning rent the heavens, and
thunder shook the very ground as, together, they sprinted the
distance to the castle. One look from Gareth sent the door

creaking open on its hinges. They raced up the stairs and stopped short at Lord Falcon's room.

Ian and Honora were standing beside the old lord's bed. In Ian's hand was a vial of poison. His eyes glinted with hatred as he turned to Felicity.

"How did you escape? And who is this stranger?"

Felicity realized that Gareth, in his diminished state, was no longer invisible.

"I am Gareth, First Lord of Falcon's Lair," he cried in a voice that rang with authority. "I command you to step away from Lord Falcon's bed."

Ian gave a chilling laugh. "How fitting. The first lord and the last. Both will die. You see, I gave my uncle his final dose of my special medicine."

"Oh, Ian!" Felicity cried. "Why do you hate your uncle so?"

"If my father had been half a man, he would have killed his brother years ago. Then I would have inherited Falcon's Lair, along with the title, instead of my wretched cousins. But at least one of us had the courage of his convictions. I will have the estate, and William's wife as well."

"You may have her with my blessing," came a voice from the doorway.

William, leaning heavily on the arm of Diana Summerville, started forward.

"What are you doing in the company of my husband?" Honora demanded harshly.

Diana's eyes flashed with an inner fire. "Bean summoned me when she couldn't find your houseguest."

"And you, William. How is it that you are alive?" Ian demanded. "I gave you the same dose of poison I gave your father."

Felicity's voice was triumphant. "Before you caught me, I gave both Lord Falcon and William an antidote. Your poison can no longer harm them."

"You fool! I told you we should have killed the American sooner!" Honora cried. "Here, Ian." Reaching over Lord Falcon's bed, she tossed her lover a jewel-handled sword.

"Since the poison hasn't worked, use this to finish all of them."

Ian caught it and advanced on Felicity. But before he could attack, Gareth dragged her roughly behind him, shielding her with his own body.

There was a time when Gareth, First Lord of Falcon's Lair, would have been agile enough to dodge the thrusts of the finest swordsmen. But in his weakened condition he was no match for the enraged Ian St. John. The blade found its mark, piercing his chest.

As Gareth fell, there was a terrible commotion, and one of the servants belowstairs shouted, "My lord! My lord! Awake and rejoice. It is Lord Chandler, your elder son, returned from the perils of the Amazon."

At that Lord Falcon rose up from his bed, his eyes wide, his senses alert. "Chandler lives? Can it be true?"

Like a proud old lion infused with new life, he seized the second sword. Tossing it to his son, he shouted, "Stop them, William! In the name of all Falcons!"

Felicity was only vaguely aware of the sound of scuffling, and the cries of Ian and Honora as they attempted to flee the wrath of William, Diana, and Lord Falcon. From the shouting, it would seem that the servants had joined in the chase. But she no longer cared what happened to Ian and Honora. All her energies were centered on the terrible drama being played out here. In the silence of the bedroom, she knelt and cradled Gareth in her arms.

"You cannot die, love," she cried. "For there is something you must know."

"I know that I have loved the finest woman ever created. Not merely in one lifetime, but in two. That is enough reward for me."

She was unaware of the tears that streamed down her cheeks. Only one thing mattered now. It was of the utmost importance that she relay to Gareth what she'd read in the family history. He must not face eternity without being granted his fondest wish.

"All these years you have believed that Adrian, your half brother, made good his threat to wed your beloved Cara and force her to bear his son. It is true that she was forced to become his wife. She died soon after giving birth to Alexander. What you didn't know, nor did Adrian, was that Cara had conceived the babe before their marriage and before your death.''

For a moment she felt the glimmer of heat. His eyes opened, struggling to focus. ''Are you saying that Alexander was my son?''

''Yes, my love. All his descendants are yours as well. You are not doomed to an eternity of loneliness. There are generations of Falcons. Hundreds of them. They all owe their lives to you.''

He clutched her hand, and she felt the chill seeping into his flesh. ''You have given me the greatest gift of all, little happy face. Now I give one to you. Know this. Though I must leave you, you will never be alone. There will be another . . .''

A sob rose up, threatening to choke her. ''No, Gareth. I won't listen to this. Please don't leave me. I don't want another. I want you.''

Lord Falcon and his sons found Felicity lying on the floor of the bedroom, weeping as though her heart were broken. The stranger who had been with her was nowhere to be seen. Though the grounds and village were searched carefully, he was never seen again.

EPILOGUE

Felicity made a slow turn around the gardens, stopping often to admire a perfect rose or to inhale the perfumed air. She would miss this. All of it. The flocks of sheep undulating gently across the rolling hills. The vast stretches of wind-swept moors. The brooding castle with its secrets. And the people. Especially the people. Bean and Simmons and Maud Atherton. Lord Falcon and his son William, and the lovely Diana, who would soon become William's wife.

And, of course, Gareth. She would carry him in her heart forever.

As she approached the terrace, she glanced toward the stand of trees, where she and Gareth had hidden away one wonderful night. As always, just thinking about him brought a lump to her throat that threatened to choke her. For a short time she had actually believed that this place could be her home. But now, without Gareth, the dream had died.

Hadn't he warned her that a sword would pierce her heart? She'd never dreamed it would be so painful. The sword that killed him had destroyed her as well. No one would ever touch her like that again.

"Miss Andrews." Chandler Falcon opened the French doors and stepped onto the terrace. Despite the fact that he'd been missing in the Amazon for months, he looked tanned and fit, and every bit the lord of the manor. He was tall, with broad, muscular shoulders and narrow hips. Dark hair, in need of a trim, seemed always slightly mussed, which only added to his appeal. He had a proud, almost haughty profile, with firm jaw, full, sensuous lips, and dark, penetrating eyes that struck a chord in her heart, though she knew not why. "The servants have gathered in the front hall to say a proper good-bye."

She nodded, but as she started to brush past him, he touched a hand to her shoulder to stop her. She felt a rush of heat and pulled back, resenting his touch.

"In all the excitement of the past few days, I've never really had the opportunity to thank you for saving my father and brother. It was a very brave thing you did. As you know, we Falcons admire those who thrive on courage and adventure."

"It was nothing," she said softly. "Just a favor between old friends."

"Nothing? You are far too modest, I'm afraid. Why, even Mrs. Atherton sings your praises." His eyes crinkled with unexpected humor. "That's rare praise indeed."

Felicity couldn't help smiling. It was true. Maud Atherton had become as friendly as Bean and Simmons and had decided that the American houseguest was no trouble at all.

"I don't believe you've heard the news of Ian and Honora."

Her head came up. "News?"

"They escaped their jailer and made off in his rig. While fleeing across the moors, something spooked their horse, and the rig tipped over, killing them both." He cleared his throat. "There are those who say it is poetic justice."

She realized that she felt nothing. Neither relief nor regret, just a chilling numbness.

When she said nothing, Chandler continued to stand in front of the door, barring her way. "I hope you won't think me too bold. But I wish you would consider staying on a while at Falcon's Lair. Not only would it make my father happy, but it would give me a chance to get to know you better."

"I'm sorry. I can't stay, Lord Falcon." She made a move to slip past him.

"It's Chandler."

"Chandler." She paused beside him, irritation deepening her tone. "Thank you for the invitation, but I really . . .''

"Your first name's Felicity, isn't it?"

She nodded.

"Did you know," he said, his smile deepening, "that 'Felicity' is Latin for happiness?" He caught a strand of her hair and watched as it sifted through his fingers. Then he shifted his dark gaze to her eyes, and she felt the jolt of recognition. "The name suits you. You have a happy face."

She felt the blood drain, leaving her pale and trembling. She tried to speak, but no words came.

A short time later Lord Falcon, William, and Diana, along with the servants, came in search of their errant houseguest. They found her still standing on the terrace, her hands linked with Chandler's.

"The carriage is here to take you to London," Lord Falcon began.

"Miss Andrews won't be leaving, Father." Chandler never took his gaze from hers. "I've convinced her that one of life's greatest adventures awaits her here at Falcon's Lair."

"I see." A slow smile spread across the old man's face. To Felicity he said, "I told you happy endings are the best, my dear." Signaling to the others, he led the party indoors, where they continued to stand at the floor-to-ceiling windows, staring at the couple on the terrace.

Chandler and Felicity never moved. Yet a shimmering light seemed to surround them. William explained to Diana that it was probably a trick of the sunlight.

Soaring above Felicity and Chandler was a magnificent falcon. It turned its head one time, as if studying the man and woman, then catching a wind current, opened its great wings and lifted high into the air.

There were many who swore it continued climbing until it reached the sun. The story was repeated until it became just another of the many legends that surrounded Falcon's Lair.

But it couldn't top the legend of the family's boldest adventurer, Chandler, who returned from the Amazon to find

Felicity, the woman of his dreams, awaiting him. Together they founded a dynasty destined for greatness.

It is said their love burned brighter than the sun and will continue to burn for all eternity.

DRAGONSPELL

MARIANNE WILLMAN

To Friends and Friendship—especially to Nora, Ruth, and Jill, whose loyalty and love are valued "above rubies"

And to Linda and Tina Blaschke, "pearls beyond price," whose friendship, love, and support eased us through a very trying time

CHAPTER 1

Once upon a time, in the days of Magic and Wonder, there lived a princess in the Kingdom of Amelonia. Like all proper princesses, she was lovely as the dawn, with fiery hair and skin like petals of the rose. But she was not like any other princess, then or now, as you will soon discover. And such an unusual princess surely deserves to win the love of a most unusual man . . .

On a warm summer's day, several noble ladies sat in the castle's solar, heads bowed over their embroidery frames. In the courtyard outside, a market day was in progress, sounds of music and laughter drifting in through the open casement window.

The only sounds inside, except for the occasional snick of tiny golden scissors, were the frequent sighs of the youngest, whose jeweled coronet sat slightly askew on her shimmering auburn hair. The amethyst cabochons were the exact color of her thickly lashed eyes.

How tedious to be stuck away on such a beautiful afternoon. *No, unbearable!* thought the Princess Tressalara. If she had her way, she would be riding out over the meadows with her hair blowing free in the sun, instead of wasting her time in such drudgery.

She stabbed the golden needle into the taut cloth in the frame . . . and into her finger, as well.

"By Saint Ethelred's beard!" she exclaimed in annoyance,

sucking her injured finger. A small drop of blood splashed onto her white silk gown.

The court ladies gasped in shock at such language from their princess. Lady Grette, the chief among the others, rose and went to her mistress's side, making soothing little noises. When the princess was annoyed, it was best to stay out of her way; but when her rosy pink mouth firmed to a hard line, an explosion was imminent.

"Now, now. Patience is a virtue to be cultivated by the wise seamstress. I know it is hard, Princess Tressalara, to remain indoors on a fine summer's day. But you must finish your work before you ride out. You are King Varro's daughter, and it is time and more that you learn all the duties and skills of a royal lady." How else was the headstrong princess ever going to mend her ways and acquire a proper husband? Heaven knew she needed one.

Tressalara's eyes darkened to violet as she eyed her handiwork ruefully. "What good is it being the king's daughter when I am kept inside like a prisoner? Why, the lowliest peasant in Amelonia has more freedom than I! Give me one good reason why I should spend any more time at this hopeless task."

The chief lady-in-waiting played her best card. "Because the king, your father, wishes it."

Tressalara fell silent. Lady Grette knew her weaknesses all too well. She would do anything to make her father proud of her. Anything to make him acknowledge that she was as capable and fit to rule after him as any man. As capable and fit as the strong sons he had longed for and never had.

Could she not ride and fence and loose her arrows to the target's heart with the best of them? Was she not clever at games of strategy? Wise in dispensing justice at the monthly assizes? And he would have her spend her days sewing posies and knotting fringes instead!

But she would do it. Because she loved him. And because she wanted him to love her in return. "Oh, very well."

Lady Grette leaned over the embroidery frame and examined Tressalara's handiwork with dismay. She certainly expected more from a princess of eighteen summers. Why, any of her youngest charges in the nursery could have done better. The stitches were all higgledy-piggledy, like the wavering progress of a rum-sotted sailor in a port town.

A shame that the king had not taken another gentle wife to raise his daughter, rather than locking himself away with his prayers and memories these past ten years. It was a wonder that the princess, motherless and raised like a boy since then, hadn't clambered out a window and escaped to the stables long ago this morning, the way she used to as a wee, naughty lass.

Ah, well. Lady Grette steeled her heart. It was for Tressalara's own good. She was a young woman now, ripe for marriage. Her father hoped to arrange a match between the princess and some foreign prince before the harvest was in. The royal scribe said that word of King Varro's intentions had been sent to kings and dukes and princes far and wide, although his messengers had not yet returned from abroad. No doubt they would, with many splendid offers for Tressalara's hand.

At least, she certainly hoped so: The lady-in-waiting did not like Lord Lector, the king's chief advisor. Grette feared that the king was considering him as a son-in-law. Certainly he had let Lector take over the reins of government to a large extent. The man was lobbying hard for the position, if half of what she heard was true.

But handsome as he was, he would make a terrible husband for a headstrong girl like Tressalara. There were those rumors that he had been responsible for bloody raids against their neighbors that had been blamed on Cador of Kildore. But Grette was sure that Lector would not have stooped so low. This was a peaceable kingdom.

In an attempt to ignore her disquiet, she turned her attention to the task at hand. "These straggling stitches will not do, your highness! You must pick them all out and start over. It is long past the time when you should have learned the gentle womanly arts."

Tressalara ground her teeth. It had taken her two hours to set those stitches. She had tried, truly tried, to do them properly. Now she tried, truly tried, to rein in her temper. As usual, it got the better of her. Instead of reaching for the tiny scissors, she rose and drew her jeweled dagger.

"*This* for the gentle *womanly* arts!" she exclaimed, slashing her blade through the faulty stitches—and through the taut linen beneath as well. It made a most satisfactory ripping sound. "There. They are all out, every one!"

While the ladies stared, aghast, their princess turned on her heel and left the room. No one followed. No one dared. She was still their royal mistress.

Tressalara's anger spurred her on. She reached her chambers and took out the boy's garb she'd hidden in one of her dower chests. The clothes had lain there for months, unused, since she had given a scrawny stable lad her best leather jerkin in exchange for the smocked shirt and trews of drab brown homespun. Rough garb indeed.

There was a time when she'd had as fine a set of hunting garb as any princeling and had ridden out in her father's train with her bow and arrows on her back. But that was before nature had made her womanhood too evident, by adding curves to what had been the figure of a spindle-shanked stripling. It was most unfair!

Worst of all was the knowledge that her changed appearance was the true reason behind her changed status. It had reminded her father that his only child was not the longed-for son. Her father felt that women were too weak to rule alone. Since he had no male heir, he had recently let slip that he intended to marry her off to some foreign prince. Fire flashed in Tressalara's eyes.

She had never met a man that she could imagine taking for a husband. And she couldn't bear to think of Amelonia being handed to some stranger like a honey cake on a platter, all because she'd had the misfortune to be born female. But the wedding ring was not yet on her hand, and there was no likely suitor in sight. Plenty of time for an enterprising young woman to prove herself worthy of guiding her people firmly and wisely.

Rebellion bloomed, and a wildness flared in Tressalara, borne with the scent of summer meadows on the warm air. She slipped out of her gown and into the stable lad's clothes.

She wished that she could cut her heavy hair short, but satisfied herself by twisting it into a thick braid.

The door to her inner chamber opened, and Elani, her youngest lady-in-waiting and closest friend, entered. Her blue eyes widened in surprise. "Oh, highness, you dare not . . . !

"Watch me and see!"

With a grin, Tressalara pinned her long braid atop her hair and covered it with a battered leather cap that pulled down to her ears. "Behold young Trev, a simple peasant lad of Amelonia, on his way to an adventure."

Before Elani could even think what to do, the princess was gone.

She was halfway down the back staircase to the lower level, her mind on nothing but escape and freedom, when she heard a scream followed by a great commotion in the main courtyard. Without pausing, she clambered to the ledge of a window that overlooked the market area.

What she saw turned her heart to a ball of ice. The portcullis had dropped, the gates were barred, and the courtyard was filled with men-at-arms in black livery. Some of the visitors threw off their cloaks to reveal the same ominous uniforms. They were everywhere. At their leader's signal they charged into the crowd.

Tables were overturned. Fruit and tools and pottery went flying as the king's bugler blew a call to arms. Chickens and piglets scattered. Women and children screamed and ran; babies wailed as men fell before the attackers' blades. Thank God—there was Jeday, her father's loyal captain of the guard arriving with his men.

He raised his arm to lead a charge, and Tressalara's relief turned to horror as Jeday was struck from behind by an assassin's knife. As he fell, lifeless, the guard behind him threw off his king's livery to show again the dread black uniform of the attackers. It had all happened in an instant.

Then Tressalara recognized their leader: the smooth-talking chief councillor, Lord Lector. No mistaking that mane of dark hair with its single silver streak, the jutting profile, and the silver scorpion emblem on his shield. A crafty and dangerous man. There was no time to lose.

As Tressalara ducked inside, the courtyard rang with fierce cries: "Death to the tyrant! Death to King Varro!"

Elani came to the head of the stairs and looked down, her usually pretty face pale as lard. "What is it?"

"Lector has turned traitor, and we are besieged. I must find my father." Tressalara was halfway down the stairs. "The enemy are within the walls. Save yourself, Elani. Hide in my chambers. You know where." She saw her friend hesitate. "That is an order from your princess! I command you!"

Then she was on the last step, plunging into the shadows along the corridor. She must reach her father in time. She must! Tressalara's heart beat so hard it seemed about to jolt out of her chest. The invaders had timed their coup well, waiting until the king had retired to the isolated chapel for his daily meditations—alone and unarmed.

Oh, the cowards! she thought, sliding back the secret panel that led to a shortcut. The castle was riddled with many such passageways, a legacy of her great-grandfather's madness. Trusting no one and fearing assassination, he had built a maze inside these walls. She knew every secret way and in the past had gotten her britches dusted a few times for hiding in them overlong and setting the castle on its ear.

But now the knowledge of these places, where she and Elani had played as children, would serve her well. If only she could get to her father in time to warn him, she could spirit him away to safety through the secret door in the chapel.

She slipped the catch that opened behind the altar. Before it had always amused her that the icon of Saint Ethelred the Dragonmaster hung upon the doorway to the heart of the secret maze. At the moment she had no thought for it.

Her father was on his knees at the altar, looking old and frail in his simple robe and without his emblems of kingship. As he humbled himself before God, his gray head bent almost to the floor, and his coronet caught the light of the tall candelabra.

At any other time Tressalara would have told herself that he was no doubt praying for a virile son-in-law to sire a male grandchild in the years to come. But now was no time to nurture old grievances.

"Father!"

"Tressalara! By all the saints!" Varro roared, taking in her boy's garb and her unorthodox arrival in one heated glance. "Do you have no sense of what is fitting in this holy . . ."

"Father, we are under attack! Lector and his men have taken the courtyard and the great hall. Jeday—" She strengthened her faltering voice. "Jeday is dead by an assassin's hand. Come this way. Hurry!"

Already they could hear the first sounds of tumult from just beyond the thick chapel walls. Voices raised in anger and fear. The clash of steel on steel. Cries of mortal agony.

"Father, come!"

He hesitated as the locked chapel door shuddered from the onslaught. The brass key fell to the stone flags with an ominous clang. The wood cracked and splintered. The king hurried to Tressalara's side, and she turned down the secret passage, assuming that he meant to follow.

Instead, he wrested her drawn dagger from her hand, then shoved her forward into the darkness with what frail strength he could muster. She fell heavily, skinning her hands on the rough stone floor. The door to the passageway thudded shut behind her.

Jumping up, Tressalara threw herself at the latch, but it refused to give. She pressed her shoulder against the panel, tears of rage and fear for her father running down her cheeks. She knew why she couldn't open it. Her father had his back firmly to the door, holding it shut so that she could not open it from the inside and reveal her hiding place. He had chosen her life over his.

Tears streaming, she could do nothing but stifle her own sobs and pray. The scuffle of feet and the shriek of metal against stone were plainly audible through the heavy wood, although the assassins' voices were muffled.

An eternity passed while she waited, hoping in vain that her father would escape yet knowing that he had no chance at all. Vowing, through her anguish, that she would have revenge upon Lector and save the kingdom.

All was suddenly quiet. Tressalara's blood chilled. She scrabbled at the edges of the wood, trying with all her might to open the panel. It wobbled slightly but did not give. Eons passed while she tried to work it free, and there was nothing but silence from the other side. Then the hidden catch gave, and the panel slowly rolled back.

The chapel was dim. The great candelabra lay on their sides, flames extinguished, among the holy icons broken on the floor. Only the ruby glow of the altar lamp illumined the chamber. "Father?"

Silence. She moved cautiously around the altar. Something skittered beneath her foot. She stooped and picked up a stone. No, a small green jewel winking at her in the half light, its center carved in the shape of an eye. She had seen it somewhere before.

Tucking it in the leather bag she wore inside her smock, she looked around. In the faint red glow, she spied the painted panel of Saint Ethelred propped against the altar. Blood dripped from the saint's painted breast. It ran in a thin diagonal line toward a dark piece of cloth on the ground.

Tressalara's breath caught. Not cloth, but a pool of blood, widening as she watched. She pushed the panel aside. "Ah, no! Father!"

How small he looked, how diminished in his bloodied robe. Cradling him in her arms, she felt for a pulse. His eyes, so like her own, flickered open.

"Foul . . . treachery," he whispered faintly. "I had been warned but I thought . . . I could not believe the reports . . . thank God and Saint Ethelred . . . I had the foresight to hide . . . the Andun Crystal."

She refused to see that he was dying before her eyes. "Save your strength. I'll hide you in the passageway . . . seek out help from our loyal soldiers. . . . You can send a messenger to Morania, asking for the duke's assistance . . ."

His voice came out in a harsh, choking whisper.

"Child, I waited too long to find you a husband. You must take the Andun Stone, daughter, and flee to Morania.

The duke has . . . several sons. Even without a kingdom you are . . . beautiful. One of them will surely . . . take you to wife.''

''I will not flee! Nor will you. We will stay and fight for our people!''

Varro gave a liquid cough, and the blood seeped through the fingers that Tressalara held to his chest to cover his wound. She put her cheek against her father's and was shocked to feel how icy it was. Her tears mingled with his.

''So . . . cold . . .'' he whispered, as if talking to himself.

Tressalara could fool herself no longer. She rose slowly and found a cushion to put beneath his head, a piece of fallen tapestry to cover him and hold the last bit of warmth in his bones. Her grief and the enormous responsibility of what it meant to be truly royal fell upon her shoulders like a cloak of lead. She could scarcely bear the weight of it. Her knees buckled, and she grasped at the panel for support, lowering herself to his side once more.

''You will be all right,'' she lied. ''Your loyal troops will overcome the enemy. I will stay here and guard you until they come.''

He clutched at her hand. His face was gray, and his eyes seemed focused on some distant sight. ''You are brave, Tressalara. Too headstrong . . . but no one can fault you for your courage.''

His head sank upon his breast, and the ominous red stains on his tunic grew and coalesced. His breathing was ragged and irregular. ''I must leave you now,'' he said.

Tressalara cradled him in her arms. ''No! Ah, saints!'' She could see the life ebbing from him second by second. ''Father, I swear to God Most High that your sacrifice will not be in vain. I will do anything that is necessary to rally the people and destroy Lector. I will avenge you!''

He looked at her and gave a little sigh: ''Ah, Tressalara, If only you had been born a son . . .''

Silence filled the chapel. Tressalara was suddenly alone in the chapel with the dregs of her life around her and the taste of bitterness on her tongue.

CHAPTER 2

In the Caverns of Mist, an apprentice sorceress and an apprentice wizard watched the tragic scene in their crystal globe. "Poor Tressalara," Niniane said sorrowfully, touching the princess's image in the glass. She turned her head away to hide a tear, and her white draperies swirled like moonbeams. "And poor King Varro."

Her companion hunched his skinny shoulders, and his spangled cloak shivered with dark light. "It's all your fault," Illusius accused. "If you hadn't mixed that eye of newt with the bladderwort syrup . . ."

"*I?*" Niniane exclaimed with icy hauteur. "*I* am not the one who broke the flask of Yann and loosed the spell that bound up Myrriden."

"Yes, but if there hadn't been newt and bladderwort lying about everywhere, it wouldn't have exploded the way it did and—"

The two glanced uneasily at the rear of the cavern, where the great wizard Myrriden was encased in a sheet of glittering Spell-Ice as clear as glass. Although Myrriden was supposed to be in a deep sleep from the spell gone awry, his gray eyes were wide open. They seemed to stare at his erstwhile students in either fury or resignation, depending upon the light. At the moment a bubble of ice glimmered like a tear on the old man's cheek.

Niniane turned hastily away, tugging at one of her silvery curls.

"Oh, hush! We won't get anywhere if we don't stop arguing about it. If only we could discover the spell that would release us from these caverns, I would find a way to save the princess.'' She sighed. ''But we can't. So you must continue to assist me in going through these endless mounds of spell-books until we find a way to unfreeze Myrriden. Then he can use his mighty powers to enable Tressalara to save her people.''

''We've been at it for ten human years now.'' The apprentice's dark brows drew together in a scowl as he scanned the stacks and stacks of cobwebbed tomes stretching up into the darkness of the cavern's mile-high roof. At their current rate of reading, it should only take, oh, about another human century. Or two. ''I need time to study for the apprentice examination. Why should I even have to get involved? She's not *my* human.''

''Hah! You're so lazy and selfish you'll never make senior wizard! No wonder you don't have a human of your own to guard.''

Illusius frowned. ''Do so! His name is Cador. He's off fighting in the mountain kingdoms. He's a highlander and a mighty warrior. The fiercest in the entire world. Why, he could save this puny little kingdom without even missing his supper.''

Niniane smiled sweetly. ''Then why don't you 'call' him? Surely so great a warrior would be up to the challenge.''

''I doubt if he could spare the time . . . even if he wanted to help Tressalara.''

The sorceress laughed. ''I shall see to it that he does.''

She picked up her book titled *Love Spells and Potions, Volume XVIII,* and turned confidently to a page marked with a wide silver ribbon. ''You're not the only one who has been cramming for the test.''

''The bastard! May he rot in hell!'' Tressalara looked magnificent in her topaz-studded gown of cloth of gold, her eyes blazing with fury. As she paced the floor of her tower bedchamber, the gown's stiff train whispered angrily over the stones. Two days since the coup and her father's murder, and she had had no time to mourn him. Lector had not allowed it. And today she would be forced to wed him.

"If only I could have escaped through the tunnel before his men returned and found me!" At least she had bloodied one and sent another to his maker. She whipped around to face Elani. "And you! You should have stayed hidden until it was safe to come out."

Elani wrung her hands. "How could I, highness, when I knew you were the villain's prisoner?"

They heard the sound of the door being unbarred, and Lector entered, resplendent in black and silver, with a massive collar of ruby-studded white gold about his neck. As his men fanned out to block the doorway, Tressalara stepped protectively in front of Elani.

"Your ignorance shows, Lector," she sneered. "It is bad luck to see the bride before the wedding."

He smiled, grasping her arm in a painful grip. "I make my own luck. And I would brave more than the threat of ill fortune for you, my sweet."

Stepping forward, he took her chin in his hand and lifted her face to his. She could not help but notice the unusual ring he wore: a gargoyle with one eye carved from an emerald. The other eye was missing. Tressalara realized that the lost emerald was the one she found in the chapel after her father was slain. So it was Lector himself who had struck her father down. Her hate chilled to a stern and icy rage.

He ran his finger along the sweet curve of her lower lip. "I shall teach you to love me," he said. "I am highly skilled in the sensual arts."

She jerked her head away. "I will never love the traitor who murdered my father, the rightful king, in cold blood!"

He saw the revulsion in her eyes and laughed softly. "There is nothing I like better than a challenge."

Pulling Tressalara into his arms, he pressed a hot kiss against her closed lips and mocked her resistance.

"I look forward to this evening and many others. In time you will come to appreciate the, ah . . . benefits, shall we say, of being my wife. With your beauty and my will, we shall forge a formidable union. I will know how to pleasure you until you beg for my favors."

She wiped her mouth with the back of her hand. ''I would rather wed a pig!''

His breath hissed out in anger, and she tried to free herself from his hold. He jerked her face back and laughed, aroused to have her completely in his power. ''It will be a pleasure to break you to bridle.''

His grip tightened. He was hurting her purposely, his fingers digging into her flesh, but she bore the pain stoically. She lifted her head defiantly, although her lips had gone white with pain.

Elani could stand no more. She leapt to her mistress's aid. Before the soldiers could even draw their swords, Lector's hand whipped out and struck the girl. Elani fell to the floor, dazed and weeping. He moved toward the door, then stopped and issued a challenge over his shoulder:

''Heed me well, Tressalara. Do not cross me! Even a princess is expendable.'' With a laugh of truimph he swaggered out of the room, followed by his soldiers.

Tressalara helped Elani to her feet. The imprint of Lector's fingers stained the girl's face like a bloody hand. ''How can a man with so handsome a face have a soul so filled with canker? It pains me to think he was once the object of my girlish admiration.''

Her maid-in-waiting wiped her tears. ''He is a cruel man. You know what tales they tell of him in the villages now. He will do what he can to break your spirit. I shudder to think of what may be in store for you this night, highness!''

''Do not fear for me. I have a plan.'' Tressalara lifted her gown's train away from her back and slid out her jeweled dagger.

''Oh! How did you get it past Lector's men?''

''I hid it in my garter. Not even they dared to search my person.'' The princess's face was cold as marble. ''If I cannot save my people, at least I will rid them of this villain Lector! I will have his life's blood before he has my maidenhead.''

''You cannot mean it. You will be tortured and put to death!''

Tressalara's violet eyes darkened to black. She twisted the bracelet on her delicate wrist, a circle of gold and amethyst that matched her coronet, even down to the dragon emblem of Amelonia carved into the central stone. "What kills once can kill twice. They will not take me alive."

Her intensity frightened Elani even more. "You must not go through with this mad scheme. Only think, you are the living symbol of Amelonia. Only you, highness, can command the powers of the Andun Stone." Her face brightened. "Can you not use the crystal's magic to overcome Lector?"

"Alas, even if I were free to discover where my father hid it, I doubt I could harness the Andun's energy." A look of savage pain flitted across Tressalara's mobile features. She should have disobeyed her father and studied the sacred scroll without his knowledge.

"When I should have been studying the Dragonmaster's teachings, I was out running through the woods like a wild creature. Now the kingdom will reap the harvest of my selfish folly. I must carry out my plan."

But Elani would not be persuaded. "I have a better one. They did not discover the secret passage behind your bed. You could conceal yourself there, highness, and I would put on your gown and veiled headpiece and go to the chapel in your stead. Once the guards were gone, you could flee in disguise. Lector would not discover the ruse until the vows were exchanged and the veil lifted. You would have ample time to make your escape."

"Yes, and let them kill you when they discover I've fled?" Tressalara took her lady-in-waiting's icy hands in hers and smiled. "You are a brave and true friend to me, dear Elani. You will do both myself and the kingdom more good if you are alive."

There was a great flapping of wings at the window, and they turned to see a large white bird fly in and settle down on the sill: Rossmine, the wild hawk that Tressalara had found wounded and nursed back to health. She had been training it as a surprise for her father. The creature was so tame now that it would feed daintily from the princess's own hand.

Tressalara went to the casement and held out her arm, and

Rossmine flew to it. The hawk settled on her wrist, curving its sharp talons so delicately that they didn't leave a scratch. She smoothed the bird's feathers with a light touch. "Rossmine, my fair companion in adventure, I give you your freedom. Fly free. Soar high!"

She tried to toss the bird into the blue void beyond the window, but the hawk only fluttered away and arced back to the sill, settling in stubbornly once more.

"She will not leave you," Elani said, "any more than I will. Rossmine wants to help. If only there were some ally to whom you might send a plea, with Rossmine as your messenger! Surely there is a man somewhere in this vast kingdom who would rally the people and come to your aid."

The hawk stretched her glorious wings and cried out piercingly: *"Cador! Cador the Warrior!"* But neither woman understood.

As Tressalara's hand drew back, the gold and amethyst bracelet gleamed in the sunlight. A daring plan took rapid form in her brain. "Your words have given me an idea, Elani. It may not work, but I believe it is our only hope!"

An hour passed before Lector's men came to escort the bride to the chapel for the marriage service. When they unbarred the door, an astonishing sight met their eyes. Elani sat in one chair before the empty hearth. The princess's golden slippers stood empty before the opposite chair, which held only her crumpled gold wedding gown—and a large white hawk.

"Where is the Princess Tressalara?" their captain demanded.

Elani pointed mutely to the bird. Rossmine turned her noble head and eyed the soldier fiercely. They saw that the hawk wore a circle of gold and amethyst upon its head. The men's mouths fell open in astonishment.

"What sorcery is this?" The captain gasped. "The creature wears the princess's crown!"

"Witchcraft!" another mumbled, making a sign to ward off the evil eye.

As they milled about in confusion, Lord Lector joined

them. "What is the delay? I am most impatient to claim my lovely bride."

The soldiers parted ranks to let him enter. "The Princess Tressalara has used the power of the Andun Crystal to turn herself into a bird."

"Idiots!" Lector pushed past them and stopped in his tracks. He would not have believed this were he not seeing it with his own eyes. The hawk hissed at him, and light winked from the carved dragon in the central amethyst upon its coronet. Lector's tan face blanched with mingled fear and fury. He lost control.

"By God, she shall not escape me through such tricks! She is of no use to me now!"

He lunged forward, intending to grab the bird and wring its neck. Instead, Rossmine spread her mighty wings and struck him in the eye with one. Before he could protect himself, a talon raked his cheek, laying it open. Then the hawk bounded to the open casement and launched herself into the air. With a mighty screech and a flap of her powerful wings, she vanished into the clouds.

Lector held a hand to his ruined face as blood dripped hot through his splayed fingers. Hate burned in his eyes. "You will pay for this, Tressalara!" he shouted.

He rounded on his soldiers. "From this moment I declare the Princess Tressalara to be a traitoress to her country. A purse of one hundred gold coins will reward the man who finds the princess and brings her to me in chains . . . alive or *dead!*"

Elani gasped, and the captain turned toward her. "What of this serving wench?"

"Lock her in and bar the door. I have no time to deal with her now. Let her starve to death for whatever part she has played in this black magic."

Lector and his men went out. Elani listened at the door until she was sure they were truly gone, then secured it with the bar on the inside, as Tressalara had instructed. When it was in place, she crossed to the enormous tester bed and tapped on the wall behind it.

Tressalara slid the panel open, grinning in relief. "I can't believe he was deceived by our ruse!"

Jumping down, she pulled out an enormous length of knotted fabric. Gowns, shifts, sheets, and cloaks had all been tied into a sturdy rope. "To think I believed that learning to knot a fringe was a waste of my time." She laughed ruefully. "Now help me tie it to the bedpost, and I will make my escape."

The drop from the tower window to the ground outside the castle walls was precipitous. If Tressalara had not been one to delight in heights and feats of daring, it would have made her dizzy with fear. White water foamed over striated boulders. A fall would mean instant death.

They fed out the makeshift rope and saw that it came woefully short of reaching the ground. Tressalara heard her maid take in a shaky breath. "Don't be concerned, Elani. I have done this before—in my younger days, you know."

She bit her lip as an unexpected sting of tears made her eyes smart. How angry her father had been at her reckless disregard! And how proud of her daring. *Oh, Father!* She dashed her tears away. She must act now and mourn later.

The two young women embraced. The princess looked solemn. "Have no fear that I will abandon you. I will return to rescue you, Elani."

Clambering to the casement, Tressalara yanked on her rope, testing its strength, then took a deep breath and began her perilous descent. One wrong move and she would be dashed to death on the rocks below. Thank Saint Ethelred that this wall was hidden from the view of anyone inside the castle and that the tall trees of the woods across the river screened her from view of the village.

She reached the end of the rope and let go, springing into a crouch to absorb the shock of impact. She rolled into a tangle of brambles and came up cursing and winded, with dirt on her face and burrs on her ripped smock. Her knuckles were scraped, and a hole was torn in her breeches. All in all, Tressalara was pleased with her appearance. She looked a proper ragamuffin now. No one would suspect that the young urchin, Trev, was actually a princess in disguise.

A princess with a price on her head.

As she slipped into the shadows of the Mystic Forest, Tressalara stopped for one final look at the turrets of the castle. "I will return, Father," she said, the words both vow and prayer. "I swear it on my life. I shall rally the people and lead an army to reclaim your kingdom."

Despite Elani's opinions, she would not need the help of any man to do so.

Niniane paced the Caverns of Mist, snagging her floating white robe on a protruding quartz crystal. She yanked it away impatiently. Her fellow apprentice was supposed to be working on a spell to help Tressalara, but there'd been no sign of him for hours.

The sorceress projected her voice until it filled the caverns. "Illusius, I have grown tired of waiting for your magic to work. I believe you aren't conjuring at all. In fact, I believe you are just off sulking somewhere!"

"Not so!"

In a puff of dark smoke the apprentice sorcerer appeared not two feet from where Niniane stood. With another wave of his hands, they were both transported to the entrance of the Caverns of Mist in a twinkling. She was very impressed but worked to hide it. "Swaggering coxcomb!"

Illusius glowered. What a tiresome girl she was. Well, this would convince her of his superior powers. "Help is on the way." He clapped his hands, and the thunder of hooves echoed through the forest. "I 'called' Lord Cador, and he has returned from the borderlands! He is meeting with Brand, leader of the rebels."

A great band of men rode by the hidden cavern mouth. They were not decked out as splendidly as Lector's men in their black and silver livery emblazoned with the scorpion emblem. Truth to tell, they looked a bit disreputable in their shabby leather jerkins, their humble tunics and cloaks. But here and there the gleam of armor shone beneath their weathered garments, and their eyes were those of warriors.

Niniane huffed. "These are your noble heroes? They look like common brigands!"

"These men are soldiers to the core. Here is Cador of Kildore, their leader."

Although his clothing was as worn as that of his companions, Cador wore it like a badge of royalty. His bronzed and windburned features were intriguing, with more than a hint of the hawk in them. His hair caught the late-afternoon sun, gleaming like gold. There was fire in his dark sapphire eyes, determination in the set of his firm mouth, strength and authority in every line of his bearing.

Niniane sighed romantically. Here was the very man for Tressalara. A king among warriors. *Well done, Illusius!* Aloud she spoke differently. "If that is the best you can do, I suppose we are stuck with him. At least he is experienced and willing to fight to restore the princess to her throne."

Illusius chewed his lip. That was something he was still working on.

It could prove a bit tricky, and he wasn't quite sure if he could pull it off. The highlander might not want to risk throwing his lot in with the Amelonian rebels. That didn't bear thinking of. If he failed, Niniane would rub it in for the next hundred years.

He felt a nervous flush rising up his face and vanished himself before she could notice.

CHAPTER 3

"Mmm! Roast dumplings and onions.''

Tressalara inhaled deeply. After failing to obtain a horse and taking many detours to avoid Lector's troops, she had needed five days' to reach the edge of the Mystic Forest. She was cold and tired and hungry. She hadn't eaten since the previous afternoon, when she'd tumbled into a stream and lost her last morsel of bread and cheese, and her empty stomach grumbled. To make matters worse, her boots were still not dry.

The glowing lights of the tavern at the edge of the woods, and the tantalizing smells emanating from it, drew her closer than was wise. The forest was ancient, and little sun penetrated through the thick leaves, but there was scarcely any vegetation to camouflage her movements here.

The tavern was filled with men in leather vests and worn clothing. Their prominent cheekbones and light eyes marked them as strangers to Amelonia. Highlanders from the border, if she was any judge. Dangerous men, like the outlawed Cador of Kildore, who raided the borderlands and whose name was used to frighten mischievous children.

Tressalara hugged her arms to herself against the chill. Toward morning she might double back to the castle's stableyard through one of the secret ways. Old Philbin would surely outfit her with a cloak and blanket, saddle and tack and one of her own horses. Meanwhile, she had to find a safe place to sleep for a few hours and some food to warm her belly.

She had thought that she might find shelter in a farmhouse, exchanging chores for a night's food and snug lodging in the hayloft. Instead she was turned away time and again: too skinny, too soft, too young. Of course her dirty and disheveled appearance didn't help the situation.

But those were not the true reasons, she knew. Lector's spies were everywhere, and strangers were suspect in these unsettled times. It was not so much the doors slamming shut in her face that had wounded Tressalara to the quick, but seeing the fear and suspicion in her subjects' faces.

Amelonia was not the happy kingdom she had always thought it to be. She realized that her people's troubles had not grown in only five days. As her father had aged and withdrawn into his personal spiritual quest, Lector had abused his authority. Now that he had usurped control of the kingdom, fear of his retribution had placed a stranglehold upon the land.

Tressalara ground her teeth. She would do everything in her power to vanquish him, even at the cost of her own life. If only she could have reached the Andun Stone before she'd had to flee! With it she would be invincible—if she could only learn the secrets of its powers. Unskilled attempts to use them would result in a terrible death. One of her first objectives would be to get the magic crystal into her possession before Lector found its hiding place. Tressalara's determination was strengthened by her discoveries of his wickedness.

She had gleaned enough information from the various bits and pieces she'd overheard to know that a ragged group of rebels lived in the Mystic Forest, and that their numbers were growing. If she could reach them, all her immediate problems would be solved. But if she meant to gather a true army to lead against the usurper, she must first see to herself. That meant food now and shelter later.

Taking a deep breath, she crept through the trees toward the tavern.

Inside the Crown and Acorn the air was dim and smoky from the torches and cookfires. Frequented by merchants and travelers, as well as people from the nearby farms, the tavern was always busy. Tonight it was as full as it could hold. Several men with the look of highlanders sat near an open window. Their leader, a lean, hawk-faced man with tousled hair like spun gold, sat slightly apart from the rest. Rough clothing hid his hard warrior's body but could not disguise his air of command.

At the moment all his attention seemed focused on his trencher of food. He tore off a tasty bit of roast fowl. "Have an eye to the fellow in the russet cloak, Brand. Chain mail hidden beneath his padded tunic."

His older companion, a husky fellow with a soldier's build disguised by simple woodcutter's garb, lifted his tankard for a quaff of ale. "Aye, I've been watching him, Cador. King's man."

"No. *Lector's* man." Cador leaned forward casually and lowered his voice. "I have an informant inside the castle walls. He says that King Varro is not ill, but dead at Lord Lector's own hand. The usurper intended to marry the princess and claim the throne in his own right. Now, my man reports, the princess is missing. Rumor says that she changed herself into a bird and flew away."

Brand made a surreptitious sign to ward off the evil eye. "By Saint Ethelred's toes, I cannot fathom why you want to mix in our business."

Cador's face hardened to stone. *"Do you not?"* His vision dimmed, clouded by memories of returning to his lands to find most of his family slain in one of Lector's border raids.

Before his companion could reply, Cador gestured for silence. He lounged back against the wall beside the window frame, seemingly at ease, But his light blue eyes held a glint that Brand recognized. His own hand moved instinctively to the sword hidden beneath his patched cape. Cador had some trick up his sleeve.

The window was so close that Tressalara could almost touch it. Her mouth watered at the sight of the trencher just inside. Succulent roasted meat dripped hot juices into the thick slab of bread beneath. It was too tempting to resist. Quick as a flash of light, she reached out and stabbed a large chunk of meat with the tip of her knife.

Quicker even than that, an arm shot out, and a strong hand clamped around her wrist like an iron band. It jerked her forward, and another hand grasped her other wrist. As she fought to squirm free she was inexorably drawn across the windowsill to sprawl on the trestle table inside. Brand relaxed. No danger was likely to come from this hungry little knave.

Cador inspected the dirty urchin with peeling, sun-reddened skin and stained clothing. He smiled wryly. "Well, well, what a scrawny little fish I have reeled in."

Tressalara uttered a curse she hadn't realized she'd even known and struggled upright. "Unhand me!" Her wrist ached, but she could not pull free from her captor.

Her tone of defiance surprised Cador. He hadn't expected it from such a young and slightly built boy. Grabbing Tressalara by the shoulders, he forced her up against the wall. "Do you know what the penalty for petty thievery is, lad?"

Although she sensed the danger in him, she glared back defiantly. "Aye. Ten lashes with a knotted whip."

He frowned. "Your information is long out of date, stripling. It is the loss of the offending hand."

Tressalara opened her mouth to protest. Then she read the truth in his eyes. How had matters deteriorated so desperately? "*Lector* again," she spat.

Instantly Cador's hard hand covered her mouth. "Watch your tongue, lad, or they'll have that, too!"

Tressalara was unable to move. It wasn't fear or even the strength of her captor that held her in thrall, but his aura of masculine presence. Her heart banged against her ribs, and her knees felt wobbly. It took her breath away. She had never experienced anything like it before. Her helplessness transformed itself into anger.

He pushed her toward the bench. "You interest me. Sit down and tell me your name . . . and why a healthy if somewhat spindly youth has to steal his supper rather than work for it. If I like the answer I will buy you a meal."

All Tressalara's desire for food was momentarily forgotten.

She bit her lip, trying to obliterate the tingling memory of his firm and calloused palm against her mouth. By the saints, the man was strong! She took in a breath and let it out in a rush. "My name is Trev. I tried to find work. None would hire me for fear I was a spy."

At Cador's signal, a tavern wench came over, bearing another trencher overflowing with meat and dumplings. She set it before Tressalara. "Looks like 'e could use some fattening up."

The enticing smell of the food almost brought tears to Tressalara's eyes. Her stomach rumbled so loud the others heard it. She was mortified. Cador leaned down, a flicker of laughter in his eyes.

"Hungry? Help yourself. Oh, but one little question first."

Turning his back to the room, Cador picked up her fallen dagger and stuck it into the table. It quivered in the wood, light reflecting from the golden hilt and the cabochon amethysts engraved with dragons.

"An interesting bauble for a starving lad. And rather inappropriate under the circumstances. I imagine it is worth a good deal."

The tension was thick. Tressalara had no choice but to tell the truth once more and hope she was believed. "It belonged to my mother," she said with quiet dignity. "A gift from the king."

Cador tipped back his head and laughed. "An unlikely story, yet I somehow believe you."

Brand rubbed his chin. "And I. Though who would have thought it of Varro. The man appeared too devout a husband to keep a doxy on the side. He seemed besotted with his lovely queen."

Tears of rage and loss sprang to Tressalara's eyes. She coughed, pretending it was the smoke of the hearth fire. She dared not defend her innocent father's reputation, though, or it might make them question her identity further. Cador clapped her on the back, far harder than she deemed necessary.

"Eat up, lad. You have earned your supper. I have need of a quick fellow to help care for our horses. Would you be interested in joining us? We offer plenty of food, a few coppers for your purse, and enough adventure to fill a dozen scrolls.''

She hesitated. Perhaps she could use the situation to her advantage. She could hide in plain sight, keep an ear out for news of her adversary, and try to discover loyal supporters for her cause. No one would suspect that a humble groom was the missing princess.

''The lad looks too soft and puny to ride all day and sleep on the hard ground at night.''

She fixed Brand with an angry look. ''I can ride like the wind!''

''Oh? And where is your horse, then?''

That silenced her. Cador looked amused.

Brand set down his tankard again. ''What a shame that the Princess Tressalara has fled the castle, Cador. Otherwise you might have used your fabled charm and had a feather bed to share with her this night, instead of a flea-bitten mattress at a common inn.''

Tressalara went rigid. *Cador!*

There was only one man by that name: Cador of Kildore. Her first reaction was shock to find herself sitting beside the outlaw reputed to be the most dangerous man in the Four Kingdoms of the West. The insult to herself registered a few seconds later.

The outlaw chief laughed at Brand's quip. ''Perhaps it is just as well. I prefer a more winsome and willing tavern wench to the crown princess. Word is that she has the temper of an angry wasp and the face of a troll!''

Stung, Tressalara set down the tankard of ale that she'd been served. ''You are wrong, sir. I have heard it said that the Princess Tressalara is a gentle and comely maid.''

Cador slanted a look her way. ''Yes, lad. And pigs fly.''

''But she is still the rightful ruler of Amelonia,'' Brand said quietly. ''Lector will never sit upon the dragon throne.''

His words, which fell into a sudden silence, the sign for which the spy had been waiting. The man in the russet cloak jumped up, sword drawn. ''Death to Cador and the rebels!''

At his signal, Lector's men-at-arms stormed into the inn,

and a wild melee broke loose. Tressalara had no time to see more than Cador and Brand lunging across the room, weapons in hand. Quick as a wink she was out the window and running for the stables.

She said silent thanks to Jeday and her old groom for teaching her to be resourceful. The second stall held a fine mare, a roan with a white blaze on her forehead. The bonus of a black and silver cloak in the saddlebag was a pleasant surprise. She threw the saddle and bridle on with ease of practice and tightened the girth, then swung herself up.

Cador and his men had found reinforcements in the others at the inn. Lector's men were being pushed backward to the door, but it was an unequal fight. More of Lector's troops were pouring out of the woods. Cador and his men were doomed.

Wisdom urged her to flee toward the main road. Something else turned her back toward the inn. Tressalara convinced herself it was the opportunity to do Lector a bad turn—and if the usurper was busy fighting outlaws, he would have less time to concentrate on finding her.

Wrapping the black and silver cloak around her, she rode up to the front door, where a soldier stood guard against any escapees. "Ho, there! I am a courier sent by Lord Lector. Follow me!" she shouted. "The Princess Tressalara is escaping on horseback along the river road! All troops are enjoined to capture her!"

Round and round the inn she rode, calling out her "news." Their captain, hearing her cries, called retreat. They scrambled to the wood where they'd hidden their mounts, then rode off after Tressalara.

It had been years since she'd ridden through the Mystic Forest, but Tressalara's memory was excellent. She led Lector's troops a merry ride through myriad twisting paths, luring them ever deeper and doubling back until they were totally confused in the darkness.

When they were hopelessly lost, she dropped back and threw off her cloak, then grabbed the branch of an overhanging tree. Her riderless horse ran on. She clambered over to a wider limb and sat hidden in the foliage, her legs hanging free. She was worse off than ever now, for the soldiers would recognize her face if they spied her again. Her hands were scraped from the bark, she had no place to go, and an army was looking for her.

She had never felt so alive.

At the sound of approaching hooves from the road behind her, she drew her legs back up and waited breathlessly. The rider reined in beneath her. Moonlight filtering through the dense leaves showed a hawklike face haloed by golden hair. *"Cador!"*

"You are a fool, young Trev, but I have never known a braver fool!" He held out his arms for her to jump. "Come. There is no time to waste."

She hesitated, but sounds from near at hand told that Lector's men were returning. Tressalara jumped.

He caught her easily in his strong clasp, wheeled his midnight-black horse about, and set off at a gallop. She felt secure and sheltered, protected by his presence, despite their peril. He seemed to know the forest well, running through the velvety stretches beneath the most ancient trees and avoiding the scrub and brambles under the younger growth. Then they reached the open meadowlands deep in the heart of the woods.

Urged on by Cador, the great gelding flew across the wild heath as if it had wings. Tressalara's blood sang with the excitement of adventure. Every sense was alert, and her whole body tingled. In the distance, light reflected off the dark waters of Mystic Lake, the place where legend said the Andun Crystal had been found in ages past. As they neared, a luminous mist rose from the lake's surface, trailing like gauzy veils along the ground. The black trees sighed and whispered. Tressalara could almost tell what they were saying.

Her journey with Cador took on a dreamlike magic as they raced beneath the stars. She didn't want their wild ride ever to end. Cloaked by night and moonbeams, temporarily insulated against grief and weariness, she would have been perfectly content to continue on this way to the ends of the earth.

The heat of Cador's hard body seeped into hers, warming her against the chill night air.

Encircled by his strong arm around her waist, pressed by the force of their speed against his wide chest, Tressalara should have felt safe, at least for the moment. Instead she had the uncanny feeling that she had never been more in danger.

CHAPTER 4

The apprentice sorceress Niniane stepped back from her gazing ball in satisfaction. "I must say that went very well!"

Illusius preened. "I told you that Cador would save the day."

"Cador? It was Tressalara who saved him and his men from the soldiers. Without her—and my magic—they would all have been lost."

The apprentice wizard drew himself up to a great height until he seemed to fill the cavern from floor to ceiling. "Enough of your boasting!"

"Are you trying to frighten me?" Niniane waved her arms and turned into a spinning wheel of flame. "Let us see who is the greater magician, then!"

Not to be outdone, Illusius changed to a whirlwind and blew her flames out. Jars rattled on the shelves and fell to the cavern's floor, spilling exotically colored powders across its width. Niniane was too incensed to notice. She became a great wave of the sea and swept the whirlwind right off his invisible feet. Illusius grabbed at a shelf and pulled it down in his wake. Bottles and flasks broke open on the floor, and sparkling liquids mingled with the powders to produce a burgeoning foam.

Niniane reformed and scrambled to separate the items. She bumped heads with Illusius in her haste. "Oh, no! My love potions! My hate potions!"

He was just as agitated. "Oh, no! Not my *shape-changing* powder! *Watch out!*"

The warning came too late. A flash of light, a clap of thunder, and a violent explosion shook the Caverns of Mist. Crystals showered down from the roof like drops of rain. A great puff of eerie red smoke filled the air. When it cleared at last, Illusius and Niniane seemed to have disappeared. In the cavern nothing was left intact except for the frozen Myrriden . . . and two large green frogs, glaring at one another.

Tressalara was weary when Cador reined in at the rebel camp, deep in the Mystic Forest. The people in the camp stopped their activities to stare, and Brand scowled from his place by the fire. Cador dismounted and helped Tressalara down. She almost stumbled from tiredness. Excitement had kept her going, but now that she had achieved her goal, she felt drained. Grief and the aftermath of her daring adventures had taken their toll. All she wanted to do was curl up in a ball and sleep.

She was taken aback when he handed her the reins. "See to my horse and gear."

Tressalara bit her tongue. Better to remain in her disguise until she scouted out the lay of the land: For all she knew, these rebels might be inclined to rid themselves of their princess and set up one of their own upon the throne. Perhaps even Cador himself.

Brand threw down the harness he was mending and rose. "You should not have brought the boy here. He is unknown to us, and there is no one to vouch for his loyalty."

His arms akimbo, Cador declared, "I vouch for him! Young Trev has proved himself to be quick-witted, brave, and no friend to Lord Lector. As his actions earlier have shown." He narrowed his eyes. "If you expect me to lead you and your men to victory, Brand, you must trust my judgment—and accept my decisions."

For a moment tension spun out between the rebel leader and the highlander. Then Brand nodded his head. "Very well. We have need of every such one we can muster. But he must swear the oath of secrecy."

Tressalara stepped forward. "I will swear."

Cador drew his sword. "Place your hand on the pommel stone in my sword."

Tressalara reached out to touch the dome of rock crystal that held a jeweled amulet in the center of the sword's hilt. A shock ran up her arm. She stared at the jewel. The glowing opalescent stone in the pommel shone with familiar blue and green and gold lights. It was surely one of the missing pieces of the Andun Crystal.

Besides the original, only one other was known to exist— and its whereabouts were unknown. Tressalara's eyes widened for just an instant before she recovered herself: she was very aware of the sharp edge of Cador's sword inches from her hand and had no doubt that the wrong word now would send it arcing in her direction. She fixed her eyes on the crystal, noticing the ancient symbols carved into its surface: ▼⟨✧Đ✧∅✧

"Do you, Trev, swear that you will never reveal the location of this camp, nor the names of these brave men and women who have gathered to free Amelonia from the hand of tyranny?"

"I so swear!"

"Rise, then, and keep your oath under pain of death." Cador sheathed his sword. "Nidd, show the newcomer around camp. After he sees to the horse."

A sullen boy stepped forward, eyeing Tressalara warily. Along with half the camp, he'd already heard tales of this slender youth's quick thinking and extraordinary riding abilities from Brand. In the course of an evening, Trev had won the unqualified approval of Cador, something he himself had not yet earned. And, he thought woefully, his own fear of horses could not be gainsaid.

"This way," he said curtly, and Tressalara followed, leading the mighty black gelding as if it were a lamb.

Several of the young ladies in camp eyed the two as they crossed to where the horses were kept. Among them was Ulfin, the pretty girl Nidd worshiped from afar. Trev would easily capture her admiration, just as he had done with Cador. Gloom descended over Nidd. He would have to find a way to put this upstart Trev in his place, once and for all.

An idea formed in his mind, but he would have to wait until Cador was gone to put it into action. Meanwhile, he could sow a few seeds as the opportunity arose. He wandered off, leaving Tressalara while she watered and rubbed down the black gelding, then returned to show her the layout of the camp.

The rumor that Princess Tressalara was missing had made its way from one end of the encampment to the other, and opinion was equally divided. Many thought she was hiding somewhere within the castle precincts; the others were sure that she was dead, either by Lector's hand or her own.

Tressalara was cheered at the size of the rebel forces. "Lector's men are better armed," she told her companion, "but your numbers are higher than I would have expected to have gathered together so quickly."

"Once Cador agreed to join forces with Brand, they came from every cot and farm. There are no fiercer fighters from the mountains to the great sea!" Nidd put on his most important-sounding voice. "Cador said his victory would be assured if he could just get his hands on the princess."

Tressalara's heart sank at those ominous words. She lapsed into silence while Nidd rattled on, thankful that she had not given in to impulse and revealed herself to the handsome highlander. It seemed that she'd jumped from the griddle straight into the hearth fire.

But later that night, sleeping on a rug at the foot of Cador's camp bed, she comforted herself. No one was likely to look for her among this ragged band of rebels. As long as she kept her identity secret she was safe here. As safe as she could be from everything except her own emotions.

She listened to the sounds of his breathing. Was he still awake? The urge to confide in him was strong; yet she must trust no one until she had reason to be sure of their loyalty. It seemed that Cador had his own eye upon the throne. If she remembered rightly, he had been outlawed for trying to overthrow his cousin, the Duke of Morania.

And, now that she thought of it, the oath he'd made her swear had been to him and to his people. There had been no mention of loyalty or duty to the House of Varro or the rightful heiress to the throne. No, better to wait and spy out the lay of the land until she knew more.

Cador lay awake long after Tressalara's breathing deepened and she drifted off, but his thoughts were much the same. He'd known her for a female the moment he'd pushed her up against the tavern wall. That had been quite a shock, and it had set him thinking of the missing princess. They were of an age. And her hands, although scraped raw, were soft and white beneath the grime, unused to hard physical labor. Definitely the hands of a lady.

Or a princess.

Certainly she had the coloring of the royal family. She might hide her hair beneath a cap, but there was no disguising those amethyst-colored eyes beneath winged brows. He smiled in the darkness. It couldn't have gone better if he'd planned it. Princess Tressalara, heiress to the throne of Amelonia, had dropped into his hands like a ripe plum.

Now he would have to figure out exactly what to do with her.

CHAPTER 5

In the Caverns of Mist two exhausted frogs squatted on the floor, eyeing one another balefully. No matter how hard they tried, they had each failed repeatedly in their attempts to clamber back up the table to where the huge spellbook lay open. The large, darker frog made one last attempt, only to flop gasping onto its back. The spots on its pale belly were curiously shaped, almost like small stars and moons.

"This is all your fault," Illusius said between gasps, flailing his webbed toes in the air.

"Nonsense," Niniane snapped, hopping fretfully back and forth in short, nervous arcs. Although human time meant little to a wizard's apprentice, she was tired, her jumping muscles ached, and there was nothing to eat but a bug perched on a rock. She'd *die* before she ate *bugs!* It took all her willpower to keep her long tongue coiled neatly in her mouth.

"Oh," she said with a sigh, "how I do wish we'd been turned into something that could fly. At least that way we could reach the table to read the spells and try to figure a way out of this fine mess you've gotten us into. And my poor princess is in terrible danger." An idea came to her. "Illusius! See how that wand is tipped up at one end? If I got on the other side and you hopped on that end, you might be able to flip me up to the tabletop. Then I could hunt through the students' handbook for a spell to free us."

The darker frog hopped over to the wand and examined it. "It might work. But how do I know you'll keep your word? You might just change yourself back and leave me here to *croak!*''

Niniane rolled her big, bulgy eyes at him. ''You'll just have to trust me.''

He didn't move, just waited with his toes splayed out. ''Oh, very well. Hop on.''

Before Niniane had even reached the wand, a curious thing happened. A puff of sparkling smoke twinkled through the caverns. When it cleared, she found herself in daylight, floating in a river's shallows on a lily pad. She was, to her intense disappointment, still a frog.

''What happened?'' Illusius croaked beside her.

''I don't have the froggiest . . . er, foggiest notion.'' She hopped a few feet to the reedy bank and looked around. ''But at least I know where we are—the rebel camp where Cador brought Tressalara last night. Let's find her and see what she's doing.''

Illusius was facing the opposite direction, across the riverbank ''I already have, Niniane. And you're not going to like it one *ribbit!*''

''Who are you calling a pimple-faced boy?'' Nidd shouted. How dare this newcomer try and make him a figure of fun before the others, especially Ulfin.

Tressalara had tried to ignore Nidd's taunting earlier, but things had finally gone too far. For the past two weeks he'd made her life miserable. Today he'd managed to push her into the horse manure, making her spill her morning's allotment of bread into it as well, and now he had splattered Cador's saddle, which she had just cleaned and polished, with claylike mud.

If she didn't stand up for herself now, he would, like all bullies, make her life hellish from dawn to dusk. She stood with her hands on her hips. ''If you have doubts, custard-face, look at your reflection in the river. Better yet, bathe in it. Saints know, it must have been long enough since your last washing, as anyone standing downwind of you can tell!''

She turned away with the laughter of the other young people ringing in her ears. That should silence Nidd for a while.

Instead, there was the unmistakable sound of a weapon sliding out of its sheath. She whirled around like a cat and found
Nidd mere paces away from her, with his rapier drawn. He
lunged at her.

"Let us see how brave you are now, Sir Trev!"

She had only her jeweled dagger. Swallowing hard against
the lump in her throat, she drew the weapon and switched to
an alert, defensive posture.

"Not fair!" someone in the crowd cried. "A dagger is no
match for a rapier blade." The speaker, a sandy-haired older
boy, took out his own weapon and tossed it to Tressalara.
"This will equal the match."

She hefted it and grinned. The balance was perfect, the
blade strong and true. "A fine piece of the swordmaker's art.
I thank you for the loan of it."

With a swish and a flourish she brandished it in the air.
Nidd was too angry to recognize the skill evident in the way
she handled the rapier. But the onlookers did, and they
looked forward to an exciting test of arms. "Have at it,
then!"

Tressalara waited for him to make the first move. Nidd
thrust wildly, and she parried it with ease. He was briefly
startled, then weighed in. Although she was well trained, with
a quick eye and the reflexes of a cat, Nidd's height and reach
gave him a slight advantage.

What she lacked in strength or reach she made up for in
wit and cunning. Tressalara danced away, darted beneath his
thrust, and came up with her blade singing against his. A fast
bit of footwork and she was out of reach again. "Catch me
if you can!"

Time and again she evaded his rapier, laughing at his be-
wilderment. She was proud of the way she handled the blade
and hoped that Cador was watching. It had become more and
more important to her that she truly win his approval.
Whether the stories told of the wicked outlaw of Kildore
were true or not, she had seen no villainy in him—and much
to admire.

Perhaps too much, for as her thoughts slid to Cador, Nidd
gained a slight advantage. She turned her wits to the task at

hand. The angry youth bore in once more, pressing her sorely. He thrust beneath her rapier, only to have his quarry slide her blade along his. He charged in once more, in deadly earnest. By the saints, he'd make this upstart Trev sorry he'd ever set foot in camp!

It took only a few moments for Tressalara to realize that Nidd was not interested in merely besting her—he intended to do her serious harm. Now that she appreciated the danger, she fought back with all the skill she'd learned from Jeday. Her only hope of escaping injury was to let him see that she could hold her own—and more. She led Nidd to give her the next opening, then darted through with a time-thrust, lightly nipping his arm. It had taken great skill to nick him without going too deep, and for a tiny moment she was proud of her control.

Then Nidd staggered back, clapping his hand over his sleeve. The fabric was stained with a small spot of red from where she'd nicked him. How many times had Jeday told her that pride and anger had no place in such a duel? Tressalara lowered her rapier, remorse flowing through her.

"Let us cry friends, Nidd. Come, I will bind up your arm for you."

The look he gave her should have been warning enough, but Tressalara didn't see it. As she stepped toward him, he stood mute, his complexion changing from red to white and back again. To be shown up publicly by this scrawny boy filled him with unbearable shame. The flurry of snickers from the onlookers was like a spear in the side of a maddened boar.

Red mist covered his vision. Nidd stood with his foil half raised, made as if to pull back, then lunged in, aiming for her heart. A gasp went up from the crowd. Tressalara was caught off guard by his cowardly attack. Although she reacted with all due speed, it was too late to fend off the blow entirely. The tip of his rapier slit her sleeve and sliced a thin line of fiery pain up her arm toward the shoulder.

Fear and anger spurred her reflexes. As she was forcing his blade away, another flashed up between their crossed weapons, and her rapier went flying out of her numbed and tingling hand

"Enough!" Cador roared.

He stood before them like an avenging angel, broadsword raised and the morning sun creating a halo around his head. There was nothing angelic about his face, though. It was dark with fury. The princess had almost been killed in a brawl, and his wrath was so great it boiled up in his chest like lava. He could scarcely contain it. Another instant and he might have lost her. Tressalara might have been dead in a pool of blood, and the fault was his. His heart thudded with the echo of fear, and with the first stirring of emotion he did not dare acknowledge.

The onlookers stepped back as one, and Nidd cringed. Tressalara stood her ground and lifted her chin defiantly. Violet lights blazed in her eyes, although her voice shook slightly. "I need no one to fight my battles for me, Cador!"

"And I need no quarreling pups to tear the loyalties of this camp asunder!"

She blanched, but he had already turned away to vent his anger on Nidd. "Nor do I need to count among my followers anyone so dastardly as first to attack an unarmed colleague and then follow it up with a coward's treachery! Nidd, son of Hewel, you are hereby banished from this company!"

He gestured with his shoulder, and two burly men stepped forward, disarmed Nidd, and ordered him out of the camp. The others watched in utter silence. Not a one spoke up in his defense.

Cador faced Tressalara. "For all your slender build, you are a noteworthy swordsman. Your teacher was a master of the art."

"Yes. Jed . . ." She caught herself before admitting that it was Jeday, King Varro's captain, who had instructed her. "My brother Jed taught me well."

Cador's eyes narrowed. Yes, he thought he'd recognized Jeday's techniques in the way she'd wielded that blade to parry Nidd's near-fatal blow. His heart had almost stopped when he'd seen it coming and known himself to be too far away to save her. He imagined the repercussions to their

cause if the Princess Tressalara was murdered while under
his protection.

There were other more disturbing considerations that he
couldn't acknowledge, even to himself. A film of sweat covered his forehead, and a fist of anger still knotted his stomach.
There must be some way he could keep her out of any further
trouble. Inspiration came.

"You need not think your swordsmanship will spare you
from my punishment for brawling in camp, Trev. For the
next few days, while I am away, you will be at the beck and
call of the women of the camp, fetching and carrying wood
and water and performing any tasks they may set you to."

Tressalara swallowed a furious response. She wanted to
protest the unfairness of being punished for a fight she hadn't
sought—but then she realized that she might discover far
more about Cador and Brand's motives among the women's
gossip than she could hope to learn from the more taciturn
men. The women were more likely to see past the facade and
into the heart of the matter. Or the man.

"As you will, Cador."

He smiled reluctantly. "I hope I may always find you so
meek and obedient." From the set of her jaw, he somehow
doubted it. All to the good. The sooner she admitted him to
her confidence, the better.

He touched her arm with surprising gentleness. "I will see
to your wound."

At the contact Tressalara jumped back like a scalded cat.
"Pah! A mere scratch. I'll tend to it myself." Clamping a
hand to her bloody sleeve, she walked away with her head
held high.

Brand joined Cador. "I see your instincts were on target.
The new lad has a cool head and a well-trained arm. I was
never more surprised."

"Nor I!" Cador watched Tressalara's proud retreat. A rare
handful, that one! At least he didn't have to worry about her
while he was away; she could take care of herself. And he
knew where to find her when the time came. Safe, among
the women who cooked and laundered and saw to the mending. He wondered if, later, she would forgive him for that.

Brand frowned as Tressalara swaggered off into the trees. "That lad bears keeping an eye on. He's got the makings of a fine warrior. I would never have suspected to find such skill at arms in a callow stripling."

An odd smile played about the corners of Cador's firm mouth, and he turned away to hide it. "Yes. I do believe that in time we will learn there's far more to young Trev than meets the eye."

It was not far to the riverbank, but the journey seemed to take an eternity to Tressalara. The strain of trying not to wince or grit her teeth against the pain took all her concentration. She was relieved to discover that the wound was superficial and would heal quickly. It would not do to have her sword arm stiff and unresponsive in the days ahead. When the rebel army attacked Lector's stronghold, she intended to lead them.

She knelt on the sloping bank. The river's cold would stanch the blood and ease the line of fire burning along her skin. It would do little, however, to put out the flame that Cador had ignited within her with his casual touch. That had had more effect on her than the deep scratch from Nidd's rapier. In the span of seconds her heart had seemed to stop, then start again, beating doubly fast. Simultaneously her throat had gone dry, and her legs had felt as if they had turned to suet.

Whatever this magic of Cador's was, Tressalara wanted none of it. She had already been in one man's power and would never willingly relinquish control to another again.

While Tressalara bared her arm and bathed it in the clear-flowing water, two frogs watched from among the reeds. "I still don't see how we escaped from the caverns," Illusius croaked in a language that only the wild creatures of the forest understand. "And I still don't know why we're here."

Niniane's eyes were trained on Cador, standing tall amid the busy routine of the camp like one of the legendary heroes from the mists of time. He was looking for Tressalara, while pretending not to.

"I'm not quite certain, either," the sorceress frog replied, "but I'm beginning to get a hint. I just wish there were some quicker way for us to get around instead of hopping. I wish we could *fly*."

She tried to remember the words of the shape-changing spell, but there seemed to be gaps in her memory. Illusius filled in the blanks. Suddenly tiny pinpricks tickled their speckled hides, and they felt themselves expanding rapidly.

Tressalara hadn't noticed any large waterfowl nearby, but a loud flapping of wings rent the air. To her surprise, a brace of birds flashed out from among the reeds and launched themselves into the sky.

Swans. One black, one white.

Lord Lector paced his chamber by flickering torchlight. The ascetic room that had belonged to King Varro was now filled with every luxurious indulgence. Two weeks had passed since Tressalara's escape, and the wizard Rill, brought at great expense, from foreign lands before the coup, had not produced the promised results. The princess and the crystal still eluded Lector.

The first was a matter of outraged pride but also, like the second, a necessity. The need to capture both princess and crystal was great. From all reports, the insurgent army was growing by the hour. His own troops had cowed the countryside with their swift and brutal punishments, but they were not sufficient to counter a full-scale rebellion. Worst of all, according to rumor, Cador, his old enemy, had joined forces with them. Cador, the one man who could bring all of Lector's plans and ambitions to naught.

That was where the Andun Crystal entered the picture. The crystal had been found in the legendary Mystic Lake by Saint Ethelred, King Varro's ancient ancestor, and could be used for good or ill. Its radiance could bring fair weather, good crops, and robust health and prosperity to all. In the wrong hands, it could bring disaster, famine, and plague.

It could also be used to bend the people's will to follow the wishes of the one who commanded its powers. Once it was in his possession, Lector knew, he would be invincible. A cruel smile twisted the usurper's lips. If Varro, that old fool, had spent more time overseeing his kingdom and less time praying on his knees, he would still be alive.

But in order to harness the energies of the crystal, Lector needed Tressalara's cooperation. The Andun Crystal was protected by an enchantment. If any but the true heir to the Dragon Throne touched the crystal, he would be burned to ash. If the true heir held the crystal out to another, however, that person would also inherit the power to hold and to use the Andun Crystal's magic, without suffering harm.

He rounded on the magician angrily. "If you have such powers as you boast of, why can you not discover the whereabouts of the princess?"

The necromancer Rill scattered more ashes into the brazier. A cloud of blue smoke rose up but quickly dissipated. "It is useless. She is under some powerful protection. If I did not know better, I would swear it is the Andun Crystal itself."

Lector cursed. "Perhaps she does have it, then."

"No." Rill was certain of it. "The Andun Crystal is somewhere within the castle walls. But, like the princess, it hides itself from us."

"I *must* have one or the other in my possession to enforce my claim to the throne. I would prefer to have both."

"It is the crystal alone that matters. Marrying the princess would only give you legal title to the crown. The Andun Crystal would ensure that you keep it."

"I have a score to settle with her." Lector's hand went to the lurid wound that scarred his cheek. "Furthermore, Tressalara is sure to know where Varro hid the crystal."

He resumed his prowling, anticipating his revenge with a dark glint in his eye. "We must have Tressalara. Once she is in my power, everything will fall in place. But first she must be found. And that," he growled, "seems a task beyond your gifts, magician!"

"We shall find the crystal eventually."

"Damn you, man! I need it for the coronation; otherwise the nobles will conspire against me. With it in my possession they will have to acknowledge me as their rightful king." His mouth twisted in a bitter smile. "They will have no choice."

Rill leaned closer and whispered in the usurper's ear. "I have prepared for this contingency. When you take your oath, my lord, it shall be upon an exact duplicate of the Andun Crystal that I commissioned."

Lector raised one eyebrow. "And what craftsman created this item of interest?"

The magician smiled. "A dead one. I saw no need for him to live once he had completed his task."

"A wise plan. But only for the interim."

"Oh, but I have another, my lord. One that will lure Princess Tressalara to the castle. Once she is here, I can use my magic to force her to lead us to the Andun Stone." His heavy lids fell to conceal the greedy gleam of anticipation in his eyes. "And then, in reward, you shall name me Keeper of the Andun Crystal, as we agreed."

Lector examined his co-conspirator with distaste. "Are you so sure you can control its magic? Or do you have some bizarre desire to be turned into a heap of smoldering ash?"

"This has not harmed me," Rill responded, pulling a glittering shard from the leather pouch at his waist. It glowed in the lamplight, turning now blue, now purple, now clear, dazzling white. "It is twin to the one owned by the Laird of Kildore and was found on the shores of Mystic Lake. It is a piece broken off the original Andun Crystal, and it has proved its power to cloud men's minds. Did I not use it to keep Jeday and Varro from getting wind of your coup?"

Lector poured himself a goblet of wine and drank it down. "Coincidence. If your shard is so powerful, why don't I have the Andun Stone and the princess in my possession yet?"

Something in the usurper's voice sent a thrill of fear along the magician's spine. He must not antagonize Lector. Not yet. "This small piece cannot work its magic over great distances, but close at hand it is deadly. I shall demonstrate to prove my point. Summon two of your servants, one or both of them expendable."

Snapping his fingers, Lector summoned two of the guards from the far end of the chamber. Rill faced them, the crystal glowing in his hand. He turned to one, said a swift phrase, and the man's eyes became unfocused, like those of a sleepwalker. The magician addressed the other soldier.

"Kill him!"

The second man paled. "Lord Magician, he is my brother!"

"How tragic for you. He is a traitor and is about to assassinate Lord Lector. You will kill him, *now!*"

The man struggled against the magician's spell but was no match for it. He drew his sword with odd, jerky movements of a stick puppet, at the same time struggling to keep the blade sheathed. Sweat broke out on his brow, and it was apparent that he fought the magician's order with every fiber in his body.

Then his vision altered. Instead of his brother's face, he saw that of a stranger. A stranger with his sword poised to strike down Lord Lector. In a flash his weapon was out, and he struck the illusionary assassin through the heart. His brother fell lifeless at his feet.

Lector was astonished. "Effective, but rather cruel, given their relationship."

The smile that distorted Rill's features was most unpleasant. "I shall show mercy, then." He turned to the soldier. "You have disgraced yourself. Fall upon your sword!"

Without the least hesitation, the second man did as he was ordered, spilling his life's blood at the magician's feet.

Lector had gone pale, but his color came flooding back. This was true black wizardry. With Rill's aid, he would soon have everything he desired: the power of the Andun Crystal, a kingdom to rule . . . and the Princess Tressalara to warm his bed. He smiled at the memory of her beautiful face, her slender, womanly figure. Subduing her would give him enormous pleasure.

Until humiliating her no longer amused him. He touched his ruined cheek again. The wound had healed badly. Her death would not be an easy one. And that would give him even more pleasure.

He fixed the magician with a grim look. "My patience is at an end. We must draw Tressalara out of hiding."

Rill hid his fear. "As I said, I have a new plan. You shall soon have the princess in your power, my lord."

"Fah! How can you accomplish what my soldiers cannot?"

In answer, the magician drew him to the window. He opened the casement and pointed to the high tower where Elani and Lady Grette were held captive.

"I shall lay my trap . . . and set it with a bait that she cannot resist!"

CHAPTER 6

Tressalara looked up between the trees along the riverbank as a white hawk circled overhead. "Rossmine!"

She whistled, and the bird plunged down like an arrow to land on a branch beside her. A thin message cylinder was tied to its left leg. Wondering, Tressalara removed it. The tiny scrap of paper bore a symbol like a crown, and three words in Elani's writing: "Beware the trap!"

Relief that her friend had not suffered for helping her escape flooded through Tressalara. So Lector was planning a trap. But what, and when? And what was the meaning of the symbol? A trap for a princess, no doubt.

She must send word back that she was alive and well, and that she had received the message. Tressalara plucked a tiny translucent pebble from the riverbank and placed it in the cylinder. To anyone else it would be meaningless, but when Elani got the message she would understand. In their younger days, Lady Grette used to scold that the princess's escapades were a constant annoyance to her. "By the heavens, highness, some days you are a sore trial to me. Like a pebble in my shoe!" she would grumble.

A sheen of tears came to Tressalara's eyes. What she would not give to turn back time. She watched as Rossmine flew off, wishing that she herself had the power to fly away to the castle and reassure her friends.

Dashing the tears away, she returned to her tasks. There was no shirking on her part. She was willing to do anything, no matter how menial or difficult, to prove her discipline and devotion to the cause of freedom. She must prove to Cador and the rebels that she was capable of sharing their worst hardships—and worthy to lead them into battle.

Tressalara winced as she lifted the water bucket from the river. Years of riding and fencing had kept her strong and supple, but every muscle in her body groaned with fatigue. So much for the idyllic country life, she thought, grimacing again. It was still better than sitting quietly in the solar, trying to learn embroidery—but not by much.

By Saint Ethelred's eyes, she would be glad when Cador returned to camp and her punishment ended. The women were working her to the bone! Dawn to dusk she was at their beck and call without a moment's respite. Fetch this, chop that, clean this one, empty that one, fill yet another. By nightfall she would gulp down her portion of stew, stoke the campfires, and then drop wearily onto her bedroll at the foot of Cador's camp bed and fall immediately asleep.

Only to toss and turn and dream of the highlander. At times they were nightmares, where his light eyes changed to dark, his golden hair to black as he suddenly turned into Lector. Those dreams left her shaken. Did they mean that he was as untrustworthy as the usurper—a greedy, ambitious man who wanted the throne for himself? Or was that only the product of her unspoken fears?

Once, though, she had dreamed that Cador remained himself, and that had been more frightening; for in that dream they had been standing on the riverbank in the moonlight, and he had looked deep into her eyes, caressing her cheek lightly with a lover's touch, pulling her to him and pressing his hot mouth to hers. Tressalara had awakened with a pounding heart, both relieved and devastated to find his bed still empty.

She had used the opportunity of her punishment to pick up gossip and learn more of the enmity between Cador and Lector. Two years before, Lector had led a party of raiders across the border in Kildore. Cador's elder brother and his pregnant wife had been killed, but not in the fighting. They had refused to reveal whatever information Lector had sought and were executed for it.

Tressalara, only fourteen at the time, had not known of the raid. Nor had her late father, who had been ill with a lung fever. But the king should have discovered Lector's perfidy later, when he recovered his health. More proof, she thought sadly, of how her father had turned away from the duties of a ruler in his quest for spiritual answers.

That phase of his life had begun with her mother's untimely death while delivering a stillborn son. That had been the start of his withdrawal. It was all very well to be unworldly, the princess thought sadly, but not when one was responsible for the welfare of worldly subjects.

She wished now that she had paid more attention to affairs of state, rather than her horses and fencing lessons. But then, she reminded herself, she would be Lector's bride now and not a free woman plotting his overthrow. Or dreaming of the outlaw known as Cador of Kildore.

A flush of pink tinged her skin and set her blood tingling. Saints, but she wished he would return!

Sunset turned the sky above the trees to a canopy of flame as Cador and Brand returned to the rebel camp. Though he had intended to be away a day or two at most, almost five had passed. The sentry greeted them with word that all was well.

"A hundred more men from the north have rallied to our cause, bringing arms and goods. More are due to arrive tomorrow."

"Excellent news, for Lector has brought in foreign mercenaries."

He rode down the wide central area between the tents and makeshift shelters. The scene was peaceful, the place orderly. A fat boar roasted over the main fire, and vast kettles of snowroot and wild verris cooked nearby.

Cador's sharp gaze went toward his tent, set off a little from the others. He was disappointed to see that no one was about. Until that moment he hadn't acknowledged that he was eager to see the disguised princess and learn how she had fared in his absence. He hadn't intended to be away so long, and she was a young woman used to silks and satins and many servants, not the hardships of a warrior's camp.

"I wonder how Trev has fared at his labors," he remarked to Brand as they dismounted.

The rebel leader glanced at him. "You seem much taken with the lad. That's the third time you've mentioned him this day."

Cador was grateful that the lurid sunset hid his flush. "It's only that I feel guilty for saddling him with the women's chores so long, when I didn't intend for it to go more than a day or two: I'm sure they've worked him long and hard. And the brawl was mainly Nidd's doing."

His intention had been only to hasten the moment that the princess would confide her identity to him. He had been certain that she would crumble under the unaccustomed work and reveal the truth rather than continue at such menial chores. Perhaps she'd found some ruse to get out of them. She was a most resourceful young woman.

And, underneath the dirt and unkempt garments, a very pretty one.

Cador pushed the unwelcome thought out of his mind. Under the circumstances, he couldn't afford any entanglements. But his thoughts had been full of her during the long nights away from camp. Yes, dirty and disheveled as she was, she had managed to get under his skin.

He made a point not to look for Tressalara until after he had taken his evening meal and the campfires burned low. He didn't refuse when Brand pulled out a bottle of the best Kildoran brandy, which he'd bought as a surprise on their travels. Finally, when he could put it off no longer, Cador decided it was time to turn in.

Pulling the curtained opening aside, he had to admit to a good deal of anticipation at seeing the princess. The tent was dark. She must have retired early. Sparking a flint, he touched it to the lantern that hung from the center pole. Everything was in good military order, polished till it shone, and in its proper place.

Except for Tressalara. Frowning, Cador set out to find her. One of the women walked past the tent as he was exiting. "Where is young Trev? Playing the truant?"

"Not that one! More likely worked to death, the way Kegi has kept the lad hopping from morn till midnight."

"The devil you say!"

"You might find him down at the river. He usually bathes after his chores, although the other lads tease him for it."

Thanking the woman, Cador set off toward the river in the rapidly failing light. He would talk to Kegi later.

There was no sound except the pleasant rushing of water over the rocks upstream, and the sigh of a gentle wind through the treetops. Overhead, a silvery moon sailed on a cloud-tossed sea. Cador stepped down to the edge of the river, where the mossy ground was soft underfoot, muffling his footsteps. There was no sign of the errant princess.

Then his eyes adjusted to the deeper gloom of the heavy tree cover. A pale form glided beneath the moon-spangled waters, like a mermaid from some ancient legend. Then the sleek shape broke the surface, and he saw Tressalara, her bare shoulders white as pearl beneath the velvety cloak of her wet hair. His pulse quickened.

She tipped back her head to wring the water from her hair and began to plait it. Her arms were graceful, her hands quick and sure. Thoughts of water nymphs and magic spells drifted through Cador's head. He was bewitched by her beauty, unable to move as she finished her task and splashed toward the shallows.

With great effort he wrenched himself free of her enchantment just in time to step into the blacker shadows of an ancient pine and avoid being seen. He was still standing there when she finished dressing and came around the clump of trees. Her disreputable cap was pulled down over her hair, but the clothes clung to her damp body, showing its lush curves.

Cador wondered how he had ever thought, even for a single moment, that she was a boy. Too many years on the run, he thought wryly. Too many years spent planning his revenge and trying to forget the pain of his losses, his needs as a man. His terrible and abiding loneliness. The pain, the need, the loneliness melded into a desire so urgent it overruled his iron will.

He stepped out into her path.

"Oh!" Tressalara gasped as if he were an apparition. Her thoughts had been full of him, and now he was here, as if her longing had conjured him up.

His nearness robbed her of breath. For the first time she acknowledged the strong hold he had over her. She couldn't even say a word in greeting for fear of giving herself away. He was expecting Trev, a callow youth—not a young woman smitten dumb by her attraction to a man who was almost a total stranger.

Cador was having his own problems and didn't notice her hesitation. He fought against the overwhelming urge to touch her. But it was imperative that he gain her confidence. If he frightened her now, it would ruin everything. He must keep that thought foremost in his mind, push away the need and longing that could undo all his careful plans.

"I came seeking you. I hear that Kegi has used you ill during my absence."

Tressalara shrugged and found her voice. As long as they talked of ordinary business, she could keep up the pretense. "There is much work to be done for so large and growing an army. I was glad to contribute my share."

She started up the incline, and her foot slipped on the mossy ground. Cador shot out a hand to catch her. As his calloused palm closed over hers, she made a small sound of pain.

"What is it?" His voice was rough. "Are you injured?"

"No. It's nothing."

"I'll be the judge of that." Drawing her into a patch of moonglow, he turned her slender hands palm up. Even in the dim light he could see that her skin was raw and blistered, covered with dozens of nicks and cuts and scrapes. All his good intentions flew out the window. Lifting her hands to his lips, he kissed her bruised fingers tenderly.

His mouth was soft and ardent, and the touch of his lips sent her blood racing through her body. Her insides were melting with heat. Tressalara was too confused by her tangled emotions to speak, to even think.

"Forgive me, my lady," he murmured. "Only a rogue would so misuse a princess."

His action sent a paralyzing languor through her body. Then his words sank in. Startled and dismayed, she jerked back. Cador kept hold of her hands, which trembled in his. She tried to recover. "What?" she asked shakily. "A princess? You have been at the ale casks, Cador."

"I am neither drunk nor blind," he answered. "You are the Princess Tressalara, heiress to the throne. You have nothing to fear from me, lady. I have known your secret from the start and kept it. No one in this camp knows your true identity. Not even Brand. It is safer that way."

The pretense was over. Tressalara lifted her head defiantly. "You must wonder, then, to find me in such a sorry state."

The story of her flight from Lector tumbled out. It was a relief to speak of it. In the past week she had almost begun to think that she *was* Trev, that her previous life had been nothing but a dream. The tears she had denied so long threatened to spill over in earnest. She blinked them away and realized that Cador still held her hand.

Her pride and courage humbled him. He had come to Amelonia seeking only revenge against Lector. But here was a woman—nay, a princess—worthy of his loyalty. And his heart. Without relinquishing her hand, he knelt at her feet and fixed his piercing blue gaze upon her face.

"All I have and all I am I pledge to you, lady. I vow that I will dedicate both my sword and my life to your cause. Will you accept my service?"

Her doubts vanished like morning mist on the river. Tressalara realized they had been just as insubstantial, and her heart overflowed with gratitude. "Gladly." A smile lurked at the corners of her mouth. "Even though you are the most obstinate, pigheaded, domineering man it has ever been my misfortune to meet!"

He laughed up at her. Something passed between them in that instant. Cador lowered his head and pressed his lips against the back of her hand. A jolt of sensation shot up Tressalara's arm until it tingled. She felt as if she'd been struck by lightning, and left giddy and confused. She could scarcely meet his eyes.

"Rise, Cador," she said quickly. "Here I am simply Trev. You must not kneel to me or treat me like the crown princess of Amelonia. It would not do. Why, you are not even my subject," she added in an attempt at a lighter note.

"No," he said slowly. "And for that I am profoundly grateful. I prefer to treat you like a woman!"

Drawing her roughly into the circle of his arms, he kissed her thoroughly. His mouth was hot on hers, possessive and demanding. His hands pressed flat against her back, molding her figure against his wide chest.

Tressalara's head swam. No one had ever dared do such a thing before. She should have been angry and indignant, totally outraged at the indignity to her royal person. Instead she melted against him even more, curving her body into his.

Cador knew he was lost then. She owned him, body and soul. Her tiny moan of surrender inflamed his blood. There was no girlish hesitation about her. She was all womanly response, warm and pliant, inviting his ardor. He smoothed his strong hands over her supple back, her neat waist, the womanly curve of her hips as he pulled her even closer. Everything was forgotten but the two of them and the passions they had both fought to deny.

There was no disguising his hunger for her, or her answering need. In another time and place, they would have been more cautious; but these were perilous times, and they were sworn to a dangerous mission. How could they wait and see what the morrow might bring, when neither knew if they would see another sunrise?

Cador slid his hand beneath her tunic and groaned at the softness of her flesh. So perfect, so warm, so yielding to his touch. He knew that, for both of them, there was no going back.

Tressalara arched her throat for his kisses. His mouth was gentle at first, then fierce. She was swept away on the wild winds of desire. She clung to his broad shoulders as he parted her lips, then took the kiss deeper. His embrace tightened until she thought her ribs might break. Or perhaps her heart.

The emotion was so intense that she pulled away a bit.

Instantly Cador released her. His eyes were dazed, like those of a man awakening from a dream. He touched her cheek. "Forgive me. I didn't mean . . ."

She slid her arms up and locked them behind his neck. "Did you not?" she replied huskily. "Then I am insulted beyond bearing, Cador of Kildore. For I have been dreaming of your kiss these past five nights!"

He laughed low in his throat. "If you insist, then!"

He backed her against a tree and tipped her head back, lowering his lips to hers once more. The perfume of her hair, her skin, surrounded him like incense. She was like a drug in his blood, and he could not deny his need for her a moment longer. Slowly, gently, he lowered her to the mossy ground. It was as soft as a feather bed beneath them, as yielding as the boundaries that marked his soul, and hers.

Tressalara twined her fingers through his hair. He smelled of green woodsy things, of leather and heady, masculine sweat. The passion surging between them was like a river in spate, a beautiful fury that would carry her away and over the threshold of womanhood in Cador's arms. She surrendered herself to it, to him.

As he removed his tunic, there was a rustling in the brush along the river path and a soft oath as someone stumbled, but neither heard it. Nor did they hear the retreating footsteps a moment later. It was drowned out by the music of the water flowing over smooth stones and the wild singing in their blood.

While they dallied by the river, Brand went weaving back to camp, shaking his head. Too much of that Kildoran brandy, no doubt. He could have sworn that was Cador and Trev by the river. He lifted one of the water buckets and upended it on his head. It didn't help. The rebel captain blearily sought out his tent with the intention of avoiding any more of the potent Kildoran liquor—and the conviction that the morning would bring him one hellacious hangover.

But two swans drifted placidly along the river, listening to the murmur of love words and the reassuring chirp of crickets. They found a safe place for the night among the reeds downstream. The black swan snapped at a bug, missed, and settled his wings.

"Very impressive," Illusius acknowledged. "Your love spells must be potent indeed."

Niniane arched her white swan's neck in pleasure. "I cannot take the credit. This was no spell of mine, but a human one, as old as time."

CHAPTER 7

The next two weeks brought nights of sweet passion for Tressalara in Cador's strong arms, and fresh hope for her cause as well. Word that the princess had escaped Lector's clutches and was in safe hiding had spread throughout the land. Dashed spirits lifted, and a new courage kindled the people's hearts.

The growing influx of rebels forced Lector's men to retreat to the very edge of the Mystic Forest. They huddled shivering around their fires by night, whispering stories of strange enchantments they had seen within the woods, such as caverns of ice impenetrable to man and a pair of talking swans.

Once more the caravans of merchants traveled along the dusty highways, and life resumed its normal tone in the forest. When Cador next rode out to the Crown and Acorn with Brand, he took Tressalara with him. Not at his wish and not without an argument.

"You cannot mean to leave me behind again," she had said when they were sharing a private moment alone, her finger trailing a line of fire over the hard muscles of his chest. He had groaned with pleasure, still sated from their lovemaking. She slanted a glance from beneath her lashes. "Since you have sworn allegiance to me, you are sworn to abide by my wishes."

Cador had groaned and taken her face between his hands for a passionate kiss. "Would that I had never given my pledge, sweetness. I would never have wanted to risk your safety; but now that we are lovers, I find myself singularly reluctant to let you risk your pretty neck in even the slightest way.''

''You are as stubborn and hardheaded as a mule!''

''Good,'' he replied. ''Then you will see it is no use arguing with me.''

But she had insisted, and he had been swayed, against his better judgment. The tavern had become their unofficial headquarters now that the area was secure. It was safer to meet and appraise new recruits and offers of aid there than to take the newcomers into the secret camp and risk betrayal.

He justified taking her along by thinking that he might hire a room for the night so that he and Tressalara could share a mattress instead of a blanket on the ground. As they wound their way through the forest, he began to feel quite cheerful about it.

There was no sign of trouble at the Crown and Acorn, and they had a hearty meal washed down with tankards of the landlord's best brew. A delegation from the southern meadow dwellers came, pledging their support. Late in the afternoon a most welcome message arrived from Morania, saying that the duke would consider sending reinforcements and arms if the princess were indeed alive.

''Bring me paper and ink,'' Tressalara ordered and immediately wrote a response, sealing it with candle wax and an impression of the signet ring, that she wore on a thong about her neck. She hoisted her tankard in a toast. ''To the swift arrival of the duke's men,'' she said, ''and to swift victory!''

A few more toasts had them feeling mellow and relaxed. Brand went out to meet with one of his contacts. Tressalara put her boots up on the bench and dreamed of an early supper followed by a hot bath before a fire, while Cador merely dreamed of a long and cozy night in a feather bed, with Tressalara in his arms.

Then Brand returned. His heavy brows were drawn together alarmingly, and the message he bore shattered their peace. ''Lector has found the Andun Stone. He plans a great reception in seven days' time, to which he has invited all the nobles and emissaries of the surrounding lands. He has vowed that he will hold the crystal aloft for all to see and name himself true king.''

"Evil news, indeed, if he has found the Andun and can touch it without being consumed. I suppose it was naught but a legend," Cador said, frowning.

Tressalara was dismayed. "I have never seen anyone but my father hold the crystal. The legend cannot be untrue. Indeed, all my life I was warned that even I could not touch it until the day my father handed it to me in solemn ceremony, or risk being consumed."

"A fairy tale for children and peasants, like most legends," Brand said. "A pity. It would have solved all our problems if Lector had been reduced to a pile of smoldering ash!"

"A pity, indeed," Cador replied grimly. "We must strike sooner than you had anticipated, Brand."

"Yes. But this grand reception will supply us with the perfect opportunity."

Tressalara looked from one to the other. "But . . . can you not see? Surely this is a trap!"

Cador shrugged. "Of course it is. But we will find a way around it and twist the scorpion's tail to sting itself."

She was unconvinced. "Perhaps the best plan is to avoid his trap entirely. Launch the attack later, when his guard is down."

Brand leaned forward and whispered something in Cador's ear. Their two glances flicked at Tressalara and away. A dull knot formed in the pit of her stomach. "You must not have secrets from me," she said with quiet force. "What new outrages has Lector committed?"

A muscle ticked at the corner of Cador's jaw. "He plans an entertainment for the people, to take place at dawn following the feast: the execution of your loyal servants. Beginning with the Lady Grette and the Lady Elani."

He'd expected an outcry of anguish from Tressalara. She went icy pale, her eyes huge pools of fear and rage and grief; yet she managed to hold her emotions in. In her quiet dignity she had never looked more royal. She was not Trev, or even merely the Princess Tressalara. She was truly Amelonia's queen.

As Cador acknowledged for the first time the great gap that lay between them, he had never loved her more, nor realized how hopeless that love was.

"Then we cannot delay. We shall go with your plan," she said firmly, "and commence our attack during the grand reception." She shifted the tankards and bread rolls on the tabletop to indicate the castle. "While you and Brand mass the troops here along outside the wall, I will take a party of soldiers and . . ."

Cador was appalled. "You will do nothing of the kind! Do you think I would let you risk your life? No, you will be safe in our hidden camp until Lector and his men are vanquished."

"I will not!" She rose and placed her hands on the table, facing him. "If I were a prince rather than a princess, you would let me ride to battle at your side. Indeed, you would think me a coward if I did not insist on leading my subjects." Her eyes flashed magnificently. "Well, I am no coward, Cador! As Amelonia's future queen, I claim my right to lead my people!"

Cador rose, too, towering over her with the width of the scrubbed planks between them. He was caught in the white heat of fury. Princess she might be, but she was still his love, and under his protection. And she was not trained to combat as he had been. "Do not pull rank with me, *highness,* or I will tie you to a tree until this is over! As it is, too many will die trying to breach the castle walls! There is not one good reason for you to risk yourself in this venture, and I forbid it!"

Tressalara was every bit as outraged. "You have no authority over me, Cador. And I have *every* right!" She struggled with her anger. "You refuse to listen to reason, and my presence is vital to the plan. There will be no reason to breach the gates, with all the loss of life that entails. I can get them opened for you—from inside."

"You are naive. Those loyal to you are either dead or Lector's captives."

"I see how little you think of my intelligence." Her frustration burst out in blistering fury. "By the saints, when I am crowned queen of Amelonia, no man will tell me what I may do or not do!"

Cador's face went hard and cold, as if a door had shut. "Yes—when you are queen. For now you are merely another rebel in hiding."

The ice in his voice tempered her anger. She struggled for control. "I am also the key that will unlock the puzzle for you. I know a secret way into the castle and I know every hidden passage within its walls."

A cold fist squeezed Cador's heart. There was truth in her statement. She did indeed hold the key. By wounding her pride, he had pushed her too far. He felt as if he had tried to take a step on solid ground and found himself plummeting through thin air. She would not forgive him for it. Nor could he ever again forget that she was born to be a queen, while he was only Cador of Kildore.

Still, he had to try. "For the love of God, then, tell me the way in. I will go myself."

"You are needed to lead the assault," she said coolly.

His anger went almost as deep as his fear for her. "After the way you have taken over," he said bitterly, "I am surprised that you feel you need me at all."

She bit her lip and turned away, afraid to let him see how much she needed him, knowing that he could never understand that her duties to her people must come before everything. Even his pride.

Even their love.

"There is no other in whom I would place such trust," she said simply. "We must return to camp and prepare." The fate of Amelonia rested upon her shoulders.

The three of them rode back through the forest in constrained silence. When they reached the open grasslands by the lake, she spurred her horse and galloped across the countryside, trying to outrun their mutually angry words and their potential consequences. Cador would have to understand that she had no choice. Wouldn't he?

That night Tressalara made up the blankets on the ground

of Cador's tent. He and his lieutenants were planning the best
route of attack once they were within the castle walls. Since
her identity must be kept secret until then, she had reluctantly
agreed to continue in her role as Trev. His anger seemed to
have dissolved, although he had seemed preoccupied upon
their return. She felt that her own anger had been justified,
though she tried not to remember the look in his eyes when
she had defied him. If they were to have only this night and
so few others together before the battle with Lector, she
wanted them to be perfect.

Hours passed, and still Cador did not come to her. She lay
with her head upon his pillow, inhaling his familiar scent and
filled with thwarted yearning. She ached to feel his strong
arms around her, his lips upon hers, and to know that their
heated words had not formed a cold wedge between them.

It was almost dawn when she heard a rustling and called
out his name. It was only faithful Rossmine, returned from
her errand of carrying Tressalara's urgent warning to Elani.

Opening the tiny tube, the princess saw that the pebble
was gone. It had been replaced instead by a tiny pink seed
pearl. She smiled. It had surely come from Elani's ring. That
meant her friend had understood the message. Her heart
warmed.

Then she saw Cador sleeping a few feet away beneath the
trees, rolled up in his heavy cloak. He had slept on the hard
dirt like a common peasant, rather than share her bed. Tressalara turned silently and went back inside with leaden heart,
knowing that whatever had been between them was over.

CHAPTER 8

The black swan flapped onto the riverbank. "I don't understand that stupid human of yours," Illusius honked. "First she wants Cador, then she doesn't."

"Of course she wants him," Niniane trumpeted, pecking at him with her bill. "And she is not a stupid human. After all, she is letting him be what he is born to be. Why is *he* trying to prevent *her* from doing the same?"

Illusius nipped back at her sharply. "You're just as silly as your human. Why don't you just fly off and leave me be?"

The white swan's ruffled feathers stood out like rounded spikes. "Very well, I will!"

Instantly there was a puff of purple smoke. When it cleared, two frogs sat on the floor of the Caverns of Mist, glaring at each other. "Oh, no!" said the darker of the two.

"Oh, yes," replied the Niniane frog. "Here we are again. But . . . something is different. Oh, look! Myrriden!"

Illusius turned his bulbous eyes toward the rear of the cavern and croaked in surprise. The great wizard was still frozen, but the block of ice that encased him was much smaller than before. A great puddle of meltwater lay over the floor like a quicksilver pool. He hopped closer. "Do you know what I think?"

Niniane sprang up and down in excitement. "Yes, I do! I do. I'm beginning to see a pattern here. Don't you remember before when I said cooperation was the key?"

"*Cooperation?* Oh. I thought you said *concentration*."

Another puff of purple smoke arose, blinding them. When it vanished, the two apprentices were back to their original forms. "Look," Niniane exclaimed, wafting the sleeves of her gown. "You were right, Illusius. Arms! And hands!"

"And lips!" Illusius shouted, whirling her off her feet in his elation and planting a kiss on her mouth before he knew what he was about.

He set her down as suddenly as he'd picked her up. Niniane stared at him, dumbfounded. For once in her entire existence she found herself speechless. Two major revelations in one short span of time were more than any apprentices should have to deal with. They blushed and looked at one another shyly.

"Uh, that was . . . *nice,* wasn't it? Would you mind very much if I, uh, did that again?" he asked.

"Why, um, not at all," she said, smiling up at him from beneath her lashes.

But before they could repeat the experiment there was a tremendous crash from the far end of the cavern. The apprentices jumped guiltily and turned toward the source of the sound.

On the night of Lector's reception, the sunset sky was like a lake of bloody fire over Cador's new camp at the forest's edge. Several of the rebels took it as an evil omen and made the signs to ward off the evil eye. Cador and Brand exchanged signals. It was time.

As the rebel chief barked out his orders, Cador went to his tent where Tressalara was dressing. When he first swept the flap aside, she was perched on the edge of his camp bed in a circle of light from the lamp, brushing her waist-length hair. It gleamed like skeins of red-gold silk. A long, slitted tunic of gleaming white silk shot with gold threads pooled around her on the mattress, and a pair of silvery white kid boots lay beside her dainty feet.

He drew in a deep breath. Cador knew he would remember this sight as long as he lived. Tressalara, with her hair like flame, sitting on the bed where they had made love only days before. Now it was almost like something he had dreamed. And, like all dreams, it had ended with the waking realization that it had been just an illusion. The gold and amethyst coronet that she wore upon her brow, emblazoned with the dragon symbol of the royal house, was proof of that.

As he entered, she looked up and caught her breath. He was so handsome in his armor of embossed leather and chased steel, so much the fierce golden warrior who had stolen her heart that Tressalara knew she would never forget this moment. The bittersweetness of it pierced her like a sword—for good or ill, it was the last time they would meet like this.

She wanted to tell him everything that was in her heart, but the stony look on his face made her forget the words she had practiced so carefully. His eyes, glowing with blue fire, melted her very bones. She remembered when they had blazed with desire for her, and felt her body respond to the memory. If only she could step into his arms and lose herself in his embrace once more.

But it was not to be. Her rank, his pride, and their bitter quarrel had driven a wedge of steel between them. Not even the passion they had once shared could overcome it. Now he addressed her only as Amelonia's future queen. Since their quarrel he had not once called her by her given name, much less touched her.

It was Cador who broke the silence. "At the risk of drawing down your wrath upon my head, I will ask you one more time, your majesty. Will you let me send you to a place of safety and go to battle myself in your place?"

Her face was pale in the lantern light. "And at the risk of invoking your wrath, I will repeat: My place is in the midst of the fight."

He started to reply, then stopped. It was no use. "Come, then. Let me present you to your army."

She twisted her mass of hair into a neat chignon at the back of her neck and held it in place with two ivory pins. The moment of truth had come. She was no longer young Trev, or even a lovelorn princess with a broken heart.

From this moment on, she was in all respects Amelonia's uncrowned queen.

The future held either death or glory.

Brand had assembled his men for an announcement. "When it comes time for battle, every man needs a symbol to remind him of what he is fighting for and what he stands to lose."

At Brand's signal a banner was raised. "Here is our standard. This white dragon you all recognize as the symbol of Amelonia's royal house and the true heir. Added to it now at the behest of the Princess Tressalara herself is this oak tree, symbol of the freedom to which every man and woman and child in this kingdom is heir."

A cheer went up from the throng. Brand stilled them with a raised hand. Cador stepped into the torchlight, leading a figure costumed in a long white tunic with flowing sleeves. She held a glittering sun mask on a gilded rod before her face, such as noblewomen used on state occasions. A hush fell over the assembly. In the stillness that followed, a great white hawk speared down from the highest tree to perch on the white-garbed woman's arm. A frisson of excitement went through the crowd.

Tressalara peered through her mask at the mass of rebels gathered in camp. The new banner, which she had designed and stitched herself during the past five days, stirred in the breeze. It gave her a strange thrill of pride, yet humbled her at the same time. She had baptized it with her own blood— and it had been worth every knot and curse and needle prick. Cador took the mask from Tressalara's hand.

"Behold, men and woman of Amelonia! I bring you another symbol, a living one this time, hidden for safety in our midst for lo, these many weeks. Behold your princess, soon to be crowned your queen!"

Tressalara stepped forward into the glare of the torches. Not a one recognized the disheveled boy Trev in the elegant woman she had become. A murmur arose from the crowd, like the whispering of a mighty wind through the ancient forest. Singly and in groups, the assembled rebels sank to their knees in homage. Then the sound grew, a low, throaty rumble changing to a mighty roar.

"Long live our royal princess! Long live Tressalara! Life and victory to our noble queen!"

Brand swung up onto his horse. "To arms, then!"

As he rounded up his men, Cador readied to help Tressalara mount a fine black mare. Once she had thrown her dark-blue hooded cloak over her shoulders she would be almost invisible in the night. He stopped and drew his sword, then nicked his palm. "My life's blood for you, lady. I swear it."

His words chilled her. "I would rather that none of yours was spilled in any cause," she replied shakily. "Guard yourself well, Cador." *My love.*

He didn't reply, only wiped his hand and prised out the dome of rock crystal set into his sword pommel. He removed the amulet inside. She saw that it was suspended from a fine chain. It caught the light with a flash of luminous fire that reminded Tressalara of the great Andun Crystal itself.

"Wear this for me," he told her, "to bring me luck. And if I fall, return it to my father, Laird of Kildore."

He slipped the chain over her head. The silver was warm from his touch. Despite the coolness between them, Tressalara felt protected and cherished by his action. "I will wear it proudly, Cador—and pray that my doing so will bring you through this night safely."

There was nothing more to be said. They mounted and rode off through the darkening forest, splitting into various groups that would rendezvous nearer the castle. Tressalara's band went with Cador. It seemed to her that the magic of the place followed them, for everywhere they went the way was smooth and safe.

By cutting through a secret path that Cador had set the men to clearing weeks before, they reached the wooded hills near the castle quickly. Too quickly for Tressalara. This was where three final groups would part ways.

First Cador's men turned off the secret path and started up the ravine that would lead them to their staging point. Although she watched, Tressalara did not see him look back.

One moment he was there, the next she saw only shadows. They seemed to fill her aching heart as well.

Then it was Brand's turn to deploy his men, while a few in costume would go with Tressalara and infiltrate the castle itself. "Godspeed, Brand. May you and your men return in safety."

He touched his helmet in salute to her. "May the angels and Saint Ethelred protect you. God willing, we shall meet again in the great hall at midnight, majesty."

He saw her lips tremble and knew the cause. Poor lass, though she would be a queen, she still felt a woman's heartache. Although their paths would take them apart in life, he knew her feelings for the Kildoran highlander ran deep.

"Do not fear for Cador. Though he takes every risk, he is said to be invincible in battle, as long as he carries his magical talisman with him."

Her heart almost stopped. "His talisman?"

"Aye, the crystal in his sword's hilt. It will fend off death and danger and keep him from all harm."

With that he rode off, leaving Tressalara to stare after him in shock. The crystal that Cador had given her, his protection from death and danger, hung cold between her breasts, like a single frozen tear.

CHAPTER 9

As Niniane and Illusius watched, the block of ice that encased the great wizard Myrriden broke asunder and crashed to the rocky floor. Sparkling spirals of light shot out in all directions, and the crystals that formed the cavern walls rang like myriad bells. The two apprentices were filled with dread: What had their spells wrought this time?

Myrriden stepped from the glittering mound of ice, scowling. "So, you young scallywamps! Broke the flask of Yann, did you?"

His wise old eyes glanced from one to the other as if assessing their guilt. Illusius stepped forward, shielding Niniane from view. He took a deep breath. "It was I."

Niniane joined him, putting her hand on her companion's sleeve. "Do not blame Illusius, Myrriden. Had I not spilled bladderwort and eye of newt everywhere, it would not have . . ."

"Silence!" the wizard commanded, but there was a hint of a smile on his face. "You are not the first of my apprentices to prove clumsy. Nor," he said with a sigh, "will you be the last. But you have evidently learned to cooperate and combine forces, which is the most important lesson at every level of existence. You are now ready for your great test—whatever it might be."

He shook his head, and fragments of ice rained down like diamonds. During the period when he'd been frozen he had suffered the strangest dreams. They seemed to go on and on. "How much human time has passed in my absence?"

The apprentices looked at one another guiltily and shuffled their feet. "Um . . . er . . . ah, about ten . . ."

"Ten hours? A record!"

"Um . . . er, not hours . . ."

"Days, then?" The wizard's shaggy white brows shot together. "By Saint Ethelred's beard! Has it been weeks?"

Before they could stammer out the truth, Myrriden's gaze fell upon Niniane's crystal globe. Earlier it had shown Tressalara approaching the old ruins; now it held the image of a glowing crystal, its natural facets forming a shape very like a dragon.

"The Andun!" Myrriden exclaimed. He looked from Niniane to Illusius. "We will settle this later, for I see that evil had been loosed in the land. It is time for your final test. Remember—the simplest solution is usually the best!"

He clapped his hands and uttered several mystic syllables. Niniane felt her limbs shrinking and looked down to see fine white fur growing up her arms. Illusius twitched his long black whiskers. "Now what?"

They found themselves plunked down in a dark passageway of hollowed rock. Niniane curled her long pink tail. "Oh, *rats!*"

Tressalara led her small party to the ruins of the old fortified tower that had stood for generations near the river falls. The rising wind almost muffled the sound of the water cascading over the rocks. "We will hide the horses here. The entrance is nearby."

She stripped off her cloak, and the others did the same, revealing their own costumes, which Cador had obtained from God only knew where. One soldier wore a fool's motley, two others the court dress of a strange and foreign land. A third had a wizard's silver stars sewn to his dark robe and a turban set with a glittering paste jewel. The rest wore the livery of Lector's men, taken from the soldiers they had slain.

The castle walls enclosed many acres. There were two separate tunnels behind the entrance hidden here, part of the maze of castle escape routes that her mad great-grandfather had planned in case of siege. Who would have expected them to prove useful in a kingdom that had been at peace with its neighbors for two centuries? One led to the main courtyard in the shadow of the stables. The rebels dressed in Lector's livery would exit there. Once inside they would subdue the guards at the entrance, then let Cador's troops in at the main gate and Brand's through the water gate on the river.

The second tunnel ran deeper, to the opposite side of the huge castle complex. Those in costume, under command of Kegi's son Zonel, would continue along it with Tressalara, with orders to infiltrate the great hall and cut off Lector before he could make good his escape. It split off near its end, with one arm running to an alcove near the minstrel's gallery above the great hall, the other into the royal apartments that had belonged to her father. Unknown to the rest, this last was Tressalara's true destination.

Leading this group to a portion of ruined wall, Tressalara felt between the mortar of the giant blocks until she found the hidden pivot point. She pushed against it. The blocks held fast. She tried again and failed. Fear shot through her. The entire plan had been based on her assertion that she could get herself and these men within the walls unseen. If Lector had found the entry and barred it from the other side, Cador and Brand were doomed.

She tried once more, this time putting her shoulder to the stone. It groaned and swung inward. A blast of dank, musty air blew past them, like the breath of some monstrous subterranean creature. Fanglike stalactites hung down from the passageway.

"Follow closely," she warned. "Beneath the castle is a maze of tunnels and natural caves. Many are built to turn back upon themselves. Others are blind ends to trick and isolate any enemy who might penetrate them. If you become lost, your bones might be found a hundred years from now."

The men huddled closer. If they had any doubts about following the princess into the hellish maze, they didn't speak them aloud. "From here on," she said, "there must be complete silence among us."

Zonel nodded and followed her into the black maw with his men, shivering as the block of stone fell back into place behind them. Their unquestioning trust buoyed her up as the darkness engulfed them. Water dripped slowly, echoing through the corridors hewn from living rock.

Tressalara struck a flint. The spark bloomed to flame in the cobwebbed lantern set into a niche. A film of crystals frosted the stone walls, attesting to their great age. Two small creatures, furry and sleek with long pink tails, squeaked and scurried into the darkness ahead. One was white, the other black.

After lighting the tapers that Zonel had brought for each of them, she led on. The way was mossy underfoot, where water had dripped from the rocky ceiling. With every step she wondered if she had made a grave error of judgment and if her stubbornness would prove to be Cador's death sentence. The die was cast. She could only go forward with their plan and pray to God that he might come through unscathed. The alternative was unthinkable. Tressalara shivered. A victory without Cador would save her kingdom, but it would shatter her heart. She would never love any man but Cador, so long as she lived.

At the first branching of the tunnels, the rebels in Lector's livery turned off on their mission. When she finally reached the second branching with the costumed group, Tressalara stopped. "That will lead you to your destination. Our ways part here. You will continue on to the minstrel's gallery without me, and I will rejoin you in the great hall. Take no action of your own, but await my signal."

"But . . . majesty!" Zonel protested.

She stopped him with a look. "There is no need for me to accompany you further. You have your orders from Cador. Meanwhile, I have other matters to which I must attend."

Zonel could only watch helplessly as the woman he was sworn to protect and defend vanished in the opposite direction. If his royal mistress came to any harm and he himself survived, Cador would roast his liver on a spit!

Lector sat alone on the dais in the great hall, watching the revelry unfold around him. The huge rubies in the eyes of the dragon's head carved upon the back of the thronelike chair winked as if they were alive. A servant filled his emerald-studded goblet with more wine, and he lifted it for a drink. The waiting had stretched his nerves like wires. He could feel them like sharp prickles beneath his skin. All the years of planning and scheming had come down to this moment. If Rill's plot succeeded, it would be a moment of great personal triumph. If not . . .

Then Rill brushed aside the curtain at the side of the dais and joined him. "All is well, my lord," the magician purred. "The fair little mouse you wished to lure to your hand has taken the bait!"

Setting down his goblet, Lector rose. "Excellent work, Rill. I shall spring the trap myself."

Tressalara made her way along the passage quietly. Two more turns to the right and she should be in the space between the castle's outer wall and the royal apartments. Ahead, a small ray of light pierced the darkness, and she smiled. She had not forgotten her way through the rocky maze. That light was a peephole into the corridor. She peered through it.

In the smoking red glare of torchlight, two guards flanked the door that led into her late father's quarters. She moved softly down the hidden passage in search of a second peephole that looked into the apartment's central chamber. It was usually closed off for privacy by an embossed medallion on the other side, but she caught a glimmer of light, showing it was unblocked. She was almost afraid to look through it to see Lector's things in place of her father's, to let grief and other emotions cloud her judgment.

When she steeled her courage, she was startled to discover that nothing had changed. The famous battle sword of King Varro I hung from the wall between the tall casements, as it had for two centuries. The same tapestries of lords and ladies a-hunting still hung upon the walls. The same two high-backed chairs, carved with the royal arms of Amelonia, were pulled up to the table where she and her father had once played at games of wit and strategy. A pang of longing for simpler, happier times smote her to the core.

But she must not dwell on the past when her country's future was at stake. Sliding the well-oiled latch aside, Tressalara stepped into the chamber. Unseen, two sleek rats slipped past her booted ankles and wiggled their way into a rolled-up rug along the wall. Two pairs of bright button eyes watched the princess from the safety of their hiding place.

The panel slid closed noiselessly behind Tressalara. Without pausing, she went straight to the hearth. The dragon symbol of the royal house was carved deeply into the central stone block of the fireplace. She traced a finger lightly over the shape, as she had seen her father do, then reached just inside the mouth of the opening and touched a minute lever hidden there. The stone block slid outward with a faint groan.

She hadn't expected it to be so heavy! It took all her strength to remove it. Dropping it would surely alert the guards outside the door. Tressalara set the block down upon the tabletop, then returned to the gaping hole. Pushing back her sleeve, she reached inside.

A sudden sound alerted her that she was no longer alone. She whipped around to find Lector standing in the open chamber door with several men-at-arms behind him. "Well met, Tressalara." He stepped aside to let the guard enter. "Seize her!"

Tressalara went for her dagger but was hampered by the flowing sleeves of her tunic. She had completely forgotten how much they restricted her freedom of movement. Before she could extricate the weapon, one of the guards pounced. As he pinned her arms, one of his comrades relieved her of the dagger.

Lector held out his hand for it. "A pretty toy. Suitable for a pretty woman." He came forward, smiling at her consternation. Lifting her dagger, he pressed its tip lightly against her cheek. "Perhaps not so pretty when I have finished."

Tressalara tried not to flinch when the point stung her skin. Lector laughed. "You have always been proud, Tressalara. Too much so for your own good. Did you think you were the only one to know of mad King Gilmere's secrets? Foolish girl!"

He stepped back and moved to the aperture above the hearth. "The only one I *didn't* know was where the Andun Crystal was kept. And now, fair Tressalara, you have led me straight to it!"

CHAPTER 10

Lector thrust his hand into the dark opening. His look of triumph changed to puzzlement. He leaned further in, up to his elbow, and felt around hurriedly.

"Empty!" he roared. For his troubles he had nothing but a scraped and bloody knuckle. He started toward Tressalara with murder in his face, but Rill intervened.

"My lord, your disappointment clouds your judgment! You will need the girl a while longer. Then you may do with her as you please."

The fire went out of Lector's eyes. "You are right. But what could Varro have done with it? Damn his soul to hell!"

His curse angered Tressalara more than his threat. Fear for Cador and his men gave her sudden strength. She struggled against her captors and almost broke free.

Lector grabbed her arms bruisingly. She expected to be shaken or thrown to the floor. Instead, he pressed a moist kiss upon her unwilling mouth. Although she tried, she could not twist her head to avoid it. When Lector had proved his point, he laughed, his humor restored. There was something about subjugating an unwilling woman that made the prize all the sweeter.

He released her. "Use your wiles on the wench, Rill. She was in her father's confidence. There must be other secret panels we have not yet discovered."

Rill stepped forward, holding his shard of the Andun aloft. Tressalara recognized it at once. "So that is how you murdered my father and overthrew the guards! Black magic." A small, cold smile curved her lips. "A warning, my lords: It is said that those who use the Andun Stone for ill will suffer tenfold for their disrespect."

"It is you who will suffer, and those foolish rebels skulking through the Mystic Forest, with an outlawed Kildoran at their head. When I find them I will crush them beneath my heel. Cador's head shall sit on a pike over the castle gates."

Hope flooded Tressalara's chest. They had been expecting only her, not Cador and his troops. They must have set a guard only on the last half of the tunnel, rather than at its beginning. Perhaps they hadn't even found the particular entrance she had taken. If she used her wits, they might still come out of this alive.

The magician wove a pattern in the air with the shard. A buzzing filled Tressalara's head. Her limbs became heavier than stone. Sound retreated, and time slowed. She felt herself shrinking to a drop of ice far in the back of her brain.

One voice seemed to fill the universe: *"Hear me, Tressalara, and obey. Do you know of another place where your father might have hidden the mighty Andun Stone?"*

Against her will, she found her mouth opening to speak. It was impossible to resist. "Yes . . ."

Rill sent Lector a glance. "You see, even the princess must respond to the power in this small shard, although it works only at close quarters. Imagine what I . . . what *you* will be able to do with both my shard and the Andun Stone in your control!"

Lector was filled with admiration. Perhaps he would not dispose of Tressalara, but keep her on as his queen: subdued to a sweet, kittenlike helplessness by day, released from the spell at night to become a spitting hellcat in his bed. The idea held great appeal.

Once more Rill wove a pattern through the air and addressed the captive princess. "Tell me where I may find this hiding place."

Again she struggled mightily. The crystal that Cador had given her warmed against her skin. It seemed to fill her whole body with heat and light. "There are many . . . places where it might be. Perhaps . . . two dozen or more. Some . . . are difficult to explain. . . . I must show you . . .''

Lector cursed. "Two dozen! We cannot spare the time to search out the Andun Stone now!''

"There is no need.'' Rill leaned closer and lowered his voice. "Remember the duplicate I had made. No one will be able to tell the difference. Shall I bring it to the great hall?''

"Yes.'' Lector relaxed, and the anger oozed out of him. "I was forgetting your wise precautions. You shall be rewarded handsomely for your services, Rill.''

The sorcerer hid his smile. He had his own ideas as to what constituted a suitable reward, and he was sure it was far greater than Lector imagined. He stepped toward the door and almost tripped over a rolled-up rug. Giving it a kick, he nodded, and the soldiers opened the door.

Niniane and Illusius rolled over as the rug hit the wall, pink-clawed feet waving futilely in the air. "It's our tails,'' the young wizard told the sorceress. "We're just not used to them.''

After a few false starts they got the hang of curling their tails exactly right and flipped back on their feet. "The princess! We must follow her!'' They shot out of the rug and into the corridor, where they vanished into the shadows just before the door shut behind them.

Lector and Rill led Tressalara away from the royal apartments. The soldiers followed. There was no need for them to restrain her now that she was under the spell: Anyone seeing her walking docilely between them would imagine that the princess was there of her own free will.

Cador waited impatiently for the signal from the east tower. A cool wind sprang up, and the crescent moon flirted from behind veils of cloud. It was long past time.

According to the plan, those infiltrating the feast were to make sure that Lector and Rill were cut off from escape, while Tressalara was hidden safely away in the minstrel's gallery until after the melee. If the guests inside were still loyal to the house of Varro, they would raise their swords in the rebel's cause. But those in stolen uniforms should have overcome the gate guards and raised the portcullis by now. He should have never let Tressalara place herself in such danger! His trust in her abilities had affected his judgment.

"Something is wrong," he said to his second-in-command. "We should have been inside an hour ago."

Before the other man could reply, the side door of the massive gatehouse opened and a lone figure stole out. Cador recognized him by his way of moving.

Using the shadows, the man vanished from view for several minutes, only to reappear nearby.

"What news?" Cador demanded. "Have all your comrades been seized?"

"Nay," the soldier said, heaving a great sigh. "Only the princess."

A terrible pain ripped through Cador, and a black rage came over him. "I swear by all that is holy, I will free Tressalara or die!"

When he fell, it would be with her name on his lips and her beloved face engraved upon his heart.

CHAPTER 11

For the first time in many weeks, Tressalara mounted the steps to her tower chamber. Lector ordered the door unbarred, and she started to pass through. He took her arm and entered with her.

"I do not put all my faith in Rill's spells, Tressalara. You escaped me once. You shall not do so again."

She looked up at him with her wide, amethyst eyes. "As you will, my lord."

Elani gasped when she recognized her princess and got up from the divan, where she and Lady Grette had been sitting over a game board. "Your highness!" She started toward Tressalara, then stopped at the blank expression on the princess's face and turned to Lector fearfully. "She is spellbound! Oh, what have you done to her?"

"Watch your tongue, wench! I bring you your royal mistress. Prepare her for a feast."

The two women dropped deep curtsies to Tressalara, pointedly ignoring Lector. His face darkened at the slight. "Tomorrow when I hold the Andun Crystal in my hand as I accept the crown, you will bend your knees to me, or you will keep your appointment on the scaffold. Now array the princess as befits my future bride."

Lady Grette gave him a look of disdain. "When you have left the chamber."

He laughed harshly. "There is nothing of the princess that I will not see when she shares my bed this night. If it offends your womanly modesty, however, she may dress behind that copper screen. While I await here.''

Tressalara walked slowly toward the hammered-metal screen. ''The sapphire silk gown with the dragon belt and collar will be appropriate,'' she told Grette in a high, flat voice. ''The matching cape as well.''

She and Elani disappeared behind the screen while Lady Grette opened the wardrobe containing the princess's special robes of state. Her soft hand smoothed out the brilliant blue silk, fluffed out the bodice and sleeves smocked with hundreds of rosy pearls. The long cape was lined with rose satin and bordered with ermine. They had never been worn before.

Tears misted Lady Grette's eyes. This was the gown she had sewn with her own hands, for the day when Tressalara reached her majority. At next year's summer solstice, King Varro was to have handed his daughter the Andun Crystal and named her his official successor to the throne. The noblewoman held back a sob. She would rather see it rent to pieces than used on such a sorry occasion.

Grette opened and shut chests, removing garments of the finest embroidered linen and a silk undergown so delicately spun that it could be drawn through a lady's signet ring. There was a delay when the right slippers could not be found.

Lector grew impatient. ''If the princess is not ready, she may accompany me in her shift, for all I care.''

''One moment,'' Grette said, lifting a golden chain from a jeweled coffer. She selected a collar as well, and disappeared behind the screen, chattering nervously about whether pearl or sapphire earrings would be more suitable.

At last Tressalara stepped out, resplendent in yards of shimmery blue, embroidered with gold thread and pearls. She looked magnificent with the queen's gold and sapphire dragon collar at her throat and the matching queen's coronet upon her brow. The light from the fireplace gilded her skin and her long, shining hair, rippling to her waist.

Even jaded Lector was struck dumb by her beauty. He felt a tightening in his loins. All this, and a kingdom to go with it! Truly this was his destiny. He held out his hand. ''Come, Tressalara. Our guests are waiting.''

She lifted her chin. "My ladies must accompany me to give dignity to the occasion, my lord."

He was too pleased with events to argue, and it would look better to the visiting dignitaries. "Very well."

They traversed the upper corridors and descended the wide, curving stone staircase, past the darkened stained-glass windows and the bright banners of Amelonia's previous rulers. Already Lector had added his scorpion insignia to their ranks. Light from the blazing torches turned the silver threads to the color of fresh blood.

As they paused at the head of the stairs, the trumpeter sounded a fanfare. Taking Tressalara by the hand, Lector led her through the stunned assemblage to the dais. Tressalara felt curiously numb and distanced from her surroundings, yet her heart turned over when she saw the simple wooden box upon the table. Rill was very thorough.

Lector stood and raised her hand. His words were like a distant, mocking echo of Cador's earlier ones in the rebel camp: "Behold the crown princess of Amelonia, soon to be my wife."

A gasp went up from the crowd. Those who had put their faith in her were dismayed. If she had thrown her lot in with Lord Lector, then hope for the brewing rebellion was lost.

Lector took the ruler's chair, its high back surmounted by a huge carved dragon's head, and seated Tressalara in the smaller consort's chair. Then he opened the top and front of a small chest that lay on the table before them. The blaze of a hundred candles and torches fell upon the magnificent crystal inside. Its clear form glimmered with fleeting opalescent colors of purple and green, blue and gold.

A hush fell over the room. All had heard of the magical Andun Crystal, but few had seen it. Its shape did indeed suggest the dragon that was emblem of the ruling house; yet after all the legends of its powers, there was general disappointment among the crowd. They had expected to see and feel a special presence, an aura of potent magic.

A new heaviness came over those who had hoped to overthrow the tyrant. Once he learned to harness the crystal's energy, Lector would be able to destroy any who opposed him with no more than a thought. The House of Varro was dead and vanquished, and hope was dead with it.

Now the House of Lector would reign supreme.

Two rodents huddled beneath the tapestry in the minstrel's gallery, watching the scene below. Servants scurried to and fro with salvers of succulent food. Illusius twitched his tail from side to side. "I don't see what Myrriden expects us to do. I . . . I've tried to run a few spells. They didn't work."

Niniane rubbed her pink paws together. "I know," she said gloomily. "Mine don't work, either. There was a time when I just wanted to pass my sorcerer's examination. Now I just wish we could save our poor mortals. Tressalara and Cador have never been in more danger."

Illusius sat up and sniffed the air. "I have an idea. A *marvelous* idea."

"You do?" she squeaked hopefully.

"Yes." Sniff, sniff. His furry body quivered with excitement. "Let's sneak down there and get some of that cheese, before they eat it all up."

"Cheese? *Cheese*?" Niniane sat up and nipped him on the nose.

Lector signaled for the musicians to begin playing. Beneath the song of harp and flute there was much mumbling and whispering during the feast. Although the princess seemed cool and remote, a strange light shone in her dark-fringed amethyst eyes. She looked vaguely out at the assembled company and gestured oddly in the vicinity of her wine cup.

"See how strangely the princess moves," a thin woman in a spangled headpiece said to her spouse. "Has she drunk too deeply of the wine?"

"Nay, 'tis foul witchcraft," an elderly knight said with more passion than wisdom. "It is plain to see that Lector and his evil sorcerer have put a spell upon her. The day he took power was a black day for Amelonia!"

A pool of silence surrounded the man, and his neighbors pulled away. Others stared fixedly at their plates. A man with drink-reddened cheeks jumped to his feet. "This man speaks treason!"

"Seize him!" Lector pushed back his chair and rose, scattering goblets and spilling wine down the table like ribbons of blood. Instantly several of Lector's men-at-arms stepped in with drawn swords. The unfortunate who had spoken out was dragged to the dais and thrown on the floor before Lector.

Elani stepped back quickly and collided with a servant carrying a silver charger filled with hot food. The tray tipped, scattering sliced beef and venison everywhere. Lector cursed as hot gravy splashed across him in an arc. Simultaneously, Tressalara jumped up with more alertness than might have been expected, given her earlier dazed appearance. Her long cape caught on the carved whorls of the other chair, and she grasped at the chiseled dragon's head to keep from falling.

Lady Grette rushed to help her mistress, while a steward helped Lector wipe away the gravy. At the same moment the serving woman and Elani tangled and went down in a heap. Somehow the brocade table runner came with them, pulling trenchers, goblets, and bowls off as well. Thuds and the tinkle of breaking glass filled the air.

In the confusion that followed, Tressalara's smaller chair was overturned. Servants scurried to repair the damage, but Lady Grette waved them back. The other guests watched the farce, too afraid of their host even to crack a smile. Chaos reigned for several minutes before order was restored.

Lector examined the man imprisoned by his soldiers. His face became grimmer as he recognized the knight. "Your years will not spare you, Sir Tron. Throw him in the dungeon!" he roared. "He will be executed with the others at dawn—an example of the fate that awaits those who dare to speak treason!"

A silence fell over the assembly. Because of it, the sounds of commotion in the outer ward came clearly to their ears. Lector drew his sword. "What is the disturbance?"

Next, a thunderous rap shook the outer doors of the great hall. Everyone froze in place. "Who dares to disturb my feast?" Lector cried out.

Tressalara, her cloak now off, stepped back and away from the dais. Cador's stone, which had protected her against Rill's spell, nestled warm between her breasts. No one noticed, nor did they see that the turbaned wizard, the courtier in blue velvet, and two men in Lector's livery silently followed. As the princess and the disguised rebels made for the musician's gallery, two others moved into position behind Lector.

Again that thunderous rap filled the chamber. The sergeant-at-arms stood before the doors and spoke through the grill as two others hurried to slide the bar in place.

"Who seeks admittance?"

"The army of Princess Tressalara, led by Cador of Kildore!"

In the next fraction of a second the doors burst inward, scattering the soldiers like leaves before a violent wind. A troop of horsemen rode into the great hall with a clatter of hooves and a flash of drawn steel blades. "Long Live Tressalara! Death to the tyrant Lector!"

Lector blanched. There was no time for more. He turned to grab Tressalara and was furious to find her gone. Meanwhile tables and benches were overturned, as those inside took up sides according to their loyalties. As more troops poured in behind Cador, another group came on foot from the corridor leading to the kitchens. Every tunic bore the white dragon insignia of the House of Varro.

The fighting was intense, and the cries of men and shrieks of horses filled the air. Cador had given orders that Lector was to be detained, but not struck down. That was a pleasure he had reserved for himself.

But as he fought his way forward he realized that something had gone awry. Brand's troops should have joined the fray by now, but there was no sign of them. Without them, Lector's men held the advantage. The rebels were outnumbered three to one. Vaulting an overturned table, he fought his way through a phalanx of enemy soldiers toward his adversary. The best way to kill a snake was to cut off its head. If he could bring Lector down, the rest would crumble.

His sword rang out like a bell and struck like lightning as he beat the enemy back like a man possessed. He stood before Lector and raised his sword to parry a vicious thrust.

"We finally meet face-to-face, you devil's spawn! Where is the princess?" he demanded.

A serving woman screamed. Rill waved his crystal and spoke from his hiding place behind Lector's chair. "Did you not hear her cry out just now? By the time you reach her, Tressalara's soft white throat will be cut."

Cador was not aware of the spell of illusion that had been placed upon him. Realizing that the scream had come from the minstrel's gallery overhead, he let his glance dart there. A terrible scene met his eyes. Where there was nothing but a cowering servant and a brocade curtain, he imagined that he saw Tressalara caught in a brawny soldier's grip, wide-eyed with fear as the man's sword bit deep into her throat.

Too late! He had come too late to save his love!

The deluge of despair froze him in place for less than an instant, then was replaced by a cold and determined fury. But that split-second was all Lector needed. His blade flashed as he lunged for Cador's heart.

CHAPTER 12

Niniane was trembling. "Do something, Illusius!"

Illusius had no thought for his sore nose. All his attention was focused on Lector's sword as its slashing tip touched Cador's chest protector, slicing through the thick leather as easily as an arrow flying through air. "Stop!" he squeaked.

"Stop!" said Niniane simultaneously.

A mighty clap of thunder resounded through the great hall, drowned out by the clash of steel upon steel.

Lector's sword caught a metal boss on Cador's leather armor, and the near-fatal blow was deflected. Although the force of it was great, Cador kept his balance, and his blade came up beneath Lector's. He thrust it away and counterattacked. The men were evenly matched in height and strength, but Cador fought like two. He backed Lector into a corner and plunged his sword through the villain's heart.

"Thus dies the traitor who murdered Amelonia's true king!"

"Curse you, Cador . . ." Lector fell, the blade still quivering in his chest. His life's blood gushed out, and he was dead.

Illusius was ecstatic. He dashed around the minstrel's gallery like a mad fox. "We did it! We did it!" He lashed his tail furiously. "But . . . *how?*"

Niniane wasn't listening. She scurried to the very edge of the platform for a better view. "Oh, dear! Oh, dear!" she squeaked. "We must do something!"

Cut off from his men, Cador still fought bravely, surrounded by Lector's troops. It seemed that he would be struck down at any moment. With Rill directing the action, the outnumbered rebels were forced back toward the armory, where they would be boxed in.

Tressalara saw her ladies to safety, wielding her dagger left and right. She longed for her own rapier, which Lector had taken from her. But the situation demanded something more. She ran back to the dais. She must save Cador, save them all. Reaching the wooden chest on the royal table, she held it aloft. The opalescent crystal inside the opened box seemed to capture the light and reflect it back. It shone blue and purple and gold and green, sending rays of glory from one end of the chamber to the other.

"Rill!" she cried. "Call off your men, or I will turn the powers of the Andun Crystal against you!"

Her voice floated over the room with incredible power, and the fighting ceased completely. Rill joined her on the dais. She stood facing him, the box containing the crystal balanced in the palm of her hand.

"Fool of a woman!" he whispered so that only she could hear. "That is not the Andun Stone. It is only carved opal that I commissioned myself. It has no powers."

Rill's mouth curled with derision as his fingers reached out. A crash of thunder shook the air, and a shock of cold fire ran up his arm. Cold changed to incredible heat. The sorcerer was unable to move or breathe.

Tressalara's voice came to his ears as if from a far distance: "You see that I was never under your puny power at all, Rill. There were only two places where my father kept the Andun Stone. One you saw. The other was in the head of the great dragon throne. And you brought me right to it. I switched the boxes earlier, during the diversion my ladies created."

Rill remembered the spilled gravy and the confusion that followed. In his mind's eye he saw the princess standing beside the dragon chair, her long cape swirled across it, with her waiting woman pretending to free it. That was the last thought he had. A towering pillar of flame erupted where he stood with the glowing crystal in his hand. The writhing fire burned so brightly that people shielded their eyes against the glare.

When the flames died, the evil wizard was totally consumed. Nothing left but a pile of ash, a small crystal shard, and the great Andun Stone was left. It swirled with opalescent color, intensifying the ancient letters that were engraved upon its base, that gave the crystal its name: 'A⟡Ñ⟡Đ⟡Ú⟡Ñ⟡.

A sudden cheer and the sound of booted feet from the direction of the kitchens announced that Brand's men had finally broken through. As they spilled into the room, Lector's men threw down their weapons and fell upon their knees, begging for mercy. In a matter of minutes it was over, and the rebels had taken control. A mighty roar went up from the crowd: "All hail Tressalara!"

She stepped upon the dais. "Where is Cador?" she demanded suddenly. Her triumph could not be complete without him to share it. This victory was his as much as hers, she wanted to celebrate the joy of the moment with him. Her moment of glory turned to bitterness. The ranks parted and Brand and their lieutenants came through to lay Cador, pale and bloody, at her feet. She felt her own blood drain from her head. "Dear God in heaven! Cador! It cannot be!"

The rebel chiefs formed a protective circle around Elani and Grette. Tressalara knelt beside Cador and touched his beloved face. Her silken sleeve trailed his blood. His cheek was already cool. All the passion, the intelligence, the lust for life was quenched. His soul had fled. In her horror she would have traded pride and wealth, throne and crown, even her very life in exchange for his. "Oh, Cador, my love!"

The words were wrenched from her. She cradled his head upon her breast, heedless of the blood that smeared her silken gown. Her heart had shattered into a thousand pieces, and every one had Cador's name engraved upon it. A part of her had died with him. She knew that she would never love again.

Her tears bathed his face, handsome even in death, and her lips gently pressed his. His amulet seemed to grow warm against her skin, and a faint flush of life seemed to color his

cheeks. Tressalara lifted her head. Once more Cador was as
still and white as wax.

Again she touched her lips to his, and again a tinge of pink
colored his face. A murmur went through the watching circle.
Another strange thing happened then. Two rats appeared—
one white, one black. They were rolling something along
ahead of them, pushing at it with their naked pink feet until
it touched the hem of her gown. Brand drew his dagger to
dispatch the rats, but she stopped him.

"Leave be! These are surely enchanted creatures."

Tressalara immediately recognized the object by the
strange symbols engraved upon it: Ð✧Ø✧▲. It was Rill's
crystal, yet the signs were similar to the ones on Cador's
amulet: ▼ǐ✧Ð✧Ø✧. Were their powers somehow linked?
There was little to lose in chancing it.

As the princess picked up the shard that Rill had dropped,
the blush of life pinked Cador's skin for a third time. The
blood that had been pouring from his wounds ceased its flow.
The crowd whispered in astonishment. The white rat and its
black twin pulled at her sleeve. Tressalara thought she understood. If these two crystals, so alike in composition to the
Andun, could do this much, what could the Andun Crystal
itself do?

The Andun Stone lay where it had fallen.

The smoldering ashes nearby gave proof of its mighty
power. But Tressalara had not been handed it by her father
and named true heir, as had always been the case before. If
she touched it, without its being given to her by the previous
heir, would she share Rill's fiery fate?

She didn't hesitate. Still touching Cador, she lifted her
other hand. As she reached out for the Andun Crystal, the
courtiers gasped in alarm. Brand stopped her. "Highness, Cador did not give his life for you only to have you risk yours
in this way."

Tressalara lifted her head with royal dignity. "I would not
be fit to govern were I not as willing to give my life for my
loyal subjects as they have been for me."

Brand looked her in the eye, then nodded and released her.
"So speaks a true queen."

Silence filled the great hall as Tressalara again reached out to the Andun Stone. Although there was fear in her heart, it was only for Cador. Her hand did not tremble as her fingers touched the cool stone.

A crash of thunder shook the air, and a shock of cold fire ran up her arm. Cold changed to incredible heat. Tressalara was unable to move or breathe. Then the power filled her, like the light of a hundred suns. It poured through her body and into Cador's.

When the great scintillating light vanished, the onlookers blinked their eyes. One moment their princess had knelt before them, the next a whirling pillar of golden flame had blinded them with its glory. When they could see clearly again they shouted out with joy. Tressalara had not been harmed.

She leaned over Cador and kissed his lips. She felt his flesh soften and warm beneath hers, heard a soft sigh of breath, and saw his eyes flutter open. She thought her heart might burst from happiness.

She raised her tear-stained face. "Cador lives!"

All the bells in the kingdom rang out as Amelonia's princess was crowned before her people. Queen Tressalara stood on the banner-decked platform that had been erected in the meadow beside the river so that all who wished might attend. Noble and commoner stood shoulder to shoulder for the ceremony.

Nearby sat a white-bearded man who greatly resembled certain portraits of Saint Ethelred, the Dragonmaster, watched the ceremonies from a grove of Linden trees. Off to the side, a young couple watched from another bower of trees. Myrriden tugged his beard and looked from his beaming apprentice wizard to his beaming apprentice sorceress and back.

"You have done me proud. Niniane, Illusius, you have passed your wizard's examination. Now for your reward. Behold, by the power that God has invested in me, I raise you to the next highest rank of beings in His hierarchy!"

A plume of sparkling smoke, a waft of incense, and the great wizard was gone. So were the wizard and sorceress. In their place stood a human lad, handsome and dark-haired, and a winsome lass with hair as golden as sunlight. Both seemed a little confused for a moment.

"Ah, don't I know you?" the lad asked. He felt quite peculiar. But perhaps it was just that the smile from this lovely girl was making his head swim. "I'm Ill-, uh, Illus. Son of a Moravian merchant here for the coronation."

The maid blushed prettily. "And I am . . . uh." Funny how for a moment she'd forgotten who she was, just from looking into his dark eyes. "My name is Nin . . . Nina. The granddaughter of the queen's head groomsman."

The lad held out his arm. "Would you care for a glass of fruit ale? Or perhaps a sweet? I saw a vendor with a tray of marchpane over yonder."

She smiled prettily. "You are very kind, sir."

The two moved off, arm in arm, in perfect charity, each feeling as if he or she had known the other for a long, long time.

It was the most beautiful day anyone could remember in years. Sunlight glittered in the clear air, and a fragrant breeze ruffled the meadow beneath the cloudless blue sky. Up on the platform Tressalara stepped forward in full regalia, a queen accepting homage from her people. Her gown of iridescent silk was spangled with diamond brilliance, so that she sparkled with the slightest movement. The emerald crown of Amelonia rested upon her head, the matching seal of state upon her finger, as the cheers resounded.

The great Andun Stone stood upon a pedestal beside her, the three pieces united into one as if it had never been broken. Tressalara held it aloft for all to see, proof of her right to claim Amelonia's throne. A wondrous light shone around her, banishing every shadow. She was a living embodiment of the Andun Stone and the peace and plenty that it would bring.

The origin of the marvelous crystal might never be known, but its powers were manifold. Famine or feast, war or peace, plague or health—death or life—the great stone could bring either. And therein lay its secret. It made and unmade. Did and undid.

Cador's shard, and Rill's as well, were part of one motto. It was only when the two were placed on either side of the Andun Stone that the legend could be read in its entirety. ▼Ï◇Đ◇Ø◇'A◇Ñ◇Đ◇Ú◇Ñ◇Đ◇Ø◇▲. So simple when one understood its message: *I DO AND UNDO.* Once more, in Tressalara's reign, the powers of the crystal would be actively used to provide good to all.

The people came forward to greet their monarch. Cador was the first to bend his knee. Sunlight turned his hair to spun gold, and his eyes were bluer than sapphires. He had never looked more virile and handsome. She held out her hand with the ring bearing the great seal of Amelonia. Her fingers shook slightly, and she prayed that he would clasp her hand in his. But the differences in their estate had built a wall between them, one that he evidently had no intention of tearing down.

Cador's eyes didn't even lift to meet hers. Since that miraculous night in the great hall he had not touched her once, or even spoken with her privately. His demeanor was always aloof and proper, that of a simple knight to a reigning queen. She bit her lip to keep it from trembling. It was a great moment for Amelonia, but without Cador's love, it was hollow.

Cador, the brave warrior of Kildore, was as nervous as she was. He wanted to speak the oath of loyalty, but his mouth was dry. Just looking at her made his throat constrict with love. She had risked everything for him, including her life. And he had treated her like a servant in his camp, then seduced her. He was not fit to kiss her dainty slipper.

Never, by word or glance or gesture, would he refer in any way to their time together, although he would treasure each memory like a precious jewel. He wished he could turn his back upon her, forget he'd ever loved her, and return to his lonely aerie in the rocky highlands of Kildore. He was not equal to the task. But although they were forever separated by her high estate, he would spend his life protecting her. Tressalara, his queen. His beautiful, forever lost, love.

He bowed over her hand, kissed the emerald ring of state,

and uttered the same words he had said to her in the rebel
camp: "All I have and all I am I pledge to you, lady. I vow
that I will dedicate both my sword and my life to your cause.
Will you accept my service?"

Tressalara lifted his chin with her fingertip, forcing him to
look square in her face. Now was the time to show her
queenly courage. Her heart gave a little leap of joy. It was
not too late. Not if the bleakness in his eyes was any reflection of what was in his heart. She took a deep breath and
threw her own pride to the winds. "Aye, I accept your offer
of service to the crown of Amelonia. But I demand far
more—of you. But only if you are willing to make the sacrifice. Rise, Cador of Kildore. You, who have shared the
power of the Andun Stone with me."

Her eyes were shining with love for all to see. "Rulership
is a lonely thing, my lord. I do not wish you to kneel at my
feet—I want you by my side as husband and king, ruling
jointly with me over this great country. With the heart and
courage and wisdom you have shown in our fight for freedom, you have earned the right."

While he stood, more shaken then he had ever been in
battle, a roar of approval went up from the crowd. "Long
live Tressalara! Long live Cador! Long live the King and
Queen of Amelonia!"

A dimple played at the corner of her sweet mouth. "Do
you, Cador of Kildore, accept this last, perhaps most difficult
task?"

She waited for his answer for what seemed like a lifetime.
Then she was pulled into his arms and soundly kissed, as if
she were a bonny farmer's maid encircled by her lover's arms
on a sunny summer's day.

A cheer went up from the throng again and again. When
he finally relinquished her lips, he kept her fast in his embrace. "One thing. If you wish a biddable husband, my
queen, you must look for another. You have stated repeatedly
that you would never tolerate a man as pigheaded, over-
bearing, obstinate, and domineering as I. Are you sure you
can put up with me?"

Tressalara smiled up at him. "A queen must be willing to
make sacrifices for her kingdom."

Cador kissed her again. They stood heart to heart, feeling the strength and love flowing between them, more powerful than any sorcerer's magic. More powerful even than the mighty Andun Crystal.

As they turned to accept the cheers of their people, Cador leaned close to Tressalara's pretty ear. Without realizing it, Cador's next words washed away the last shadow over Tressalara's coronation.

"I wish your father had lived to see this day. How proud he would be of all you have accomplished!" He pressed a light kiss against her temple.

"Although you are as brave and capable as any man, I must admit this to you, love: I am heartily glad that King Varro's only child was a daughter!"

He swept her into his arms and kissed her again.

Some say that on Tressalara and Cador's wedding day, rebels and nobles danced together, and many a happy match was made. Still others say that the Andun Stone rang out like a great golden bell or the voice of an angel and was heard in every corner of the Four Countries.

As in all good fairy tales, Tressalara and Cador ruled Amelonia and its people long and wisely. They raised many merry children, some sharing their mother's amethyst eyes and auburn hair, others exactly like their father with sapphire eyes and golden hair. And, of course, they all lived happily ever after . . .